THE ROSWELL WOMEN

Frances Patton Statham lives in Atlanta, Georgia. She has
received two national and two regional awards for her
novels, including the prestigious Author of the Year
award in fiction from the Dixie Council of Authors and
Journalists in 1978 – the first time this award went to the
author of an original paperback. She has conducted
numerous seminars throughout the south of America and
has appeared at many writers' conferences.

THE ROSWELL WOMEN

Frances Patton Statham

Pan Books
London, Sydney and Auckland

First published in the US 1987 by Ballantine Books
First published in Great Britain 1989 by Pan Books Ltd,
Cavaye Place, London SW10 9PG
9 8 7 6 5 4 3
© Frances Patton Statham 1987
ISBN 0 330 30478 X
Printed and bound in Great Britain by
Cox and Wyman Ltd, Reading, Berks

To Charlsey

CHAPTER

I

The magnificent white columns of Rose Mallow appeared beyond the rise of early morning fog. Coin Forsyth loved this part of the day best—before the river mist burned away and the soft cool breeze vanished under the searing heat of the summer sun.

As he viewed the house, his lips formed the name of the woman he loved: Allison. She was the reason he'd built the mansion on the bluffs of the gently flowing north Georgia creek. From the moment he'd first met her in Savannah, he had coveted her as his wife.

Half hidden by the fog, Coin watched as the front door opened. Then Allison slowly walked onto the wisteria-sheltered porch and gazed down the long, graveled vista in the direction of the Roswell road. Seeing her, he was replete with happiness. She was his, and nothing would ever part them.

With a sudden urge to close the distance between them, Coin Forsyth mounted his horse Roan and moved from the hidden copse of willow trees. He smiled, raised his hand in greeting, and then galloped toward the woman standing on the porch.

"Cap'n Forsyth?"

"Allison?"

"Beg pardon, sir, for wakin' you, but General Gordon wants to see you."

All at once, the weary Confederate captain opened his eyes and sat up. The early morning fog still lay heavily on the damp earth. But Rose Mallow had vanished. The wisteria scent had given way to the odor of rotting vegetation and the lofty trees were now charred stumps that silently cursed the spoilers of the Virginia wilderness.

"What is it, Corporal?"

"The general, sir. He's sent for you."

"Where is he?" Coin asked.

"Over on Plank Road. There's a man waitin' with the picket to lead you to him. Lee's in trouble."

"Then more than likely we'll be moving out soon."

"Yes, sir. Seems a shame, though, after we spent half the night throwin' up these earthworks for the guns."

Coin ignored the corporal's comment. "Get Sergeant Gibbs for me," he said.

"Yes, sir."

The name was taken up and whispered down the line. Within a few minutes, the sergeant, crawling on his belly in the brackish watered trench, reached the earthworks, hoisted his body, and tumbled over the pile of dirt. "You sent for me, Cap'n?"

"Gibbs?"

"It's me, all right, even if I *do* look more like a mummichog flappin' around in all this mud."

"Well, scrape the mud off your beard, Sergeant, so the men will recognize you. I want you to take over the company, or what's left of it, until I get back.

"And don't waste any shot," Coin added, "before you see the blue."

The sergeant nodded. "We killed enough of our own, I reckon, to last us a while."

A sadness clouded Coin Forsyth's blue eyes, for the armies were hopelessly entangled in the dense undergrowth of laurel bushes and prickly briars, interspersed with stagnant streams and marshes.

The previous evening, darkness had crept along the ridge like a ghost probing for its prey—spread out, hollow—with no substance except terror in the air. Then the muskets started flashing, with a response from the larger guns. Battle lines disappeared, while the soldiers, two hundred thousand of them, exchanged bullets, killing almost as many of their own comrades as they did the enemy. But then the woods caught fire, and the eerie cries of the trapped soldiers rose on the hot breath of the wind. Suddenly, the color of uniform had no longer mattered—only the wounded, damned in the raging inferno.

Coin glanced down at his blistered hands. He had rescued only a few men before being driven back by the solid sheet of fire.

"Allison," he whispered as he picked up his Enfield musket and left the earthworks. But her face eluded him. The nightmare of living was too powerful for him to recapture the dreams of his sleep.

CHAPTER
2

For two weeks, the June rains had not ceased.

Even now, the torrential downpour splashed against the tall, beveled glass windows of Rose Mallow, hit the ground, and rushed past the boxwood hedge to follow the easiest route toward the Chattahoochee River.

Etched in red, ditches along each side of the drive threatened to overflow, taking with them the gravel that made the road halfway passable in such weather.

Inside the house, Allison Forsyth sat alone in the parlor. She was oblivious to the storm that snapped the black ribbons of the wreath back and forth against the heavy oak front door. In her hands, she held a wedding picture, the only reminder of her tall, handsome husband.

"Would you like a cup of blackberry leaf tea, Miss Allison, before the carriage comes?"

Allison turned her head in the direction of the voice. Her servant, Rebecca Smiley, stood in the doorway and waited for a reply.

Finally, Allison spoke. "No, thank you, Rebecca." She grasped the photograph even tighter. "I think I'll just sit here for a while longer."

Suddenly, a gust of wind blew the front door open, and Rebecca rushed into the hallway to shut it before the rain came in. "I see the carriage comin' down the drive now," she called out. "I'll go and get the baby ready."

Reluctantly, Allison stood and placed the treasured photograph on the mantel. Wet violet eyes stared from the photograph to the face in the mirror and back again. The change was remarkable. Just as vividly as the picture captured her joy of another day, so the mirror reflected Allison's immediate sorrow.

Coin was dead. Nothing would ever bring him home again. Even the solace of his tombstone in the church cemetery was denied her, for her husband was buried along with his men in one common grave in the Virginia wilderness.

Allison turned from the mirror and put on the bombazine cape. On her head, she placed a matching black bonnet and tied the ribbons under her chin.

When the carriage pulled up to the steps of Rose Mallow and the driver held the horses steady, Allison climbed inside. Rebecca followed, carrying Morrow, her mistress's three-month-old daughter, dressed in her christening gown, which was now bordered with black.

Once she was seated, Allison held out her arms. "I'll

take her now," she said, with a sudden need to be reminded of Coin's love.

The carriage began its slippery way down the tree-lined drive, but Allison did not protest the swaying of the carriage. She was too intent on examining the baby's face. "She looks a little like her father, don't you think, Rebecca?"

The black woman hesitated. The baby was a replica of her mistress, with the same soft, moonbeam hair, the identical fair complexion, but it would not do to tell her so today. "She's got Cap'n Forsyth's smile, I think."

"But not his eyes," Allison said. "I couldn't bear that, having her look at me with his eyes."

Even in the rain, the land surrounding Rose Mallow was incredibly beautiful. Flame-colored azaleas dotted the nearby woods, with dogwood trees and sweet shrubs perfuming the air of the hillsides. Not far below, the roar of water rushing over the dam filled the air as the waterwheel turned to give power for the spindles and looms of the three mills built along the banks of Vickery Creek.

A sad, bittersweet smile came to Allison's lips as she noticed the people standing respectfully on each side of the road while they waited for the carriage to pass. Ordinarily, the people who had once owned horses and carriages would have joined the slow procession on its way to the church, but the war had lasted too long. Most of the barns were empty, including her own. And so there was only one carriage, one matched pair of horses on the road—those belonging to the Reverend Nathaniel Pratt, who had been kind enough to send for Allison.

The roar of the waterfall was soon replaced by the doleful toll of the church bell. As if on cue, the citizens of Roswell took their places behind the carriage and began to follow it toward the church for the memorial service.

"Rebecca, they should have gone to the church and waited," Allison lamented. "All this mud . . ."

"They can wipe the mud off their shoes better than they can live with shame on their souls, Miss Allison. I know how the folks in this town always loved Cap'n Forsyth, even when he was a little boy. They wouldn't feel it was fittin' for his widow and baby to travel alone to the church today."

Accepting Rebecca's explanation, Allison nodded and became introspective until her memories forced her to speak again. "I remember how my brother Jonathan loved him, too. And how pleased he was when Coin came to visit him that first time at Cypress Manor."

Rebecca made a noise in her throat. "Now the war's taken both of them."

"Yes." Allison bit her lip and fought back the tears, for they had come within sight of Great Oaks, the property belonging to Dr. Pratt.

It was not the sight of the plantation house that caused her such anguish. Rather, it was the small cottage on the grounds in which the minister had tutored young men from all over the state for their entrance exams to Princeton and Harvard. It was here that her brother Jonathan had stayed while a student. And it was here that he had made friends with another student, Coin Forsyth, who had later become her husband.

The carriage slowly passed the Pratt property and turned on the opposite side of the street into the driveway of the Presbyterian church. For Allison, it was strange how grief gave a different perspective to familiar surroundings. Now, she saw the sanctuary as if it were that first Sunday, when Coin had brought her there as his bride and they had walked down the aisle together to the enclosed family pew.

She remembered thinking how alien the church had

looked on the outside that day: a Connecticut meeting house transplanted to the South, with its short bell tower taking the place of the more traditional spire and its walls made of white clapboard rather than red Savannah brick. It looked just as unfamiliar today, and she felt the same trepidation. She didn't want to go inside. And yet she knew she must.

The carriage came to a stop before the white-columned portico. Allison returned the sleeping baby to Rebecca as the carriage door was flung open and a hand reached out to draw her up the steps.

When she was inside, Allison stopped and waited for Rebecca. Her lips trembled. With a sense of urgency, she whispered to the woman, "Rebecca, I want you to sit with me."

"But my place is in the balcony . . ."

"Your place is with me. You're the only family I have left."

The black woman glanced toward the filled pews. "Then I'd better keep on carryin' the baby," she said, and followed her mistress down the aisle.

As the Reverend Pratt began his opening prayer in memory of the town's fallen hero, the steady din of guns in the distance interrupted him. Members of the congregation lifted their heads to listen for a brief moment.

Chattanooga and Dalton had fallen, and the war was coming even closer to Roswell. Several miles to the north, General Sherman's troops were carrying on a thrust-and-parry campaign around Kennesaw Mountain. But so far, they had been unable to breach the ten-mile defense line set up by Joe Johnston and his Confederate troops. But everyone knew that Sherman had received an ultimatum from Lincoln. He desperately needed a Union victory, especially after the devastating Wilderness campaign, and he was looking to Sherman to give him that victory.

As if sensing the uneasiness of the congregation, Morrow awoke and began to cry. Rebecca rocked her in her arms to quiet her, but the baby refused to be comforted until Allison reached over and took her.

Concentrating on the tall, imposing figure of Dr. Pratt standing in the center pulpit, Allison asked only that the service be over as quickly as possible. She wanted no public display of tears to mar the service, but she wasn't sure how much longer she could remain composed. The sound of the guns had brought renewed pain to her heart. "Oh, Coin," she whispered, and hid her face close to that of her child. Once again, the baby began to cry, and she kept up her plaintive wail for the remainder of the service.

". . . And give Thy peace and courage to each widow, each orphan, in the dark days ahead. Amen."

The communion silver rattled as the guns in the distance renewed their onslaught against the mountain. Then the doleful rumbling of the bass notes on the organ drowned out the guns.

Like someone caught in a bad dream not of her own design, Allison touched hands, acknowledged condolences with a nod, and then, mercifully, was once again inside the carriage. The memorial service was over.

Morrow finally drifted off to sleep again to the lulling roll of the wheels. No words were spoken aloud between Allison and Rebecca, for fear of waking the baby. Yet Allison's mind was busy. The church service had given a finality to her life as the wife of Captain Coin Forsyth. She was now a widow—with no money. A widow—with a small child to support. The only food in the house had been brought by kind neighbors, sharing the little they had out of respect for the dead. The only money left was the gold eagle given to her by Jonathan on the day of her marriage. She would never part with that.

For the rest of the day, the rain came down, beating its steady rhythm against the wisteria-vined porch of Rose Mallow, trickling through the roof to the tin tub in the hallway, and making a pond of the graveled courtyard.

At last, Allison rose from her desk and walked to the parlor window. The solid lay of the land had vanished with the rain and in its place the silent, illusive fog had begun its evening journey from the lowlands to the bluff above. Steadily, the mist moved, devouring with its silent steps portions of the land until it finally reached the porch of Rose Mallow.

Allison turned from the window and went to find Rebecca. Her steps were resolute. She had made up her mind.

The summer kitchen was attached to the main house by a covered walkway. From the door, which was opened to catch the breeze once the rain had stopped, Allison could see the faint flicker of the fire in the kitchen. Negotiating the passageway with quick steps, she stopped and watched Rebecca taking the hot stew from the kettle and placing in the soup tureen.

"Rebecca, I want to talk with you."

"I'll be in the dinin' room in a minute, Miss Allison."

"There's no need for that. Just put the tureen on the table on the back porch."

At the sight of Rebecca's raised eyebrows, Allison added, "I don't have time to waste in empty ceremony. We need to make plans about our future."

"You'll be served in the dinin' room," Rebecca said in a firm tone, "the way you always have. Cap'n Forsyth might be dead, Miss Allison, but you're still the mistress of Rose Mallow. And tonight's no time to forget it."

For a moment, the two women stood and stared at each other. Allison, realizing the battle to come later, allowed Rebecca her small victory.

"All right, Rebecca. In the dining room."

Allison turned and retraced her steps through the breeze-way, down the hall, and into the formal dining room, where she raised a window to allow the slight breeze to penetrate the room that still smelled of funeral flowers and beeswax.

On the wall on the far side, facing the windows, the French scenic wallpaper was faded by the strong southern sun. The wide-planked boards of pine, pegged together to make up the flooring, rippled slightly from the leak in the roof that she had been unable to stop. In trying to run the small working plantation, Allison had done the best she could without adequate help or money. So much of the furniture was now gone—as well as most of the silver and the fine Persian rugs.

Yet she was glad that she had not complained about such trivial matters in her letters to Coin. It had been far more important for him to hold in his memory the way Rose Mallow had looked on his last visit. A full year ago. Now he lived through their child, who had been conceived in love during those too brief days.

Rebecca walked into the room and placed the tureen on the table. "Shall I light the pine knot on the hearth, Miss Allison?"

"No, Rebecca. We'll save it."

The woman nodded. "I'll be back with the bread."

A pensive Allison sat in the shadows and slowly ladled the soup into her bowl, the English Spode that had once belonged to her grandmother and had become part of her

13

own bridal chest. Allison remembered how carefully she had packed each piece for the long trip to this upcountry colony. Founded by wealthy coastal planters of Savannah and Darien as a summer escape from the pestilence of the lowland marshes, Roswell was already a permanent town long before Allison undertook the journey north as Coin Forsyth's bride.

"Your soup's gettin' cold."

With a start, Allison looked up at Rebecca, who had come into the room again. "It doesn't matter. I'm not hungry, anyway. I have too much on my mind." She didn't give the woman time to protest. "I wrote a letter to Araminta this afternoon. There's nothing left for me in Roswell now that Coin is dead. So as soon as I hear from her, I suppose I'll take Morrow and go back to Cypress Manor."

"Livin' in the same house with Mr. Jonathan's widow won't be no life for you, Miss Allison. She never liked you, even before your brother was killed. And it'll be worse now."

"But I don't plan to go to her as a charity case. I've decided to ask Théophile Roche for a job in the woolen mill. That way, I'll have some money of my own.

"Don't look at me like that, Rebecca. I'm destitute, with no money at all. If the other women of the town can take the place of the men in the mills, then so can I."

"But you're not like the other women. You're Cap'n Coin Forsyth's wife. It'll be a disgrace."

"No one in Savannah need ever know. And have you forgotten so soon? I'm not a wife—only an impoverished widow who hasn't been able to pay her one servant for the past six months."

"Have you heard me complainin'?"

"Well, you should. And if you're smart, you'll let me ask Mr. Roche for a job for you, too."

"Who'll take care of the baby?"

"I'll put her in a basket and take her to the mill with me. That is, if Mr. Roche will give me the job."

"And if he doesn't?"

"Then the baby and I will probably starve."

"Looks like you might starve, as it is. You haven't touched the little bit of food before you."

Allison picked up her spoon and began to eat the soup. Rebecca was right, of course. A nursing mother had to keep up her strength—if not for herself, then for her baby.

For a long time, Allison sat in the shadows, where memories from the past lurked and called to each other. Finally, when she could stand it no longer, she rose, fled from the room and, unmindful of the dense fog, left Rose Mallow, to wander along the bluffs of Vickery Creek.

CHAPTER
3

High on the bluffs overlooking the waterfall that supplied power for the Roswell mills, Théophile Roche, the French manager of the Ivy Woolen Mill, awoke.

He could already hear the warning bell that heralded the opening of the millrace gate for the great rush of water to the mill wheel. He loved the whirr and hum of the machinery that signaled the full production of cloth—the Roswell gray material used for Confederate uniforms.

He remembered how uneasy he'd been when the workers had gone off to war and he had been forced to hire their wives and daughters to take over their jobs. Yet he need not have worried. The Roswell women had proved more than adequate for the task. And they didn't complain like the men, either, when they had to work longer hours to make up for those days when there was no power for the spindles and the looms.

Roche smiled. He was probably the only one in the town who welcomed the gullywashers that poured down from the mountains and into the creeks and rivers. For without the steady stream of water to turn the mill wheel, his mill had to close down. The last two weeks of rain now assured him of enough power for quite a while to come. He could rest easily on that count.

The smile left his face as the heavy guns in the distance began their daily bombardment. They sounded even closer this morning, like a knocking at the door of the town itself. Lately, he'd begun thinking about what he would do if Sherman's troops slipped past the Kennesaw defense line, for burning the mills would be their first priority. But Roche was a French citizen, not a Confederate. And he was now part owner of the mill. If he raised the French flag above the mill . . . Yes, that's what he would do. Hurriedly, Roche got dressed and then went up to the attic of his house to search for the flag he'd brought with him from France.

At Rose Mallow, Allison Forsyth finished nursing her baby and then dressed for her appointment with Théophile Roche. At the last moment, she put on the old boots belonging to Coin and took down a parasol to protect her head from the sun.

"I still think you're makin' a mistake, Miss Allison," Rebecca said. "Can't be nothin' but trouble comin' from it."

"My actions are not open for discussion, Rebecca. Just take care of Morrow until I get back. That's all I ask."

Allison didn't look at the woman standing in the breezeway. With a stubborn tilt to her chin, she walked down the garden steps and, holding up her skirts to avoid the wet places, hurried through the side yard, toward the orchard, and on to the creek bluffs beyond.

For some time, Allison walked, edging her way past the vines that spread out in a tangled network of lush greenery. Threatening the most careful of travelers, the woods provided a formidable barrier for a woman in long skirts. Finally, in frustration, Allison began to use her parasol to brush past the thorny vines hanging from the tree limbs above.

The ground beneath her suddenly shook in a convulsive quake, and Allison reached out for support, only to feel excruciating pain as she pulled one of the vines loose from the nearest tree and the thorns punctured her shabby black glove. Unmindful of the damp earth, Allison sat down, hurriedly removed the glove from her hand and stared at the ugly, jagged pattern in her palm. Like a child, she lifted her hand to her mouth and, with a sucking motion, drew blood and the thorn from the wound.

The Union guns. They had caused her pain. Now she had another reason for hating them. With her hand still hurting, Allison put on her glove again, stood up, and wiped the debris from her skirts. She did not want to be late for her appointment with Théophile Roche. That would make a bad impression on the mill manager, and he might not give her a job because of it.

Finally, the mill village came into view, with tall, slanted little cottages following the meandering trails that passed for roads. And at a slightly higher elevation sat The Bricks, the two apartment buildings that had also been erected to house the employees of the mills.

Then the two-story brick house that served as both residence and office for the manager of the woolen mill appeared. Allison stopped, took a deep breath, and shored up her courage to face the Frenchman. A few minutes later, a composed Allison stood before Roche in his office.

'You wished to see me, Madame Forsyth?" he inquired in his pleasantly accented voice.

Allison cleared her throat and stared at the window that was slightly above the manager's head. "I have come with two requests, Mr. Roche. As you may have heard, my husband is dead. I can no longer afford to pay my servant, Rebecca Smiley. She's an excellent worker and knowledgeable about wool, so I was hoping that you might hire her as a weaver in your mill."

The small, dark-haired manager looked at Allison for a moment without speaking. He sat back in his comfortable chair and slowly rubbed his hands together in a pensive pose. "It is very commendable of you, madame, to concern yourself with a servant's welfare. I trust you can vouch for her honesty and integrity?"

"Oh, yes. Otherwise, I would not have come to you with such a request."

The man nodded and sat forward. "She is a free black woman?"

"Yes. Not every family in the South owns slaves, Mr. Roche. Rebecca was born free and is at liberty to work for anyone who can pay her."

Roche hesitated. "It's true, we desperately need good workers in the mill. But I cannot provide housing for her . . ."

"That's not necessary. She has her lodgings at Rose Mallow."

"Then tell her to report to me at dawn tomorrow in front of the mill."

"Thank you, Mr. Roche."

19

Allison made no attempt to leave. She twisted the worn white lace handkerchief and cleared her throat again. "I mentioned, Mr. Roche, that I had two requests."

"And the other?"

Allison's voice became so low that Roche had trouble understanding her. "I had hoped that you might hire me also."

"I beg your pardon, madame?"

"I have the same qualifications as Rebecca. I also know how to spin and weave. And anyone in the town will vouch for my honesty and integrity, if you ask."

The full import of her words shocked him. "Do you realize what you're asking, madame? To agree to hire your servant is one thing. But for me to hire the lady of Rose Mallow as a worker in the mill . . . That is impossible."

"In wartime, Mr. Roche, there *are* no ladies. We're all women, fighting to survive. Using our hands to scrounge for food, to work the land left in our care. And to spin cloth to clothe the poor soldiers on the battlefields."

"Does this mean that you need the money, madame?"

"Yes."

"But you must have relatives that you could go to. That would solve the problem, would it not?"

"Working in the woolen mill, Mr. Roche, would solve my problem, too. I only ask that you hire me for one month. No longer."

Still Roche was hesitant. "But I understand you are the mother of a small child."

"Some of your other workers also have babies. One more in a basket nearby won't disrupt the production of the mill."

Théophile Roche could not bear the intensity of the violet eyes staring at him. He lowered his head and tapped his finger on the edge of the mahogany desk. "If I grant this shameful request, it will be on one condition."

"Yes?"

"That you will promise to contact your relatives to ask for shelter. If you do that, Madame Forsyth, I will hire you until you can make plans to leave."

Allison smiled. "I promise. And thank you, Mr. Roche." She stood and held out her hand.

"*Enchanté*," he said, taking it and holding it to his lips.

"Tomorrow? At dawn?" she asked, as if she were merely inquiring the time of the next church social.

"Yes. Tomorrow. And may *le bon Dieu* forgive me for what I have promised today."

"May the good Lord bless you instead, Mr. Roche. For you have just saved my life."

"I hope you will still feel that way, madame, a month from now. As for myself, I'm not so sure."

That evening, as Allison and Rebecca prepared for bed, Madrigal O'Laney was returning from the mill commissary to her apartment at The Bricks. Her usual exuberance was missing. At seventeen years old, with a shapely body and a saucy face, Madrigal felt that fate had dealt her a mortal blow. Her high, young breasts strained at the calico material of her bodice as she attempted to control her anger. Nearly all of the men in the mill town were gone. It wasn't fair, just when she had bloomed into womanhood. Not that she wanted a husband. Heavens, no. Husbands never gave their wives anything more than brats. What she wanted was fun. And the war had seen to it that she had missed out in that category. But the ultimate humiliation had just happened. She had been waylaid by Puckka Knox, a smelly, twelve-year-old twit of a boy.

21

"What's the matter, Madrigal? Your face is as red as your hair. You mad about somethin'?"

"Furious is more like it, Ellie," she replied to the friend who'd rushed to catch up with her and was now trying to keep pace alongside her.

Gazing at the half-filled satchel, Ellie said, "I told you last week that you were gonna get into trouble with old Mr. Rowdybush, chargin' as much as you did at the commissary. I see he didn't let you have half the amount this time."

"Oh, pish, Ellie. It's not Mr. Rowdybush. He'd give me anything I want, just for the askin'."

"Then what's wrong?"

"Everything. The war, lastin' as long as it has. The soldiers just over the mountain and not even allowed to come around here. I could make a list as long as Fannie Morton's wash line. But the worst thing of all just happened."

"You gonna tell me or not?"

"Promise you won't breathe it to a single, livin' soul, hope to die and spit on your mother's grave if you do?"

Ellie made the appropriate sign.

Madrigal stopped beyond the posts that braced the shed roof of the store buildings and gazed toward the empty town square. Finally, she spoke. "You know that Puckka Knox?"

"Sure. Everybody in the mill village knows the little bully."

"Well, he's not so little anymore. He just asked me to meet him in the blacksmith's barn as soon as it got good and dark."

Ellie's whoop swept over the square until Madrigal admonished her. "Hush, Ellie. You want everybody, includin' Reverend Pratt, to hear you?"

"Sorry, Madrigal. But it's so funny. No wonder you

22

looked ready to spit nails. But tell me. What did you say back to him?"

Madrigal's eyes lost their angry look. A smile began, getting broader and broader until she, too, broke into a laugh. "It's too terrible to repeat. But I'll bet one thing, Ellie, Puckka won't ever bother me again."

"It was that bad, huh?"

"Yeah. But promise me you won't mention his name again. I want to forget him. Let's talk about somethin' else. Somethin' pleasant."

"I got a letter today. From my brother Bedford. Miss Tilly brought it in her mail hack all the way from the train station in Marietta."

"What did he say?"

"Nothin' much. Just that he was all right and that he was sure sorry about Cap'n Forsyth and his men. Said when his platoon went back to look for them in the wilderness, there wasn't a trace. They got blown up in the trench."

"Ellie, I'm tired of hearin' about the war. I told you to talk about somethin' pleasant."

"You wanna go pick blackberries tomorrow as soon as we get off work? I know a good spot near the bridge."

Madrigal nodded. "If I can still move after workin' ten hours."

"I know. Sometimes my back hurts so bad I wish the creek would dry up. Then I think about Bedford. And imagine I might be weavin' the very cloth that'll go on his—"

"Ellie, you're talkin' about the war again."

"Well, what else is there to talk about? You said you wanted to forget Puckka Knox."

Madrigal quickened her pace and her teeth chewed at her lower lip—a sure sign that her brain was busy. She shifted the weight of her shopping bag and smiled. "A celebration.

That's what we need in this town. Everybody's had the mubblefubbles for so long, they've forgotten how to have a little fun."

"What kind of celebration?" a wary Ellie asked.

"I don't know yet. But I'll think of somethin' before tomorrow. Has to have some dancin' and singin' to it. And somethin' good to eat."

The two young women stopped at the division in the road. The summer twilight had lasted a long time. Now the fireflies lit up the air as the sun sank below the trees and the river mist began to settle in the low places.

"I'll see you tomorrow," Madrigal called out as the two started in opposite directions.

"Don't forget the basket for the blackberries," Ellie reminded her.

"I won't." Madrigal suddenly felt better. She always perked up when Ellie was around. She was the only one who could help the time pass when they worked such long hours together at the mill. That is, if Ellie didn't launch into a boring discussion of the war, as she was sometimes prone to do.

Madrigal opened the gate that led into the small courtyard of The Bricks. She raced up the steps to the front door of her apartment and pushed it open. For a moment she stood there, getting acclimated to the dark. Slowly, her yellow cat's eyes adjusted to the dimness, and the surroundings took on familiar shapes.

A sense of elation took over as she mentally caressed each piece of furniture in the combination living room–kitchen. The day she had moved into the apartment had been the most exciting day of her life, for the two-story abode, with its two fireplaces and polished pine flooring, represented quite a change from the shack at the edge of town where Madrigal had spent most of her life.

It took her a number of weeks to get used to an upstairs bedroom. And with a fireplace, too. Cooking, eating, and sleeping in one room, with a blanket hanging from a rope to hide the bed shared by her mother, Maisie, and her steppa, Ben, had been a way of life, even if the blanket never masked the sounds coming from the other side. That used to scare her until her mother explained the nature of men. So on the nights Ben came home drunk, Madrigal stuffed cotton in her ears, pulled her quilt over her head, and went to sleep. Now, Madrigal had a place to herself—an unexpected luxury.

She put down her satchel and groped for the Confederate candle on the kitchen table. The tallow-dipped wick was coarsely woven and wrapped in a coil around the bottle, to make it last longer.

Just as Madrigal lit it, there was a tap on the door. "Madrigal, are you home?"

She recognized the voice of the woman. "Come on in, Flood. The door's open."

The candle flared, throwing the shadow of the large, heavyset woman onto the opposite wall as she walked across the flooring toward the kitchen.

Flood Tompkins was the best worker at the Ivy Woolen Mill. She did the same work as any man and that's why Mr. Roche had made her a foreman. Sometimes, when she wore her husband's trousers and stuffed her hair into a cap, Madrigal thought Flood resembled a man more than she did her own sex.

"Come and sit a spell, Flood," Madrigal invited. "I was just goin' to put up my food supplies in the cupboard."

"Can't stay but a minute, Madrigal. I came to warn you about tomorrow at the mill."

"What's wrong? Has Mr. Roche complained about me again?"

"No. Not that he doesn't have just cause. It's about two new workers he's hired. We're to train them tomorrow, and I want you to help me."

"Not if one of 'em is Puckka Knox's little sister. I refuse to have anything to do with that family."

"No, Caddie is still too young. But you'd never guess in a month of Sundays. One of 'em is Mrs. Forsyth's Rebecca."

"So what's so special about *her?* It's not like she's the first black woman at the mill. Hettie's been there as long as I have."

"But you didn't let me tell you who the other one is."

"Who?"

"Mrs. Forsyth herself."

"I don't believe it."

"Neither did I, until Mr. Roche told me for truth."

Madrigal stared at the woman whose parents had named her for the disaster that had taken place on the day she was born. "I hope this doesn't mean that I'll have to stay any later than usual, Flood. I promised Ellie we'd pick blackberries right after work."

"That depends on how good a teacher you are, Madrigal."

"Then let me take Rebecca. At least she's used to workin'. That Mrs. Forsyth will probably ruin the heddles, first thing."

"No, Madrigal. I'm givin' Rebecca to Hettie. You're to help Mrs. Forsyth at the loom. I've made up my mind. And it won't hurt you none when Mr. Roche finds out I've selected you for the job. That might put you back in his good graces."

"What a merry-go-sorry bit of luck."

Flood ignored the face Madrigal made. "Be sure you're on time in the mornin'," she warned. "Good night, Madrigal."

"Good night, Flood."

The candle sputtered, and Madrigal hurried to get her supper so that she could go to bed on time. If Flood had appointed her as a nursemaid to the mistress of Rose Mallow, then she would have to get plenty of rest for the difficult task ahead.

CHAPTER 4

Like the glow of fireflies caught at twilight, the rare piece of phosphorus took on its magical power as Allison carefully inserted it onto a piece of cotton in the small glass flask. Just as suddenly, the light vanished when she screwed the lid tight and dropped the bottle into the pocket of her dress. She would have need of its light once she reached the bluff along the creek.

Allison had slept little, but that was not surprising. She was nervous and unsure of herself despite her confident avowal to Mr. Roche the previous day. Spinning and weaving at home were not the same as working on the water-powered looms in the mill. But she was determined to learn as quickly as possible so that the Frenchman would have no regret in hiring her.

"Rebecca, are you ready?" Allison asked.

The woman at the other end of the kitchen looked up from her chore. The beehive oven was still aglow with embers as she opened the lid wide and removed the freshly baked bread with a long-handled spatula.

"Just as soon as I wrap the hot bread in the napkins, Miss Allison. Then the basket will be ready for you to tote."

"You're sure you don't mind carrying the baby?"

"No'm. I'd rather you go first with the light, and I'll follow behind."

They left Rose Mallow by the same route Allison had traveled the previous day, going past the orchard and walking through the wooded area to the bluffs of the creek. Allison stopped and took the bottle from her pocket. The phosphorus began to glow, making a faint light for the two women with their burdens—the basket containing their food supply for the day and the heavier one holding the sleeping baby.

They had not gone far when the darkness vanished with a tremendous roar and whistle. The ground shook in protest as the sky lit up with fireworks exploding into exotic designs, their beauty denying the inherent danger of each shell burst. Allison, clutching the small glass flask, hurriedly returned it to her pocket. There was no need now for the dim light provided by the phosphorus. The tremendous guns on the mountain had started their onslaught for the day, lighting up the entire path along Vickery Creek.

"Lord have mercy," Rebecca murmured, defending the basket containing Morrow as if the guns might snatch the baby from her. "You think we'd better go on back home?"

Allison stopped and turned her head. "Sherman isn't interested in this little town, Rebecca. He's headed for Atlanta. And he might even bypass Roswell completely. Let's keep going."

A wary Rebecca followed her mistress through the dense growth, past the road leading into the mill village; then they reached the property of the woolen mill, where the women workers were already congregating to wait for the mill doors to open.

Conscious of the hush that greeted their arrival and the open, curious stares of the workers, Allison searched for some sign of Théophile Roche. But he was nowhere to be seen.

Finally, a large, heavyset woman stepped forward from the crowd. "Mrs. Forsyth?"

"Yes?"

"I'm Flood Tompkins. Mr. Roche told me to look out for you today."

"Thank you, Mrs. Tompkins. And this is Rebecca Smiley. We'll both be grateful for your guidance."

"Forget the 'Mrs.'," the woman said. "Nobody calls me anything but Flood." She frowned as she spoke. But the frown disappeared when Madrigal, late as usual, came into view, sauntering down the trail with a basket swinging from her arm. Flood waited until an unrepentant Madrigal stood before her.

"Well, here I am, Flood."

Flood nodded and again faced Allison. "I'm turnin' you over to Madrigal O'Laney here, Mrs. Forsyth. She'll show you how to operate the loom." Then she motioned to the black woman standing a few feet away. "Hettie, take Rebecca. It's time for the mill to start up."

Walking beside Allison, who now carried the basket containing the baby, Madrigal said, "Flood didn't tell me you were bringin' a brat with you."

Allison's voice was defensive. "Mr. Roche is aware of her." Then, with a slight smile, she added, "Her name is Morrow."

The morning's work began, with Allison initiated into the mystery of operating the loom.

"You got to watch the tension of the warp, Mrs. Forsyth," Madrigal reminded her.

Allison nodded, throwing the shuttle across and beating it. She watched the even threads, and then the odd, lifting up and kept her eye on the tension to make sure that the selvages remained even. She continued working, to the steady accompaniment of the guns in the distance. Women stared openly at Allison until Flood forced them to turn their attention to their own work.

At Kennesaw Mountain, where Angus Smithwick of the Georgia Militia had been hidden behind breastworks for the past two weeks, the Union troops were in a dilemma. The flanking movements, to draw the Johnny Rebs into the open, had met with little success, for they were like foxes in a secure den, protected by an abatis of pines sharpened to prevent anyone from scaling the mountain. But on this day, Sherman had decided to change the battle plans.

At first, Private Smithwick was not alarmed when he awoke to the reveille of Union guns. He was used to the constant bombardment, to eating his one meal of bacon and hardtack to the midday noise, and to going to sleep at night with the strident lullaby of shells still ringing in his ears. So the morning appeared to be no different from any other of the past two weeks except that the rain had finally stopped.

31

Then, in the light of the shell bursts, he saw a solid line of blue running at a steady pace. He couldn't believe his eyes. Sherman's soldiers were advancing straight toward the Confederate lines, jumping over the rifle pits of their own forward line.

"Jeb, wake up," he yelled to the friend beside him. "The Feds are headin' straight toward us." He grabbed his musket and scampered through the small hole in the abatis to alert the other troops.

They took up their positions and began to fire, hitting one blue uniform after another. Still the enemy kept coming, closing up the gaps in the line, taking a few hundred yards at a time, while Angus and the other Confederate troops fought to keep the high ground.

In the steady advance up the foothill, Federal troops fell right and left. For two solid hours, column after column of soldiers appeared and rushed upward, tearing through the twisted vines and undergrowth that clothed the mountainside but never reaching their goal.

"Poor devils," Angus murmured, loading his rifle and firing at will. It didn't seem to matter in which direction he aimed his rifle. The soldiers in blue were like a covey of quails flying straight in front of the hunter's blind.

In the past few weeks, during the brief lulls of battle when the men themselves decided they'd had enough fighting, the forward pickets had gone in for a bit of swapping with the other side. Angus couldn't help but remember his own conversation with a Yank picket just two nights before.

"Hey, Butternut, you got any tobacco?"

"And if I do, what'll you give for it?" Angus had asked, used to the name the Feds called him because of the color of his homespun.

"How about some real Lincoln coffee?"

"Fair enough."

Angus had put down his rifle, crawled out of his hole to leave the tobacco and claim his coffee, and then fallen back into his fox's den.

Now the truce was over. The war had begun again in earnest with three early morning volleys and a constant stream of blue-uniformed men running, falling to the ground, with their places taken up by others to maintain the line. For two hours, they kept coming, then falling, with the senseless carnage that made Angus sick to his stomach.

But Sherman was determined to cross the Chattahoochee River, the primary obstacle keeping him from Atlanta. And if he had to sacrifice some of his men, so be it. His armies would not stop except to bury the dead.

By nightfall, the pendulum had swung in favor of the Union troops. McPherson, one of Sherman's generals, found another way to the Chattahoochee via Marietta, and Johnston's troops, who had fought so well, were forced to evacuate their stronghold on the mountaintop or risk being trapped from the south.

Interspersed with the retreating troops were groups of civilians using any type of conveyance they could find to transport their few goods across the Chattahoochee River. Most of the wealthier families from the area had already gone, removing the bulk of their fine furniture from the mansions and hiding it in small, unpretentious houses that offered no temptation to conquerors interested only in ransacking the finer homes.

Along the creek, where the giant looms of the mill hummed, a worried Théophile Roche forgot about the two new workers, Allison Forsyth and her servant, Rebecca. His mind was on the retreating Confederate soldiers passing through the town. If there were no one left to defend Roswell, then saving the mill from destruction was entirely in his hands. And he couldn't wait any longer to run the French flag up over the woolen mill.

The whistle signaled the midday break, and a relieved Madrigal turned to Allison. "You can go on outside and eat your lunch now, Mrs. Forsyth. When you come back inside, you'll be on your own."

Allison was already tired, but she forced herself to smile. "Thank you, Madrigal, for helping me this morning."

Her words went unheeded. Madrigal had already vanished down the aisle. Walking over to the place where the fretful Morrow lay in her basket, Allison lifted the baby and followed the other workers out of the mill.

The women congregated under the trees in small, intimate groups to laugh and chat as they ate. Allison searched for a place to herself, secluded from the others, where she could attend to Morrow, who was ravenously hungry and extremely wet.

It was by the creek, not far from the mill wheel, that Rebecca found her. "I'll take the baby now, so you can eat, Miss Allison. Hettie says we don't get much time."

Allison did not hesitate. And she needed no prompting to eat, for, like Morrow, she was hungry. "Are you getting along well, Rebecca?" she asked as she opened her jar containing the soup.

"I'd rather be workin' on a loom than carding wool," she admitted, brushing away the lint from her hair and dress. "But what about you? That Miss Madrigal doesn't look like she'd be much interested in helpin' anybody but herself."

"She evidently thinks I've learned enough to be on my own this afternoon."

"Well, be real careful, Miss Allison. Those wool threads make your fingers awful sore."

"I've found that out, Rebecca. And, heaven knows, my hand is sore enough from the thorn," Allison acknowledged.

As Allison began to eat, Théophile Roche returned to the mill from his office. In his hand, he carried the French flag, and walking by his side was twelve-year-old Puckka Knox, who also worked in the mill.

"Look, Miss Allison. They're takin' down the Confederate flag," Rebecca said.

The two watched uneasily as one flag was replaced by another. "That's the French flag," Allison said, recognizing the tricolor of red, white, and blue. "I suppose Mr. Roche is taking precautions in case the enemy tries to burn down the mill."

A great silence fell over the area along the creek. Only the water rushing over the falls seemed the same. A cloud passed over the noonday sun, an omen that caused Rebecca to mutter under her breath and to hold the baby closer to her breast.

"If the soldiers do come," the black woman said, "a little piece of cloth flappin' in the breeze ain't gonna protect the mill."

"But it might stir up an international incident since Mr. Roche is still a citizen of France."

The whistle blew again, indicating that the short lunch break was over and it was time to start work again. Hurriedly, Allison returned the half-empty jar to the basket and stood up. "I'll wait for you at the footbridge, Rebecca, after work."

"I wish I could look after the baby this afternoon."

35

"No. It's best if I keep her near me. We'll be all right, Rebecca. Truly we will."

The two rejoined the crowd, while the French flag, with no breeze stirring, hung limply above the Roswell woolen mill.

CHAPTER 5

An uneasiness swept through the air and settled into the low places along the river like haunted, wild mallards searching for evening sanctuary.

Through the fog, a curious Madrigal O'Laney stood by the covered bridge and watched for some sign of the Confederate rearguard retreating from the mountain. All she heard was the murmur of water dashing against the rocks off the northern bank of the Chattahoochee River. By placing her ear to the ground, she felt a vibration that signaled that an army might be approaching.

A few minutes before, she had waved to a man fleeing in a wagon with his life's goods. He was as old as his mules, and a stranger, too. Where he had come from, she had no idea. But one thing was certain. He was headed south, in front of the Army of the Tennessee.

"I want to go home, Madrigal," Ellie said, tugging at her friend's arm. "It's gettin' dark, and I'm scared."

"You're as safe here as you are in the village. Safer, maybe. But if you want to go back, it's all right with me."

"Will you come with me?"

"No. I want to stay and watch the soldiers go by." Madrigal stood up and reached for her basket of blackberries. As she popped a ripe berry into her mouth, she added, "Mr. Rowdybush said the soldiers in the rearguard are goin' to burn the bridge after they get across so the Union troops can't follow."

"But how will the enemy know that? I mean, they could still come this way."

"Then they'll have to swim across the river. Or build a new bridge. And you know how long that would take."

"But—"

"Quick, Ellie, I think I see someone comin'. We've got to hide." Madrigal ran toward a small group of laurel bushes on the bank with Ellie following immediately behind her. "Keep your head down and don't move."

Ellie did as she was told, not even scratching where the chiggers had burrowed into her skin although the itching was something fierce. She shut her eyes, but Madrigal pushed back a small branch of the laurel bush to get a better view.

Through the mist, the Confederate soldiers appeared in small groups, not at all like an army marching in step to martial music. At first, Madrigal was disappointed, for they were a motley crew dressed in homespun, tattered and mud-stained. A few wore enemy tunics, with the collar and cuffs edged in sky blue, the color signifying the infantry they had just faced at the mountain. Some of the men wore shoes, but most were barefooted. Madrigal didn't see a single foot soldier with boots on, for the lesson had been learned early in the war. Boots were for the cavalry, not for men who marched on foot.

"Oh, no," Madrigal murmured, releasing the branch with a snap.

"What is it?" Ellie whispered.

"A soldier's headin' straight toward us. He'll find us for sure."

A terrified Ellie opened her eyes. She saw a soldier with his bayonet probing the nearby bushes. "Please don't shoot," she called out.

In surprise, Private Angus Smithwick halted. "Identify yourself," he ordered, peering through the fog and aiming his rifle in the direction of the voice.

Slowly, Madrigal and Ellie stood up.

"What are you two doin' here?" he asked in a gruff voice. "You coulda been shot."

"We were . . ." Ellie stopped. She looked at Madrigal to finish the sentence for her.

Eyeing the soldier, who was handsome despite his ragged appearance, Madrigal smiled. "Why, we were pickin' blackberries along the riverbank. And when we heard somethin', we thought it might be some of those Yankees comin' down the road, so we hid."

Angus laughed and lowered his rifle.

"What is it, Private?" a voice called out to him.

Angus suddenly turned. "Two young ladies, sir, from the village."

"Well, tell them to get home immediately."

"Yes, sir."

A regretful Angus looked at Madrigal again. "What's your name, ma'am?"

"Madrigal O'Laney. What's yours?"

"Angus. Private Angus Smithwick from Resaca." He stared back in the direction of the bridge. "You'd better get goin'. You heard the sergeant."

"Want some blackberries, Angus?" Madrigal asked, holding out the basket.

Again he looked in the direction of the sergeant before grabbing a handful. "You think you could bring me somethin' more rib-stickin' to eat in about two hours?" he inquired, wolfing down the berries. "I got to guard the bridge and then set fire to it after everybody else has crossed over."

"We'd be too scared,'" Ellie replied, "to come back."

"Don't pay any attention to Ellie. Sure, we'll bring you somethin', Angus. Maybe some fresh biscuits and ham."

"I'd be much obliged. But just to make sure I know it's you, give me some sign."

"Like what?"

"Can you whistle like a whippoorwill, Miss Madrigal?"

The red-haired young woman pursed her lips and made the soft, sweet sound of the bird. Almost immediately, the sound was repeated in the wooded area upriver.

Angus grinned. "That'll do fine," he said, and then disappeared in the direction of the bridge.

"Come on, Ellie. Let's get goin'."

"You're not really goin' to do it, are you, Madrigal?"

"What? Come back later? Who knows? Maybe I will. And maybe I won't."

Several miles west of Roswell, Captain Mars Ferrell of the Union army had just left General Garrard's tent to return to his own when two Federal scouts rode into camp. Seeing them, Mars hurried toward them to get the news.

"Were you successful, Corporal?" he asked one of the men.

"I think so, sir. There's a bridge crossing the river near a town called Roswell. It was still standing a few hours ago."

Ferrell nodded. "Come with me, Corporal. The general might want to question you himself."

The soldier dismounted, turned his horse's reins over to the other scout, and followed the captain to General Garrard's tent. Within a few minutes, he was summoned inside.

The bearded general, large and imposing, sat at his campaign desk with the lantern light casting grotesque shadows on the canvas. He lit a cigar, blew the smoke upward, and then motioned for the corporal to come closer. "Captain Ferrell here tells me you found a bridge still intact, Corporal."

"Yes, sir. Or it was, several hours ago. But those Johnny Rebs move pretty fast when they want to."

"Then we must move even faster to capture it." The general spread his map. "Show me just where the bridge is located, Corporal."

The young soldier gazed down at the military map and found the meandering Chattahoochee River. Then he pointed his finger at the small dot. "Here, sir. Right below this little town."

The general took his pen and circled the area. Then pushing the map aside, he said, "That's all, Corporal. You may go now."

As the scout left the tent, Garrard turned to Mars Ferrell. "Rouse the men, Captain. We'll move out in an hour. If we wait until morning, it might be too late."

A few minutes later, the tent held only one man—Kenner Garrard. He stared down at the open map with the two cities, Atlanta and Savannah, marked in red. Between the two cities lay the entire state, marked for destruction—its roads, its crops, its homes. Sherman had ordered that nothing be left standing that would feed or sustain the Confederacy, either military or civilian. Understanding what was ahead, Garrard folded the map and made ready to move out.

The retreating Confederate soldiers steadily crossed the Chattahoochee bridge with all the equipment they had been able to drag from the mountain. But their hearts were heavy. The general they had fought under for so long had been replaced by Hood. And the men who had been so proud to serve under Johnston felt betrayed, almost as if Jefferson Davis had asked Mr. Lincoln himself which general he'd rather fight against in the battle of Atlanta.

Angus Smithwick, looking for some sign of Perkins's men, was getting worried. He couldn't wait much longer. Straining his ears, he heard only the sound of a whippoorwill in the distance.

Madrigal stood alone in the fog where the sandy white road emerged from the woods. Holding the basket of food on her arm, she waited, but no birdsong answered her call. She pursed her lips again and this time whistled louder. Then a similar sound answered her.

She walked forward until a soldier suddenly appeared out of the mist before her.

"Gosh, Angus, you don't have to scare a girl to death."

"I'm sorry, Miss Madrigal. But I wasn't expectin' you back this soon."

"I know I'm early, but I came to tell you that the Federal

troops have been spotted headin' this way. Here, take the basket and get on across the bridge quick as you can."

"I can't leave yet. Perkins's men haven't showed up."

"They're not goin' to, Angus. They got captured."

"How do you know that?"

"A man came into the commissary less than half an hour ago. He told Mr. Rowdybush, the manager."

"Then I'd better get on with settin' fire to the bridge."

"I brought some people to help you, Angus. That is, if you want them to."

"Where are they?"

"Back in the woods a few hundred yards. I'll go and get them."

Quickly, Madrigal turned and disappeared, while Angus grabbed a ham biscuit from the basket and began to eat.

Through the fog the town people moved stealthily, with Flood, Ellie, and some of the children gathering small twigs and pieces of pine. Mr. Rowdybush carried a bucket filled with kerosene oil from the store. With Angus directing the women, they crept onto the bridge and placed the pine knots and the debris from the nearby woods into a pattern along the full stretch of the covered bridge. Coming up behind them, Angus and Mr. Rowdybush poured the kerosene oil over the wood and trailed the remainder down the sides, to soak the wooden trusses supporting the planked bridge.

Then Angus came back and stood beside Madrigal on the north approach. "Better get on home, ma'am. There's goin' to be an awful bonfire now. Wouldn't want you to get hurt. Especially after you've been so kind."

"You think I'd leave now, Angus? Just when the fun's beginnin'?"

Angus grinned. "Then, at least, take cover upriver. If

43

there're any Yankees around, the fire and gunpowder's sure to draw them here."

"Well, good-bye, Angus. And take care of yourself."

Quickly looking to his left and then to his right, the young soldier leaned over and whispered, "You sure are pretty, Miss Madrigal."

She smiled and said in a saucy manner, "Would you like to kiss me good-bye, Angus?"

He needed no further urging. Quickly, he touched her lips with his own, then turned and started running onto the bridge, while a smiling Madrigal watched him disappear.

"You gonna give me a kiss, too, Miss Madrigal?" a mocking voice called out from the dark.

Madrigal whirled to find the culprit who had witnessed her exchange with Angus. "You shut up, Puckka Knox. I'd rather kiss a spit frog than you."

Puckka hoisted himself from the truss and followed Madrigal. "You want me to tell Mr. Roche he's got a tart for a worker?" he threatened.

"That's not fair. And you know it."

"Well, then, give me a kiss 'cause I'm goin' off to fight, too."

"Your mama won't let you."

"She won't know till it's too late to stop me. Come on, Madrigal. One kiss and I'll keep your secret."

Madrigal didn't believe him, but she disguised her anger. With her voice as sweet as she could make it, she said, "All right, Puckka. You win. But let's get farther away, so nobody will see us."

The boy followed Madrigal into the wooded area. She stopped and turned around in an inviting manner. Puckka reached for her, pressing himself against her.

"Damn you, Madrigal. You didn't have to bite me." He

wiped the blood from his mouth and said in a threatening voice, "I'll get even with you for this. I swear I will."

A satisfied Madrigal walked away and vanished into the crowd with the others. But Puckka, stung by Madrigal's contempt for him, raced across the bridge to join the soldiers on the other side.

Angus bored a hole in the middle of the bridge, then inserted the pipe filled with gunpowder. It was especially designed by the Federals for blowing up bridges, but now it was being used against them. Taking the slow-burning cigar lighter, Angus attached it to the piece of metal. He gave the signal for Mr. Rowdybush to set fire to his end of the bridge. Then he began to run for all he was worth to the other end of the bridge.

The fire from the bridge lit up the river, with the fog only partially blanketing the deed that had been done that night.

At Rose Mallow, a tired Allison lifted her head from her pillow. The explosion had awakened her. Quickly, she got up, checked on the sleeping baby, and then put on her robe. By the time she reached the front porch, Rebecca was already there.

"The noise wake you, too, Miss Allison?" Rebecca asked.

"Yes. What do you think it was?"

"There's a fire down by the river, looks like."

"Then it must be the bridge."

The two women stood on the porch in silence while they watched the night sky light up with flames. The guns that had bombarded the land for weeks were strangely silent. But that fact gave Allison no comfort. The Federal troops were on the march now. Burning the bridge wouldn't stop them.

"Rebecca, I'd like for you to get your bedclothes and move into the bedroom next to Morrow and me."

"Yes, Miss Allison. I'll do it right away."

Rebecca left the porch and returned to her quarters, built on the side of the summer kitchen. A woman alone in a big house was extremely vulnerable to the bummers and looters that traveled in the ruts left by an invading army. Especially so when that house was isolated from any near neighbors and the woman was as pretty as Captain Forsyth's widow.

Rebecca reached under the mattress and removed her knife. With the bedclothes in the basket and the knife re-hidden in the pillowcase, Rebecca left her room to bed down in the main house.

"I'm moved now, Miss Allison," she said, returning to the porch via the hallway.

"Thank you, Rebecca. I'll rest easier tonight knowing that you're in the next room."

"Wouldn't hurt none to put the cap'n's pistol by your side, too."

"I haven't fired it since . . . Coin was here on furlough. I'm not sure I remember how to use it."

"Then you'd better start practicin' in the orchard. I have a feelin' you might need it sooner than you think."

"Let's go back to bed, Rebecca. It's the *dawn* that will get here sooner than we think. Or want."

The two disappeared into the house while flames devoured the Chattahoochee bridge below, denying Garrard's troops an immediate access to Atlanta, the rail center of the South.

CHAPTER
6

In that area of river bottom land between Smyrna and Roswell, the hot July sun bore down on devastated farm yards. Carcasses of piglets, slaughtered needlessly, were spread out beside young laying chickens with their necks wrung. Fences had been pulled down, gardens trampled over, and in one yard a rosewood piano had been dragged from the house to serve as a trough to water the horses.

The Union army had already foraged the land, carting off what it wanted and then leaving behind nothing of value that the Rebels might use. Sherman's scorched-earth policy was apparent everywhere as General Kenner Garrard and his cavalry rode upstream to occupy the town of Roswell.

Captain Mars Ferrell rode at the general's side, his blue

eyes taking in the rape of the land, his nose recording the stench that could not be denied. The hostile, accusing looks of the women and children standing by their burned-out houses caused Mars to keep his hand on his revolver in case he needed to defend his general from ambush.

At that moment, Mars had no sense of pride and honor as a Union officer. Foraging by an invading army was to be expected, but wanton destruction that left women and children hungry and homeless was not the reason he had joined the army. He thought of his own mother and sisters, safe at home with plenty to eat, clothes to wear, and adequate shelter. Then he remembered Vicksburg, and his cousin Emily and her two children, hiding in the caves and starving to death during the siege of that city.

The general's voice prompted him to return his thoughts to the military imperative before him. "Captain, make a note of these orders for my men," Garrard said. "They are not to burn down any private homes, or they will answer personally to me."

"Yes, General," a relieved Mars replied.

"And pass the word to the other officers. I want them to discourage the troops, as much as possible, from plundering and pillaging the countryside."

Mars nodded. He knew the first order would be much easier to implement than the second.

They rode at a steady pace beyond the few scattered remnants of civilization and the burned-out ruins of a cotton mill on Sope's Creek. The Confederate army had fallen back across the river, leaving a small band of Georgia Militia, made up of young boys and old men. They were no match for Garrard's troops. With only one man killed and a few wounded, the Union soldiers reached the banks of Willeo

Creek, a few miles to the north of Roswell. There, they halted and made camp for the night.

In the town below, the hopes that the small manufacturing center would be bypassed had been crushed. And the people made plans for its imminent occupation by the enemy.

That night, Pheenie Peters, of the militia, rode out to warn the people in the isolated areas away from the town square. It was his knock at the front door of Rose Mallow that awoke Rebecca.

Armed with her knife, Rebecca crept down the hall and cautiously peered through the beveled glass by the front door.

"Who are you, and what do you want?" she called out, not recognizing the dim figure framed by moonlight.

"It's me, Pheenie Peters. Tell Miss Allison to hide anything she wants to keep. The Yankees are fixin' to occupy the town."

With that, Rebecca put down her knife and opened the door. She walked onto the porch and talked in low tones with Pheenie. Then, a few minutes later, she walked back into the house to wake up her mistress.

Anxious not to wake Morrow also, Rebecca tiptoed into Allison's bedroom and leaned over the bed. "Miss Allison," she whispered. "You need to get up." Her voice had no effect on the sleeping woman. "Miss Allison," she repeated, and this time touched her on the arm. Rebecca's action brought immediate results. Startled out of a sound sleep, Allison sat up and reached for the pistol hidden under her pillow.

"It's all right, Miss Allison. I didn't mean to startle you, but we've got work to do."

"What's wrong, Rebecca?"

"Pheenie Peters just came to tell us the Yankees will be here by mornin'. We got to hide what's left of your silver. The Spode, too, and anything else they might want to cart off."

A sleepy Allison put on her robe, followed Rebecca out of the bedroom, and lit the candle in the dining room. "You find some baskets, Rebecca, while I get the linen to wrap the china in."

By the dim light of the lone candle on the dining room table, the two women carefully packed the precious china and the few remaining pieces of silver.

As they worked, Rebecca began to talk to help them both stay awake. "Pheenie said two of the Reverend Pratt's sons slipped into town earlier tonight. They wanted to make sure the family was all right. Then they helped them hide their valuables in the eaves of Great Oaks."

"It seems to me that would be one of the first places the soldiers would look."

"Not if they think they're already gone. The boys named the west side of the attic 'Macon' and the east side 'Augusta,' so their papa wouldn't be lyin', in case the Yankees ask him where his valuables are. He can look at them straight as an arrow and say they were sent on to Macon or Augusta for safekeeping."

Allison looked at the pitifully small valuables on her own table. "Looks like we'll only need to say 'Jonesborough,' if it comes to that."

"But you've got your trunk with your beautiful weddin' dress and lace veil. I hear that a woman's clothes aren't even safe from them. We'll have to hide your blue silk dress, too."

"Yes. I would hate to lose it. I was saving the dress for the day Coin came home." Allison turned her head and became busy, wrapping another piece of china to put in the basket.

Soon they were finished, taking the few goods up the stairs and placing them under the eaves of Rose Mallow. With that done, the two women went back to bed to await the morning and the invaders.

Not all of the citizens were as destitute as Allison Forsyth and the other widows whose husbands had fallen in battle. Dr. Pratt and his wife, a member of the King family who had founded the town, had chosen not to flee as so many others had done, but to remain at Great Oaks, the large, redbrick plantation house.

Situated in the heart of the town, Great Oaks was surrounded by oak-shaded lawns; thirty acres of tall, young corn; several acres of sorghum; and outbuildings holding bushels of wheat, cured hams, and other supplies for the winter ahead. Too green to be harvested or too bulky to be carted away, the crops, unlike the nonperishables hidden in the attic, remained in sight, vulnerable to the approaching army.

They came with the thunder of hoofbeats—the men dressed in regulation blue, their polished muskets, like their leather boots, catching the glint of the early morning sun.

Behind the cavalry came six thousand mules harnessed to a thousand springless wagons. Their progress was recorded in the deep, rutted roads that no longer resembled roads once the army had passed.

By midmorning, General Garrard, after allowing the Pratts to remain, set up headquarters at Great Oaks, while the cottage and school dormitory on the grounds housed Mars Ferrell and some of the other officers on Garrard's staff.

All morning, the air was filled with oaths, whistles, and shouts as orders were barked back and forth.

"Private, unhitch those mules and get them into the corral."

"Sergeant, take a squad of men across the street to the church and remove the pews to make room for the wounded."

"Corporal, take two men with you and stand guard at the commissary to discourage the men from looting."

With the sound of pegs being hammered into the ground, a tented city for an occupying army began to take shape under the oaks as far as the eye could see. The noise was compounded by the stubborn hee-haws of mules, the creak of wagon wheels, and the sound of the church organ, wheezing its last, as the soldiers ripped it from the church sanctuary along with the pews.

Within a few hours, the Union troops had turned the town into an army camp, complete with quartermaster stores for their provisions. With one enemy subdued, they now faced a new one, less visible but just as deadly—the harsh July sun.

Along Vickery Creek, the mill wheel turned, the spindles and looms made their usual noise, while the French flag drooped in the listless heat.

Inside the mill, a nervous Allison worked at her loom, her concentration broken by the murmurings of the other workeers as Madrigal came back down the aisle. "I saw a soldier on horseback," the red-haired girl announced. "He watched the mill wheel turnin' for a while, and now he's disappeared."

"Get back to work, Madrigal," Flood said, motioning for her to return to her loom across the aisle from Allison. "We still have work to do."

"Don't you think I'd better go and tell Mr. Roche first about the man on horseback?"

"I'm sure he knows what's goin' on."

Reluctantly, Madrigal went back to her loom, but her head turned every few minutes toward the open door of the mill. The soldier on horseback did not reappear, so she eventually stopped watching the door.

Morrow began to cry and Allison tried to quiet her with a soothing voice. "Hush, baby. Don't cry now. Go back to sleep." She moved her foot and started to rock the basket.

"That's not goin' to help," Madrigal said with a frown. "She's probably wet."

Allison nodded. "Hungry, too."

"Well, I'm sure Flood won't mind if you change her and feed her a little early."

Madrigal's encouragement was all that Allison needed. "If Flood asks for me, please tell her I won't be long." Allison picked up the basket with the baby and hurried out of the mill to a cool spot under a tree facing the water.

"Oh, I'm sorry. I didn't realize anyone was here." She gazed at the other woman, already seated and nursing her child who was little older than Morrow.

"That's all right. Plenty of room for both of us. I'm Alma Brady and this here's my little boy, Robert, named for General Robert E. Lee. What's your baby's name?"

Allison hesitated only briefly. She looked down at the baby in her arms. Beads of perspiration lined the pink cherub mouth, and the blond wisps of her hair were matted together from the heat. For the sake of the baby, she could not afford to be modest. She needed to remain under the shade of the water oak.

"Her name is Morrow," she replied, sitting down. "And I'm Allison."

"Oh, I know who you are. Ellie told me. Looks like we're both in the same fix. My husband, Henry, was killed at Snake Creek Gap, right below Dalton."

"Captain Forsyth was in Virginia."

The woman politely ignored the tears in Allison's eyes. "When this war's over, I'm goin' to take the fancy blue silk material I bought from my first mill money, have a dress made from it, then move to Atlanta. And if I'm lucky, I'll find a new papa for my little Robert." She stared down at Morrow, who was hungrily nursing. "You ought to do the same for your young'un."

A startled Allison looked up. "I'll never marry again, Alma. I loved Coin—Captain Forsyth too much."

"I loved my Henry, too. But when your man's dead and gone, you got to think of the livin'. That's what my mama always used to say. Well, I better get goin'. I've stayed out here 'bout as long as I can without gettin' into trouble with Flood."

Alma stood up, rebuttoned the front of her dress, lifted the baby boy to her shoulder, and began to walk away, leaving the tree-shaded spot to Allison.

Once the child had been satisfied, Allison returned to the redbrick mill, where she took up her place again in front of the loom. She had worked only a few minutes when the whistle blew three short blasts.

"What's wrong, Flood?" a voice called out. "It's not near quittin' time."

The women looked toward the door. An unsmiling Théophile Roche stood beside Captain Ferrell. "Evacuate the women and children, Mr. Roche. I have orders to destroy the mill."

"But, monsieur, did you not see the French flag flying overhead?"

"I did. But there's no Union flag flying beside it. You are manufacturing goods to be used by the Rebel forces. That is unlawful."

"How can it be unlawful, monsieur? I am not a Confederate. I am a citizen of France. If you burn down this mill, it will be against international law."

"I have my orders from General Garrard, Mr. Roche. Nothing you say can change those orders. See to your workers, if you don't wish them harmed."

The women and children fled from the mill as the soldiers entered and began to rip loose the overhead shafts powered by the waterwheel. Standing, helpless, in groups on the hillside, they watched while the machinery they had worked on a few minutes before was dismantled, dragged outside, and relegated to the watery grave of Vickery Creek.

"Save the overhead beams, Corporal," Mars ordered. "We can use them later in rebuilding the bridge."

With that, done, the mill was put to the torch. Flames licked at the structure, with a burnt offering of wool permeating the air with its acrid odor.

Rebecca and Allison stood together, observing the destruction. "Let's go home, Rebecca," Allison urged.

Not looking back at the engulfing flames, the two, taking turns carrying Morrow, dejectedly retraced their route along the banks of Vickery Creek. They continued walking in complete silence until they reached the small orchard belonging to Rose Mallow.

Allison stopped. "Look, Rebecca. Someone has stripped the last apples from our trees."

But Rebecca was not looking at the trees. She was staring instead at a group of soldiers standing in the breezeway between the house and the summer kitchen. And while she

55

watched, another soldier came into view carrying the utensils from the kitchen.

An irate Rebecca began to run toward the soldiers, shouting, "You put that stuff down. Ain't right for you to steal Miss Allison's things."

"No, Rebecca. Stop," Allison called out, afraid that some harm would come to the woman. But it was too late. The soldiers had already seen her.

CHAPTER
7

There were six of them. For a moment, the surprised soldiers stood like guilty schoolboys. But with Rebecca's steady progress resembling an angry hen scuttling to protect her brood, their mood changed. They no longer looked like schoolboys but men, hardened in battle, accustomed to taking what they wanted by force.

"Rebecca," Allison called again. "Stop."

Allison's sharp warning had little effect on the woman. She paused only long enough to glance at Allison and then continued toward the soldiers, who were filling their sack with confiscated goods.

Quickly, Allison placed the basket containing Morrow on the ground and then took the baby in her arms. She hurried to catch up with Rebecca before she reached the back steps of Rose Mallow, for she knew that the black woman lost all caution when she became angry.

"I'll deal with the men," Allison said. "Here, you see to the baby, Rebecca." Disguising her fear, Allison looked at the soldiers, her violet eyes studying one face and then another until she came to the one who looked the most uncomfortable at being caught stealing.

"Gentlemen, as you have already learned, I have few possessions. So I would appreciate your leaving quietly, without taking anything that belongs to Rose Mallow."

The boy with the guilty expression made as if to put back the stolen goods, but an ugly voice admonished him. "No, Robby boy. Drop the kitchen wares into the sack with the other things. We'll be needing them to cook with tonight."

"But, Raynor, it's not quite right, is it, to steal from a woman?"

"Who said anything about stealing? This is a Rebel household. We're foraging, my boy, for what we need. Take the sack on to the wagon in front and don't pay any attention to the woman."

The boy glanced apologetically at Allison. Then he picked up the sack and left the breezeway.

"Miss Allison!" Rebecca protested, moving forward with the baby in her arms.

"Stay where you are, black woman. Or I'll slit your gizzard with this here knife."

The look on the leader's face showed that it was no idle threat.

"Do as he says, Rebecca."

The two women remained motionless before the steps of the breezeway until they heard the wagon leave the front yard. Then, taking Morrow with her, Rebecca rushed up the back steps and into the house. But Allison, wanting to put off the sight of her ransacked house for as long as she could, slowly walked to the front entrance of Rose Mallow and sat down by the wisteria-vined steps.

She watched the dark smoke from the burning mill rise steadily over the treetops and spread its cloud beyond the town square. Not only had the Confederacy lost an important source of cloth, but the women had lost their livelihood, too. For Allison and Rebecca, it was even worse. It was not likely that Roche would pay them for the little work they had done. Now they had no hope of acquiring enough money to hire someone to take them all the way to Savannah. They would have to wait for Araminta to send a carriage.

"What are we going to do?" Allison asked aloud, with no one to hear her. Tugging at the collar of her calico dress because of the heat, she stood and went inside just as Rebecca was walking down the steps from the attic.

"Morrow and I made a tour of the house, but I guess you want to see for yourself what the soldiers took away. While you look, I'll go ahead and give the baby her bath and get her ready for bed. At least they didn't take away the cradle."

The long shadows of the evening spread along the length of the hallway. The tin washtub, used to catch the rain, had disappeared along with the fainting couch beyond the stairs. The crystal vase in the hall niche was gone, too, with the wilting flowers trampled on the floor.

"What about the trunk in the attic, Rebecca?"

The woman was silent.

"The silver? My grandmother's Spode?"

"They're all gone, Miss Allison."

She nodded her head and began to walk slowly into the front parlor. As she did so, Rebecca went to the kitchen with the baby. She knew her mistress would want to be alone.

The parlor mantel was bare. Allison's most prized possession, the wedding picture in its silver frame, was gone. "No," she cried out, responding for the first time to the pillage of her house. But somehow she couldn't blame the soldiers—only herself. "Oh, Coin, please forgive me."

She knew she should have buried the picture in the orchard for safety. But she'd been selfish. She had wanted it where she could look at it each day. Now, because of her, Morrow would never know the joy of seeing her father's likeness.

As she had on the day of the memorial service, Allison remained in the parlor and grieved. She found no comfort in her sorrow. As much as she wanted to deny it, Allison knew that her own memory of Coin's face would diminish with time. So it was a double loss—for the child who had never seen her father and for the wife who had loved him dearly but would never see him again.

That night, the sounds of an alien army celebrating its latest victory floated along the banks of the Chattahoochee. And the people in the occupied town of Roswell rested uneasily.

With the burning of the mill, there was no need for the two women at Rose Mallow to rise before dawn. Allison slept fitfully until Morrow demanded her morning feeding. Then she rose and dressed in the only dress that the soldiers had missed—the black one hanging out to air in the shade of the pergola. In its place, she hung the newly washed calico muslin she'd worn to the mill the day before.

As the sun crept past the old dial in the garden, a man on horseback rode up Roswell Road and turned into the long, graveled drive that led to Rose Mallow. The man's military uniform was covered with dust, making it difficult to tell its color—blue or gray.

Allison stood on the porch and watched the rider approach. Her heart began to beat rapidly. There was something about the way the man sat his horse that reminded her of Coin. But, of course, that was impossible. Coin was dead, and the town was occupied by the enemy. Seeing a sack slung over the horse, Allison called to Rebecca and fled into the house.

"Go to the door, Rebecca. And inform the soldier that he's too late. Everything of value in the house has already been confiscated." Even her pistol had been taken along with her bed pillow, so Allison was at the mercy of anyone who came.

She stood near the empty fireplace and looked out the long window that faced the porch. She watched the soldier dismount, remove the sack from his horse, and walk up the front steps.

Then came Rebecca's voice. "You're too late, soldier. There's nothin' left in this house for you to take. So you can just go back where you came from."

"My name is Captain Mars Ferrell. Please give my compliments to your mistress and inform her that I wish to see her on an important matter."

Rebecca eyed him suspiciously but did as she was told, leaving him to wait on the porch while she went into the parlor.

"You heard him, Miss Allison?"

"Yes."

"You want me to let him in?"

61

"I don't have much choice, do I, Rebecca?"

"No'm."

"Then send him in."

The soldier paused in the parlor doorway. "Mistress Forsyth?"

"Yes?"

Allison turned slowly to face the Union officer. Her violet eyes revealed her pain, for her first impression had been correct. The man before her resembled her husband in stance and manner. He had the same boyish look on his face, the same color eyes. But the slight resemblance worked to the man's disadvantage, for he was alive and Coin was dead.

"Captain Mars Ferrell, at your service, ma'am."

Allison's voice was harsher than she intended. "I'm afraid I can't ask you to be seated, Captain. As you see, even my chairs have been taken by your men."

"My apologies. If it were possible, I would return them to you. But it's too late. However, I do have a few things in the sack that I would like you to examine. I was told by a Mistress Pratt that they might belong to you."

The soldier proceeded to remove the items one by one, laying them on the floor at Allison's feet—the long-handled spatula that had come from the kitchen, the lace veil to her wedding dress, a large serving spoon of her silverware, and the teapot and three cups of her Spode china. She viewed them all without emotion until she saw the familiar silver frame. Allison gave a cry and immediately stooped to retrieve the treasured picture.

With tears blurring her vision, she hugged the wedding picture and, for the first time, showed her gratitude. "Thank you, Captain Ferrell. You don't know how much this means to me to have the picture of my husband returned." Abruptly, she stood up, walked to the mantel, and put it in its place of honor. The sun, coming through the open window, picked up the gold in Allison's hair.

Mars Ferrell found himself unable to take his eyes from the woman. He had first seen her likeness in the wedding portrait the men were passing around the campfire the previous evening. There had been something vulnerable about her that had caused him to want to protect her from the ribald comments of the soldiers. By the light of the flames, she had seemed too beautiful to be real. Now, seeing her in person, he realized the picture had not flattered her. She was even more beautiful. And even more vulnerable.

For the first time, he became aware of the black dress. "Your husband is dead?" Mars inquired.

She turned from the mantelpiece. "Yes. He was killed in Virginia. That's why I'm so grateful to you, Captain Ferrell, for returning his picture to me."

"He should have seen to your well-being, madam. Sent you somewhere safe, out of reach of the war, instead of leaving you here at the mercy of any bushwhacker who happened to come along."

His comment caused a bitterness to her voice. "He thought I would be safe in my own home, Captain. The fault doesn't lie with him, only with—" Allison stopped. It would not do to offend the man who had taken the trouble to return her few possessions to her.

But the Union captain had no hesitation in completing her thoughts aloud. "Only with the foraging soldiers, I think you were going to say." He moved toward the hallway. "I beg your pardon, ma'am, but I have to get back to headquarters."

Allison followed him to the open front door and watched as he removed his horse's reins from the hitching post and mounted. "By the way, madam, a guard will be stationed at the road to prevent a recurrence of yesterday."

"Thank you, Captain."

She watched until the rider disappeared down the long, tree-lined drive. By the time Rebecca reappeared, Allison was alone again.

"I suppose I should have invited him to have some blackberry leaf tea, Rebecca. Especially since he was nice enough to return the teapot and three of the cups."

"Miss Emma would turn over in her grave if she thought a Yankee was drinkin' out of one of her prize Spode teacups."

"But he was a gentleman, Rebecca. You could tell that by his manner."

"A *Yankee* gentleman, Miss Allison. That's the worst kind."

"Well, let's be grateful for the few things he was able to rescue. Why don't you fix a pot of tea and we'll have it on the porch. Then you can help me find a place to bury the wedding picture. I don't want to risk losing it again."

"We're out of blackberry leaves," Rebecca said. "I'll have to gather some more, to brew."

Allison nodded. "Do we still have some parched okra seeds?"

"Yes'm. That's the one thing they didn't take yesterday."

"Then, we'll have make-believe coffee instead." A wistful Allison added, "When this war is over, Rebecca, I vow I'm going to have *real* coffee, with cream. And Morrow will have a bonnet of soft silk instead of woven cornshucks."

"And I'm gonna have real pearl buttons instead of these

64

persimmon seeds," Rebecca added, looking down at her patched calico dress.

The two women stared at each other and laughed. "Things have to get better, don't they?"

"I guess so. Seems they can't get much worse, Miss Allison."

CHAPTER 8

At The Bricks, Madrigal O'Laney finished eating her breakfast and watched the open door for Ellie. A large horsefly zoomed inside, and Madrigal, taking her apron from the kitchen chair, began chasing the insect throughout the apartment.

"What're you doin', Madrigal?" a voice inquired.

"Oh, hello, Ellie. Come on in," she said. "I'll be ready to go just as soon as I chase this horsefly out the door."

"Won't do a bit of good," the tall, slender Ellie advised her. "They're all over the place. Ten to every horse, I reckon. Flood says she's never seen so many horses and wagons. Or soldiers, either. They're spread all over Preacher

Pratt's lawn, and ruinin' his fields, too. Just like they ruined the mills."

"And they're probably takin' everything from the commissary," Madrigal added. "But if we hurry, maybe there'll still be a little food left."

Putting down her apron, once she had shooed the fly outside, Madrigal picked up her basket, motioned for Ellie to follow, and then closed the door to her apartment. "Wish I had some way of lockin' the door behind me," she commented.

"Wouldn't do you much good," Ellie remarked. "I hear they went to poor Mrs. Forsyth's house and took everything while she was standin' there. Flood said it would be better for us not to try to lock up in the village. They'd just break our doors down, to boot."

"Well, they'd better not try to get in here. I got my steppa's old gun, and I don't mind usin' it."

The two, cautious at first, began walking toward the square and the commissary. "You hear what happened to Mr. Roche?" Ellie asked.

"What?"

"He's been arrested for treason."

"Treason? That's the silliest thing I ever heard of," Madrigal said, stopping in the middle of the road to gaze at Ellie. "You have to betray your country for treason. You must have it all wrong, Ellie."

"Alma Brady told me, and she should know." Ellie was suddenly defensive. "She overheard one of the soldiers talkin' about it. The order came from General Sherman himself. He was mad because Mr. Roche was manufacturing cloth for our army to use. And there was even talk of hangin' him."

Madrigal snorted in disbelief. "And I suppose the next thing you're going to tell me is that we're all goin' to be arrested, too. It would make just about as much sense."

Two soldiers, dressed in blue, leaned against one of the posts supporting the shed roof of the stores and watched Ellie and Madrigal approaching. As they came within a few feet, one of the men took off his field cap and said, "Good morning, ma'am."

Madrigal lifted her head, stared past him, and kept walking. But then she heard the steps on the wooden walkway behind her and knew they were being followed.

"Looks like she's got a temper to go with her hair," one soldier commented. "Snooty, too."

"I always did like a little red-haired gal," the other commented with a laugh. "Didn't matter which side of the Mason-Dixon line she came from."

Ellie stuck closely to Madrigal until they reached the commissary and walked inside.

"Good mornin', Miss Madrigal." Mr. Rowdybush's face brightened when he recognized her. Then, nodding to the young woman with her, he added, "Miss Ellie."

"Good mornin', Mr. Rowdybush," the two said in unison.

With the bright sun still impairing her vision, Madrigal waited for her eyes to become adjusted to the light inside the store.

"What can I do for you?" Mr. Rowdybush asked.

"I need some flour, if you have some," Madrigal answered. "A little fatback, too."

"You're in luck today. But when this supply is gone, don't know when we'll be gettin' in any more." He stared at the two soldiers lingering by the door and whispered, "They burned the flour mill up the creek two days ago."

Madrigal made no pretense at keeping her voice low. "They seem to enjoy burnin' things, don't they? I hear they've burned so many houses, people have started calling the lone chimneys 'Sherman's Sentinels.'"

"Miss Madrigal," the man warned, "you better be careful what you say."

She turned around and stared in the direction of the two soldiers. "Law, I'm not afraid of them, Mr. Rowdybush." Then she placed her basket on the counter and began to bargain with the man, who could never resist Madrigal's smile.

When Ellie had also completed her shopping, the two said good-bye and left the store. The same soldiers smiled and bowed as Madrigal swept by.

"A pleasant day to you, Miss Madrigal."

"And to you, Miss Ellie," the other one said.

This time, Madrigal gave a curt nod and walked on. Maybe Mr. Rowdybush was right. Her tongue had always gotten her into trouble. Maybe she should be more careful, after all.

"They're still followin' us, Madrigal," Ellie whispered.

"Well, pretend you don't notice them, Ellie. Just keep walkin'. We'll reach home soon enough."

But it was hard to ignore them. And not only the two trailing them, but all of the other soldiers that now swarmed over the town. In the churchyard, the pews that had been ripped from the sanctuary to make room for the wounded were scattered under the trees, and men, with nothing else to do, sat in them and held spitting contests to while away the time. An occasional moan coming from the open door of the church mingled with the laughter of the men outside.

Madrigal's faced hardened when she saw the remnants of the organ, a pathetic thing, lying near the street. She had loved the music played on it each Sunday. But from the looks of it, nobody would ever be able to put it back together once the Union army had left.

Horses galloping down the road sent Madrigal and Ellie scurrying to the green strip of grass beyond the road. They waited for the cavalry to pass, and then, looking both ways, they crossed the dusty road and headed for home.

The two soldiers, who had been following them all this time, stopped. Seeing Madrigal disappear into The Bricks, they turned around and retraced their steps to the churchyard where they, too, found a pew and sat down.

"You know how long it is, Maybry, since I've been with a woman?"

"Too long, I guess, from the way you were looking at that little redheaded gal."

Caleb laughed. "She's sure something, ain't she? Miss Madri-gal." He placed the emphasis on the last syllable of her name.

Captain Ferrell walked by, took one look at the lolling soldiers, and put them all to work clearing the churchyard of its debris. "We can use the wood to help rebuild the bridge," he said. "Get a wagon, Private, and begin loading." He stared straight at Caleb.

"Yes, Captain. Right away."

"And when you're through here, go down to the mill and pick up the wood there."

"What do you want us to do with it, sir?"

"Haul it to the river and unload it for the men to start rebuilding the bridge."

Two hours later, Caleb and Maybry were still working. "Never should have sat down where the captain could see us," Maybry complained.

"Wouldn't have made a bit o' difference. The general has

everybody working. Saw Jed a little while ago. He's been foraging all day gathering grain for the horses." Caleb wiped his perspiring face with his bandanna. "Hotter 'n hell in the fields, I can tell you. Jed's face was every bit as red as this here bandanna."

Maybry nodded. "I never *seen* weather this hot before." He threw another large piece of wood from the wagon onto the huge pile at the riverbank. "You know what I'd like to do right this minute?" he asked.

"What?"

"Go skinny-dippin' in the crick behind the mill. You wanna go?"

Caleb laughed. "Not with you, Maybry. But I wouldn't mind if I could persuade that little redheaded gal to go with me."

"She's been on your mind all day, ain't she?"

"Not much else to think about," Caleb confessed.

"Well, there's the whiskey ration that General Garrard is gonna issue us tonight for supper."

A surprised Caleb said, "What brought that on? He's only done it one other time in all these months of fighting."

"General Sherman. He's that pleased to be back in his good graces again."

They finished unloading the wood. "Gee haw," Caleb shouted, and whistling to the mules, he brought the wagon around and headed back from the Chattahoochee River toward the burned-out mill. By the time they took one more load to the river, it would be almost dark and they could quit.

Two hours later, Caleb and Maybry sat around the campfire and scraped their mess kits clean. The allotment of whiskey had not lasted long with the two. They looked over at young Orville, who hadn't bothered to taste his.

"You gonna drink your whiskey, Orville?" Caleb asked.

"No. I promised my granny I wouldn't touch the stuff till I was nineteen. Got a year to go." Then he said, "Why? You want it?"

"I could use a little extra."

"So could I," Maybry said.

"How 'bout a game of cards for it?" another voice piped up. "Winner take all."

"Yeah. Let's play for it," a fourth voice agreed. "Everybody who has a gill they don't want, put it under this tree. And everybody who wants to play for it, get out the dice and cards."

Soon, by the light of the campfire, the men began to play, with the rations of whiskey as the prize. At the end of each round, the winner picked up a gill from the stockpile and downed it before the next round began.

Caleb, Maybry, and Jed were lucky. Within two hours, all of the gills were gone, with a decidedly drunk core of soldiers sitting around the fire at the last.

The men who had lost got up and began to drift in various directions. But Caleb, Maybry, and some of the others were in no mood for the festivities to stop.

"Hey, I know where there're some of the cutest little mill gals just waitin' for us," Caleb said.

"Where?" Jed asked.

"Me and Maybry will take you there," Caleb offered.

'You'd better not let Captain Ferrell hear you," someone whispered, motioning for Caleb to be quiet until the captain passed by.

"Good evenin', Captain," Jed called out.

"Time to break it up, boys," he advised. "We've got a long day ahead of us."

"Just as soon as we finish our smokes, sir."

"Well, put out the fire before you leave. There's been enough burning to last a while."

"Till we get to Atlanta, I reckon," a voice piped up in the dark. The soldiers laughed and watched until Mars Ferrell was out of sight. Taking their time with their cigarettes, some lingered by the fire. Then, conspiratorially, the soldiers left two by two, crossing the road and waiting until Caleb had put out the fire and joined them.

In her apartment at The Bricks, Madrigal was still awake. The night air was heavy with the odor of horses, and the slight breeze that found its way through the upstairs window also smelled of dust, as if the June rains had never happened. In the distance was the sound of the waterfall cascading over the dam. But the mill wheel was silent.

Poor Mr. Roche. Ellie had been right, after all. The Frenchman *had* been arrested and taken to Marietta. Thinking about him, Madrigal climbed out of the black-iron bed and walked to the window. The moon was hidden behind the clouds. But an occasinal red glare flashed in the distance, lighting up the sky. Madrigal's mind turned from the manager of the mill to Private Angus Smithwick, who had kissed her by the bridge. All of the Georgia Militia were gone now, with Roswell occupied by thousands of enemy soldiers.

A slight movement along the white-graveled road caught her attention. For a moment, Madrigal strained her eyes, but she saw nothing out of the ordinary. Then voices penetrated the silence—stealthy voices, moving along in a whisper. The moon came from behind the clouds, bringing momentary light. Soldiers in blue uniforms, perhaps a dozen or more, were walking down the road. She saw them clearly until the moon went back behind the clouds.

Madrigal rushed to put on her wrapper. The gun was still hidden in the kitchen behind the cracker barrel. With bare feet, she fled down the narrow steps to retrieve it and take it upstairs with her. But before she reached the bottom of the stairs, she heard an impatient knock at the door.

"Miss Madrigal," a voice called out, "can you hear me? I want you to open this door right now."

Madrigal froze. She looked in the direction of the kitchen and then toward the door with its wooden bar in place.

"Miss Madri-gal, I know you're in there. Open up!"

She heard the door rattle, and her hand flew to her throat. Finally, she spoke. "What's wrong? Who are you, and what do you want?"

"It's me—Caleb. And I've come to keep you company for the night."

"Go away, Caleb. Leave me alone."

The door rattled again. "You can't get rid of me easy as you did today, Miss Snooty."

Alarmed, Madrigal rushed toward the cracker barrel. Before she had a chance to retrieve the pistol, she heard a board splinter, and the door to her apartment fell open.

CHAPTER

9

As Caleb stumbled past the door and into the apartment, Madrigal blew out her candle, leaving the room in complete darkness. She didn't move.

Swearing, Caleb struck a match, and in its brief glare, he saw Madrigal standing only a few feet away. She came to life and began to move forward, trying to get past him and out the door, but he blocked her way.

"Oh, no, you don't, Madri-gal. I'm not letting you run away from me this time."

"What do you want, Caleb?" she repeated.

"A little company, that's all. A soldier gets mighty lonesome around here."

He reeked with the odor of whiskey, and Madrigal knew

he was drunk. Remembering the earlier days when Ben, her steppa, had come home in the same condition, she knew the best thing to do was to humor him before he started to get ugly.

"Well, why didn't you say so, Caleb? Wait a minute till I can light the candle again."

"I'll light it for you."

Disappointed at not being allowed to reach the kitchen, she held the candle steady while Caleb lit another match. Then she placed the candle on the table and sat down in one of the rush-bottomed chairs.

He looked at the door hanging on its hinges. "You stay where you are while I fix the door," he said, walking back to the opening and lifting the door into place. He then anchored it by placing the slat of wood back into the groove on each side.

By now, Madrigal could hear the commotion along the row of apartments and she knew that no one in The Bricks was safe from the soldiers. She thought of Ellie and Flood in the village and wondered if they were also having trouble. Poor Ellie. She was such a 'fraidy cat. And she was frightened of men more than of anything else.

"What have you been doin' today, Caleb?" Madrigal inquired, as if she didn't have a care in the world.

"Hauling wood to rebuild the bridge," he answered, coming back to stand beside her at the table.

Madrigal tightened the sash of her wrapper and pushed the long red hair from her eyes.

"That must have been hard work in all this heat. When will the engineers get started on the bridge, and how long will it take?"

"You're awful talkative, Madrigal. Why do you want to know?"

"You don't have to answer if you don't want to. I was just makin' conversation." She indicated the empty chair opposite her. "Sit down, Caleb. If you're goin' to stay awhile, you might as well get comfortable. Can I fix you a cup of coffee or tea?"

Madrigal *had* to get into the kitchen to retrieve the gun. But Caleb shook his head. He looked at the stairs and then back at Madrigal. "What's upstairs?"

"Oh, just another fireplace—and the rest of the apartment."

"And a nice feather mattress, I'll bet." He stared again at Madrigal. "I been sleepin' on the ground for the past three months. I sure would like to sleep in a nice soft bed tonight."

"Well, if you want the mattress, there's not much I can do to stop you from takin' it."

"And not much you can do to stop me from taking you, too."

"Now, Caleb, you're drunk. So I'll just pretend you didn't say that. But I sure do feel sorry for you, sleepin' on the ground for so long. I wouldn't mind a bit if you went on upstairs and slept off the whiskey."

He looked at her in a questioning manner, as if he couldn't quite comprehend what she was saying. "Go on, Caleb. It's all right. I'll just stay here in the kitchen and put on a pot of coffee that we can drink together when you wake up."

"Oh, no. I'm not that stupid, little redhead. Think you can get me to go upstairs, do you, just so you can run out the door?"

"Why, sir, that never entered my mind."

"Wouldn't do you any good if it had. Take the candle, Madrigal. We'll go see that feather mattress together."

"You're sure you're not hungry? I got some nice left-overs . . ."

Caleb's laugh was ugly. "I'm hungry for something besides food," he admitted. "I'm hungry for *you*, redhead. And I been thinking this livelong day, ever since I saw you, what I was going to do about it."

Caleb suddenly grabbed her arm and began to propel her toward the stairs. "Go on, girl, up the stairs you go. I'm getting impatient."

Slowly, she walked up each step, wondering what she could do to defend herself. The only weapon at hand was the candle. At the head of the stairs, Madrigal stopped, turned around like lightning, and pushed the candle into Caleb's face. A yelp of pain echoed through the apartment as the light went out and Caleb lost his footing. "You little bitch," he shouted. " Now you're going to pay for that."

Madrigal didn't get far in her flight. In the darkness, she felt Caleb's hand reach out and grab her ankle as she tried to flee down the steps. Only the railing kept her from taking a nasty spill.

"No, leave me alone," she cried.

But it was too late. Caleb was stronger than she. He dragged her like a rag doll toward the iron bed, faintly framed by the light coming through the open window.

In the bedroom, Madrigal struggled, twisting and turning, to avoid the drunken Caleb. It made no difference. He was soon on top of her, pinning her to the bed as he fumbled with his uniform. And he began to touch her, just as her drunken steppa had touched her sometimes when she was younger.

Caleb's actions brought back the part of her life that she had relegated to the past, with a curtain drawn over the memory, just like the curtain that had separated the bed belonging to her mother and Ben from her own bed.

But then the flames that had only been banked were stirred up again, awakening the erotic appetite that had been force-fed by Ben. Despite herself, she began to twist and turn in a different manner—not against Caleb, but with him, becoming the willing receptacle for his every thrust. And she hated him, for he had made her a twelve-year-old again, alone in the shack with her steppa. *He* was the one who was on top of her.

"You're bad, Madrigal. And it's gonna be your fault when I leave your ma one of these days. I can see her face cave in when I tell her what we've been doin' behind her back."

"But it wasn't my fault, Ben, I didn't want you to do it."

"Not at first, anyway. But you love it now, girl. Don't you? Admit it feels good, Madrigal."

"Yes, Ben. It feels good." And she began to cry in shame.

The heat of the room now clothed the two bodies wet with perspiration. Caleb teased her breast and laughed. "You can't tell me you didn't enjoy that, too, redhead."

Madrigal moved away from him and was silent. He may have had his way, but she wasn't through with him yet. She rolled over again and whispered, "I wanted you, Caleb. The minute I saw you today, I wanted you."

He reached up and touched the burn on his cheek. "Well, if you were that sure, girl, why did you have to push the candle in my face?"

"I'm sorry about that, Caleb. I really am. Come on, let's get up and let me show you how sorry I am. I'll fix you somethin' to eat. And some coffee would taste mighty good, too, don't you think?"

"I reckon so, but I can't stay much longer. Got to sneak

back into camp before that Captain Ferrell comes poking his nose around the tents."

Madrigal reached out for her wrapper, put it on, and then leaned over toward Caleb. "I'll be downstairs when you're ready."

While Caleb began to put on his uniform again, Madrigal walked down the steps like a sleepwalker. Not lighting a candle, she groped her way to the cracker barrel in the kitchen to retrieve the gun.

In the mill village, with its meandering trails connecting one house to the other, a frightened Ellie ran to Flood's house. She had heard the drunken soldiers.

"Quick, Flood, let me in," Ellie called, knocking at the door.

"What's wrong, Ellie?" Flood asked, opening the door to the frightened girl.

"There're some soldiers comin' into the village. They're up to no good, I know."

"Ellie, nobody's goin' to harm you. You're scared of your own shadow these days."

"But I heard somebody cry out, Flood, down the road. It sounded like Alma. But I was too scared to go and see."

"Well, stay here with me till you get over bein' so scared."

"Thank you, Flood. I don't know what I'd do without you."

The large, heavyset woman listened to the noise along the road. And she, too, began to grow a little uneasy.

"I think I'll just go and get out of these nightclothes, Ellie. I won't be gone long."

Lighting another candle, Flood moved from the living area into her bedroom. But instead of dressing in the calico dress that she'd taken off an hour before, she pulled out her husband's clothes instead and put them on. It wouldn't hurt any, if the soldiers happened to come by. Better than having two females alone in a house.

She had managed to twist her hair up and put it under her husband's cap when a knock sounded at the door. Quickly, she walked back to the living area where Ellie was standing, ready to flee at the sound.

"Ellie, get in the bedroom."

The young girl needed no prompting. She ran from the room while Flood went to stand by the closed door.

Lowering her voice, she said, "Who's there?"

"Private Maybry Elliot, on official army business. Will you please open the door?"

Flood debated with herself, but in the end there was nothing to do but open the door. She had already heard what happened to Mr. Roche. And she knew there was some survey going on about the workers in the mill that had been burned down.

She stood in the dim light with Maybry Elliot and his friend, Jed Riley, staring at her. But the clothes had done their work.

"May we come in, sir," Maybry asked, "to ask you a few questions concerning the mill?"

Flood stood back to allow them to enter. Maybry pulled an official-looking paper from his pocket and then began to question Flood. "You were a worker at the Ivy Woolen Mill?"

"Yes."

"Are there any other workers, besides you, here in this house? A wife or a daughter, maybe?"

"No one else livin' here," Flood answered curtly, recognizing the smell of whiskey about them.

Ellie, overhearing the conversation, was relieved. She left the safety of the bedroom to return to the living area.

"Good evenin', Miss Ellie," Maybry said, grinning as he recognized the young girl from the encounter that morning.

"Good evenin'."

At a nod from Maybry, Jed walked toward Flood. "Sit down, mister. In that chair yonder."

Taken by surprise, an angry Flood saw the revolver pointed at her. "Why?"

"Because we aim to have a little fun with your daughter here. And we don't intend to be interrupted. Sit down, mister," he said again, this time in a harsher voice.

"Ellie, run—"

Flood's admonition came too late. Maybry had already grasped the girl's arm. "Now, don't be scared, Miss Ellie," Maybry cautioned. "If you treat Jed and me right, no harm will come to your pa."

Flood got up from the chair, but Jed said, "Sit down, mister, or else I'll knock you sidewinded."

"Please. Let us go," Ellie begged. "We haven't done any harm to you."

Both Maybry and Jed ignored the pleading of the young girl. "You ready to go first, Maybry?" Jed asked.

"Yeah. Since it was my idea. I think I deserve the first try. Come on, Miss Ellie. Let's find someplace private where your pa won't be causin' a stir."

"W-what do you plan to do?" Ellie's voice was barely above a whisper.

"Don't you know, Miss Ellie? I'm plannin' to treat you right."

"I—I want you to go instead."

Maybry laughed. "If we do, it won't be for a long while. Now, don't be scared of *me*, Miss Ellie. I'll be very gentle."

"Flood!" Ellie's pathetic voice caused Flood to jump from her chair to go to her aid, but Jed took the revolver and hit her on the head, sending her reeling.

"That's right. Sit back in the chair, mister. There's not one earthly thing you can do to stop our little bit of fun tonight."

Flood felt the blood dripping from her head. She put her hand up and then, dazed, glanced at the redness on her hand. In a few minutes, Ellie's cry caused Flood to grit her teeth and she acted as if she were going to leave the chair. But Jed, watching her, said, "You want another blow, mister?"

She sank down in the chair again and closed her eyes to fight back the tears. She waited; no sounds came from the room beyond. Then, finally Maybry appeared.

"All right, Jed. It's your turn now. I'll take over the gun to keep Papa to his chair."

"You were gone a mighty long time, Maybry. I just hope there's enough left for me."

Twenty minutes later, the two soldiers left Flood's house. For a moment longer, Flood sat in the chair. Then, with a heaviness of heart, she began to walk slowly into the bedroom. "Ellie?" she called out. "Are you all right, Ellie?"

At The Bricks, Madrigal O'Laney waited for Caleb to appear in the kitchen. As arrogantly as his drunkenness would allow him, he walked down the stairs and toward the table that had been set with two plates and two mugs.

"You have it ready, Madri-gal?"

"Yes, Caleb."

She turned around and pointed the pistol at Caleb's heart. As the candle flickered, the gun fired.

"You bitch," Caleb cried out for the second time that

evening. He gazed at her in disbelief, but seeing her with the gun still aimed at him, he staggered toward the doorway while he held his side.

For a long time after the wounded Caleb had left, Madrigal sat at the kitchen table with Ben's gun in her hand. The candle burned low and then went out. But Madrigal O'Laney didn't seem to notice.

CHAPTER 10

At Great Oaks, where General Kenner Garrard maintained his headquarters, there had been a flurry of activity since early morning. People of the town had come and gone to protest the ravaging of the mill village and The Bricks.

In the dining room, now the personal office of the general, Garrard stood up and walked to the window to look out. His face was stern as he viewed the tents in all directions. At the knock on the door, he turned around.

"Yes?"

"Captain Ferrell reporting to you, General."

Garrard looked at his secretary. "Send him in."

"General," Mars said, saluting his commander.

"Sit down, Captain Ferrell." Garrard indicated the chair

at the end of the dining-room table. "You corroborated the story?"

"I'm afraid so, sir."

"How many men were involved?"

"They're all closemouthed, but, as far as I can determine, about twelve, all from the same brigade. One man was shot rather badly by one of the young women. A Private Caleb Rabb. He was taken to the church by his friends. I haven't questioned him. The surgeon says he's too weak to talk since he's lost so much blood. But there's no doubt who shot him—a Madrigal O'Laney who worked in the woolen mill. Shall I bring her in, General?"

Garrard's eyes were piercing as he stared straight at his subordinate. "Ferrell, what would you do if a Confederate soldier broke into your house and raped your sister?"

"Beg pardon, sir, but I'd kill the bastard."

"Exactly. The private got what he deserved. So I see no need to arrest the young woman yet. Especially with the orders I've just received from General Sherman."

Garrard did not elaborate. Instead, he sat and tapped the table with his thumb. Then he looked through the window again at the tents.

"As much as I deplore their actions, those twelve men are my soldiers, and I'm afraid if they stay in this town, their lives won't be worth Confederate scrip. Ferrell, have that entire brigade moved back to Willeo Creek. Immediately."

"Yes, sir."

"And, Ferrell, we're getting too many casualties for the church to hold. The Bricks will soon be empty. Direct the surgeon to be ready to move most of his heatstroke victims when I give the word."

Once Mars Ferrell was gone, the general returned to

Sherman's letter, in which was in front of him. He didn't like the orders stated in it any more than he liked dealing with the aftermath of his own order for whiskey for the soldiers.

In the Field, near Chattahoochee.
General Garrard.
GENERAL:

I assure you, in spite of any little disappointment I may have expressed, I feel for you personally not only respect but affection, and wish for your unmeasured success and reputation, but I do wish to inspire all cavalry with my conviction that caution and prudence should be but a small element in their characters.

I repeat my orders that you arrest all people, male and female, connected with those factories, no matter what the clamor, and let them foot it, under guard, to Marietta, whence I will send them by cars to the North. . . .

The poor women will make a howl. Let them take along their children and clothing, providing they have the means of hauling or you can spare them. . . .

In your next letter, give me as much information as you can as to the size and dimensions of the burned bridge. . . .

I am, with respect, yours truly.

W. T. SHERMAN
Major General, Commanding.

By midmorning, Sherman's orders had been set in motion. Armed with the names of the mill workers, the soldiers began to round up the women and children, over four hundred of them.

Madrigal, sitting by the bed in Flood's house, stared down at Ellie. She held her hand and continued talking to her, but Ellie made no response. She acted as if she were far away—too far away for Madrigal's voice to reach her.

"Poor Ellie. She's been like that ever since last night when I found her," Flood said. "I'd hoped that seeing you might make some difference."

Madrigal looked at Flood. "Is your head feelin' better, Flood?"

"A little. And what about you, Madrigal?"

"Oh, I'll be all right. I've had bad things happen to me before."

"Rena Knox is spreadin' the rumor that *you're* to blame for all this. And some of the other women believe her. I just wanted you to know, Madrigal, that I don't think that at all."

"Thank you, Flood."

"You figure you'll get into any trouble for shootin' the soldier?"

"I don't know. But it's too late to worry about it. And I'd do it again if it happened today." Madrigal stood up. "I have to get back to the apartment. Mr. Rowdybush said he'd send someone to fix my door. But I'll be back soon as I can."

Madrigal left the village and began to walk back to The Bricks. But the events that occurred during the next hour kept her from returning to Flood's house.

Deeming it too heartless to make the women and children walk the sixteen miles to Marietta in the intense heat, General Garrard requisitioned one hundred and ten springless army wagons and put one of his captains, Worth Good-fellow, in charge of rounding up the women.

Down into the meandering roads of the mill village the wagons went, stopping at each house while the drivers and guards checked the names from a master list. A great wail ascended once the women realized what was happening. Just as Théophile Roche had been arrested for treason for running the mill, so were the women, whose only crime had been in taking the places of their husbands, fathers, and brothers now fighting in the Confederate army.

A tearful, crying Alma was torn from her aged grand-mother's arms and loaded onto a wagon. "Mama Lou," she screamed as the old woman stood, tears streaming down her face, seeing her granddaughter and the baby Robert for the last time in her life.

The same scene was repeated over and over—young women torn from their families and loaded on the wagons with their few possessions tied up in a bundle, while the drivers and guards looked the other way and pretended they had no part in what was taking place.

"Wait. Please wait," a woman begged. "I have to find my Caddie. I can't leave without my child."

Flood, dressed in her brown calico dress, hurriedly bundled her few possessions, including her husband's clothes, and then lifted Ellie, dressed in her calico dress and wrapped in a counterpane, to carry out to the wagon.

Up and down the mill village roads the wagons went, with the July sun bearing down on the women and children. As each wagon was filled, the vehicle took its place in the massive convoy for the trip to the Georgia Military Institute in Marietta, where the women were to be placed under guard until arrangements could be made to ship them north by rail.

As he sat under the shade of one of the old trees at Great Oaks, a reporter from the New York *Tribune*, Harry Newman, was bored. He had been assigned to General Garrard's cavalry, and while they were engaged in battle he had written many stirring pieces for the civilians back home. Now, with the fighting at a near standstill, he had little to write about until the crossing of the Chattahoochee and the taking of Atlanta. His last piece had been a human-interest story about the men who had gathered ripe, juicy blackberries in the woods and thrown them into a boiling pot of water with sugar, cornstarch, and crackers to make a dessert fit for the gods.

But as the army wagons began their trek out of the mill village and onto the main road, Harry realized that something unusual was happening. The air was filled with the cries of terrified women, of babies crying, and of old women trailing behind the wagons and weeping like Rachel for her lost children.

"What's happening?" he asked one of the officers coming out of headquarters. "Why are these women being taken from the village?"

"They're being arrested for treason."

"What's their crime, Captain?"

"They had the misfortune of working in the mills."

Harry left headquarters and began to run in the direction of the village. He knew he had the news scoop that all reporters dream of but seldom get.

He followed the progress of the wagons, saw the women and children being forced from their homes. Then he sat down at the entrance to the village, pulled his paper and pencil out of his pocket, and began to write.

. . . Only think of it! Four hundred weeping and terrified Ellens, Susans, and Maggies transported in the seatless and springless army wagons, away from their lovers and brothers of the sunny South; and all this for the offense of weaving tent cloth and spinning stocking yarn.

Newman continued to observe and to write. Seventy-two hours later, the village was empty and he had finished his story.

As he saw one of Garrard's aides climbing into a wagon, he called out, "Captain Ferrell, do you care to make a statement for the newspaper concerning the Roswell women?"

"No."

"But it's true, isn't it? They're going to be sent north by rail on the express orders of General Sherman?"

"That's correct, Newman. Now, if you will excuse me, I have my own orders to carry out."

At Rose Mallow, an unsuspecting Allison sat in the shade of the pergola and rocked her baby to sleep. She had always loved the pergola with its scuppernong vines giving it shade. But now she loved it even more, for it was under the pergola that she had chosen to bury the silver frame holding the picture of her husband.

The guard stationed at the entrance to her long driveway had made her feel relatively safe. But she had made a vow to herself to protect the portrait for her daughter. As soon as she heard from Araminta, she would dig it up again to take with her to Savannah.

She was no better off than she had been before her brief sojourn as a weaver in the mill. Her food supply was very low. Even the blackberries, once so plenteous in the woods, had been stripped by the soldiers, leaving the Roswell residents with none for their own bowls. And she had even dug up the smallest potatoes from the hill.

"Miss Allison?"

"Yes, Rebecca?"

"That Captain Ferrell is here to see you again."

"Send him here to the pergola, Rebecca."

"Yes'm."

Seeing him in full military uniform striding toward her, Allison stood. "Good afternoon, Captain."

"Mrs. Forsyth, I'm afraid I have bad news for you."

His face was severe, the lines between his eyes wrinkling against the sun.

"Yes?"

"You worked in the Roswell woolen mill with your servant, Rebecca, did you not?"

Allison nodded. "But I'm afraid my career didn't last long, Captain. I worked for two days before the mill was burned down. Why do you ask? Are you making reparations for the lost salary?"

"No. Merely ascertaining for myself that you were a worker in the mill, however short."

"And how does this concern you, Captain?"

"I'm afraid I'll have to ask you to come with me. General Sherman has ordered that all mill workers are to be arrested for treason."

"I don't understand, Captain Ferrell. Are you trying to tell me that *I* am under arrest, like a common criminal? Surely there's some mistake."

"I only wish it were, ma'am. I have a wagon waiting outside to take you to Marietta. You and your servant have fifteen minutes to gather any possessions you want to take with you."

"This is ridiculous. I demand to see General Garrard to clear up this terrible misunderstanding."

"There is no misunderstanding, I assure you. Your name is on Théophile Roche's ledger. The others in the mill village have already been gathered up and are on their way, at the direct insistence of General Garrard. Nothing you could say to him would cause him to make an exception to General Sherman's orders."

"But why is he sending us to Marietta?"

"You're going to be shipped north, over the lines."

An unsmiling Allison took up the baby basket from the pergola while the Union officer walked to the front of the house where the wagon and its driver waited.

"Rebecca," Allison called out, rushing inside the house to find her servant.

Mars Ferrell was true to his word. In fifteen minutes, he left the porch and walked into Rose Mallow to find Allison and to escort her to the army wagon.

As the wagon pulled out of the long driveway, Allison turned and kept her eyes on Rose Mallow until it was no longer visible. With Rebecca at her side and Morrow in her arms, she realized the nightmare that had started the previous month had never stopped.

The long, slow drive was far different from the one she had taken in June when the Reverend Pratt had sent his comfortable carriage for her. That day had been stormy and raining, with the wheels of the carriage bogged down in the muddy ruts of the road. Now there was no elegant carriage to cushion the jolts of the road or to shield the burning July sun from her face.

But two things were the same. The people who had stood on the side of the road the day of the memorial service and watched her pass were also there today.

She felt their curiosity now, even as she had felt their sympathy a month ago. And the same sense of desolation overwhelmed her. "Oh, Coin," Allison whispered, barely moving her lips. "I'm glad you can't see what has befallen us."

In bitterness, she remembered her conversation with Théophile Roche.

"May *le bon Dieu* forgive me for what I have promised today."

"May the good Lord bless you instead, Mr. Roche. For you have just saved my life."

"I hope you will still feel that way, madame, a month from now. As for myself, I'm not so sure."

CHAPTER

II

While the frightened women from the three mills settled into the barracks of the institute and waited helplessly for the military authorities to arrange their rail passage, Harry Newman's report generated an incredulous response from the North.

A new correspondent publishes a story, which, we trust, for the sake of the officer implicated, as well as our own good national name, may prove to be unfounded. It is to the effect that General Sherman, finding at Roswell, in Georgia, four hundred factory girls, employed in a large cotton factory at that point, ordered the whole of the unfortunate creatures to be sent

north of the Ohio. General Sherman has shown on
two or three occasions that ability as a military commander is quite compatible with something not far
removed from imbecility in respect to civil matters.
He writes stupendishly foolish orders on things political, and is evidently incapable of administering a
village on practical principle.

But it is hardly conceivable that an Officer, wearing
the United States commission of Major General,
should so far have forgotten the commonest dictates
of decency and humanity (Christianity apart), as to
drive four hundred penniless girls hundreds of miles
away from their homes and friends to seek a livelihood
amid a strange and hostile people.

We repeat our most earnest hope that further information may redeem the name of General Sherman
and our own from the frightful disgrace which this
story, as it comes to us, must inflict upon one or the
other. (New York *Commercial*)

At the Georgia Military Institute, the women were unaware of the furor churning on their account.

In the heat of the crowded barracks near the Marietta
train station, Madrigal sat by the cot where her friend Ellie
lay. Each small freckle across Ellie's nose seemed magnified
because of the ashen color of her skin.

A worried Flood hovered nearby. "The wagon trip wasn't
good for her, with all the jolts. I see she's bleedin' again,
and that can't be a good sign."

"I wish I knew what to do for her," Madrigal said. "It
breaks my heart to see her like this."

As the door to the barracks opened, Flood and Madrigal
looked up. They saw Allison Forsyth, with the crying

baby, and her servant, Rebecca, escorted through the door by the guard, who pointed toward the two vacant bunks. Then the door was locked again.

"Well, just look who's come in, Flood," Madrigal said. "The lady of Rose Mallow herself. Good evenin', Mrs. Forsyth."

"Madrigal, be civil," Flood warned.

Allison, burned by the hot sun, removed her bonnet and sat on the vacant bunk not far from Ellie's. She nodded to Madrigal and Flood but said nothing. She was still an outsider and she felt it. The two short days working in the mill had not been sufficient to forge a bond with any of the women.

Within a few minutes, Rebecca had draped Allison's cape to shield her from the curious eyes in the room. Soon, Morrow was nursing noisily at Allison's breast.

Later, Allison lay on her cot with the baby finally asleep beside her. She still did not comprehend fully what had happened to her. But she knew she didn't belong in this room with the other women. It was apparent by the curious looks directed at her, the shutting out from the intimate little groups that had gathered around the room.

Gazing at nothing in particular, she became aware of blood seeping through the counterpane on the cot next to hers. Quickly, she sat up and, forgetting that she was an outsider, said, "Madrigal, what's wrong?"

At first, Madrigal stared at her the way the other women had done. But then her worry compelled her to answer. "It's my friend. Ellie. She's hurt awful bad. And me and Flood don't know what to do for her."

"What happened?"

"It was the soldiers, comin' into the village several nights ago, that did it. Ellie hasn't been the same since. She hasn't spoken a word, either. Just stares like a voodoo doll with a pin stuck in her."

"We must get a doctor for her."

A puzzled expression swept over Madrigal's face, as if questioning why Allison Forsyth would be concerned for one of them.

"We tried, Mrs. Forsyth. There's not one anywhere near here."

"Then we'll have to take care of her ourselves, or she might bleed to death." Allison reached into her bundle and pulled out a white cotton petticoat. "Quick, Madrigal, tear this into tiny strips for me."

Madrigal needed no further prompting. Both she and Flood began to rip the petticoat into shreds while Allison gazed around the room. "Does anybody in the room have some Spanish moss?"

No one spoke. Finally, a voice said, "Addie Wickes has a pillow stuffed with it."

"Nobody's takin' my pillow from me. It came all the way from Darien, and I'm not partin' with it."

"Give Mrs. Forsyth the pillow, Addie," Flood ordered.

"Well, if you ruin it, you'll have to pay me for it."

Allison ignored the woman's remark. She worked quickly, with Rebecca helping her, while Flood and Madrigal, unable to do anything else, held the cape a second time for privacy.

Allison was no stranger in dealing with hemorrhage, for she had been afflicted with it immediately after Morrow was born. Within a few minutes, Allison had used the small strips and moss until the surgical packing was tight. "Now we need to prop your friend up, to make the blood clot. She mustn't be allowed to lie flat.

"Someone, go to the door and inform the guard that we need more water."

The women around Allison stared at her, not certain that what she was doing would be of any help to Ellie. And they resented her using most of their small supply of water.

Rebecca, keeping an eye on the baby, rushed over to the cot just in time to prevent her from rolling onto the floor. "I declare she's gettin' strong," she said. "You see that? She turned right over and nearly fell off the cot."

"Then I suppose we'll have to put her back in the basket, although I hate to do it," Allison said, realizing how little air was circulating in the hot room.

"You won't have to put her back in that hot basket, Mrs. Forsyth. I'll sit on the cot and watch her for a while."

Allison looked up to see Flood standing by the cot. "It's the least I can do while you help poor Ellie."

For the next hour, Allison attended to the sick young woman, changing the surgical packing when needed. She glanced up from time to time to make sure her child was all right. And she smiled when she saw that Flood was holding Morrow in her lap and fanning her while she talked to the baby.

Later, when food for the women was brought, Ellie seemed better, so Rebecca and Allison returned to their own allotted space in the barracks while Madrigal stayed by Ellie's side, spoon-feeding her as if she were no older than Morrow.

That night, in the darkness, the tears of the women began again. All around her, Allison heard weeping, but by that time she was too tired and numb to join in.

Along a dark, deserted road in the Shenandoah Valley of Virginia, a night rider galloped at full pace with only the moonlight to guide him. His saddlebag was filled with official Confederate dispatches intended for General Jubal Early's headquarters.

The general had routed the Federals at Kernstown, and his cavalry was pursuing the retreating General Crook, who was headed for Williamsport on the Potomac.

As the rider passed by a dark wooded area, his horse grew nervous as if sensing danger within the woods. The rider lifted his head for a brief moment and peered at the trees, but the woods revealed nothing. He spurred his animal, which needed no further urging. The horse picked up speed, its hoofbeats pounding against the road in a lonely race with the wind.

In the woods beyond, night sounds began to follow the progress of the rider—a whistle here, answered by a birdsong in the distance.

Suddenly, a shot rang out; then another. The rider fell from his horse and landed with a thud upon the hard earth. The riderless horse continued its steady pace along the stretch of woods until another shot brought the animal down.

Within seconds, a small band of Union soldiers emerged from the woods. "Get the saddlebag, Horace," a voice whispered.

When that was done, the group took to the woods without looking back at the Confederate courier lying on the road with the pale moon shining down upon him.

Later that night, one of General Crook's staff officers sat in his tent and by lantern light sorted out the mail from the contraband saddlebag. The general would be interested only in the official dispatches, not in the personal letters of Confederates writing home. He had his orders to destroy those. Taking the personal letters, he threw them into the waste bucket. Early the next morning, one of the men would come, as usual, to pick up the trash for burning.

Soon after reveille, when the soldiers had eaten their breakfasts, Private Ledlie Grosvener walked toward the officer's tent. He was careful to touch nothing but the bucket set in the tent opening. Hoisting it onto his shoulder, he began to walk toward the barrels, which were already smoking with the morning's trash. Ledlie was always curious about the contents of the buckets he picked up from the officers' tents each morning, so this time he lazily perused each piece of paper before relegating it to the flames.

"Looky here. Here's a letter from a Confederate captain to his wife. Just look at that fancy handwriting."

He spoke to his friend, Zach Turner, who was standing a few feet away.

"I didn't know you could read, dumbhead."

"Better than *you* can, I betcha."

"Well, then, why don't you just prove it and read that letter to me?"

Ledlie scowled at Zach. "And how would you know whether I was readin' it or just makin' it up?"

"That's easy, Ledlie. If you start out by readin' 'I take my pen in hand,' then I know you're makin' it up."

"And what's wrong with that? Both letters I wrote to my pa this year I started that way. Everybody does."

"Not those Johnny Reb officers. I hear they write fancy things, just like their penmanship."

"We'll just see how fancy." The soldier was irritated, and he tore open the letter as he backed away from the burning barrels.

"'My darling wife,'" Ledlie read, "'It is with a sense of extreme gratefulness that I am able to write you to let you know I am alive.'"

Ledlie looked up at Zach. "Seems to me that ain't much different from 'I take my pen in hand.'"

"Keep readin'."

You must have heard by now of the terrible battle in the wilderness, where the counterattack of the Federals killed many of our Army. If a picket had not brought a message for me, I would have been buried with my men.

As it was, I was severely injured and lay unconscious in a woodsman's hut for ten days. When I came to, the wound in my leg kept me immobile.

Any day now, I will go back to my regiment. They need officers so desperately. I count the months and days until I see my beloved family once more. Take care of Morrow. It is for these little ones that we are fighting so hard to save our land. Be strong and know that I love you more than words can tell.

Your devoted husband, Coin Forsyth, Captain, C.S.A.

Ledlie looked up at Zach. "Well, guess that proves to you I can read 'bout anything."

"You stumbled over a lot of words," Zach teased. Then, grinning, he said, "But I guess you couldna made the letter up. Ain't your style."

An officer walking by stopped when he saw the two soldiers seated on the ground. "Don't you have work to do, Private?" He gazed directly at Ledlie as he spoke.

"Yes, sir. Right away." Ledlie hopped up, took the large waste bucket, and emptied it into the burning barrel. Flames licked at the name "Allison," and soon there was nothing left of the letter.

• • •

At Marietta, the general in charge of arranging rail transportation as far as Nashville for the mill women was upset. In his headquarters at the rail yard, he glared at the man standing before him.

"We've got one track to bring in all the supplies—forage for the horses and ammunition and medical supplies for the battle of Atlanta. My men are being picked off like flies by the Johnny Rebs, hiding behind the trees and dynamiting the rails and bridges. It's hostile territory all the way between Marietta and Nashville, and here I get this durn-fool order to stop the military supplies and use my rolling stock to transport a bunch of women."

The general stopped as the sound of an engine whistle penetrated the yard. Then he continued with renewed fervor. "I've seen some mighty ridiculous orders in my day, but this one is the worst of the lot. No, Sergeant. You can go and tell your general that *I'm* running these trains, and I'm not about to take on four hundred and fifty women and squalling children. I have a war to fight. And a break in the rails up at Snake Gap Tunnel that needs fixing."

"General, you better look to see who personally signed those orders."

The general picked up the orders. "My God, he can't mean it."

"But he does, sir. And the sooner you start, the sooner you'll be rid of them."

That night, the officer in charge of the Marietta station requisitioned the food supply listed in the orders—nine days of rations for each woman and child. And he began the mammoth task of allotting boxcars for the train to carry the women prisoners as far north as Nashville. After that, they were General Webster's concern, not his.

CHAPTER

12

With guards surrounding the barracks to keep them from escaping, the women settled into another night of waiting. The cots were far too close together for the slight breeze to circulate. Already some of the women were ill with fever, and the close confinement had caused tempers to flare periodically.

Allison lay awake, her face wet with perspiration. She longed to get up and walk onto the porch of Rose Mallow to seek some relief from the stifling heat, but that was impossible. They were all prisoners with no control over what their fate might be.

Each day had passed more slowly than the previous one until a week had gone by. But the passage of time, however slow, had brought an ever-growing hope to some of the women that Sherman might rescind his orders and allow them to return home.

That prospect was on Madrigal O'Laney's mind as she lay awake in the dark.

"Miss Allison?" she whispered. "Are you still awake?"

"Yes, Madrigal. What is it?"

"Fannie Morton heard someone talkin' about us tonight. It sounded like we might be moved from here soon. You think maybe they've changed their minds and might let us go back home?"

"I doubt it, Madrigal. Especially now that our army is trying to retake Roswell."

"Have you ever been north?" The young woman didn't sound afraid, merely curious.

"Only as far as Virginia. Then I sailed from Savannah to Newport on the northeast coast one time."

The hungry baby awoke and began to cry, ending the conversation.

By morning, the women's hopes of returning to Roswell were crushed. After a scanty breakfast, the door to the barracks opened for a second time. A scowling Union officer demanded silence and attention from the women as he stood before them. Then, in a monotonous voice, he read from the paper in his hand.

"Now hear this. In approximately one hour, you are to be ready to move out. Arrangements have finally been made for your transportation north. Take only what you can carry. Once you have been checked off the list for loading, you will each be given nine days' food rations. You must not squander the food. It will have to last you until after you cross the Ohio River into Indiana."

The officer didn't wait to answer any questions. He left, and the door was locked behind him.

"I want to go home," a child's voice cried. "Mama, I want to go home."

"Hush, Maggie," Fannie Morton admonished her child.

"This is all your fault, Madrigal O'Laney," a woman accused. "If you hadn't shot that soldier, we'd all be home now."

Flood challenged her statement. "That's not true, Addie, and you know it. There's no need to be blamin' Madrigal for all our troubles."

But the woman paid no attention to Flood. She continued her tirade, directing her anger against Madrigal. A baby started crying, and soon the cry was taken up by other babies until the barracks were filled with the noise of crying women and children.

But within the hour, a quietness had come over the group. Sitting on the edge of cots, with their few possessions tied in bundles, they sat and listened for the sound of soldiers coming to march them to the train.

Allison looked at the window, for the sky had taken on that strange hue that presages an electrical storm, so prevalent in the scorching days of summer in the South. As a child, she had been able to smell an approaching storm, a blanket of heaviness in the air, long before it became apparent to her father or brother. And that same feeling now hung over the grounds of the institute.

Outside, the activity was stepped up—mules and wagons drawn from the supply sheds to the rail yard; men loading the boxcars with fresh straw, not to feed a shipment of horses but to spread over the floor for the women to sleep on. Other wagons brought the limited rations to be allotted to each woman for her journey.

Then a jagged chain of lightning appeared fleetingly in the air, followed by a crack of thunder that sent the mules bolting. And the military manager in charge stood at the window of his office and watched the pandemonium that followed.

The rains began and the trees on the grounds of the institute responded to the wind. The sudden storm intensified as if the belligerent gods had waited for this day to unleash their awful retribution against the land.

Within a few minutes, lightning had struck again, killing two of the mules and a guard who had been leaning against the steam engine of the train. A tall oak tree nearest to the barracks where Allison was lodged took a direct hit, splintering its wood in missiles over the lawn.

Inside the military rail office, the sergeant responsible for carrying out the orders to move the women was clearly uneasy. "Are you superstitious, Colonel Ramsbottom?"

"No. But I'm not a nitwit, either. We'll hold up awhile and wait until the worst of the storm is over before proceeding."

Twenty minutes later, the rain showed no sign of abating. But the pandemonium in the rail yard had been dealt with, and the colonel, realizing they couldn't wait any longer without running the risk of a flooded tunnel ahead, gave the order to begin the migration from barracks to boxcar.

Because of the steep grade of the roadbed through the mountains, the engine could pull only twenty boxcars. Ramsbottom didn't like loading each one with over twenty women and children, for that would give them little space to lie down, but there was no help for it. He could spare only one train.

His main concern was the one hundred and thirty miles

of single track from Marietta to Chattanooga. That was the most dangerous because of the Rebels. The next hundred and fifty miles to Nashville was a little less so. But once he got the women to Nashville, General Webster could worry about the next one hundred and eighty miles to Louisville. For by that time, he would have washed his hands of the women and started carrying military supplies again.

"All right, Edwards. We've wasted enough time. Start moving them out."

"Yes, sir."

In the barracks, the women, sobered by the storm, still sat surrounded by their bundles in silent groups.

"I hate this waitin'," Madrigal said, looking at Flood. "Why can't they hurry up and get it over with?"

"Well, you might be glad to leave Roswell behind, Madrigal O'Laney, but you'll never be able to escape your reputation. Puckka told me the kind of girl you are. And I'm gonna make sure nobody forgets it." Rena Knox glared at Madrigal as she held on to her daughter Caddie.

Madrigal lifted her head and smiled. "No wonder Puckka is such a bastard. I see he takes after his mother."

"How dare you—"

"Now, Rena. Just hush. You're the one who started it." Flood frowned at Rena and then turned to Madrigal. "It won't help matters if we get into a fight with each other. We got a long way to go, and the goin' is gonna be mighty rough without any added fussin'."

The door opened, and soldiers armed with muskets walked into the room to herd the women out, row by row.

Allison covered the basket holding Morrow with her shawl, to keep the rain from her face. And Rebecca, following beside her, carried both bundles of clothes.

Out into the rain they went, with the wind slashing across

their faces and whipping their clothes against their bodies. Ellie, still silent, was supported by Madrigal and Flood. Following them were those ill with fever who were also unable to walk without help from friends.

As they approached the platform, Madrigal recognized some of the women from the mill at Sweet Water. A few men, including Mr. Bonfoir, the superintendent of the Roswell mills, were walking from another direction.

"Miss Madrigal."

The red-haired young woman looked up at the sound of the man calling to her. "Mr. Rowdybush, what are you doin' here?"

"They arrested me, too, Miss Madrigal. Said the commissary was part of the mill." Seeing Ellie being supported, he asked, "How is Miss Ellie?"

"Be quiet, old man, and stay in line."

The soldier's voice brought instant silence to the timid, old white-haired man.

The women were marched to the boxcar openings, where wooden ramps had been placed for entrance. As soon as twenty-two were counted off and ordered inside, the ramp was removed, the door closed, and the bolt slipped into place.

The guards had started loading from the rear of the train. Now the women and children were halfway down the track. Allison, caught in the crowd, held on to the basket containing the baby.

Surging forward, she saw the soldier standing and counting each woman as she went by. Suddenly he stepped between her and Rebecca. "All right. You're the last for this car. In you go."

Frantically, Allison felt his hand pulling her onto the

ramp while Rebecca struggled to reach her. "Miss Allison, wait for me."

"Please," Allison protested, "I can't be separated from my—" She stopped. She realized it would do no good to say the word *servant*. She began again. "My baby can't be separated from her . . . wet nurse."

At that moment, as if on cue, Morrow began crying.

"All right, get back in line for the next car. I need another woman. You, over there. Swap places with this woman."

A relieved Allison returned to the waiting line, and when the car had been closed, she and Rebecca were pushed toward car eleven.

It had never occurred to Allison that she might be separated from Rebecca Smiley. The woman had been with her from the moment she was born. And though she might call her her servant to other people, she considered Rebecca her friend and the only family she had left. The bond between them was strong.

Behind Allison and Rebecca came Flood, Ellie, and Madrigal. They were followed by Rena Knox and her daughter, Caddie; Fannie Morton with six-year-old Maggie; and Alma and her baby son, Robert.

The sliding in place of the wooden door brought darkness and a finality to the women's dreams of going home. Holding on to their few possessions and the small bundle of rations that meant the difference between life and death for the next nine days, the women in boxcar eleven sat in silence and began to count the distinctive sounds of the other cars closing. Then the whistle of the steam engine announced that the prisoner train was ready to leave Marietta on the first leg of the long journey north.

"You think we'll ever see home again?" a quivering voice inquired.

No one answered.

With the rain pelting against the sides of the boxcars, the engine gathered steam and, with one giant groan and jolt, the wheels began to move, metal against metal, on the tracks of the Western and Atlantic Railroad.

Once they passed Big Shanty, they would be traveling the same route as the great locomotive chase of the *General*, which had been stolen earlier in the war. But no one would be pursuing them to stop the locomotive of this train. The women and the few men in the boxcars were merely civilian casualties of a war that had torn the land asunder.

CHAPTER
13

The siege of Atlanta began, but the Roswell women had no knowledge of the battle. Their minds were attuned to their own struggle for survival as they sought to find more comfortable positions in the darkened boxcars.

To the women, the continuous rain slashing against the wooden car meant little. They became accustomed to it, like the darkness inside the car. Instead they listened for rifle or cannon sounds, indicating that their own Confederate troops were somewhere nearby. For without speaking it aloud, each one still hoped for rescue by their own army.

Allison leaned her head against the hard wood siding and also listened. It wasn't eyes that played tricks on a person, she decided, but ears—straining to make meaning out of the most insignificant sounds while allowing the more important ones to go by without notice.

No one came to rescue them. The quarter miles multiplied into miles, with the steady clacking of the wheels, the puffing of the engine taking them farther from home. Allison felt the steady uphill pull, which was followed by a sudden sharp curve in the tracks that sent her tumbling against her nearest neighbor.

"Watch where you're going," a voice called out.

"Sorry."

Occasionally, the train stopped to take on water, and each time the women waited in hope that one of the guards might take pity on them and let them out of the boxcars to stretch their legs. But then the engine would start up again, leaving all of the women disappointed.

In the space of three hours, they slept, soothed their crying babies, and then wept themselves. Some women sang low, mournful tunes while others prayed. Silences were interrupted with a sudden need to speak, to reach out for comfort, for reassurance. And through it all the rains came down, steadily, unceasingly.

"I wonder where we are," Madrigal finally said.

"Must be close to Resaca by now," Flood answered.

"You hear that, Ellie? That's where that Private Angus Smithwick was from. You remember that day we picked blackberries by the river?" Madrigal asked.

Ellie gave no response.

"I don't think she even hears you, Madrigal," Flood said.

"But she's a lot better, thanks to Allison."

In the darkness, Allison smiled. What a difference two weeks had made. At the mill, Madrigal had called her Mrs. Forsyth. At the institute, it had been Miss Allison. Now, in the boxcar, she was merely Allison—no better, no worse than any of the other mill women.

The train continued on for another hour. Then it began to slow again. With brakes wheezing, the metal wheels screeched against the metal rails, jolting the boxcars against each other until the train came to a full stop.

At first, there was no other sound beyond the steaming engine. Then the guards began to talk, their voices growing louder as they passed by a boxcar and then diminishing as they walked on by.

"I wonder what's happening, Rebecca. We shouldn't be stopping again this soon, should we?" Allison asked.

"Maybe something's happened to the track."

"Listen. I hear the guards comin' back," Madrigal said. She crawled to the tiny slit in the door and tried to peer out. She moved quickly back when she heard the bolt being removed.

Accustomed to the darkness, the women blinked at the sudden light when the door was slid open.

"All right. Out you come," one of the guards commanded. "The engineer says you're going to have to walk a little ways by foot. Leave all your belongings in the boxcar."

"Well, I don't mind that a bit," Madrigal said. "The walkin', I mean." And she was the first one to jump down from the boxcar. When she was on the ground, she called out, "Come on, Ellie. I'll catch you."

Flood slowly lifted Ellie to Madrigal, and then she herself jumped.

Fannie Morton and Rena Knox, with their children, Maggie and Caddie, came next. Then the others jumped or were helped down, until the last ones remaining were Allison and Rebecca.

The rain had changed into a gray mist, covering the entire landscape with a fine veil. Peering through the mist, Allison sought to get her bearings.

They were now in the mountainous region of Georgia, with red clay hills covered in pines and hardwoods and fertile valleys cut wide into the land. Low-hanging clouds sat on the peaks and disintegrated into the mist that partially obscured the valleys below.

Standing at the higher elevation and looking downward, Allison felt an unexplainable sadness encompass her, almost like a cognizance of another time.

She was moved by the relentless majesty of the Cherokee land where Indians had once fished and hunted until their hunting grounds had been taken from them. And she felt the anguish of the people walking along the interminable trail of tears, bleached with the bones of the weak.

The feeling was strong: another time binding her to the present; a people being torn from their homeland by military decree.

For the first time since leaving Marietta, Allison brushed an unwanted tear from her cheek. At that moment, she didn't know whether the sadness was for herself or for the Indians.

The women began to murmur and shrink back, making an opening through which Allison could finally see ahead.

A tall, wooden cornstalk bridge, built over the swollen gorge, rose up before her, curving and bending in endless length, its iron rails mounted on awkward stilts of impossible height. It would have been shattering enough to ride over the gorge on the train. But hearing the roaring, swollen stream below bombarding the wooden pilings, Allison realized now why they had been ordered to walk. The engineer must have deemed it far too dangerous to take a fully loaded train across the weakened track.

"Golly! Have you ever seen such a terrible sight," Madrigal said, also catching a glimpse of the awesome trestle bridge.

Motioning for the small band of women who were standing back to join the others, a soldier ordered, "All right. Start walking."

"Not me. I'm scared of heights," Alma Brady said. "I couldn't carry my little Robert and keep my balance at the same time."

"There's no other way, ma'am, to get across," the second guard said.

"Can't I just climb back inside the boxcar?"

"No. The orders are for everybody to walk across."

Amid the protesting cries, the women began to walk slowly along the narrow roadbed past the other boxcars and finally came to a stop in front of the engine.

A terrified Rebecca gazed in horror at the vast expanse ahead of her. "Miss Allison," she whispered. "That soldier just might as well shoot me now. I can't walk across that trestle."

Allison disguised her own fear. "Yes, you can, Rebecca. It's the only way we'll ever get across."

"But the baby . . . How're you goin' to get Morrow across? You'll lose your balance for sure."

The image of Indian mothers carrying their babies upon their backs became a fleeting picture in her mind and then was gone. Of course. The basket. She could tie it to her back, leaving her hands free to balance herself on the tracks.

"Hurry, Rebecca. Go to the boxcar and get the basket— and a strong piece of linen. I'll strap Morrow to my back."

The guard, Tom Traymore, allowed the black woman

116

to retrieve the basket from the boxcar. With Rebecca's help, Allison tied the basket to her body and slipped her arms through the loops of the strong linen cloth.

When Alma saw what Allison was doing, she followed her example, making a cloth swing for little Robert. But she placed him in front, where she could see him.

The engineer watched in consternation at the slow progress of the women. With only one track and no siding until they reached Chattanooga, the railroad track was dangerous with the constant threat of another train bearing down upon them from the opposite direction. Once they started the hazardous journey of walking over the gorge, there was no turning back. And if an unscheduled train happened to come along before the women reached the other side, they would all be killed.

"Come on, Ellie. Put your foot on the crosstie. And be careful." Madrigal held on to the silent Ellie while Flood walked directly behind them.

A woman cried out as she stumbled, and her cry swept over the valley, a mocking echo answering her from the next mountain peak. An anxious Alma closed her eyes, prayed, and then stepped onto the trestle. To lull her child and to take her mind off the raging flood beneath her, she began to sing in a low voice, "Hush, little baby, don't you cry. Mama's gonna sing you a lullaby." And she thought of Mama Lou, who had always been the one to sing to little Robert.

Next came Allison and Morrow, with Rebecca at her side. Rebecca took one look downward and stepped back.

"Go on, woman. You're holding up the others," a guard's harsh voice said behind her.

Allison held out her hand to her servant. "Don't look

down,"she advised. "Just one step at the time, Rebecca. You can do that."

Tentatively, Rebecca placed one foot on the crosstie of the trestle. She had taken only a few steps when a strange creaking noise assailed her. "The bridge isn't gonna hold," she cried out. "I'm gettin' off the bridge."

But Rebecca had nowhere else to go. As she turned around, she saw other women behind her, cutting off her retreat. Allison took her hand again and gave her an encouraging nod. "You can do it, Rebecca."

More women came onto the trestle while Rebecca slowly made progress from crosstie to crosstie. Then it was Addie's turn and she rebelled. She started wailing, but the guard near her had run out of patience.

"Stop your sniveling and start walking. Or else I'll shoot you."

A terrified Addie, seeing the musket aimed at her, rushed onto the trestle. "It's all your fault, Madrigal O'Laney," she screamed. "If somebody dies on this trestle, the sin will be on your head."

"Shut up, woman. I said, walk."

The summer rain began again, with flashes of lightning connecting the mountain peaks in the distance. Now the crossties of the trestle were more slippery than ever, with the rain cutting off even the slight view below.

Yet the sound of the water was fierce, with logs and uprooted trees caught in the swirling gorge, bumping against the trusses of the bridge before being dislodged by the rush of water forcing the debris onward toward the rocky cataracts farther downstream.

Then a new sound pierced the mountains—a train whistle signaling an approach to the trestle.

The women couldn't tell in which direction the sound

came. They only knew that they were in the middle of the trestle bridge with the roaring gorge beneath them and the safety of solid ground too far away.

In panic, they slipped and stumbled as they rushed toward the other end of the trestle.

"Maggie," a woman screamed. "Maggie."

Allison turned around. The six-year-old was no longer in sight. Fannie Morton fell onto the track, with one foot between the crossties and her arms frantically reaching downward.

"What's happening?" a guard asked.

"I think a little girl fell off the bridge," Allison said.

"Maggie! Maggie!"

The guard's face was severe. "I'm sorry," he said, and walked over to Fannie Morton. "Get up, ma'am. Can't you hear the train coming?"

"But it's my little Maggie. She's fallen. We've got to save her."

The guard shook his head. "It's too late. We have to keep going."

"But we can't leave her. She's down there somewhere in the water."

The guard took her arm, helped her up, and began to walk with her. "We've got to keep going," he reiterated.

Through the driving rain, the women finally reached the land beyond the trestle. Forming lines on each side of the tracks, they kept moving, while behind them the impatient engineer who had caused the panic by blowing the locomotive whistle began to edge the empty train onto the rickety cornstalk bridge.

Twenty minutes later, the women and children were loaded once more onto the train.

In boxcar eleven, sadness was mixed with relief. The

119

women with children held them close, grateful that disaster had not come to them; while at the same time, they grieved for Fannie Morton in the loss of her child.

Flood had always liked Fannie. She'd been a good worker in the mill. With a sudden need to comfort her, Flood called out in the darkness, "Fannie?"

There was no answer.

"Fannie? Where are you?"

Still there was no answer.

"I didn't see her get in the boxcar again," Madrigal said.

"Where could she be?" Rebecca whispered to Allison. "You think she got into the wrong boxcar?"

"No. I think she's probably making her way down to the gorge at this very moment," Allison replied.

"If she went to look for Maggie, she'll never find the child in all that water."

"But don't you see, Rebecca? She has to try. No mother would do less."

Allison bit her lip to keep from joining in the weeping. The Roswell women were now no different from the Indians. A new trail of tears had begun. Regardless of the loss of lives, they would still be forced onward to an alien land.

She held Morrow even closer and thought of her dead husband, Coin. Silently, Allison Forsyth made a vow to him to protect their child with her very life.

CHAPTER
14

Two evenings later, the long, mournful whistle of a train cut through the quietness of the Tennessee countryside as the engineer signaled his approach into Chattanooga.

The sound came as no surprise to the mayor and fifty other townspeople, both men and women, who were bunched together in small groups and lined up along the platform of the Western and Atlantic Railroad. They had been waiting for over an hour for the deportation train to arrive.

The news had come over the wire that afternoon. Used to seeing troop trains with cannons, horses, and wagons on their way south to the battlefields, they now waited to see the human cargo being shipped north.

Lanterns gave a dim light to the railroad yard, with the office of the provost marshal in the background resembling a country store with its porch and tin shed roof. On the siding, away from the main track, empty wooden boxcars, stamped with the initials USMRR, the official logo for Mr. Lincoln's military railroad, rose in the semidarkness.

"It's comin'. I saw it just around the bend," a young boy called out, rushing onto the platform to join the others.

All eyes were directed toward the tracks. Then the bright light beam of the diamond stack woodburner locomotive came into view, its large pilot truck wheels making sparks on the track as the engineer applied the brakes. The train passed by the roundhouse and then the depot itself. The wheels continued rolling slowly until all twenty boxcars had passed from the main track and come to a full stop in the siding yard.

Tom Traymore and Alonzo Puckett, the guards for boxcar eleven, didn't wait for the new guards to relieve them for the night. Impatiently, they swung down from the train and began to walk back toward the depot. They had little enough free time before resuming the trip to Nashville the next morning.

One of the first in military uniform to reach the platform where the mayor waited, Tom looked up as the man stepped in front of him.

"Corporal, is it true," the mayor asked, "that this train actually contains four hundred and fifty Southern women and children?"

"A few men, too," Tom said. "All mill workers."

The corporal, off duty until morning, hurriedly passed through the crowd. He could feel their hostility, and he was glad the other troops were visible. He had no stomach for this job of guarding women. But lately he hadn't had much stomach for fighting, either.

"Come on, Puckett," he said to the soldier beside him. "Let's go find the nearest tavern and get drunk."

The new guards swept into action, walking along the boxcars to take over their evening duties.

In the darkness of boxcar eleven, Allison Forsyth listened and waited for the sound of the sliding bolt. Being confined for so long had already taken its toll among the women, as if by being treated like animals they had lost part of their humanity.

Petty arguments had erupted in the boxcar over the most trivial things. But above the pettiness was the fear that they might all starve before they reached their final destination.

Allison was almost certain that someone had stolen part of her food ration, but she would say nothing about it until she could examine the bundle in the light. But when the light came, she was too anxious to smell clean, fresh air again. As soon as the guards slid the door open, she and Rebecca were in the first line to jump from the car.

Once on the ground, she turned around to watch Flood and Madrigal attempting to get Ellie down. For the past several hours, the young girl's brow had felt hot to Allison's touch. Seeing her now in the lantern light, Allison realized the hazards of the trip were doubly dangerous for the girl who had lost so much blood.

Gathering what dignity she had left after being shut in the boxcar for two full days, Allison smoothed her skirts, lifted her chin, and began to walk alongside Rebecca, while the guards closed in to take them to a shelter for the night.

Seeing Allison with her baby, a man stepped from the crowd. "Excuse me, ma'am," he said. "Can we get anything for you and your baby?"

Allison looked down at Morrow, asleep in her arms. And then she remembered the others in equal need.

"Anything will be appreciated," she replied. "All of us with babies especially need fresh linen. But if you have any influence at all with the military authorities, perhaps you could get them to send a doctor. So many of our women are ill with fever . . ."

"Please move on," the guard's curt voice commanded the civilian. "You're to have no conversation with any of these women."

"I'll see to a doctor," the man called out. "And we'll bring food to you, too."

"Poor things," a woman's voice murmured. "They look so exhausted."

"Keep your chins up," another voice called out. "This war ain't over yet."

The second man quickly faded into the background to avoid the soldiers on guard.

That night, the women, divided into groups by boxcar numbers, had little to say to each other. They ate the food brought to them by the townspeople and, still hungry, they lay down to sleep in a ramshackle old building with guards posted outside to keep them from running away.

Bone-weary and dirty from the jolting, grimy trip along the rails, Allison longed for a cool, refreshing bath and a change of clothes. But the women had been allowed only enough water to drink, with a surreptitious dipping of their handkerchiefs to rub the dirt from their faces when the guards weren't looking. Allison, who had always prided herself on her immaculate appearance, even in her faded calico, made one small obeisance to tidiness. She took out her brush to remove the tangles of her long blond hair, then did the same for Morrow, gently gathering the small wisps of hair into a curl on the top of her head.

Then the doctor, promised to them, came and looked over the women and children ill with fever. Allison watched as the kindhearted man examined Ellie and merely shook his head. From his action, Allison knew that Ellie's chances for survival were not good.

But to the women, even kindness shown to them was at a premium, and they were grateful to the doctor despite his being unable to help them.

In a restless manner, Allison struggled to find a more comfortable spot for the night. And she reached out to re-assure herself that Morrow, so quiet in the basket beside her, was still all right.

A few minutes later, the same doctor stood before the provost marshal. He had been appalled at the poor condition of some of the women, including Ellie Barnes. And he had decided to seek out the only man who could do something about it. But so far he had not met with any success.

"Some of these women are much too ill to be moved," Dr. Powers warned. "If you have a shred of humanity about you, you will allow them to stay here until they either get well or die."

The provost marshal shook his head. "I'm sorry, Doctor, but orders are orders. If I don't reload them all on the train first thing in the morning, there'll be hell to pay." He stood up and began to walk toward the open door. "You'll be gratified to know, I'm sure, that provision has been made for them to take several days' rest once they get to Nashville."

"Some of the women won't make it all the way to Nash-ville," the white-haired old doctor warned.

"It's a fact of life, Doctor, that many lives are lost in wartime."

"Soldiers, yes. But not innocent women and children—"

"The general evidently doesn't see them as innocent," the provost marshal interrupted. "Else he would not have arrested them for treason. Now, if you will excuse me, we've got to put down fresh straw in the boxcars."

The mayor, who had been standing silently by Dr. Powers all this time, shook his head. "Well, we tried, Hiram. Heaven knows we tried."

The doctor, tight-lipped and grim, said nothing in reply. He began to walk down the steps, feeling his way along the rustic banister until his feet touched the muddy ground.

"Mark my words, Edward," the doctor said finally. "We'll all live to regret this act of inhumanity."

But the mayor was not so sure. "People forget too easily, Hiram. I'll bet within six months no one will remember the plight of these women—especially if Grant and Sherman bring the South to her knees in that time."

Still, the old doctor shook his head. "A dastardly business. That's what it is. A dastardly business."

Holding his lantern and doctor's satchel, Dr. Powers parted company with the mayor. In the distance, the sound of music in the saloon penetrated the air as he made his way to the house on the corner.

Inside the saloon, Tom Traymore took another swig of whiskey. It burned going down his dry throat like the first swallow of rotgut Tennessee mountain moonshine fresh from the still.

He held up the glass to the light to see the sediment in the bottom. But his mind was on something other than the whiskey.

"You noticed that little redhead on the train?" Tom Traymore asked his friend, Alonzo.

"Yeah. But we'd better steer clear of her. I heard one of the women say she shot a soldier back in Roswell."

"I heard that, too. But can't say as I blame her. He broke her door down."

"I think he broke more than her door," Alonzo answered with a laugh.

Tom Traymore didn't respond. He sat and finished his whiskey. He was damned tired of the war. And he began to think of the family farm farther back in the hills. He always became maudlin when he had too much to drink. That was the time the "lonelies" set in, when he longed for the sight of the sun first rising up over the mountain, shining on the tall slash pines and the hardwoods—that first sun-tipped sight that told him autumn was coming soon.

He thought of the apples in the orchard, now turning ripe and red, and of the rows of corn beyond, bending low under the weight of the full-kerneled ears.

His pa was old now, too old to work the farm alone. Tom hadn't intended to stay away for three whole years. Most of the other soldiers had left the army after two years, slipping back home to help plant the crops, with some forgetting to return to the fighting once the fields were planted.

He banged his empty glass against the counter. "Another whiskey," he bellowed, hoping for the next drink to dull his mind and stop the lonelies.

"We'd better go, Tom," Alonzo said. "Drunk or sober, we got to get back on that train tomorrow morning."

"One more drink, Puckett. That's all I want. Then we'll go."

"All right, Tom."

A few minutes later, the two staggered out of the saloon

to sleep off the whiskey in an empty boxcar in the siding yard next to the rail station.

In the building where the women slept, Flood Tompkins lay awake and listened to Ellie's shallow, rapid breathing. She reached up to touch the bruise on her head, wanting to feel the pain, to remember, for she still felt responsible for what had happened to Ellie.

Tonight, she was glad she didn't have any children of her own—for the pain would be even worse, if that was possible. Earlier in her marriage, she'd been disappointed not to give Sproule any babies—a big, strapping woman like herself. But then they'd both gotten over the disappointment and gone on to live their own lives.

Sproule was the only man who'd ever made her feel like a woman. Now he was dead, and she sorely missed him. Maybe that was why she dressed so often in his old clothes—to feel closer to him and to remember the years they'd been together.

In the dark, Flood patted her chemise to make sure the small packet was still there. It wasn't much money, but at least it was Union money, which was the only kind that was any good now. If she could, she would have bought some medicine for Ellie, but Dr. Powers had said that there wasn't any medicine that could help her now even if he could get some.

Ellie began to moan, and Flood sat up. "What is it, Ellie?"

"Please. Please don't hurt me."

"It's all right, Ellie. Truly it is. Flood's right here beside you."

But Ellie refused to be comforted. Speechless for almost two weeks since the ravaging in the village, she now began to talk as her fever reached a dangerous pitch and swept her into delirium. Her cry became an animal's cry as she seemed to relive those terrible moments when Flood had been unable to come to her aid.

Allison, reaching into the pocket of her dress, pulled out the small flask containing the phosphorus. Its brief glow lit up the small corner where Ellie lay. The bloodcurdling scream coming from Ellie's throat brought Flood to her knees and the guards rapping on the door.

"Quiet in there," a guard yelled. "You want to wake the dead?"

Allison knelt over the young woman as the babies in the room, awakened by the noise, joined in the crying. "Rebecca, can you see to Morrow?" she asked.

'Yes, Miss Allison."

Allison turned her full attention to Ellie, now caught in the throes of a convulsion. Her body began its awful trembling, and Allison, afraid she would harm herself, thrust a linen cloth between her teeth, while Flood held her down, keeping her confined until the shaking began to subside.

During that time, Madrigal stood by helplessly.

In the distance, the sound of music and the high, tinkly laughter of women—camp followers—floated over that portion of town. Madrigal lifted her head to listen. It wasn't fair. She and Ellie should be the ones having fun that night instead of being cooped up like chickens waiting for someone's Sunday dinner.

They'd never even had time to plan the celebration they talked about that day before the Union troops came to Roswell. But one day soon, she vowed, she and Ellie would have all the fun, all the music—and, yes, all the men—that they wanted.

Ellie was not aware of Madrigal's hopes and dreams that

night. Her fever continued, with her screams bringing a
renewed rapping on the door by the guards.

All during that night, Flood and Allison took turns sitting
up with Ellie. If Ellie was lucky, by morning the fever
would be broken and perhaps all the ghosts that had previously silenced her would also be banished from her mind.

CHAPTER
15

The railroad yard came alive in early morning light; the sound of a rooster vied with the irritating, high-pitched buzz of a sawmill somewhere along the tracks.

Tom Traymore awoke with a headache and a bad taste in his mouth. Then he remembered the terrible whiskey of the night before and was not surprised. With his eyes bloodshot and his head reeling, he sat up and called out to his partner, Lonnie Puckett.

"Come on, Lonnie. We'd better get a move on," he said, gathering his equipment and musket before jumping from the boxcar.

The telltale aroma of coffee brewing and bacon frying floated through the air as the two began to walk along the tracks. Tom knew that if they wanted to get in on the coffee, they wouldn't have much time. And he suspected that Puckett needed a hot cup of coffee about as bad as he did.

The two walked past the deportation train where contrabands—the blacks who followed the Union army—were already hard at work loading wood for the locomotive to burn on its way to Nashville.

Then the irritating noise that had awakened Tom began again. The sawmill, mounted on railroad wheels, stood on the siding track with black smoke rising out of the tall funnel while logs were cut—the larger ones to replace crossties or bridge timbers and the smaller pieces for fuel for the engines.

Tom stopped to watch the process for a few moments. He hoped they would cut a plentiful supply, for he was afraid the woods along the rail tracks to Nashville had been stripped clean already. That made it dangerous for the guards. The farther away from the train they went in search of wood to burn, the more likely it was that they would run into a bunch of Rebels.

They continued walking, crossing the deep-rutted road on the other side of the provost marshal's headquarters, where a row of pointed Sibley tents stood with a cookstove set on rocks in front of each tent.

"Want a cuppa coffee, soldier? You look like you could do with one this morning."

Tom looked at a huge, bearded cook with his dirty apron wrapped around his protruding front. The man stood in front of his grated iron stove and leaned toward the metal coffeepot already steaming.

Tom nodded and took his tin dipper cup from his musket, where he had tied it so that he wouldn't lose it.

Puckett did the same, and then, with full cups, the two

walked back to the steps of the provost marshal's head-quarters, where they pulled out some hardtack and dipped it into the hot coffee to soften it before eating.

Everywhere he looked, Tom saw plentiful supplies and smelled food cooking. If his stomach wasn't so queasy, he would take out his creeper pan and fry up some bacon, too. But he didn't have much desire for army rations that morning.

"Wish I had me a big, juicy red apple from home," Tom said, putting down the hardtack.

"That would be nice," Lonnie agreed.

"Even better than all those blackberries we ate back in Georgia."

"I expect Lee wouldn't be mindin' the blackberries *or* the apples 'bout now," Lonnie said. "I heard tell he said it was awful hard fightin' a war on ashcakes and water."

"You notice that's about all the women have been eatin' for the past two days?" Tom said.

"Now, don't be goin' soft on those women, Tom. We got a job to do, and it won't help none for you to start worryin' about what they get to eat."

"But have you wondered what's gonna happen to them? I mean, once they get to Indiana and we just dump them out to forage for themselves?"

"No. I got other things to worry about—like goin' to ordnance supply to get some more powder for my musket before we pull out of here."

"I wouldn't be a bit surprised if we ran into some Rebs today."

"Yeah. That's why I need me some gunpowder."

Tom watched Lonnie chew on his hardtack and finish off his coffee. He stared down at his own half-empty cup and finally poured the coffee on the ground.

"Now what did you go and do that for?" Lonnie asked.

"I ain't hungry, or thirsty, either. I got a great big knot in my stomach. Had it ever since last night when I started thinkin' of my pa and the farm back home."

"You're not that far away, are you?"

"No. Just over the mountain, past Nashville."

"Sometimes, Tom, I think your mind just ain't on fightin' Rebs."

"It sure would be better than doin' what we're doin' right now. I won't ever forget that woman's scream when her little girl fell off the trestle."

"Ain't no use worryin' about what happened yesterday, Tom Traymore. You better keep your mind on today."

"I reckon so." The train whistle blew several short blasts, and Tom stood up. "And I reckon we better get goin' back to the train. Sounds like we're 'bout ready to leave again."

"Well, I'll hurry on over to get me some more powder. I'll see you back at the boxcar."

The two parted company, with Tom headed once again for the tracks where the locomotive was beginning to build up power. Smoke from the woodburner rose in the air in great white puffs, resembling Indian messages from the hills. And like an answer to the smoke signals, the women walked in a slow procession toward the rail yard.

This time, Ellie was too weak to walk. Flood, with the same strength she had used to sling a sack of wool over her shoulders at the mill, now carried the young mill worker to boxcar eleven and hoisted her up into Madrigal's waiting arms.

Rebecca, walking beside Allison, suddenly said, "You know what day it is, today?"

"I'm not sure, but I think it's Thursday," Allison replied.

Overhearing them, Alma, who was directly behind the

two, joined in the conversation. "Wonder how long it'll be before we reach Nashville?"

"Several more days at least. That is, if we don't run into trouble along the line."

"My little Robert was sickly last night," Alma confided. "I sure hope he's not comin' down with the fever, too."

"I pray not," Allison replied. She passed the basket containing Morrow to Rebecca after the woman had climbed aboard the train.

Once the twenty-one women were all accounted for, the bolts were slid into place, cutting off most of the light and making them prisoners once more.

To Madrigal, the sound of the door being shut that morning was particularly jarring. She didn't like the trapped feeling any more than she liked the darkness.

As the train pulled from the station, low-hanging clouds, heavy with the seeds of rain, obscured the top of Lookout Mountain and the terraces of Missionary Ridge, where the trenches and foxholes of the recent battles waged by Bragg and Sherman pockmarked the land.

The train approached the wide Tennessee River in the valley, settled onto the trestle bridge, and began its journey through the early morning fog enveloping the tracks.

Now, as the locomotive crossed it, Tom Traymore viewed the landscape from the top of the caboose. Normally, that car was attached to the end of a train, but for this trip it had been placed directly behind the locomotive as additional protection from possible attack.

All of the guards on the train would have to be especially careful, for the area between Chattanooga and Nashville contained small bands of Confederate irregulars. If word got out to any of the Rebs that they were transporting Confederate women, Tom knew the lives of the engineer and the guards wouldn't be worth a lead nickel.

"What are you thinking, Tom?"

A startled Tom came out of his deep reverie. He shifted his body and said, "Oh, more than likely what you're thinkin', Lonnie. The sooner we get to Nashville, the better off we'll be."

The uneasiness the guards felt was similar to that element of hidden danger that always lurks beneath the surface of consciousness, like a child's nightmare that no amount of gentle persuasion will rout. Their fear was transferred to the prisoners, but for the women, it was an inverse fear—that the Confederates would *not* come. And the one who worried the most, besides Madrigal, was Flood Tompkins.

The train began the upgrade climb out of the valley and onto more rugged land, the engine straining and puffing to carry the twenty loaded boxcars.

The women's thoughts turned from possible rescue to the problem of maintaining their equilibrium against the sharp incline until the locomotive, hugging the roadbed, could reach the more level ground beyond the ridge.

They had been traveling for less than thirty minutes when Flood, losing her balance, fell against Ellie, who was lying prone on the straw before her. As Flood's hand touched Ellie's face, she knew that something was different about her. Instead of being on fire, her brow was now cool to the touch. Relieved, Flood decided the fever must have broken some time that morning, even though Ellie had given no sign of coming out of her delirium. Then Flood began to get worried.

"Allison?" she called. "Could you bring out that phosphorus light for just a moment? So I can check on Ellie?"

"Of course." Allison reached into her pocket, but the flask was gone. "I can't find it, Flood. It isn't in my pocket."

Madrigal spoke up with a fierceness in her voice. "All right. Whoever took Allison's pocket light last night, you'd better give it back. Now, I'm gonna go sit by the door. I'll hold out my hand, and I want to feel that flask in my hand in less than a minute. If not, you'll answer to me as soon as we make the next stop."

Allison listened. No one in the boxcar moved near the door once Madrigal had stationed herself there.

Then Flood spoke up. "All right, Addie. We're waitin'."

"What do you want to pick on me for, Flood? I didn't take it."

"You forget, Addie. I have the second sight. I know you're the one who took it."

"Well, what if I *did* take it? She ruined my moss-filled pillow. It's only fair I get to keep somethin' in its place."

"If you're speakin' of Allison, Addie, you know she didn't use the pillow for herself. It was to stop Ellie's bleedin'."

There was a rustle of straw and a movement toward the bit of light coming through the crack in the bolted door. "All right, Madrigal, if that's your hand I feel. Take the old bottle."

Once again, there was a rustle of straw as Addie turned over the bottle and rushed back to her place.

"I've got it, Allison. Where are you?" Madrigal called out.

"Right beside Flood."

The flask changed hands again. Removing its lid, Allison held up the flask until the phosphorus began to glow. Faces gathered around her assumed an eerie greenish shade. Then she moved it to illuminate Ellie's face, and what she saw almost caused her to drop the flask in the straw.

Ellie lay stiffly, her unseeing eyes staring upward. She was no longer feverish. Her skin, cold and clammy, proclaimed a new disaster.

"Ellie?" Madrigal called out. "Can you hear me, Ellie?"

Her question went unnoticed. "Ellie, you've got to answer me."

Allison leaned over to feel the pulse at Ellie's throat. There was no trace. She placed her head on Ellie's chest. There was no sign of a heartbeat, however fragile. Ellie was dead.

With the same gentleness she had used to close her own father's eyes at death, Allison Forsyth moved her fingers in a downward motion and closed the frightened blue eyes.

"She can't hear you, Madrigal," she said. "She won't ever hear you again."

"I know."

Madrigal moved away as the phosphorus light went out. She shed no tears for her friend. Instead, she hugged her knees and put her head down to think. Ellie was the only reason she had remained on the train this far. Now she no longer had to stay. At the first opportunity, she would escape, just as Fannie Morton had. And she knew the very person who would help her—the guard, Tom Traymore, who kept watching her every time the train stopped for water or fuel.

Whatever she had to promise him, she would.

Flood Tompkins was not so stoic. With great heaving sobs, she grieved, and soon the babies in the boxcar joined in.

"I'll take Morrow and try to quiet her, Miss Allison," Rebecca said.

"Thank you, Rebecca. I've just fed her, so she can't be hungry."

138

At the other end of the boxcar, Alma's low, mournful voice began to comfort her feverish child. "Hush, little baby, don't you cry. Mama's gonna sing you a lullaby."

Rebecca joined in the singing, lulling Morrow to sleep, while Allison comforted Flood.

But the red-haired young woman remained by herself. Madrigal O'Laney wanted no one to comfort her. She wanted to feel the grief sweeping over her like the waters rushing into the millrace gate; she wanted to remember Ellie as she had been that day by the Chattahoochee when the retreating soldiers had crossed the bridge before it was burned.

She waited, but no grief came. Her heart was empty— every bit as empty as it had been that night she had shot Caleb Rabb.

CHAPTER
16

By late afternoon, the train had stopped.

Beyond the tracks, in a small meadow where yellow bit-terweed mingled with green blades of grass and the mountains were tiered in varied shades of blue to the east, the women stood with bowed heads.

Nineteen bodies were being consigned to the earth that had once given them sustenance. Ellie was in the group. And Mr. Rowdybush, too—both dead of the fever that had swept through the mill workers like wildfire.

Long, deep trenches had been dug by the guards. And in one corner of the meadow, slightly apart from the others, a smaller trench had been shallowed out from the hard red clay for Alma's son, little Robert E. Lee Brady.

The smell of the earth was in the air—a fine red dust choked the nostrils like pungent incense sprinkled over the land. But in place of a priest's accompanying bell, the jarring, raucous whistle of the engine sounded, signaling that it was past time to go. And so, with a final prayer, the women began to return to the train—all except Alma, who sat by the small mound of earth and smoothed the dirt where she had transplanted a clump of blue flowers.

Allison stood back, waiting to walk with the woman to the boxcar, but Alma seemed in no hurry to leave the grave site.

Once she had finished the contouring of the mound, Alma placed little Robert's baby bonnet upon the small cross, made from the green twigs of a nearby weeping willow. Then she reached into her apron pocket, took out a bone rattle, and tied it to the ribbons of the bonnet.

Her thin voice began to sing. "Hush, little baby, don't you cry. Mama's gonna sing you a lullaby."

The train whistle again signaled the engineer's impatience, but Alma, unmindful of anything else, kept singing in a hypnotic manner over and over, until Tom Traymore motioned for Allison to help the woman back to the boxcar.

"Alma, we have to go now."

The woman stood up. "He's so little to be by himself, Allison. But I'm gonna sing to him every night of my life. You think he'll be able to hear me?"

"Yes, Alma. He'll hear you."

"It was Mama Lou who always sang to him before. But she doesn't even know he's dead."

As Allison put her hand on Alma's arm and drew her toward the boxcar, two yellow monarch butterflies lit on the clump of flowers and folded their wings, while in the tree beyond, a bird began to chirp a strange, sweet song.

And if Allison had not known better, she would have vowed that a mockingbird had taken up Alma's song and was now singing to little Robert in his lonely grave.

Tom Traymore walked behind the two women. When Allison turned around, he quickly averted his face. But it was too late. She had already seen the tear rolling down his cheek.

Once the train started again, it picked up speed, with a constant, punishing strain against the elevated grade of the roadbed, as if to make up for the time lost that afternoon.

An uncommon silence gripped the women in boxcar eleven, and they seemed oblivious to the jolting and the metallic grinding noise that accompanied the turning of wheels. On tracks fired to anvil heat by the full day's absorption of the summer sun, they continued to travel, with Nashville as the destination of the more fortunate ones. Even the babies, enervated by the heat, refused to cry. And with each mile the unceasing clack of the wheels mocked them all with a subtle warning: Too far. Too far now. You'll never get home again.

Several miles to the north, at one of the military outposts where a sentry shack had been erected to protect that area of track from the enemy, an impatient Marcus Stagg paced up and down under the shade of a sweet gum tree while he took out his gold watch to recheck the time. The train carrying the women was late. It should have gotten to the siding at least an hour ago.

"You don't think something has happened to the train, do you?" Marcus asked one of the guards.

"No, Mr. Stagg. It'll get here eventually. Just takes a little longer sometimes. Got to expect delays with a war going on."

Stagg grunted. He replaced his watch and, uncomfortable from the heat, he pulled out his handkerchief to wipe the sweat from his brow, mopping it as he walked toward his carriage and horses. Despite himself, he smiled. It had taken quite a bit of doing to bribe the officer at the army post to sign the papers, giving him the pick of the mill workers for his own mill. It had cost him a pretty penny, too, but it wasn't every day that a man had a chance to get fifty or sixty skilled workers for nothing beyond a little food and shelter.

He could count the profits already—even greater than he'd ever dreamed of. Making cloth for the Union army was a lucrative business. The fact that his goods hadn't held up very well was of little concern to him. The army didn't seem to mind, either. They kept ordering more goods without saying a word about the quality of the material or the exorbitant prices he charged.

Marcus looked at his three empty wagons and the drivers sitting under the shade of the tree. "You'd better go ahead and feed the mules," he called out. "Looks like the train is going to be a while coming."

He seated himself on the leather cushion of the carriage and waited. Three-fourths of an hour later, Marcus heard the train. Relieved, he climbed out of his buggy and began to walk back toward the tracks.

Inside boxcar eleven, the women heard the whistle of another train. Immediately, they felt the uneven swerve as their own train responded, veering off to the right.

"Feels like we're pulling off to a side track," Rebecca commented to no one in particular.

"Well, I sure hope we aren't on the same track as that other engine," Madrigal answered. "Else the guards will have to dig some more graves today."

"But they'd be dead, too," Flood said, "if that happened. Unless they jumped off the train in time."

Allison was silent until Madrigal said, "What about it, Allison? You think any of 'em would really give a whoopubb as to what happened to any of us?"

Allison remembered the tear on Tom Traymore's face. "Yes. There's at least one who wouldn't desert us."

"And who might that be?" Madrigal asked.

"The same one who watches you every time you get out of the boxcar."

"Oh. *Him*." Madrigal made a face, but it was too dark inside the boxcar for Allison to notice.

But there was something else that Allison had noticed beyond Tom Traymore's obvious attraction to Madrigal. It was Madrigal herself and her reaction to her friend's demise. No tears had been shed over Ellie at the graveside. It was almost as if Madrigal had removed herself emotionally from Ellie long before the last rites. It couldn't be that the young girl was unfeeling. Madrigal had demonstrated her concern for Ellie over and over again, while she was still living. But now that she was dead, it was a different matter. Still, whatever prompted Madrigal's present reaction was her own concern. Not Allison's. She was prepared to accept Madrigal without judgment or reservation.

Being in the boxcar with twenty other women was an experience that Allison would never forget. For no two women were alike. Each had an inherent rhythm of her own that manifested itself in variations day after day— women who accepted, women who blamed. Their aura was ever present in the darkness of the boxcar: Madrigal, with her fidgety and impulsive behavior; Flood, with her quiet, calm strength, soothing and familiar; Addie Wickes and Rena Knox, carved from a darker hue, breathing with a vehemence that so often wounded. And dear, quiet Alma, so accepting of life's harshest measures. But it was Rebecca Smiley who had been the greatest source of comfort to Allison. As always, she was both rose and thorn, offering Allison that strange combination of friendship and servitude, with Rebecca herself choosing the time when she would be one or the other—mentor or servant.

The women sat in the boxcar, listening to the approach of the other train. The wooden boxcar rattled as the powerful engine passed by. But then voices were heard again, and the train carrying the women made no effort to pull out. Soon, Allison heard the door sliding open.

"All right. Out you come," Alonzo Puckett said, once the brief light of the late afternoon was visible.

They needed no urging. With an agility acquired in the past few days, the women jumped onto the ground

A puzzled Allison looked around her. Wondering at first if they had stopped for the night, she quickly decided there must be another reason, for there was no visible shelter for them unless they were to remain in the boxcars. But that possibility was much too cruel to contemplate.

The countryside seemed desolate, with only a rough, wooded sentry house built along the periphery of the tracks. A few curious guards in blue left their posts and walked closer to stare openly at the women streaming out of the cars.

On the rise above the sentry house, in a small grove of trees, Allison saw Stagg's fine leather-trimmed carriage with two chestnut horses resting in the shade. And slightly beyond the trees, the three empty wagons, with their drivers tending to the teams of mules. The blond-haired woman took a few steps forward to get a better view, but Alonzo

Puckett admonished her, "You're not to get out of line, ma'am. We got to wait for Mr. Stagg."

"Who's he?" Madrigal asked.

"You'll find out soon enough."

"Well, pardon me for askin'." Her sarcasm was lost on the soldier.

While the women watched, the man, Marcus Stagg, approached the train.

He was rotund, with a plaid vest partially obscuring the mound of flesh that shook as he walked. Muttonchop side-whiskers framed his round face, giving him the appearance of an old gray lion. But the resemblance stopped there. His walk was not that of a jungle cat, lean and sinuous, but rather a waddle on thin, stovepipe legs that seemed much too small to carry the bulk of his upper body.

Seeing him in all his sartorial splendor, with the gold chain of his watch fob stretched across his enormous stomach, Madrigal whistled and said, "Just look at the prick-medainty comin' toward us."

"Madrigal, watch your language, girl. He must be some important person. And it wouldn't do to rouse his ire."

Madrigal glared at Flood and then returned her attention to the man disappearing toward the front of the train.

Marcus Stagg stopped at the first boxcar, made a brief perusal of the women, and, evidently not liking what he saw, walked on to the next. Narrowing his eyes, he began to point, first to one woman and then another.

"Step over here, please," the guard called out to each one so selected. A brief murmur rose in the group, who was slow to respond. And fear gripped the women around Allison. They had dreamed of being rescued by their own soldiers. But this was different.

"You notice he's only picking out the strongest?" Rebecca whispered.

"And the ones without children," Madrigal added, moving closer to Flood.

"I don't like it," Flood said. "Don't like it one bit. There's something shady about that man."

"I saw a man like him in Savannah once. At a slave auction," Allison said. Suddenly realizing the effect her words had on Rebecca, she quickly assured her, "Don't worry, Rebecca. I won't let him take you from me. Here, hold Morrow."

Allison took the shawl from around her shoulders, wrapped the baby in it, and handed Morrow to the black woman.

Realizing what Allison intended, Rebecca said, "No man's gonna think this is *my* baby, Miss Allison."

"He might if you keep her covered up and her face turned away from him."

"But what about you?"

"I'll worry about that when he gets closer."

"We can all pretend to be sick or something," Madrigal said. "He wouldn't want to choose anybody sick with the fever."

Marcus Stagg continued to edge his way past each boxcar, pointing to certain women and then moving on, as if he knew exactly what he was looking for. Finally, he approached the women at boxcar eleven.

Surveying the twenty women, he first pointed to Madrigal and then abruptly changed his mind. "No, not that one. She isn't quite right in the head. A pity."

Madrigal didn't move. She was too intent on keeping her eyes crossed and her mouth open, like the harmless village idiot who had drowned the previous year near the millrace

147

gate. As much as she wanted to escape from the train, she felt it in her bones that it would be disastrous to leave with this man, whoever he might be.

The man walked on, selecting first one and then the other, rapidly moving down the line until he saw Allison Forsyth.

She stood quietly, with her eyes looking at the ground. Small and fine-boned, she exuded grace and beauty. Even though her clothes were no better than any of the others around her, there was something different about the woman that caused Marcus Stagg to stop and examine her more closely.

Still looking down at the ground, Allison felt his presence and heard his raspy breathing as two enormous feet, encased in polished leather and splayed at angles, came into view. Startled, she felt a hand lift her chin, and despite her resolution, she met the curious gaze of the man before her, full force.

Marcus Stagg smiled while his eyes took in her face and then traveled insolently over the length and breadth of Allison's figure. With a satisfied nod, he finally turned to the soldier beside him and ordered, "Guard, put this woman in my personal carriage. I have better plans for her."

CHAPTER
17

The sinking sun hurled its final rays past the sweet gum trees on the nearby hill, hovered on the horizon, and then disappeared, leaving only elongated shadows as a remembrance of its former presence. Along the line of trees, an ungainly crow suddenly flew toward the west, its raucous cry causing one of the mules to bolt.

"Whoa, mule," the surprised driver shouted, using an oath for emphasis. The wagon halted, and then the quiet of the late afternoon returned.

Rebecca Smiley, standing a few feet away from Allison, mercilessly pinched the baby she was holding, and at its cry, she stepped forward, removed the shawl, and thrust the child toward Allison.

"Here, you'll have to take your sickly baby back, Miss Allison. I'm scared to take care of her any longer. I think she's comin' down with the smallpox like some of the others we buried today."

At her words, Stagg jumped back and placed his handkerchief over his nose. "Stay where you are, woman," he said to Rebecca, and then stared at Allison in a new light. She didn't look nearly so enticing to him now. As he stared at her, he decided her amethyst eyes were a little too bright and her cheeks a little too pink—not at all a good sign for such a fair-headed woman.

"Let's move on, guard, to another car. I've changed my mind. I don't want any of these women from number eleven."

"What about the women you already selected?"

"You know which ones they are. Tell them they can go back to the boxcar."

"And the blond-haired woman?"

"Don't you dare sully my carriage with her," Stagg snapped. "I'd be dead of the pox in less than a month if I were to take her with me."

"The black woman isn't speaking the truth, Mr. Stagg," Alonzo Puckett said. "No one on this train has come down with smallpox."

"And what would you call the spots on my little Robert's face?" Alma asked. "The baby you buried this afternoon?"

Marcus Stagg glared at Alonzo Puckett and moved on quickly, placing as much distance as possible from the supposedly infected boxcar. "It's getting dark and I don't have any more time to waste."

Once the man was out of hearing distance, Rebecca said, "I'm sorry I spoke so uppity to you just now, Miss Allison. I'll take the baby back now if you want me to."

Far from being miffed, Allison was grateful. "You saved us all, Rebecca. Thank you. But I'll hold on to Morrow in case he comes back this way."

"Well, I never thought I'd see the day," Madrigal said. "Alma, of all people, makin' up such a lie. And with a straight face, too."

"Speakin' of faces . . ." Flood laughed in spite of herself. "Looks like you've suddenly come to your senses again, Madrigal."

But Addie was not so grateful at the turn of events. Pushed out of one of the wagons, she marched angrily back to the boxcar and stood in front of Madrigal, the one she'd blamed for all her ills ever since that night in the village. "My one chance to leave this godawful train and somethin' had to spoil it. What did you do, Madrigal, to make Mr. Stagg so mad?"

"Shut up, Addie. You don't know what you're talkin' about."

"I see you're still stickin' up for the little hussy, Flood. Seems to me that you'd have found her out by now, like Rena and me."

"Mama, I'm hungry," Caddie Knox cried.

"Hush, Caddie. We've got other things to think about besides our stomachs right now."

The three wagons soon disappeared over the hill with sixty of the women. For a few minutes longer, Marcus Stagg sat in his carriage and stared at the siding where Allison still stood holding her baby. Yes, it was a good thing that the black woman had spoken up when she did. A few minutes later, both she and the heavyset woman would have been in one of the wagons, and the blond-haired beauty, despite having a child, would have been sitting beside him in his own carriage and then infecting him in his own bed that very night.

Marcus pulled out his handkerchief again, wiped his brow, and brooded over the close call he'd had. But then his mind turned to the sixty skilled workers. Even if a few of them died, he would still have enough to make a difference in his textile mill. Only now he planned to stay away from them all until he made sure they weren't sick. He'd let his manager work with them until the threat of infection was gone.

Leaving the hillside beyond the tracks, he clucked his tongue and whistled through his teeth. With the response of his nervous horses, he quickly disappeared in the direction his wagons had taken. At the speed he was going, it wouldn't take long to catch up with them and then leave them in the dust.

Back at the train, the engineer was busy consulting with the sentries. And when it was agreed that the best course was to remain where they were for the night and get a quick start early the next morning, he signaled the guards with several short toots of the whistle and allowed the fire in the engine to die down to stoked embers.

By now the women could read the signs as well as the guards. "Looks like we're gonna camp here after all," Flood said.

For Allison, the heat had been uncommonly irksome all day and she longed for a nice, cool bath. She gazed longingly through the last vestiges of light at the stream running in an easterly direction from the track. "If we stay here for the night, I wonder if they would allow us to take a bath in the creek?" Allison said.

"Why don't I ask Tom Traymore?" Madrigal quickly suggested.

"Oh, you wouldn't have any trouble gettin' him to say yes, Madrigal. In fact, he would probably take great pleasure in watchin' you bathe." Addie spoke with her usual venom. "But don't think the rest of us are goin' to take a bath in front of a man."

"We'd all keep our dresses on, Addie." By now, Allison had become impatient with the woman. "There's nothing wrong in that."

"Suit yourself. As for me, I'll keep my dignity."

"And something else, too," Flood said sarcastically, wrinkling her nose as she spoke.

While some of the women settled down to make fires to cook the rancid bacon, others walked toward the creek to get water to heat for coffee.

Madrigal deliberately went farther down the creek than the others. As she looked back, she saw Tom Traymore heading her way. And the plan she had nourished ever since Ellie died took full root in her mind.

"Can I help you with that bucket, Madrigal?"

The red-haired woman turned around and smiled. "No, thank you, Tom. But there's somethin' else you could do if you had a mind to."

"And what's that?"

"Let me go swimmin' in the creek tonight."

"I couldn't let you do that, Madrigal. The other women would get mad."

"Not if you let them do the same thing. The women were the ones who asked me to speak to you about it. We've all been cooped up in those hot boxcars for so long we resemble draggle-tail chickens gettin' ready to molt."

When she saw that he was mulling it over, Madrigal smiled again and leaned toward him, moistening her lips with her tongue. "I'd make it worth your while, Tom."

"What do you mean by that?"

"We could swim together later tonight—just the two of us, without anybody watchin'."

From the look on his face, Madrigal knew she had won. But her ultimate goal was not the swim in the creek. It was *escape* before they reached Nashville—with Tom Traymore helping her.

"I'll see what I can do."

"I'll be waitin' for you tonight after everybody else has gone to sleep."

Later, at supper, the announcement was made. The women who wished to bathe would be allowed to do so, boxcar by boxcar, with the guards standing watch on the banks.

It was such a small concession toward the women to cause such pleasure. Forgotten were the hard day, the sadness at the burial site, and the less than human treatment that had been their lot from the moment they had been removed from the town of Roswell.

With a sense of anticipation, the women from Allison's boxcar awaited their turn, holding on to the carefully hoarded small bits of soap and removing the remaining pins from their hair.

Allison took her hairbrush out of her bundle, and with deft, sure strokes, she worked on the tangles, listening all the while to the numbers being called in succession. When she heard number eleven, she stood up and began to walk toward the creek with Rebecca, holding the baby, walking by her side.

A torch light flickered on the water, still muddy from the recent rains. But Allison didn't care. She sank into the shallow part of water not far from the bank and, taking the soap, lathered herself—calico dress and all. Her petticoats

154

floated on the water like sails, and her blond hair, with all of the pins removed, hung over her shoulders in heavy strands. When she had finished bathing, she reached out for Morrow, who cried at the first trickling handful of cool water gently cupped onto her small body.

But then the sounds of delight took over, up and down the creekbank, as the women laughed and splashed together.

Allison only remained at the edge of the creek long enough to give Morrow a quick rinse; then she climbed out to dry the baby with a linen from her bundle before she became chilled.

"I didn't know water could feel so good to tired old bones," Flood commented, sinking into the creek like a small behemoth, with only her head visible above the water-line. "I certainly am grateful to Madrigal for speaking up for us."

"Where *is* Madrigal, anyway?" Rebecca asked.

"Time to get out," Alonzo Puckett ordered, before anyone could pursue the subject.

"Oh, can't we stay in just a little bit longer?" one of the women begged.

"No. The other women are waiting their turns."

With a small amount of grumbling, the women emerged and stood on the banks. Those who had washed their hair twisted the strands dry and plaited them into one long pigtail down their backs. Now they didn't even mind that they were to spend the night in the boxcars with the sliding door closed. They were cool and clean—a nice reprieve from the humid, sweaty day. And some of them carried fresh twigs to place in the boxcars as a freshener for the stale air.

"Oh, there you are, Madrigal. I didn't see you down at the creek. What happened to you?"

She looked at Flood but was glad it was too dark for the woman to see her eyes. Flood could always tell when she was lying.

"Oh, I decided to have another cup of coffee instead."

"And since when did you start drinkin' coffee, Madrigal?" Rena Knox inquired.

"When my steppa's cow got hit by a wagon."

At Rena's disbelieving snort, Madrigal said, "I never said I actually *liked* the stuff. But sometimes when you're hungry, you eat or drink a lot of things you don't really like— just so your stomach won't bleat like a goat."

"That's right, Mama," Caddie defended.

"Hush up, Caddie. Nobody asked you."

An hour later, all of the women except Allison and Madrigal were asleep, with a soft snore coming from the corner where Flood lay.

Then the stealthy sound of the door being slid back caused Allison to lift her head in the dark and listen.

She recognized Tom Traymore's voice. "Madrigal," he whispered. "I've come for you."

Allison heard a slight movement near her and felt a foot stumble over her outstretched leg. Quickly, she drew it up, sighed, and turned on her side, while Madrigal squeezed through the opening made for her. With another creak, the boxcar door was slid shut again.

"What's happening?" Rebecca whispered.

"Nothing. Go back to sleep, Rebecca."

If Madrigal had a chance to escape, then Allison would not spread the alarm.

Neither Tom nor Madrigal said a word as they crept past the tracks and the sentry house. The pale moon had risen in the sky, giving the landscape a silver patina and painting the clumps of birches along the water with the same fool's-silver tints. In the distance, an owl hooted and a hyena howled, causing a deer to scamper into the wooded area downstream.

At the water's edge, Tom suddenly disappeared, leaving Madrigal alone for a few minutes. Madrigal smiled and proceeded to remove her clothes—dress first, then her pantaloons, her one petticoat, and finally her shoes. Making little noise, she slid into the water, as she had done so many times along the Chattahoochee, and began to tread water, while her eyes remained on the bank.

It wasn't long before Tom reappeared. Spread upon a nearby bush were the girl's dress and underthings. Seeing them, Tom quickly removed his uniform and then stood upon the bank, straining his eyes for a glimpse of Madrigal in the water.

She rose slowly out of the shallows, walking toward him, with the moonglow caressing her body. Tom wasted no more time on the shore. He, too, slid into the creek and purposefully made his way toward Madrigal. As they met, she opened her arms to embrace him, offering her lips to his own eager mouth.

"Madrigal," he whispered, feeling the soft skin of her body as part of his own. With a shiver, he moved his hands along the curves of her firm young breasts until he could stand it no longer. They went down together in the water, rose upward again for air, meeting and parting in a mating ritual as primitive as the land and water around them. In the distance, the hyena continued to howl, but Tom Traymore was only aware of his powerful hunger for the red-haired girl he had watched from the moment the train had pulled out of Marietta.

And when his urgent need had received gratification,

Tom continued to hold Madrigal and stroke her hair—a gentle thing that she had never known before.

"I love you, Madrigal."

She quickly dispelled the feeling that had surged within her. Her goal was more important. "By tomorrow, you won't even remember this happened between us."

The sadness in her voice made him deny her words. "That's not true. I'll always remember. And I'll always love you. When this nightmare is over, I give you my word that I'll find you, Madrigal, and I'll take you to my farm in the hills."

She shook her head. "No, Tom. You must forget me. I have this dreadful feeling that I'll die before we get to Nashville."

"Don't say such a thing. That's tempting fate."

Madrigal hesitated. "If only . . ." She sank against him and could feel his excitement begin to stir again.

"What if I was to help you escape? I could do that—but only after we reach the city and I'm relieved of duty. Once General Webster takes over . . ."

"You'd do that for me, Tom?"

"I'd do anything for you. You know that."

A noise along the bank stopped their conversation. Madrigal put her hand to his lips. "Let me get out first. So no one will catch us together."

Later, Allison, who was still awake, heard the boxcar door slide open and then shut. She felt Madrigal brush against her as the red-haired girl groped her way toward the sleeping space next to Flood. A few drops of water landed on Allison's face. So Madrigal had not escaped, after all. She'd gone swimming instead. Probably with Tom Traymore.

At that moment, Allison's only desire was to protect

Madrigal from being found out by the others, especially Rena and Addie. Perhaps it was because she felt guilty and partly responsible for the young girl's behavior. If Allison had not longed for a refreshing bath, she never would have urged Madrigal to seek Tom out.

Now it was too late. Whatever had happened between the two was beyond calling back. Both she and Madrigal would have to live with the consequences of that night.

CHAPTER
18

Now the hunger began. All rations were gone. Tempers flared, babies cried, and the great cast-iron water buckets chained to the sides of the train had little liquid left in them. It grew increasingly difficult to find a spring or a watering hole along the way, and many of the women, already ill, suffered even more from the lack of water in the summer heat.

Allison, ill with the fever that had spread through the boxcars, had not yet fallen into delirium as some of the others had. It was left to her to be aware of Addie's smug, satisfied voice admonishing them all.

"I told you not to bathe in the creek. But no. Nobody listened." In a particularly crowing manner, she had a few personal words for Allison. "I guess you're sorry now, Allison, that *you*, of all people, didn't heed what I said. Especially with a baby to take care of. And your milk gone sour with the fever."

Allison had no strength to argue with the woman. Perhaps Addie was right. If so, she had done a terrible thing, risking Morrow's life as well as her own.

But how she longed for the cool feeling of the water on her skin, even now—the same longing as on that other night. All she could think to say was "My poor Morrow. My poor baby."

She tried to lift her head, to get a glimpse of the child lying in Rebecca's arms, but she was stopped.

"Just lie still, Allison," Alma Brady said, wiping Allison's brow. "Don't try to get up."

"But Morrow . . . I have to see to Morrow."

"She's all right, now. She's asleep."

"Are you sure she isn't ill, too? She's so quiet, and I haven't even fed her."

"Rebecca's watchin' over her."

Allison returned her head to the small bundle of goods that served as a pillow. It was strange to have Alma Brady take over, mopping her face, sitting beside her, and talking in a soothing, reassuring manner. Only several days before, Alma had been the one needing consolation.

But life changed swiftly from day to day, hour to hour, on the train the women had labeled "Sorrow." They were the forgotten, cast from memory as surely as if their names had been obliterated from the pages of a family Bible, with no hope left of being returned to their families. The railroad was now secure against the Confederates, even though Hood, thinking only of military expediency and not of the women, had sent Wheeler's cavalry to raid the lines above

Atlanta. But Sherman had gotten through the supplies he needed for the siege of that city, making the unnecessary removal of Wheeler's cavalry from the battle one more blunder in Hood's defense of Atlanta.

Realizing she was growing weaker, Allison spoke to the woman sitting beside her. "Rebecca, I think it's time to get out the shears."

Rebecca understood. But she mourned the task ahead—the cutting of Allison Forsyth's beautiful blond hair to conserve her strength.

The woman removed the shears from the bundle, but still she couldn't bring herself to begin until Allison urged her on. "Go ahead, Rebecca. Cut it."

"Yes, Miss Allison."

A few minutes later, Allison's head was compeltely shorn and the beautiful blond hair lay at Rebecca's feet.

But the cutting of her hair did not help. Allison grew continually worse, threatening to lapse into delirium, that dangerous twilight of the mind. It was Alma who attempted to draw her back to reality by recalling their first meeting under the water oak.

"Do you remember that day, Allison, at the mill when we sat together and fed our babies?"

The hypnotic tempo of the train wheels became, in Allison's mind, the same unceasing rhythm of the mill wheel with the water rushing over it. Allison smiled. "I remember. You were going to make a dress out of blue silk and move to Atlanta."

"Yes. To find a new papa for my little Robert." Alma leaned over and whispered, "I brought the material with me, Allison. It's in my bundle. But I don't need it now. When you get well, I want *you* to have it."

Allison's violet eyes became sad. "No, Alma. You keep it. I won't have need of it, either."

"Oh, but you will. You're goin' to get well, Allison. I can tell. And it'll look so pretty on you. A lot better than on me. I think I knew even when I bought it that *silk* was much too fancy for the likes of me."

Alma wiped Allison's brow again and then nodded to Rebecca to change places with her. Unknown to the sick woman, Alma took Morrow, settled down in the corner of the boxcar, and unpinned her calico dress. Soon, the hungry baby was nursing greedily at Alma's full breast. A subtle change came over the woman. Allison, the mother, was forgotten, as Alma's full attention was now lavished upon the baby.

Despite Flood's and Rebecca's efforts, Allison continued to grow worse with each mile traveled. As the fever took over her body, fear—a nebulous, ugly thing—took over her mind like the fog that crept over the Chattahoochee, obliterating the landscape. Still, she struggled—to see, to hear, to feel, to be reassured time and again that her baby was not dead beside her.

While the train made its appointed stops for water, for the women to scavenge for food along the way, and for the guards to dig other graves, Allison knew little of what was going on. Yet a cool, wet cloth, a strong hand forcing her to drink from a cup—all these became landmarks along her dark, unknown journey, with voices constantly probing, urging her back to reality.

"My Miss Allison is a strong woman," Rebecca said, more to bolster her own troubled mind than to reassure any of the others. "I remember when she and Mr. Jonathan were little. It was always Miss Allison who got over things quicker—while Mr. Jonathan took twice as long to get well."

Another day passed and by midafternoon Flood, sweeping her large hand along Allison's face and brow, felt encouraged. "She doesn't appear nearly so hot today. Maybe the fever is beginnin' to break."

Flood was right. Just as insidiously as the fever had come upon Allison, so it began to leave her. And when the train stopped one evening not long after that, Allison, although weak, was lifted out of the boxcar by Flood and placed in a comfortable position on the ground, where Rebecca had spread her shawl as protection against the evening dew. Then the women left her alone to forage for food for their evening meal before it got too dark.

They spread out into the woods, searching for sheep sorrel, wild carrot, berries, nuts, and roots, with the children admonished not to eat anything until it had been declared safe by one of the women experienced in wild plants.

Madrigal was the first woman to return from the woods. In the boxcar, she had kept to herself, not helping with nursing Allison back to health. Or with taking care of the baby, either. She was no good at that sort of thing. But when it came to finding food to eat, she was one of the best.

"Here, I've brought some pine nuts and blackberries for you," she said to Allison, and thrust them in her lap.

A surprised Allison, with dark smudges under her eyes attesting to her illness, looked up and said, "Thank you, Madrigal. This is very kind of you."

"Just consider it part of a debt paid," Madrigal said, and then flounced off to eat by herself. She had not intended to gather food for anybody else. But the blackberries had reminded her of poor Ellie and that day at the bridge. And then she remembered it was Allison Forsyth who had come to Ellie's rescue at the institute, keeping her from bleeding to death that night.

Soon the other women returned. Some had been lucky; others not so lucky. But the table became a communal one, with small offerings set forth—a meager spread for the hungry women.

Then Rebecca, sitting beside Allison, recognized the faint, tantalizing aroma of meat cooking in the open not far from them. With a sudden longing for real food, she looked down at the few berries remaining in the palm of her hand. "Somebody musta raided a henhouse," she said to Allison.

One by one, like animals scenting their prey on the wings of the wind, the other women lifted their heads to get the full benefit of the aroma, all the while knowing, like Rebecca, that their still empty stomachs would never taste the coveted meat.

"Probably Alonzo Puckett," Flood said. "I notice he always manages to eat better than any of the other guards."

But Allison began to lift her head in another direction, with her eyes searching the northern sky, now filled with stars. "Surely we should be reaching Nashville soon. And then we'll *all* be having a nice meal, don't you think?"

"Well, it won't be a bit too soon for me." Flood placed the last pine nut in her mouth and made a crunching sound with her teeth. Her clothes now hung loosely on her large frame, and her hair, stringy and dirty, held the grime and soot of the train journey.

"Rebecca, could you please bring Morrow to me? I think I'll try to feed her now."

"You sure you feel up to it, Miss Allison? Alma won't mind a day or two longer."

"That's just it, Rebecca. I can't rely on Alma forever. A day or two longer and I may not have any milk left."

Rebecca stood up and went off to find Alma. And as she did so, Madrigal, alone in a small copse, finished her food and wiped the berry juice from her chin.

"Madrigal? Are you in there?"

She recognized Tom's voice. "Yes, Tom."

Soon he was sitting beside her, offering her a piece of chicken. "Here, I brought you a drumstick. Hurry and eat it before the other women find out."

Madrigal needed no further prompting. She tore into the half-cooked meat with a ferocious appetite. And she didn't stop until the bone was picked clean. During that time, Tom sat beside her and watched, his eyes shining with the love he bore the young, red-haired woman.

When she was finished, she suddenly felt guilty. "Did you have any chicken, Tom? Or was that your piece?"

He hesitated. "I won't ever lie to you, Madrigal. It was mine. But I got more pleasure out of watching you enjoy it than I would have if I'd eaten it myself."

Madrigal nodded and accepted Tom's love offering, dismissing a momentary twinge of guilt as she thought of her plans when they finally reached Nashville.

Like Madrigal, Alma had also sought out a secret place, apart from the other women. In her arms she held Allison's baby. No. *Her* baby now. She'd even changed her name, for *Morrow* sounded too highfalutin to suit her. As the baby began to cry, Alma rocked her in her arms. "That's all right, Lovey Lou," she crooned. "You don't have to cry. Mama's gonna take care of you from now on."

At that moment, the past week's events became confusing to Alma. She vaguely remembered a baby being buried along the tracks some time back. And she even remembered his name. Robert. At times, she'd thought that the baby might have been her own, but then all she had to do was to gaze down at the pretty, little fair-haired baby at her breast to know it wasn't true. *Her* baby, little Lovey Lou, named for her grandmother, was alive.

Then she remembered Allison by the gravesite. "Poor Allison," she murmured. It must be awful sad to lose your own baby. At that thought, Alma tightened her hold on Lovey Lou.

"Alma, where are you?" Rebecca called out. Alma listened and smiled but did not respond. She had deliberately chosen the secluded spot so that she and her baby wouldn't be disturbed by the others.

Rebecca kept calling, but the voice was now farther away and Alma relaxed. But then other voices took up the cry and Alma knew that she should go back to camp with the others.

"Alma, where are you?" Rebecca's voice was closer now.

Alma sighed and emerged from her hiding place. "I'm here, Rebecca. But please be quiet. Or you'll wake little Lovey Lou with all your shoutin'."

Rebecca frowned at the name. "Why didn't you answer before?"

"I was too busy feedin' my baby."

"You mean Miss Allison's baby."

"No, Rebecca. This is *my* baby girl, Lovey Lou. Don't you remember? We buried Allison's little boy, Robert, by the railroad tracks."

Alma began to croon as she walked along the moonlit path with Rebecca. She took no notice of the other woman's moan or the tightening fist that clutched at her troubled bosom. Alma was far too intent on the baby in her arms.

By the time they reached the edge of camp, Rebecca was aware of the problem that faced her. Her mistress would have to know. But how to tell her? And what to do about

Alma, especially if Allison were still too sick to feed her child?

"Don't you want me to carry the baby a while?" Rebecca suggested.

"That's awful kind of you, Rebecca. Maybe if you hold her for a minute or so, I'll take care of the necessaries."

Rebecca took the baby and said in a careful, soothing voice, "We'll be in camp, Alma."

They parted, and Rebecca hurried as fast as she dared to the area where Allison lay. "I found her, Miss Allison. Here she is." Rebecca gave Morrow to Allison, and without any explanation as to where she'd found her, she hurriedly left Allison's side to seek out Flood.

Allison held the baby in her arms for the first time since her illness. Her arms were weak and the baby felt heavy, but she didn't mind. "Hello, Morrow," she said, gazing down at her child. "I've missed you. Did you know that?"

In the full moonlight, the baby resembled a small cherub, peaceful and asleep. It was a pity to awaken her, yet Allison knew that she must try to feed her. Once awake, the baby did not cooperate. Instead, she set her mouth rigidly and turned her head away, causing a sense of rejection to overwhelm the weakened Allison.

There was no mistaking Flood's large bulk as she ambled down the path. Rebecca, waiting for her, stepped in front of her. "Flood, can I speak to you for a minute? We've got a terrible problem."

"What is it, Rebecca?"

"It's Alma."

"Has she got the fever, too?"

"Not that I know of. But her mind's powerfully confused. She thinks Miss Allison's baby is her own."

"You must be mistaken, Rebecca."

"I don't think so. Just a few minutes ago, she told me how sorry she was for Miss Allison losin' her baby boy, Robert."

"My Lord. You mean she can't remember whose baby died?"

"Looks that way. She's even changed Morrow's name. Calls her Lovey Lou instead. What are we gonna do about it, Flood?"

"Have you told Allison yet?"

"No. I was waitin' to talk to you first."

But before Flood and Rebecca reached camp, Allison had become aware that Alma's fierce maternal love had been transferred to Morrow.

"You got no business holdin' my baby, Allison, in your weakened condition," Alma said, rushing over to where Allison sat. "Here, give her to me."

"I beg your pardon, Alma?" A startled Allison stared up at the angry woman.

"I said, I want my baby back. You got no business holdin' Lovey Lou like that. *Rebecca* was s'posed to watch after her till I got back."

Morrow was torn from Allison's arms, while Madrigal, sauntering into camp, looked on in amazement. She saw the anguished look on Allison's face and went to her defense. "Alma, give Morrow back to Allison."

"No, Madrigal. Leave Alma alone for now."

In triumph, Alma gazed at the two and then hurried to the edge of the camp, where she carefully wrapped the baby in her shawl and lay down beside her to go to sleep.

"Alma's gone feather-headed, Allison. Why did you let her get away with taking your baby from you?"

"For Morrow's survival, Madrigal. My milk evidently isn't to her liking."

Allison turned her head, and a tear escaped down her cheek. "Oh, Coin," she said, with a great longing for her dead husband.

And in the quietness, Allison wept.

CHAPTER
19

Addie and Rena, aware of Alma's delusion concerning Allison's baby, were strangely silent. No barbed remarks struck an unsuspecting target. It was almost as if the two troublemakers were now bystanders, watching this new development and waiting to see what would happen next between Allison and Alma. Then, too, Rena's mind was on Caddie, who'd evidently eaten something in the woods that had made her sick.

For Allison, this part of the journey was extremely difficult. As her strength began to return slowly, she longed to resume the total care of her child, but Alma Brady had moved to the innermost corner of the boxcar and taken Morrow with her. Allison couldn't help but feel rejected, for the baby seemed content being nourished by the other woman.

Rebecca sensed Allison's sadness as the monotonous sound of the train lulled them into a near stupor. "Have you decided what you're gonna do about Alma, Miss Allison?"

"I can't see that any good will come with a battle over the baby, especially in this crowded boxcar. Perhaps when the train stops, I can take Alma aside and talk with her."

Several hours later, that opportunity came when the train ran out of fuel and had to make an emergency stop. It was a hazardous spot, situated as it was on the other side of a tunnel blasted from the stone heart of the mountain terrain.

While half the guards took their axes and went in search of wood to feed the dying engine, the others set up a well-planned watch around the women who were allowed out of the boxcars to stretch.

In front of them, a chalky bluff, with a few straggly cedars bent at angles by the wind, delineated the boundary where land ended in a steep precipice and low-hanging clouds began, obscuring the valley below. Directly above them, the train sat, wheezing its last fiery breath.

Allison, too weak to go far, had chosen a spot to rest while Rebecca went foraging for both of them. Because of the heat, she removed the widow's cap to allow the sun on her hair. Cropped short, it stuck out in small bunches, reminding her of the difficult time she'd come through.

As she looked back at the train, she saw a guard standing on top of one of the boxcars and watching them all. His legs were spread apart, and he held the musket in his hands as if he were ready to use it at the first sign of mutiny among the women. She had noticed him before—a man totally without compassion. He was tall and broad of shoulder, with an undisguised line of cruelty running from the corners of his mouth to his granite-gray eyes. For a brief second, their eyes met. And then Allison, feeling vulnerable, covered her head again and, with a shiver, turned her back to him.

The guard, Wolf Perkin, saw Allison's reaction to him and was gratified. Several of the women from his boxcar had escaped the day before, and he had been blamed for it—a blemish on his record, coming at a bad time because he was waiting for a promotion. He had sworn that no others would escape while he was guarding them.

As he surveyed the women before him, he sensed their desperation. Haunted expressions marked their faces. He had seen the same look on his hunting dogs that he starved for days before a big hunt. That made them better hunters, with no quarter given for any animal they tracked down in the forest. But he had to be careful. If he waited too long to feed them, the dogs would turn on their own pack.

He continued to watch the woman who had lost her beautiful, long blond hair. Finally, he saw her get up and walk over to another woman sitting by herself. A baby rested on a shawl on the ground beside her.

"Alma?"

"What is it?"

Allison swallowed and prayed that the speech she'd rehearsed for two days would come out right. "You've been so wonderful these past few days while I was ill. And I owe you so much."

"For what?"

"For taking care of Morrow and feeding her when I was unable to do so."

"Morrow? Who's she?"

"My child. The one sleeping beside you."

173

"You must be mistaken, Allison. This is Lovey Lou."

"No, Alma. You're only pretending. But I understand. You see, I know how much it hurt to bury your little Robert back there along the tracks, and if taking care of Morrow and pretending she's yours helped to ease some of the pain for a while, then I'm glad. But it isn't good for you to keep on pretending. The child is mine and you'll have to give her back to me soon."

Before Allison could stop her, Alma snatched up the baby and began to run toward the precipice. "You'll *never* take Lovey Lou from me."

"Alma, stop! Please don't go any farther."

Rebecca, returning from foraging, heard Allison's cry before she saw what was happening. And then she saw Alma running toward the bluff with the baby in her arms. "Lordy! Lordy! Alma's gonna jump with the baby. We've got to stop her."

Rebecca's warning alerted Flood and Madrigal, also returning from gathering pods and green shoots along the mountainside. In amazement, they heard Alma scream, "Don't you come near me, Allison. I'll jump. I swear it."

While Allison remained frozen where she was, Flood slowly edged her way around the others.

In a soothing voice, Flood called out, "Alma, I found some queen-of-the-meadow roots for you. I know you've been lookin' for some these past few days." She watched Alma pause, then continued, "Madrigal's makin' a fire right now. I thought we'd boil the roots for tea. Would you like that?"

When Alma still hesitated, she said, "Bring Lovey Lou over to the fire. I expect you're real thirsty."

Alma's head lifted and she gazed at Allison, who still

hadn't moved. "I *might* join you. That is, if you keep Allison away."

"Why, sure, Alma. It'll be just the two of us. With Lovey Lou, of course."

Allison was immensely relieved when she saw Alma turn from the bluff and begin to follow Flood.

Later, a dejected Allison sat apart, hunched over and clasping her arms around her knees. She was still shaking from the near tragedy. Sitting down beside her, Rebecca reached over and squeezed her hand in sympathy. "We got to be more'n careful, Miss Allison."

"I know, Rebecca. I handled that badly. But I never dreamed that Morrow would be placed in such danger."

"I guess it caught all of us off guard. Alma's sicker than anybody ever imagined. But we'll stick together, Miss Allison, closer'n a tick to a dog's ear. And when the right time comes, we'll get Morrow back. Don't you worry."

But Allison made no further attempt that day to settle matters with Alma Brady.

Within a half hour, with the wood loaded in the hopper behind the engine, the women were summoned to the train and the engine, making up for lost time, hurtled its way toward Nashville.

Two years previously, the Tennessee city built on the banks of the Cumberland River had been an important rail center for the Confederacy, with a junction of three main lines—the Nashville and Chattanooga, the Central of Alabama, and the Louisville and Nashville. With its giant depots filled with munitions and supplies, the city had been a prime target for General Grant's gunboats and his successful Army of the Tennessee.

On a bitterly cold winter day in 1862, when the sleet and

the defeated troops from Fort Donelson arrived at the same time, Nashville's citizens, in a state of panic, had vied with the wounded for places on the last Confederate trains leaving Nashville.

Now, in 1864, in the heat of waning summer, the same platform was crowded with other civilians as the long train, with too many empty places in the boxcars, finally drew into the station. Many of the people waiting to catch a glimpse of its passengers were merely curious; others were truly concerned over the condition of the deported Confederate women prisoners.

In the headquarters of the military Division of Mississippi, General Webster heard the news—that the women and children had finally arrived. And he rued that July day he had received Sherman's message. Even the northern newspapers were having a field day following the progress of the women.

Webster stared down at the Philadelphia *Patriot and Union* that some anonymous officer on his staff had left on his desk.

. . . Our generals out West are very busy sending the ladies back and forth. Sherman sends from Georgia 200 or 300 helpless factory girls north—to starve— while Rosecrans is packing them by the dozens south from Missouri. Between the vandalism of Hunter, the barbarity of Sherman and Rosecrans, and the lawlessness of Banks, the country will need peace to keep us all from the horrors of a Tartar civilization.

But the reporter didn't have his numbers correct. Webster already had on his hands a total of fifteen hundred women, children, and babies—to feed and to shelter. And if these women from Roswell and Sweet Water were in no better condition than the ones who had arrived earlier, then he would have the added expense of pine coffins, too.

"General Webster, sir?"

The Union general looked up from his desk. "Yes, Curry?"

"The deportation train has pulled into the station."

"Have the engineer brought to me."

"Yes, sir."

The soldier did as he was told. He walked through the crowd that jammed the platform and approached the engine just as the engineer climbed down from his tall perch.

"Just a minute, mister," the soldier called out. "General Webster wants to see you."

"Then tell him I'll be over at the Watauga Saloon rinsing the dust out of my throat."

"I don't think you understand, mister. The general has jurisdiction over everybody on this train, including you. He's waiting at headquarters. And I'd advise you not to make him wait much longer. He's not in the best of moods."

While the unwilling engineer went with Curry, the guards who had traveled with the train all the way from Marietta to Nashville began to open the boxcars for the last time. Their duty was ended once the women were put in the care of General Webster.

"I never knew a train trip could be so long," Alonzo Puckett complained to Tom. "I feel like I've been to hell and back. And just look at the blisters on my hands from chopping all that wood for the engine."

While Puckett complained, Tom helped the women down from the boxcar, going to the rescue of several of the older ones whose legs doubled under them when they tried to stand and some of the younger ones too small to negotiate the jump by themselves.

Tom watched for Madrigal. When she appeared, he leaned toward her and whispered, "I'll find you tonight. After you get settled."

"You promise?"

With a silent gesture, he used his hand to cross his heart, but with Puckett staring, he quickly returned his attention to the other women.

He saw Alma Brady standing in the opening of the wooden car. For a moment, she clutched Morrow to her bosom and hesitated to jump until Tom came to her aid. He held out his arms to take the baby as he had done with Caddie and some of the other children.

When she finally relinquished the child to Tom, Alma said, "Be careful of my Lovey Lou. I wouldn't want you to drop her."

Tom frowned. He knew that the baby's name was Morrow and that she didn't belong to Alma, for he had dug the grave for Alma's little boy in the meadow. He would never forget how it had torn his insides to watch her smoothing the dirt mound and to hear her sing that strange song over and over before Allison got her back to the train. But Allison Forsyth had been ill for the past week or more. Maybe that was why Alma was still caring for the baby.

As soon as Alma jumped to the ground, she was followed by Flood. Then came Rebecca, helping Allison. The woman still looked pale and weak, but she smiled when she saw Tom with the baby. As a matter of course he held out the baby for her to take.

Suddenly, Alma pushed herself between Tom and Allison and shrieked. "Don't you dare give my Lovey Lou to anybody but me."

"Ma'am?" Tom looked from one woman to the other. By that time, the people on the platform had become interested in the exchange. Morrow started to cry, and Allison, realizing that the platform was too public a place to have it out with Alma, finally nodded and said to the guard, "Give the baby to Alma for the moment, Mr. Traymore."

After he had done so, Tom stood by the boxcar and watched the procession with Alma being carefully escorted by four women—Flood and Madrigal on either side of her, and Allison and Rebecca following closely behind.

An hour later, the women were resting in refugee quarters. New guards were now assigned to watch over them, to keep them from escaping. But they were in no condition to do anything but eat the first hot meal they'd had in days and then find rest on the narrow cots that seemed like heaven after the discomfort of the boxcars. Allison, choosing a cot not too far from Alma, kept her eye on her child, all the while praying that it wouldn't be too much longer before she was able to nurse her again.

That night, with the eruption of every little noise, Madrigal, close to the window, lifted her head and waited to be summoned to the gate. But Tom Traymore never came. Finally, in the wee hours of the night, when she could no longer stay awake, a disappointed Madrigal laid her head on the makeshift pillow and went to sleep.

For two days, Madrigal waited for Tom to reappear. But by the third day, when the women were separated into smaller units to be moved to another building, she became reconciled to the fact that she would never see him again. She would have to find some other means of escape. It galled her that she had allowed Tom all those liberties, especially that night at the creek. But she knew that he wasn't the one responsible for her present condition. The culprit was

Caleb, taking her that night in her apartment at The Bricks. She hadn't told anyone what she suspected. Not even Flood. With a slight feeling of nausea, she slung her small clothing bundle over her shoulder and followed Rebecca, Allison, and Alma out of the gate toward the smaller building a hundred yards away.

Standing outside the gate was Tom Traymore. When Madrigal saw him, her eyes darkened and she turned her head away so that she wouldn't have to speak to the soldier who had betrayed her.

"Madrigal, wait!"

His insistent voice caused her to look around. He motioned for her to come closer and the faint hope of escape was born again.

"Be ready around midnight tonight, Madrigal. I'm coming for you then."

"I got no timepiece, Tom."

"Just listen for the hoot of an owl outside the window. That'll be the signal to slip out. I've already arranged it with one of the guards to be looking the other way."

Madrigal didn't know why she felt so stubborn. And when she'd said it, she was even more surprised than Tom. "I can't leave without my friends."

For a moment, he stared at her. Then he said, "How many?"

"Well, there's Flood. And Allison, with her baby. And Rebecca, too."

A soldier escorting the small group of women stopped and pointed a finger at Madrigal. "You, young woman, stop loitering."

"I'll be there in a minute."

The love shone in Tom's eyes. "All right, Madrigal. Have your way. I guess there'll be enough room for them, too."

A pleased Madrigal rushed to catch up with the others. Once she was in the group, Addie, as usual, had her say about the red-haired girl's flirting with the Union soldier. But Madrigal didn't even respond. By midnight, she was going to be free. And Addie wasn't.

Madrigal skipped along, making a slight pirouette in her shabby calico dress. Her red hair was matted, but her skin was white and smooth. With her topaz eyes showing her excitement, she reached out and tugged at Allison's sleeve.

"I've got the answer, Allison. Tonight, you'll have your brat to yourself again."

CHAPTER
20

Situated in a small wooden building not far from the rail tracks, Allison had listened all day to the familiar whistles of incoming and outgoing trains; had heard the shifting back and forth of locomotives and the abrupt, clanging noises that accompanied the uncoupling of cars. The steady songs of the work crew had also filled the air—the rich, hypnotic rhythm so peculiar to the field songs of the South.

But once darkness descended on the town, the work songs gave way to peals of female laughter answered by a masculine roar, a shot fired, and pigs squealing in the street. That first night, on her arrival in Nashville, Allison had noticed the pigs running loose, rooting around in the garbage that lined the ditches. Filled with oozing mud and debris, the ditches crisscrossed the alleyways, ran parallel to the wooden walkways, and provided a stench that the women, penned up in the boxcars for days, hardly noticed.

Allison had immediate sympathy for the animals looking for food. After having to subsist on roots, berries, and nuts, the women and children had been driven into near frenzy at the aroma of potatoes and a little fat meat served to them. What consternation it had produced when they had eaten so ravenously and then, one by one, lost it all. If it had not been for Flood's saving a queen-of-the-meadow root for soothing tea, Allison doubted that either she or Madrigal would have survived the night.

Only now, after several days' rest, were the women beginning to realize what they had been through. And, even worse, what was still ahead of them. They had come only halfway in their journey north. Allison could sense the hopelessness in some of the less sturdy women—that they might not be alive when the deportation train reached its final destination beyond the Ohio River. That was one of the reasons why Allison, still weak from the fever, had not wrested Morrow from Alma once and for all. For Alma was one of the strong ones. Her round face, with its freckles sprinkled across her nose, did not resemble a mask of death but of life. If Allison died, she knew her child would be taken by Alma as her own.

Now Madrigal had given Allison reprieve, hope, and the opportunity to reclaim her baby.

She waited in the dark for the signal Madrigal had told her to listen for. But she was so tired. She fought the sleep that threatened her. She *must* remain awake, for when the signal came she had only a moment to get to Alma's cot, take the baby, and then slip out of the building to go to the wagon hidden in the alley.

Close to the window, Madrigal O'Laney lay on her cot and listened to every sound. The night noises outside were subsiding, and she was glad. Inside the small barracks, Flood's snore was conspicuously absent. That meant the woman was still awake.

Then a child coughed. A baby began to cry, and Madrigal sat up, peering through the dark with her topaz eyes to make sure that it was not Morrow who had awakened. It would be dangerous enough without a crying brat to spoil it all. She almost regretted what she'd done—making Tom agree to take along the others, too. It would have been so much easier for only one person to slip past the guards. But it was too late now. She had already spoiled it.

The time passed slowly—an hourglass stretched toward eternity. But Madrigal's only knowledge of time passing was the cramp in her foot that kept getting more painful with each minute. Then an owl hooted from a nearby tree. It was midnight.

Quickly, Madrigal rose, grabbed the bundle from her cot, and headed toward the door. She didn't look back, for she had told the others that she would give them no more warning than the one on which Tom had decided.

Flood, adjacent to Madrigal, grimaced at the noise her own cot made as she attempted to get up. She waited a moment longer, and on the second try, she heaved herself to her feet just as Rebecca began to edge her way around the other side of the room. The black woman carried the double bundle containing Allison's few clothes as well as her own. And tightly wrapped in a cloth was the food each had hoarded from previous meals.

Three women—Madrigal, Flood, and Rebecca—met outside the building. "Where's Allison?" Flood asked.

"I thought she was right behind me," Rebecca whispered.

"Well, we can't wait for her. She'll have to catch up with us or stay here." Madrigal's voice was emphatic.

"I'll go back for her."

"No, Rebecca. It's too dangerous."

With a start, Allison opened her eyes. She realized then that she had been dozing. A sense of panic enveloped her. What if she had missed the signal and the others had already gone? She sat up and gazed around her, getting her bearings. In the filtered moonlight, she stared at Rebecca's cot. It looked empty. Groping for the shawl at the foot of her cot, she immediately stood and began to walk rapidly toward the one where Alma lay. But someone had moved a cot out of line and Allison stumbled against it. She held her breath as the woman rolled over onto her other side.

More slowly now, Allison began to move, walking in the narrow aisle like a tightrope walker, holding on to her shawl to balance herself in the dark. As she walked, she counted the number of cots, as she had done that afternoon. And then she stood before Alma's cot.

Carefully, Allison removed the woman's hand from Morrow's body. She picked up her child and, not taking time to wrap her in the shawl, fled down the aisle away from Alma.

The baby squirmed and grunted as she began to awaken. "No, Morrow. Please stay asleep," Allison begged, rushing toward the barrack's door.

"Lovey Lou?" Alma's voice was faint. "Where are you, Lovey Lou?"

Then Allison heard the woman shriek. "My baby! Someone's stolen my baby!"

"Oh, God, help me!" At the door, Allison could see no one. And the ground beyond looked deserted. She was too late. The others had already gone.

"Miss Allison?"

"Rebecca?"

The woman stepped from the side of the building. "Yes'm. I waited for you. If we hurry, we can still catch up with Madrigal and Flood."

The two women sped past the barricade and headed for the alley behind the Watauga Saloon while a lantern light suddenly appeared in the barrack's window behind them. With Alma's triggering cry, the alarm was spread. Walter, the guard who had been bribed by Tom, slowly walked into the room where most of the women were now waking up.

"All right, what's going on?" he inquired.

"My baby has been stolen."

In the dim light, the woman whose cot Allison had stumbled into heard Alma's hysterical voice. Now she knew who had escaped—Allison. And she had taken her baby with her. Good. But if the guards started looking for her this soon, she would have no chance at all. Quickly, the woman said, "Pay no attention to Alma. She's always cryin' out for her baby. But, you see, we buried the child along the tracks a number of days ago."

"Yes," a voice in the dark agreed. "She's just confused. Let's all go back to sleep."

Wolf Perkin, waiting for reassignment after guard duty on the train, had enjoyed his few days of leisure, swapping hunting stories with some of the other soldiers and drinking a few bottles of beer each night with them at the Watauga Saloon. Now it was a little past midnight and he walked alongside Beacher, who was scheduled to go on duty at the building from which Allison and the others had escaped a few minutes earlier.

As the two approached the building, they saw a flickering lantern light and heard a woman shrieking.

"My Lord!" Beacher said. "No wonder the trip was such hell for you if you had to put up with caterwauling like that."

Wolf frowned and listened. He remembered hearing that same sound that afternoon on the bluff when the stuckup blond woman had caused such a ruckus. He'd watched her all along—the way she had held herself aloof and acted as if she was so much better than all the rest, with her black servant taking care of her. But he'd seen her back off soon enough when that other woman put up such a howl. And now it sounded as if the two women might be at each other's throats again.

"Beacher, you're going to have to be firm with those women. If you want me to, I'll go in with you and show you how to handle them."

"I sure would appreciate it, Wolf. There's two things I'm scairt to death of—and one of 'em is a screaming woman."

"What's the trouble, soldier?" Wolf asked the guard coming out with the lantern.

"Oh, some woman in hysterics," Walter replied. "Claims somebody's made off with her baby."

"Is it true? Is her baby missing?"

"Naw. Poor woman. She doesn't have one. It died somewhere along the way."

"Doesn't happen to be a woman called Alma, does it?"

"How did you know?"

"Because several days ago she *did* have a baby and some woman was trying to take it away from her then."

"But two of the women vouched that her baby was dead."

"They just might be covering up for someone." Wolf remembered the escape from the train and how the other women had reacted, keeping it quiet until it was too late

187

for him to do anything about it. Even though he had been relieved of duty, Wolf grabbed the lantern from the guard and said, "Come on, Beacher. We might as well get them all up and count them. And if anybody's missing, we'll have to sound the alarm."

Behind the Watauga Saloon, Tom Traymore sat in an ambulance wagon and waited for Madrigal to appear. He was even more nervous than the two horses he'd borrowed from the officers' corral and hitched up to the wagon. Yet he congratulated himself on his choice of transportation. It had come to him the night before when the soldiers at the saloon had laughed about the fist fight the general had gotten into with the surgeon.

"Seems the general had requisitioned the ambulance wagon for his own transportation," the fellow beside him at the bar rail had said. "That made the surgeon madder'n a rooster havin' his favorite pullet taken away from 'im. He stormed into the general's office and demanded his ambulance back. Said he needed it to transport his patients from the riverboats to the hospital."

"Well, what happened?" Tom had asked.

"They fought for it."

"Who won?"

"The surgeon. After the general drew his gun on 'im, the doctor threatened to report the general to the president."

Tom laughed. "Then I guess that was the end of it."

"No. Durned if the general didn't steal it back the very next day."

Now Tom sat in that same ambulance wagon and waited for the women to appear. To the casual observer, it wouldn't seem unusual for the ambulance to be out and about at night, especially with all the wounded soldiers coming in from the battles near Corinth.

"Tom?"

'Madrigal?"

"Yes, it's me. Have any of the others gotten here yet?"

"No, you're the first. But hush talking and climb in the back."

Madrigal did so, throwing her small bundle inside first and then climbing into the covered wagon with its canvas stretchers lashed to each side. Hiding behind the bundle, she kept her eyes on the alleyway. Soon she saw a large bulk heading their way. At first, she couldn't tell whether it was Flood or a man. But as the figure drew closer, Madrigal recognized Flood, dressed in her husband's clothes and with her hair hidden under a cap.

As Flood approached the wagon, Madrigal reached out from the back and took the bundle she carried. Without a word, the large woman followed the bundle and hoisted herself to the ambulance floor, which was still stained with blood.

Now, all three kept watch—for Allison and Rebecca. The horses neighed, and at the sight of two drunken soldiers passing in the alley, Tom clicked his teeth and began to edge slowly down the alley.

"Where're you going, soldier?"

Tom swallowed. "I'm waiting for the hospital boat to come in."

One of the soldiers laughed. "This ain't the dock, soldier. It's in the other direction. Here, we'll just get in the back and ride with you to the levee."

"I wouldn't advise that if I was you."

"And why not? We got just as much right as anybody else to hitch a ride."

"The general wouldn't take kindly to you crowding him out," Tom whispered in a confidential tone.

189

"You mean the general's stolen it back from the surgeon?"

"Yeah, but you don't have to go telling everybody about it."

The two laughed and then stumbled on down the alleyway. Listening to the exchange, Madrigal had held her breath. It had been a close call. Deciding they couldn't wait any longer, Madrigal crawled toward the driver's perch. "Tom, we might as well go now. The other two must not be comin'."

Tom was of the same opinion. He snapped the reins and urged the horses into action, leaving the alleyway just as a breathless Allison and Rebecca stopped and hid in a doorway to avoid the two drunken soldiers making their way down the garbage-filled street.

CHAPTER
21

The Nashville Basin, situated in the heart of Tennessee, is bordered by the Highland Rim, a large upland plateau with steep hills that finally drop into the basin on three sides.

Turnpike roads, built in the 1800s, lead out of the city in all directions, following the old Indian traces to Natchez, Corinth, and other towns along the banks of the Mississippi River.

On the plateau itself, prosperous farms with cotton and tobacco crops sprinkle the area, but as the land sprawls to the east, the farms become smaller and less prosperous.

Tom Traymore, in the dead of night, hurried the horses along one of the pike roads toward the east and his own farm, which was a little west of Lebanon. And once they had left the city, Madrigal came to sit beside him.

"Where're we goin', Tom?" she asked.

"Me and my pa have a farm several days away from here. That's where I'm headed."

"You don't think they'll be lookin' for you?"

"I doubt anybody will be concerned about me since my time in the army is almost up. And even if they did decide to come after me, they probably couldn't find the farm since it's so far off the main road."

Madrigal tugged at her lip as she thought hard. An isolated farm wasn't where she intended to spend the rest of her life.

"I feel homesick already," Tom continued. "It's the smell of red cedars I remember. And the limestone caverns I used to explore as a boy. Why, I remember one time I was tracking a lynx, and I made one of the biggest mistakes of my life. Outside of joining the army, that is."

"And what was that?"

"I followed the cat into one of the caves. You see this mark on my arm?"

"I noticed it once before," Madrigal whispered. "That night at the creek."

"But you never said anything about it."

"I . . . my mind was on other things." Madrigal turned her head to make sure Flood and the other two had not overheard her.

Tom reached over and touched Madrigal's hand. "I'll never forget that night, Madrigal. In fact, my mind hasn't been on much else since then."

Madrigal rolled her eyes at Tom's confession. It was a pity the night swim had meant so little to her.

In the back of the ambulance wagon, Flood, Rebecca,

and Allison sat upright. With Morrow at her breast, Allison felt the first contentment in days.

"Looks like Morrow doesn't miss Alma at all," Rebecca said, hearing a satisfied burp coming from the baby.

"But I'm so sorry for Alma. Tonight, she must feel that she's lost *two* babies," Allison said.

"I wouldn't waste a split second worryin' over it, Allison. Alma was the one who almost caused you to get caught. Have you thought of that?"

"Still . . ."

"Flood's right, Miss Allison. And I got a feelin' we haven't heard the last of it."

"You think someone might be trying to catch up with us?" Allison took Morrow from her shoulder, wrapped the shawl around her, and placed her on her lap.

"You never can tell," Flood said. "I'll feel a whole lot safer once we get off this main road."

"I haven't even thanked you properly for coming back to look for us. If it hadn't been for you, Flood, Rebecca and I probably wouldn't have made it."

"Well, I knew what danger you were both in. And Rebecca, most of all, if it happened she was out by herself after curfew. Without you to vouch for her, I could just see her locked up as a runaway and then sold to some disreputable fellow, like that Marcus Stagg."

Rebecca shuddered. She'd been free all her life, with the papers to prove it. Still, that didn't give her liberty to go where she wanted to go or when she wanted to go—by herself. The color of her skin had decreed that her freedom was limited—set between sunrise and sunset. And, even worse, she'd lost her papers. If she'd been caught that night while waiting for Miss Allison, neither heaven nor Mr. Lincoln's proclamation could have helped her. If she hadn't been returned to the barracks with the other Roswell women, then she would more than likely have wound up in a place equally as bad. And it could still happen. Their escape was not assured.

Rebecca had good cause to be anxious. Almost directly behind them, Wolf Perkin was tracking their progress. He had already discovered the two discarded Saterlee litters, the canvas stretchers thrown from the ambulance wagon. It wouldn't be long now before he caught up with them, even though they'd had a good head start.

Riding on horseback, with a hound at his side, Wolf felt exhilarated, like old times—tracking his prey. The recent rain was making it easier, for the mud in the road revealed newly made ruts of a wagon pulled by two animals. The hoof marks indicated that the animals were shoeless and broken down—like the nags turned in at the post by the officers in line for replacements. The man who had taken them would have done better raiding the corral at the levee, where the new shipment of horses had just been unloaded.

Wolf had gotten the name of the soldier, too. He had forced it from Walter with a promise that he would not be reported, in exchange for his information. Of course, he'd covered up his part in it, while implicating one of the guards who'd come in on the deportation train. Wolf could have told which one, even before Walter opened his mouth. He'd seen how Tom Traymore had completely lost his head over that Madrigal O'Laney.

Wolf, kneeling in the road to pick up a baby's shoe that the dog had found, got back in the saddle and, whistling to the hound, began to gallop again, following the telltale trail of the wagon prints east.

Farther into the night, the wagon traveled, until it reached the road to Fort Donelson, where numerous wagon and caisson tracks had already made patterns in the mud. On purpose, Tom blended the ambulance wagon wheel tracks into those already made, coming and going. Then he left the wagon for a while to cut some limbs from a nearby tree. Once he'd returned, he had Madrigal take over the reins of the horses while he traveled behind the wagon, using the branches of the tree to obliterate the telltale marks of the wheels until Madrigal pulled the vehicle into the woods beyond and stopped.

Now, it was time to attend to the wagon itself, disguising the vehicle's military appearance, for they would be traveling in areas where people would look askance at an ambulance so far from the river and the fighting area. Tom took his knife and cut out the medical insignia painted on the canvas, then stuffed the opening with rags borrowed from Flood.

After giving the horses a rest, Tom took the wagon over rough terrain, staying clear of the roads—threading his way between trees, with the swish of smaller saplings caught under the wagon and the thud of rocks hurled against the wheels providing a percussive rhythm to the journey. At last, when he could go no farther because of the increasing density of the forest, Tom pulled out into a clearing until he'd come to a small path, little better than the forest route.

Twenty minutes behind them, Wolf stopped at the road to the fort where the wagon wheels that he had followed all the way from Nashville suddenly disappeared. Disappointed at first, he began to wonder if he had been following the wrong vehicle. But then he took out the baby shoe from his saddle, let the hound sniff it, and then watched as the dog disappeared into the wooded area beyond.

Wolf's laugh was triumphant. Tom Traymore had used

an old Indian ploy, but it was not going to work this time. Within a few hours, they would all be caught, and he, Wolf Perkin, would finally get the promotion that had been denied him.

He whistled for the dog, which bounded out of the woods and returned to Wolf. Now that he knew where the wagon was headed, he decided he could do with some help. He wheeled his horse around and raced toward the fort, demanding entrance from the night guard, who had been dozing while on duty.

Within minutes, Wolf rode out of the fort. With him this time were four cavalry men, their horses headed toward the woods off the road, with the hound barking and bounding ahead of them, stopping to sniff along the way and then following a zigzag pattern eastward.

The horses attached to the ambulance wagon were winded. Foam and lather drifted from them into the night breeze. They needed water; they needed rest. Tom knew they could travel no farther for the remainder of the night.

Toward the east, the thin moon had disappeared. A rim of light was barely perceptible on the horizon—a dull foreplay for the anticipated brilliance of sun that would burst through the cedars at any moment.

"We'll stop here and rest," Tom said, turning his head to look at the women hidden under the wagon's canvas hood. He had reached the entrance to one of the familiar caves that sprinkled the landscape. And a spring of water was not far beyond.

Madrigal, who had elected to return to her place with the other women, raised her sleepy head and looked out. The area Tom had chosen seemed desolate and raw, with outcroppings of limestone—the barrenness of the land giving an unwelcoming appearance with no promise of shelter or water. But Madrigal had no call to question the soldier who had brought them this far.

"All right, Tom," she said, and then jumped from the wagon. She brushed her hand through her hair, and with sleep still disturbing her equilibrium, she stumbled over the back wheel as she began to walk toward the soldier, who was busy unhitching the horses.

Rebecca, Flood, and Allison joined Madrigal, their reactions to the land much the same. But their spirits were light. The time of stress had gone from them, with their wariness gradually subsiding at each stretch of road they put behind them.

Allison, in a burst of thankfulness, looked at Rebecca and smiled. "Just think, Rebecca. Because of Tom Traymore and Madrigal, we might be in Savannah less than a mouth from now."

"And whatever Miss Araminta chooses to do or say to us will be just like water off a duck's back. Won't it, Miss Allison?"

Allison laughed. "We've come through a lot together, to be sure. Do you realize how lucky we are to be here at this very moment?"

"We're not out of the woods yet," Flood warned, "in more ways than one. We still got a long way to go."

Madrigal was silent. She looked at the women and then gazed back at Tom, who had stopped unhitching the horses to listen.

Suddenly, all of the women were doing the same, their sense of security severely shattered as they heard the telltale bark of a hound and a stealthy movement in the woods not far from them.

"Quick, we've got to hide," Tom said.

"But where?" Madrigal asked.

"In the cave ahead. I'll show you. But once you're in, don't utter a single word."

"What about the horses, Tom? And the wagon?" Madrigal was still worried that their presence would betray them.

"I'll lead them away from the cave."

"But, Tom—"

"Don't worry, Madrigal. Here, take my revolver. And whatever happens, don't come out of the cave until you hear my voice telling you to."

The women fled through the underbrush, with Tom, barely visible, leading the way. Rebecca held on to Allison to keep her from stumbling with the baby, and Flood and Madrigal clasped hands so that they wouldn't get separated.

Tom stopped when he reached the cave entrance. Stepping aside, he motioned for Madrigal to go in.

Seeing the uninviting black hole, she wailed, "I'm scared of caves."

"Hush, child. And get yourself on in. We don't have time to be afraid." Flood gave her a push, walked in herself, and Allison and Rebecca followed.

A flapping of wings greeted their invasion. Madrigal mourned as the creature brushed past her face to escape into the openness of the woods.

Tom disappeared. In total blackness, the women crouched in the cave and listened. They tried to separate the creak and roll of the ambulance wagon from the alien sounds that crept closer from the opposite direction. And in that suspension of time, as they held their breath and strained to hear what was going on in the wooded area beyond the cave, the same erosion of spirit that had threatened to paralyze them during those last days of captivity now descended upon them in heavy measure.

No one was more aware of what was at stake than Allison. For her, the idea of freedom had become a powerful hunger, a constant struggle to regain it once it had been lost. Looking at Morrow, blessedly asleep in her arms, Allison forgot all else but that single hunger, far surpassing the needs of the flesh. The debilitating fever, the lack of food and cleanliness—all these degradations of the body had merely served to make that spirit stronger.

A voice finally came roaring through the woods. "I know you're in there. We have the traitor who helped you. So, you might as well give yourselves up."

No one inside the cave moved. Allison, Rebecca, Flood, and Madrigal merely waited and listened.

"Did you hear me? This is Wolf Perkin, your guard. I'll give you thirty seconds longer. If you're not out by then, I'm sending the dog in."

Still, no one responded except Madrigal, who slowly drew up Tom's gun and waited.

". . . twenty-eight, twenty-nine . . . Thirty."

Wolf Perkin took the baby shoe and held it before the hound's nose. Then he released the dog. "Sic 'em, Devil," he ordered and, standing astride as he had done that day on the boxcar, the guard smiled and waited for the hungry dog to reach its quarry.

CHAPTER
22

The baying of the hound as it leaped through the opening of the cave caused Morrow to awaken and begin to cry. Suddenly, another sound shattered the isolated terrain— the shot coming from the revolver in Madrigal's hand.

With a surprised whimper, the wounded hound fell to the limestone floor of the cavern.

Morrow continued to cry as the four women remained in the darkness with the feral eyes of the hound gazing upward.

"Devil, boy!" Wolf Perkin called out. The hound whimpered again in response, attempted to get up, and then slid back to earth with his wounded front leg refusing to support him.

Wolf Perkin had not counted on the firearm. And he certainly hadn't counted on his hound being wounded or killed. The anger that comes when a cornered animal turns to defend itself and harms the chaser swept over Wolf, clouding his judgment. Devil had been with him during his entire tour of duty. The dog had served him well, but now he was of no use to Wolf anymore. Still, he deserved to be avenged. Cold-bloodedly, Wolf raised his rifle and aimed it toward the opening of the cave.

"No, Wolf. You can't shoot the women." Tom Traymore's voice held an uncommon anguish. His words brought back a semblance of sanity to the other men standing with Wolf.

"He's right, soldier," one of the men agreed. "You can't shoot the women. Put your gun down."

"They hurt my dog."

"They were merely defending themselves. I'd do the same in their situation."

But Wolf was still angry. The women deserved to be punished, especially the one who'd used the gun.

"Then I want the one who shot my dog," Wolf insisted. "Come out, whichever one of you did it. If you don't, heaven help every last one of you."

Inside the cave, the four women remained huddled together. "Give me the gun, Madrigal," Allison insisted.

"No, Allison. I can't let you take the blame for somethin' I did."

"The authorities know you've already shot a soldier, Madrigal," she argued. "There's no telling what they'll do to you for a second offense. No, it's safer to let me walk out with the gun."

"I'll take the blame," Rebecca said, moving in front of the others.

"No, you can't," Flood said. "It's too dangerous for you, too. Here, give me the gun."

The stalemate continued with each offering to take the blame until Madrigal said, "Why don't we just throw away the gun and walk out together?"

But Allison did not consider it a good idea. One of them would have to answer for it eventually. "There's no need for all of us to be punished equally," Allison said. "And I believe the authorities will be kinder with a mother and her child."

Before anyone could stop her, Allison called out, "All right. I'm coming out." She took the gun from Madrigal and whispered, "Wipe your hands in case you have any gunpowder on them."

It was not so much a sense of bravery that made Allison take over. She felt guilty. It was her fault for slowing them all down. If it had not been for Madrigal and Tom waiting for her, while Flood went back to find her, they would have stood a better change of escaping.

Tom Traymore was just as surprised as Wolf Perkin when Allison, with Morrow, emerged from the cavern opening. A small baby foot was barely visible in the folds of the shawl. And on the ground where Wolf Perkin stood, lay the matching baby shoe that Wolf had dropped.

The first vestige of sun came through the trees, encircling Allison and the baby in her arms with an ethereal halo of light. For a brief moment, the men, seeing the fragile blond-haired woman standing there and looking at them with a mystical sadness in her eyes, were suddenly tempted to kneel, as if they were in the presence of some sacred vision. Then the image of the revolver in her hand was superimposed over the other, eradicating that puzzling, fleeting feeling in the hearts of the men before it could take root.

Allison walked over to Wolf and handed him the gun. "I think your dog is merely wounded."

The other three women were close behind Allison, for they did not wish any harm to come to her. Wolf gazed at Allison, and then he looked at the others. He narrowed his eyes and then barked instructions to the men with him. "All right, put those three back in the wagon with the traitor. And you, Allison Forsyth—wait here, while I see to my hound."

Wolf whistled. "Devil, come here, boy. Come here."

Inside the cave, the dog whimpered. Slowly he began to move, his bloody foreleg forgotten at the sound of his master's voice.

As the dog struggled to reach Wolf, the man looked at him and raised his rifle again.

"No," Allison cried out. "Please don't. The dog isn't hurt that badly."

Wolf Perkin ignored Allison's cry. The shot rang out as Wolf put a finish to the hound at his feet.

"Come, give your baby to one of the women in the wagon," he said. "You're riding back with me."

"No. Morrow stays with me."

He raised his hand as if to strike Allison. "You'll do what I tell you without arguing."

"I think that's enough, soldier," one of the cavalrymen intervened. "The woman and her child should ride in the wagon with the others."

Wolf whirled at the sound of the voice. "I'm in charge here. And if I say this woman is riding with me, she'll do it without any interference from you."

"What's your rank, soldier?"

"I'm a corporal, on special assignment, charged with guarding these women."

"I believe your jurisdiction ended, Mister Perkin," Allison commented softly, "once we reached Nashville and were put under General Webster's command."

At her words, a slight smile hovered on the cavalryman's face and then disappeared. "As your superior officer, Corporal Perkin, I order you to allow this woman to return to the wagon."

Wolf Perkin glared at the other soldier, seeing in the faint light his sergeant's stripes.

"Don't worry, Corporal. You'll be given full credit for their capture in my official report."

Wolf turned and, swallowing the bile in his throat, strode toward his horse tethered to a nearby cedar.

"All right, ma'am," the sergeant said. "Take your baby and climb into the wagon. We've got a long trip back to Nashville ahead of us."

The arduous trip began again, over the same rough terrain they had traveled, until they hit Donelson Pike, the road that led back to Nashville.

With one of the soldiers driving the ambulance wagon, the others, including Wolf Perkin, rode in convoy, determined that no one would escape this time.

"I'm sorry, Madrigal." Tom Traymore, with his hands and feet tied, leaned his head against the inside of the wagon.

"It's not your fault, Tom," she answered.

"Maybe if I'd gotten a boat instead . . ."

His lament hung on the air, like a wisp of smoke curling and then disappearing. No one blamed him for their capture. He had done his best, but their dash for freedom had been aborted. It was as simple as that.

That night, Tom Traymore was in the military stockade, while the four women, resting in a more closely guarded cell away from Alma and the others, waited to be shipped northward toward Louisville, Kentucky.

John Hunt Morgan, a Confederate cavalry officer from Kentucky, had been luckier than the Roswell women. For two years, the officer led his troops on raids throughout Kentucky, Mississippi, and Tennessee, striking at the heart of the Union arsenals and supplies and taking hundreds of prisoners. Then, with a series of raids into Ohio, his luck ran out and he was captured. But after four months in the Ohio Penitentiary, his bid for freedom was successful. And now, in the late days of August 1864, he was back with his men, riding through the countryside and striking at strategic supplies and railroads. His actions were so daring and swift that the damage to Union morale was even worse than the damage done to their military supplies.

Because of his exploits, the women on the deportation train took on new hope, praying that the man would become their deliverer.

At the same time, the news of Morgan's exploits was being followed closely by another Kentuckian—Captain Glenn Meadors, wounded in the skirmish at Ashby's Gap and now recuperating at home on the horse and tobacco plantation that he owned jointly with his elder brother, Rad.

The sandy-haired, medium-height soldier sprawled in a porch chaise and gazed out at the fenced acres of bluegrass meadow. On the table in front of him, he had deliberately set his empty julep glass on his brother's letter, causing the ink to blur and run.

Thinking of Morgan's exploits, he smiled. Rad was probably incensed by now. And anything that made Rad angry afforded Glenn additional pleasure.

It had been that way for as long as Glenn could remember—the two brothers pitted against each other, always on opposite sides. Just like Kentucky itself, divided in loyalty, Glenn had thrown in his lot with the Confederacy, while Rad had chosen to remain in the Union.

Still, the plantation was a mutual problem, binding them together as family despite their differences in politics.

The land, caught in the long shadows of early evening, was still beautiful, albeit a shabby version of the way it had been before the war. The fences now needed painting. The tall bluegrass begged for mares and their capering foals. And the fields, once so golden with burley tobacco, lay fallow, like the curing sheds with no smoke spiraling from the chimneys. Even the servants' houses were empty, with the last two black men conscripted into the Union army to dig ditches and to keep the levees from overflowing.

The house was empty, too, except for the young woman Glenn had brought from town to cook his meals and to tend to his other needs.

As he moved his injured shoulder, a slight stiffness was all that remained. He was almost well, and it wouldn't be long before he left and rejoined his outfit. But the letter that had been waiting for him at Bluegrass Meadors reprimanded him even as it fluttered with the sudden breeze sweeping the porch. Only the julep glass anchored it and kept it from sailing into the wind that kicked up the gravel dust in swirls down the long driveway.

Glenn didn't need to renew his memory as to his brother's instructions. He remembered them well. But he couldn't follow them even if he wanted to. He'd already spent the money earmarked to hire someone to take care of the place until they both returned from the war. Only a miracle would do. But Glenn had run out of miracles as well as money. There wasn't a chance to hire someone now. And he could see his brother scowling at the empty fields and a vandalized house when he returned. As usual, he, Glenn Meadors, would get the blame for it.

"Your supper's ready, Glenn."

The soldier glanced up at the young girl standing in the doorway.

"I'll be in, in a minute." Glenn continued to sit, watching the darkness creep along the fields like some slow, devouring creature swallowing the land that his brother loved.

In the same darkness, the deportation train struggled over the rough terrain, stopping at times so that the new guards, who had no sympathy for their cargo, could remove the tree trunks placed across the Louisville and Nashville Railroad tracks to hamper its progress toward the Ohio River.

The present train was no better and no more comfortable than the first. The only difference was that Allison, Madrigal, Flood, and Rebecca had been separated from their companions in boxcar eleven and placed in another boxcar with those women and children earmarked for incarceration at the refugee prison barracks in Louisville, if they were still lucky enough to reach that city.

Allison wiped the perspiration from her face. Morrow had finally gone to sleep after a fretful afternoon that had been nerve-wracking to them all. "Madrigal, have you heard any of the guards say how much longer it will be before we reach Louisville?"

Madrigal fought hard to control her nausea. Her voice was brittle. "I'm not the one you should ask, Allison. These new guards won't have a thing to do with me. They look at me like I'm poison."

"I guess they're afraid they'll wind up like poor Tom," Flood said.

Rebecca, who had been silent for well over an hour, finally spoke. "If this trip's the same length as the one from Marietta to Nashville, then I expect it'll be another week at least."

"Oh, I hope not," Allison said. Then she brightened. "Maybe only six more days. Remember, we lost nearly a whole day crossing the trestle bridge on foot and then stopping for Marcus Stagg."

"You shoulda gone on with the man, Allison. I expect you'd be better off with him than you are now."

"That's not true, Madrigal. And you know it as well as I do. No, whatever happens, we're much better off sticking together."

The train whistle tooted, but the wheels gave no evidence of slowing down. In fact, the train picked up speed, hurtling through the darkness in record time and causing the women to lose their balance as it shunted from side to side.

Allison coughed, and like the others, she stretched and searched for a more comfortable position on the stale straw. But the comfort she sought eluded her.

As sleep finally came to her bone-weary body, Allison had a disturbing dream of Rose Mallow and the decaying gazebo where she had hidden her husband's picture. In the dream she frantically dug up the box. But when she opened it, the wedding picture had been ruined by the passage of time. She carried the box to the gazebo seat and sat down. Like viewing a stranger from a distance, an unemotional Allison Forsyth watched the blond woman holding the box and weeping. Then the sleeping Allison curved her body around her child and dreamed no more.

CHAPTER
23

In the port city of Louisville, Brown General Hospital, situated on Broadway between Ninth and Tenth streets, had been confiscated as refugee headquarters for the Confederate women and children arriving from Nashville.

Ironically, the building was only a short distance away from the military prison where many of the Roswell Battalion soldiers, captured after the burning of the Chattahoochee bridge, were also lodged as prisoners.

Late one afternoon, when the women and children had been in the city for only a short time, Puckka Knox, who had seen little action with the battalion before being captured, began to gather together his few clothes and possessions prior to being set free.

He glanced at Private Angus Smithwick, who was lounging on the nearby cot. At the man's hostile glare, Puckka quickly averted his eyes and continued to stuff his possessions into the haversack.

"So you took the Oath of Loyalty," Angus accused.

Puckka swallowed as his face turned red. Then he grew angry. "You don't have to look at me like I'm some traitor, Angus. Plenty of the others have done the same. And if you didn't have such a stubborn streak in you, you could be leavin' today, too."

"I'd rather rot in jail than go against my principles." After his harsh words, Angus began to feel sorry for the overgrown boy. His tone softened. "Still, I guess if you're only thirteen years old, it's mighty hard to make any sense out of this war."

Puckka nodded. "I just found out my ma and Caddie— they're here in Louisville, too. I'm gonna go and get them out of that awful place. And I hear tell there're lots of jobs in the mills in Indiana. Maybe we'll go there and get work till the war's over."

"If that's the case, you'd better be extra careful. The Confederate scouts, I'm told, hang every man they find goin' over to the other side."

At Angus's warning, Puckka quickly pulled out his uniform from the bundle and threw it on his cot. He walked to the cell door and immediately yelled, "Guard, I'm ready now. You can come and unlock the door."

Once the guard had come and gone, Angus grabbed his crutch and hobbled to the locked door. "Puckka?"

The boy stopped. "What is it, Angus?"

"When you get over to the hospital, if you happen to see a pretty, little redheaded gal named Madrigal O'Laney, tell 'er I'm close by."

"Sure thing, Angus."

Puckka continued walking toward freedom. He thought about Angus and remembered that the man had been good to him while he was in the prison barracks. And if it had been anybody else, he would have done it. But after hearing Madrigal's name, Puckka had no intention of relaying the message.

With quick steps, he walked to Broadway and traveled down the street until he came to the two-storied brown building. He walked past the few shade trees and finally knocked at the locked gate.

"I come for a woman—Rena Knox and her child, Caddie."

The guard looked at Puckka. Because of his size, he did not suspect that the boy was so young.

"You must be answering the advertisement in the paper," the guard said, and waited for the young man to verify it.

Puckka hesitated. "The advertisement?"

"Yes. You know, the one sanctioned by the provost marshal. It's a pretty good deal, getting one of these women as a bond servant for nothing. Especially since the proclamation's put a stop to getting any other servants."

When Puckka remained silent, the talkative guard continued, "You getting her for a seamstress or a house servant?"

"Er, a s-seamstress."

"Then you might not want her little girl, too. If it's the one I'm thinking about, she was sorta sickly when they came in."

Quickly, Puckka said, "That's all right. I'll take the girl, too."

"Well, you could be right. She's a pretty little thing. You

might find a use for her a little later on, if you get what I mean."

If Puckka had learned one thing in military prison, it was how to control his temper. He grinned at the guard and said, "Tell me where I can find them."

The guard consulted his chart. "Up on the second floor, toward the back of the building."

Puckka walked down the long hall, where the doors to the rooms were open to catch the slight breeze. He saw children playing hopscotch between the beds where women sat and sewed. At the sound of his footsteps, the women looked up in curiosity, but the children continued playing.

The boy hurried past, walked up the stairs to the second floor, and then began his search for his mother.

"Why, Puckka Knox, what are you doin' here?" Flood Tompkins inquired on seeing the boy who had worked in the woolen mill.

"I'm lookin' for my ma. And Caddie. You know where they are, Flood?"

The larger woman hesitated. "They're not here, Puckka. They moved Caddie down to a room in the back of the building. Rena's there watchin' after her."

"What's wrong with Caddie?"

"She's got the fever, Puckka—after comin' down with the measles. She's over them now, but the fever's still hangin' on."

Puckka hurried back along the hall. Through one of the open doors, he saw the Forsyth woman and her servant. But nowhere did he catch a glimpse of Madrigal O'Laney, which was just as well.

Once he reached the rooms at the back of the building, he began to get worried. There was something about bodies burning up with fever that no amount of sweet-smelling flowers could disguise. It was true in the prison and it was true here in that portion of the building he had come through.

Puckka stumbled past some of the cots where emaciated forms lay. Some moaned in pain; others were silent, their eyes staring up at the ceiling.

"Ma?" He waited for the woman to look up. "It's me—Puckka."

Her face was severe as she looked at the boy. "You've grown a lot, Puckka, since I last saw you."

"I . . . I come to get you, Ma. You and Caddie."

"How'd you find us, son?"

"I heard—over at the prison—about the train that come in. I was hopin' you and Caddie were on it."

"But how did you get free?"

"I signed the loyalty oath, Ma."

"Hush, Puckka. Not so loud. Somebody might hear you." Rena Knox looked around the room, but no one acted as if Puckka's confession had been uttered. "Where're we goin'?"

"On to Indiana. I got me a little money, Ma. Maybe just enough to get us there. I already signed for you, so I'll stay with Caddie while you go and get your things."

"Don't talk to a soul while I'm gone, Puckka."

"No, ma'am."

A few minutes later, after saying good-bye to Addie and no one else, Rena Knox followed her son out of the building. He carried Caddie in his arms. Her face was still splotched with a few remaining measles spots, and Puckka could feel the heat of her body through the thin sheet.

Through an upstairs window, Madrigal O'Laney saw the three step into the open grounds. She watched the guard unlock the gate. And she stood at the window until they had completely disappeared from view.

Madrigal felt none of the old animosity for Puckka. Those innocent days by the river seemed a thousand years ago. Ellie was gone. And so was Private Angus Smithwick. For a fleeting moment, she traced her finger along her mouth and remembered the gentle kiss she'd given to the soldier.

Finally, Madrigal wrapped her robe around her and turned from the window. Flood already suspected her condition, and it wouldn't be too much longer before everyone else knew, too.

Even though Puckka Knox had not read the advertisement placed in the *Constitution Union* newspaper by the provost marshal, there was another man who had—Captain Glenn Meadors. And he immediately realized the miracle he'd sought had fallen into his hands like a ripe fig.

It had been a long way to Louisville from the plantation, which was located between Shelbyville and Lexington. But if he were successful, the trip would be worth it.

In anticipation of hiring someone, he had brought the carriage, with his own horse tied to the back of it. And he'd been careful, too, to carry some identification belonging to his brother, Rad. Otherwise, as a Confederate officer in a military supply town full of Union soldiers, he might wind up in the military prison not far from the refugee headquarters.

He threaded his way through the streets, trying to avoid hitting the roaming pigs that plagued Louisville even worse than Nashville. He traveled along the railroad tracks, casually watching the military supplies being loaded for the battles going on in Arkansas and Missouri. But spying on military shipments was not his main objective. And so he hurried past the large strawberry fields not far from the tracks and reached Broadway, where he tied up his horses and walked to the same gate into the hospital that Puckka Knox had used.

Another guard was on duty this time, a Corporal Massey whose fighting days were over because of the loss of his right arm. Assuming his brother's identity, Glenn straightened and began to walk with the swinging, self-confident stride of the tall, dark-haired Rad. His easygoing manner disappeared, too, and was replaced by a no-nonsense, unsmiling face.

Glenn approached the gate. "I'm Major Rad Meadors, Fifth Cavalry," he announced. "I'd like to look over your prisoners to see if you have anyone suitable to work on my plantation."

"Of course, Major Meadors," the guard said, hurrying to unlock the gate.

After turning the key in the lock, the guard began to follow the man through the open grounds. "Some of the prisoners are taking the air on the grounds," he announced. "Perhaps you'd like to start your inspection outside."

"Yes, that would be fine. Thank you, Corporal."

"Sir, may I say something?"

"Corporal?"

"Just that I'm one of your staunchest admirers. You see, I was in the battle when you captured some of Morgan's raiders up in Ohio."

Glenn kept his face bland. "A pity Morgan escaped. But we'll catch up with him one of these days, won't we, Corporal?"

"That we will, sir. That we will."

With a nod so typical of his brother, Glenn dismissed the guard. He stood alone and watched the people milling about in the yard. Suddenly he walked up to one of the prisoners.

"What's your name, mister?"

Flood Tompkins, dressed in her dead husband's clothes, with her hair pulled into a knot and hidden by the cap, turned toward the man. "Flood," she said. "Flood Tompkins."

"My name is Major Rad Meadors. Do you know anything about horses or tobacco?"

Flood hesitated. "A little about both."

"How would you like to leave this place to work on a beautiful farm in bluegrass country?"

"For you?"

"Yes. Only I'll be going back to my cavalry unit soon. I need somebody to plant the next crop of tobacco and watch over my few horses until I return home."

"How much does the job pay?"

"Depends on how well you look after the farm."

Flood had seen that look in other men's eyes. The man was desperate but appeared not to be. And Flood, realizing she had some bargaining power, took advantage of it. "I dunno. I've always worked for straight wages before. I got a family, you know."

"Are they here at the prison with you?"

"Yes."

"Well, speak up, man. How many?"

"Two, plus the baby. And our black woman, of course."

Glenn tried to disguise his delight. Rad would certainly be pleased if he learned Glenn had been able to hire an entire family with that many additional hands to work on the farm.

"All right. Room and board, with a place for your entire

family. And if you do a fine job of it, then you'll certainly be rewarded upon my return. Is it a bargain?"

"Yes, sir."

"Well, then, go and round up your family. I want to get back to the farm before morning. Oh, and Flood?"

"Yes, sir?"

'Give me the names of your family members, so I won't have to waste any time signing you out."

"Allison and Madrigal. And the servant's name is Rebecca."

"Well, step on it, man. We've got a long way to go."

Flood hurried out of the yard, past the apple tree, and disappeared into the dingy brown building. She tugged at a wisp of hair that had come loose from the knot and adjusted her cap.

While Glenn waited for Flood to reappear, he strolled along the grounds. He was in no hurry for further conversation with the guard.

Ten minutes later, Flood appeared, and directly behind her came Allison, with the baby, and the other two. "We're ready, Major," Flood said.

"Good. Then just follow me to the carriage."

As soon as Glenn approached the guard's station, the corporal said. "You find anybody to suit you, Major?"

"These people will do," he admitted grudgingly.

"If you'll just sign here, Major, and then I'll write down their names."

In a hurry, Glenn scribbled his brother's name. He turned to the guard. "Just send them to my carriage as soon as they sign out."

The guard carefully checked off the names of Allison Forsyth, Madrigal O'Laney, Rebecca Smiley, and Flood

Tompkins. As an afterthought, he wrote, "Morrow Forsyth, age 5 months."

As the carriage carrying the women began its journey past Ninth Street, an overturned supply wagon was being righted by four men.

While Glenn waited for the street to be cleared enough for him to get through, one of the men looked up. "Hey, Glenn. Glenn Meadors. I thought you was off fighting. When did you get home?"

Glenn tightened his hands on the horses' reins and stared straight ahead. He ignored the worker's greeting, and as soon as an opening was made, he rushed the carriage past the spilled debris in the street.

With the disconcerting stare of the blond-haired woman, the man forced a smile. "I'm often mistaken for my brother," he explained.

Allison returned his smile and relaxed against the comfortable seat of the well-sprung carriage. She didn't speak, for she was well aware of Flood's subterfuge and didn't want to do anything to mar their chances.

Although Flood and Madrigal knew absolutely nothing about running a plantation, Allison and Rebecca did. And so Major Meadors would have no cause for regrets. The four of them, working together, would make sure that the horse and tobacco farm would not suffer neglect because of them.

CHAPTER
24

Known as the "dark and bloody ground," from the early days when pioneers had fought Indians, Kentucky was still a land of bloodshed, with families and neighbors divided over the war. Entire families had disappeared overnight, leaving their houses and barns vacant, as the military regime imprisoned civilians on the flimsiest of charges, tried them in military court, and then executed them without recourse.

The lawlessness and erosion of civil liberties in those states bordering the Ohio River had been the reason for the creation of the "Paw-Paw Militia," named for the fruit they subsisted on in the wild. Made up of refugees, deserters, oath takers, and those who had escaped from the military prisons, they were a mysterious group of men sympathetic to the Confederate cause who retaliated—eye for eye, tooth for tooth—for the more flagrant offenses committed against the people. And so it was a time of vengeance on both sides, with political events doing nothing to lessen that animosity. Even Bluegrass Meadors had been victim to the exorbitant fees demanded of all suspected Confederate sympathizers for the relief of Union orphans and widows.

As Glenn Meadors, captain in the Confederate army, directed the carriage eastward toward the rolling meadows where the blue haze of grass spread over the land, he was still resentful of the cavalier manner in which *his* share of Bluegrass Meadors had been assessed. But he'd gotten back at the Unionists, after all, by hiring the Confederates from the refugee prison. And when he wrote to his brother, he certainly wouldn't be foolish enough to tell Rad where he'd found the workers. He'd be more careful than that.

With his sense of caution relaxed somewhat since leaving the outskirts of Louisville, Glenn came alive again. Although he'd gotten away with posing as his brother in the city, he was traveling closer to his own home, and it would be easier now for someone to recognize him.

"You think we could stop for water at the next house, Major Meadors?"

Glenn turned to stare at the red-haired girl. He was thirsty, too, and the horses needed watering. But he'd rather remain thirsty than risk his head—for the next house belonged to Royal Freemont, a Union sympathizer, who knew both of the brothers.

"I doubt the owners would allow you the use of their well," Glenn explained. "They have no regard for Rebels. Anyway, my house is just over the next hill. We should be there before dark."

His explanation caused Madrigal to tighten her lips.

"Well, drive on. I'd rather be a thirsty Rebel than a galvanized Yankee anyday!"

Despite himself, Glenn laughed. She was a feisty little thing—Rebel through and through—and it amused him. Prison had evidently not done much to her spirit. He gazed again at her, noticing the tight calico dress straining against her full breasts. And then, catching himself, he quickly returned his attention to the horses.

There was one other thing he'd noticed, too. The family was a motley group. The woman, Allison, though she had spoken only a few words during the entire trip, had a more genteel accent than any of the others. In fact, she reminded him a little of his mother. Except for the chopped hair, of course. But despite the loss of the woman's hair, she held her head in a regal manner. He had observed her posture right away, too, which was at odds with the way the young girl, Madrigal, sat.

Finally, when the haze of blue spread in every direction and the swallows began to fly toward the tall trees of oak and ash to roost for the night, Glenn stopped the carriage for a moment and pointed toward the house in the distance.

"That's Bluegrass Meadors," he announced.

A tall, stately redbrick mansion with large white Doric columns appeared in the distance beyond the tree-lined drive. Dark green shutters framed the windows of the first two stories, while the setting sun caught its reflection in smaller dormer windows that announced a third story.

Rebecca Smiley watched Allison's reaction to the elegant house. She saw the pain dull her eyes as recognition came, swift and sure.

The house was nothing like Rose Mallow. Rather, it was a companion in style and elegance to Allison's childhood home in Savannah. Only the moss on the oaks was missing.

"Rebecca . . ."

"I know, Miss Allison. It reminds me of it, too."

Allison's lip quivered. She turned her head and watched the white fence trail by as the man clicked his teeth and urged the horses on past the front of the mansion, past the stone paddocks, and on toward a smaller house that sat amid its own cathedral of trees.

"This is where you'll live," Glenn explained. "You'll find almost everything you need for the night—including food for your supper."

"Will you be wanting us to do any work tonight, Major?" Flood asked.

"Not after the horses are put up. It's been a long trip. Just get settled, and I'll see you first thing tomorrow, Mr. Tompkins."

Madrigal giggled at Flood's being called "mister," but she quickly stopped when Rebecca's frown chastised her.

Glenn turned to Madrigal. "There's a water pump in the yard." He watched in amusement as Madrigal held up her skirts and jumped from the carriage. Without waiting to retrieve her bundle, she ran toward the pump.

The others were more sedate in getting down from the carriage. Flood went first, then the black woman with the baby. And finally Allison stepped down, smoothed her skirts, and turned to Glenn.

"Thank you, Major, for your kindness to us. We'll make certain that you won't ever regret taking us in."

He felt vaguely uncomfortable with her amethyst eyes looking at him with such sincerity. "There's a lot to do, ma'am, to keep this place running. It won't be an easy job, what with the tobacco to be harvested and dried, and the vegetables and fruits to be preserved for the winter."

"Will you be here for the harvest season?" Allison asked.

"No. I leave in two days to rejoin my cavalry unit." He turned to Flood. "You'll find fodder in the barn for the horses and foals, Mr. Tompkins. Be sure to give these two animals a rubdown before you feed them."

Flood's eyes widened as he motioned for her to take over the carriage. Seeing her distress, Allison quickly said, "I think I'll ride with you, Flood, if you don't mind. Maybe I can help you rub down the horses."

Glenn turned the reins over to Flood and strolled down the lane, past the scuppernong arbor, and walked into the house from the flagstone terrace.

"Be careful, Flood," Allison whispered. "Just give the horses a slight nudge with the reins and they'll head to the barn."

"Oh, Lordy, Allison. I'm so glad you're with me. I thought for a scared second I was gonna have to shut my peepers and go it blind."

Allison laughed. "You sound just like Madrigal."

"Well, I expect I *feel* better than she does. I didn't want to say anything in front of her, but we got us a problem, Allison. I think Madrigal's in the family way."

A worried Allison put her hand over to adjust the reins in Flood's hands while the horses continued to the barn. "I was afraid of that."

The stone-walled paddocks held only a few foals, loping and kicking up their heels in a last romp before they settled down for the night. They were beautiful, with glistening brown coats and straight, finely boned legs—the mark of excellent blood stock.

Beyond the barn, golden fields of tobacco had already matured, with the plant tops cut off, giving strength to the few carefully selected leaves on each stalk.

Looking at the ventilated barns set in the middle of the

fields, Allison knew that an arduous, backbreaking task awaited them. She would have been so much more sure of herself if the fields had contained cotton instead.

"Tomorrow, Flood, you'll have to listen extra well to Major Meadors when he explains how to cut and cure the tobacco."

"You don't know how to do it, either, Allison?"

"Not really. I did visit an uncle in Virginia one time. But the tobacco barns looked different in his fields. I guess the thing you'll have to make certain about is whether the tobacco is supposed to be sun-cured or fire-cured."

"Maybe you could talk with Major Meadors tomorrow, Allison."

"No, that wouldn't do at all, Flood. He thinks you're a man. And for the next two days, we don't dare tell him any different. The conversation will have to be man to man."

As the horses came to a stop before the barn, Allison climbed down and began to show Flood how to remove the harness reins from the animals. "You might ask him, though, if he has a book or pamphlet on tobacco. He wouldn't mind that. And then we could read it together."

Flood sighed. "Now, if this was a mill . . ."

Allison felt sorry for Flood, looking so lost and dejected. "We'll manage, Flood. I know we will."

"I hope you're right, Allison."

While the two women worked in the barn rubbing down the carriage horses, the other two were equally busy. Rebecca built a fire on the kitchen hearth of the cottage as the hungry Madrigal raced to the vegetable garden for fresh beans and tomatoes. And then, when the foals had been brought in from the paddock and they bellied up to the trough of oats mixed with sorghum, Rebecca's batter bread was baking in the beehive oven, a smaller version of the one at Rose Mallow.

Later, in the candlelight, when Morrow had been put to bed in one of the drawers taken from the bedroom chest and the four exhausted women were sitting around the kitchen table, a peacefulness bound them to each other. They bowed their heads and held hands as they began their nightly ritual of thanksgiving. "Lord, you have delivered us out of the wilderness," Allison prayed. "Give us strength for the tasks ahead. Amen."

The women rose, snuffed out the candle, and went to bed. They slept soundly for the first time in many days.

Inside the redbrick mansion, another ritual was taking place—and Glenn Meadors was conducting it—a meeting of the Sons of Liberty: Northerners and Westerners sympathetic to the Confederacy. The secret society, composed of 23,000 men divided into lodges, had spread from Missouri to Indiana, Kentucky and Illinois, with a lodge in New York as well.

"Gentlemen, I leave two days from now to join Shelby's cavalry in time for General Price's invasion of Arkansas. And we won't stop until we've wrested all of Missouri from Rosecrans. Once the flag flies in St. Louis, that will be your signal to show which side you're on."

"Have you heard what's happened to our lodge brother, the Belgian consul in St. Louis?"

"Rosecrans has arrested him for the second time—even after Lincoln ordered the general to release him."

"I find that hard to believe, especially since the man has resorted to no attack whatsoever upon the Union."

"Rosecrans doesn't *need* a reason. He sees Confederate sympathizers behind every tree."

The six men laughed. Then they stood up as Glenn stood. The meeting was terminated.

"It's been a long day, gentlemen," Glenn said. "But the future seems a little brighter tonight, with Price headed toward Rosecrans."

The men shook hands. "Godspeed to you, Captain Meadors," one whispered. And in the dark of night they crept out of the house, one by one, mounted their horses, and galloped down the long-fenced drive away from the red-brick mansion.

In the cottage, Allison awoke. She lifted her head and listened to the pounding of hoofbeats for a moment. At their disappearance, she placed her head on her pillow and went back to sleep.

That night, the rains began, slowly at first, delicately trickling down the large leaves of tobacco and settling the dust along the paths and lanes. In steady tempo, the drops upon the cottage roof became a rhythmic, musical sound— a fragile Chinese tune played upon a tin flute.

Farther west, along the banks of the Ohio River, the rain had changed into a deluge, with the added fury of sound and thunder. Lightning flashed, revealing a rider suddenly veering off from the main path and pulling up into a cane-brake only moments before other riders galloped by.

The man's blue uniform, covered in the dusty legacy of the long road he had just traveled, was now soaking wet. Water cascaded in rivulets from his wide-brimmed felt hat down his strong, severe face, but he didn't appear to notice. Like some stone statue in the middle of a town square, he sat immobile. Then, finally deeming it safe to move, he came to life again and left the canebrake behind.

Major Rad Meadors, dark of eye, with hair as black as

night, seldom smiled even in the best of times. Heaven knows, he'd had little to smile about lately. The worry over the way the war was going had been compounded by his worry over the plantation he'd left behind.

God, how he missed the land—the smell of the tobacco leaves drying in the fields and the fragrant breath of the blue flowers covering the meadows. He reached down and patted Bourbon Red, the sire of the only foals he'd been able to keep—the last of the bloodline.

"One day soon we'll go home, old boy," he promised. He looked toward the southeast where angry clouds had gathered in a dark funnel. Bluegrass Meadors was in that same direction.

As Bourbon Red broke into a gallop, Major Rad Meadors, of the U.S. Cavalry, prayed that his brother, Glenn, had been able to find someone suitable to work the farm until the war was over.

CHAPTER
25

Allison paced up and down while she waited for Flood to return from her interview with Major Meadors. The rain had not let up. On this late August day in Kentucky, the rains announced a new season just as surely as the June rains along the Chattahoochee had christened the beginning of summer.

But a lifetime had elapsed—a way of life had vanished forever in the space of those three short months. Allison was no longer the woman she'd been that day at the memorial service for her husband. A new creature, tempered by hardship, now inhabited the same body. Her dreams were gone, dying a little at a time on the rail line from

Marietta to Louisville—a trip into hell as certain as the one Dante had taken into his Inferno.

Now, through a stroke of luck, she had emerged from that hell with the other three women, and for that she was grateful.

While she watched, Flood began walking down the path. Allison released the lace curtain of the cottage window and walked out to meet her on the small porch that only partially sheltered her from the rain.

Eagerly, Allison said, "Well, Flood, how did the interview go?"

"As well as could be expected, I suppose. At least it's over with."

"He didn't question your . . . manhood?"

"No, I don't think so. He was in a hurry, really, to get the interview behind him. Because of the rain, the major's decided to leave early this afternoon rather than wait until tomorrow."

"Did you find out about the tobacco?"

"Yes. It's supposed to be sun-dried. We'll have to start cutting as soon as the sun comes out and soaks up the rain."

As Flood followed Allison inside, she pulled out a small ledger from her pocket. "He gave me this when I asked for something on growin' tobacco. It's one of the journals he kept. Said it might come in useful, with a record of everything—when he planted, when he harvested, and where he got some more seed when they lost the plants to hail one year. And the major said there're others in the library if this one doesn't have everything in it we need."

"That's wonderful, Flood." Allison took the proffered journal and placed it on the desk in the parlor. She would begin reading it that very afternoon once the women had gathered together for a meeting. The chores needed to be divided up so that no one would have more than she could do.

"Where's Madrigal?" Flood asked.

"She's eating her breakfast," Allison responded. "I didn't say anything to her about sleeping late. She seemed so tired and I knew we couldn't do much today because of the rain."

"Madrigal will take advantage of your sympathy if you're not careful, Allison. Half the time she was late gettin' to work at the mill. In the family way or not, she's gonna have to pull her own weight around here. There's too much to do. And *I* for one don't have the remotest idea where to start."

"But you have the major's instructions." Allison's voice sounded certain. Yet her look was questioning.

"Well, such as they are."

"What do you mean?"

"He's not like Mr. Roche, spellin' everything out. Seems he's more interested in gettin' back to the fightin' than worryin' about this plantation."

It wasn't long after that conversation when the two saw Glenn Meadors, dressed in civilian clothes, walk past the cottage and head toward the barn. Within a few short minutes, a horse galloped down the drive. The rider didn't look back.

"The major isn't wearing his uniform," Flood said. "Isn't that strange?"

"Perhaps he doesn't want to get it soaking wet."

"Or maybe he's decided not to broadcast the fact that he's headed back to the fightin'."

Allison frowned at Flood's words. "Are you suggesting that the major might be afraid of meeting up with some Rebels along the way?"

She couldn't see a major in the Union army being cowardly. There had to be some other reason for his leaving in a clandestine manner. It must have something to do with the whispers on the terrace the previous evening and the sound of the riders on horseback leaving Bluegrass Meadors in the dead of night.

"I'm not suggestin' anything. I just think it's strange, that's all," Flood replied.

"Well, I'm glad he wasn't wearin' a Union uniform," Madrigal said, joining in the conversation as she came to sit on the settee in the parlor. "Otherwise, I might have been tempted to shoot him myself."

"That's not very charitable of you, Madrigal, especially since he was the one to rescue us."

Allison suddenly turned from the window. "Rebecca," she called out. "It's time the four of us had our meeting."

Wiping her hands on her apron, Rebecca came into the parlor and took a seat on the small bench near the fireplace. Then Allison and the other two looked to Flood to begin.

Halfway through the meeting, an impatient Madrigal said, "How much money did the major give you?"

Flood hesitated. "None. He said we would be self-sufficient until he got back."

Rebecca spoke up. "You mean he didn't leave as much as a shin plaster?"

At Flood's silence, Madrigal grew angry. "Well, I don't expect to work my fingers to the bone without bein' paid for it."

"He'll pay us for our work when he comes home," Flood reiterated.

Allison, just as appalled as the others, attempted to reconcile them all. "Perhaps it's not so bad as it sounds. I'm sure he didn't mean to be miserly with us. And we have to remember that even if we get absolutely nothing, we're better off here than in the prison in Louisville."

Allison's comment calmed the others, and Flood was grateful to her. Still, she wished that Allison had been along at the interview.

The decisions that day formed the routine of the four women for the next several weeks. When the rains stopped, they took to their assigned chores. Apples and pears were gathered from the orchards. Vegetables were stripped from the garden, and herbs picked and dried. During the time of canning and preserving, the women moved into the kitchen of the main house as well, with Allison supervising in both kitchens while Madrigal and Rebecca stirred ingredients in the black kettles over hot coals.

Each day, Allison grew stronger and her child became more active, crawling through the cottage and pulling herself up on the furniture. And each night, by candlelight, Allison read the journals belonging to Rad Meadors. His handwriting became familiar to her, his words at odds with the man who had hired them. Outwardly, he'd appeared callous to the land, but his words revealed a different man—one who loved the land and what it stood for. There was a gentleness underlying the unemotional entries of the journal, and Allison began to look forward to each evening when the chores were done and she could take up one of the journals to educate herself in the running of the plantation. She had not stopped with the first one, but had taken others from the library as well. And in the process, the journals unknowingly had served another purpose—to bind her to the man himself.

One early afternoon, when Allison sat on the front porch of the cottage and finished feeding the baby, she gazed at Rebecca, who was busy stringing beans. An idea had come to Allison the previous night when she'd read Rad Meador's comments concerning his herd of cattle, which no longer existed.

"We need a milk cow, Rebecca."

The black woman looked up from her work. "You thinkin' of Morrow?"

"Yes. And the tobacco. Flood and I have to begin the harvesting no later than Wednesday. According to the major's journal, the leaves are ready. That means I'll be away from Morrow nearly all day."

"But we got no money."

"I still have the gold eagle—Jonathan's wedding gift to me."

"You said you'd never part with it. Remember?"

"I said a lot of things in the past, but times are different now. We need a cow, and Mr. Freemont has a number of them. I saw them grazing as we passed his place. I expect he'll be happy to sell me one."

"But you heard the major. That man hates Rebels. He wouldn't give you the time of day, Miss Allison. Much less a prize milk cow."

"Well, it won't hurt to try. I think I'll hitch up the horse to the carriage and ride over there this afternoon."

"Then somebody needs to go with you."

"I'll take Morrow with me. The rest of you need to stay and finish your chores."

Allison had her way. Carefully, she dressed in the clean calico dress and brushed her hair. It had grown, curling and waving into ringlets on her head. She picked up the onyx tuck-comb and anchored it to the top of her head, although there was no need for it except as decoration. Wrapping the dark shawl around her shoulders, she picked up

233

the basket that Morrow had outgrown, placed her in it, anyway, and walked down to the stables.

In a slow trot, the horse pulled the carriage down the drive. Allison noticed that the paint on sections of the fence was beginning to peel. She filed that observation in the back of her mind. Once the tobacco was harvested and sold, and the canning finished, they needed to start on the fence. Or perhaps it would be better to wait until after the winter.

As she traveled down the road toward Royal Freemont's house, Allison stopped the carriage for a moment and looked back at the redbrick mansion she'd left. Framed by the tall trees, their leaves beginning to turn a golden yellow, almost like the tobacco leaves, the house became a symbol of what she'd lost.

But Sherman had taken away more than her home, her way of life. His action had breached the very foundation of her soul, the mores and principles by which she'd always lived and viewed the world, that same vision that governed all women brought up in the gentle traditions of the South.

These ideals had been stripped away from her as surely as bark splitting from a tree. With each mile, each further humiliation, the dead past had fallen away. For a time, when she was struggling with the loss, she had felt the vacuum. Then, gradually, without her becoming really aware of it, a stronger Allison had emerged, until now she could look at her situation and realize that, from now on, she would be responsible for her own fate.

Allison turned to her child and smiled. "It's always a shock, isn't it, little one, when you let go of a dream and begin to face reality."

Morrow waved her arms. "Ma-ma," she said, showing two small teeth as she smiled and attempted to climb from the basket.

Royal Freemont's house was situated a distance from the main road, the same as Bluegrass Meadors. In the distance, it, too, was framed by trees, but the fence bordering the drive was made of unpainted split rails, a more rustic approach to a house not quite so elegant as the one she'd just left. But as Allison turned into the avenue of trees, she stifled the nervous feeling in the pit of her stomach.

The white-haired man seated on the porch pushed his straw hat back off his forehead and gazed myopically at the carriage making its way up his drive. Big Ceasar, his black man that he'd hidden from the conscription officer, was barely visible in the cotton field as he harvested the second picking from the stalks.

Royal Freemont, taking a break from the fields, set down his glass of bourbon, calmly reached for his rifle, and waited for the carriage to come closer.

He hated the war—and most of the men involved, Rebel and Yankee alike. Nothing made sense—the abolitionists in the Northeast saying they were fighting to free the poor black man from slavery while the draft riots in New York had resulted in blacks being hunted down throughout the city and killed. And the Colored Orphan Asylum being burned. And the South saying they were fighting for state's rights, liberty, and independence, while the men in the West straddled both sides of the fence. And all the time, one section of the country was growing prosperous while another section was starving—with the war giving an excuse for lawless bands from both camps to rove the countryside to plunder and pillage.

The carriage came closer. Royal now recognized a lone woman heading up his driveway. He hated all women, too. And he'd just as soon have this one turn right around and go back to where she came from.

Instead, Allison pulled the carriage up to the steps and, taking the baby into her arms, climbed down. "Mr. Freemont?"

The man relaxed his hold on the rifle. "Yes?"

"My name is Allison and this is my child, Morrow. We're part of the family that Major Meadors, your neighbor, hired to run Bluegrass Meadors while he's away."

"You're a Rebel, aren't you?" the man inquired. "Taken from the prison over in Louisville."

Allison didn't deny it. "I have come, Mr. Freemont, to see if I might purchase one of your milk cows."

"Your husband should have come. I don't do business with a woman."

Allison's face flushed. "My husband is—" She stopped. She could not tell him that her husband was dead. And she certainly couldn't tell him that Major Meadors had made the mistake of hiring four women and no man. "He's busy in the fields, Mr. Freemont."

Morrow chose that moment to smile and reach out toward the man. He looked at the baby for a moment and then said, "You have any money? I mean, *good* money?"

"Yes." She reached into her pocket and pulled out the knotted handkerchief. "A gold eagle."

At the sight of the gold coin, Royal called out to the man in the nearby field. "Big Caesar, go to the pasture and bring up Daisy Belle."

The black man set down his crocker sack. He walked to the railing and he repeated, as if he hadn't heard the man correctly, "Daisy Belle?"

"You heard me. Daisy Belle."

Big Caesar looked at Allison. Slowly, he began to walk past the barn and then disappeared into the clump of trees at the edge of the pasture.

Frances Patton Statham

"Well, you might as well sit down on the steps and wait."

"Thank you, Mr. Freemont."

The man picked up his bourbon glass, and pretending to ignore the woman, he began to sip the last of the liquid.

"What happened to your hair?"

"I had the fever."

"A pity. A woman doesn't look right with such short hair."

Allison shrugged. "It doesn't matter. It will grow out again."

A few minutes later, Big Caesar returned with the Guernsey cow. Royal stood up and walked over to the animal. "Well, here she is. Shall I have my man tie her to the back of your carriage?"

Allison took one look at the cow. She cleared her throat and then said, "I don't like the looks of this animal, Mr. Freemont, especially for the money I'm paying you. Don't you have a better one—one without the bloat?"

Big Caesar coughed and turned his head away from his master.

Allison couldn't tell which action had made the man so furious—hers, in refusing the animal, or Big Caesar's.

"Well, don't stand there, Big Caesar. You heard the woman. Take Daisy Belle back to the pasture and bring one more to her liking."

"Yes. Mr. Freemont."

It didn't take the black man long to return. This time the milk cow chosen looked like a prize specimen. Big Caesar waited for Allison to inspect the animal.

With a nod, Alllison said, "She'll do fine, Mr. Freemont."

"Of course she will. Big Caesar has just given you one of the best cows in my pasture."

As the black man went back to the cotton field and picked

237

up his crocker sack, Allison slowly left the driveway of the house belonging to Royal Freemont. Tied to the back of the carriage was the milk cow purchased for her daughter Morrow.

While Allison made her way back to Bluegrass Meadors, she inwardly thanked Major Rad Meadors and the only humorous entry in his journal—concerning Royal Freemont and his cow, Daisy Belle. Otherwise, the problem cow might now be tied to the rear of her carriage.

The purchase of the cow by Allison heralded a new era. The gold coin that she had clung to ever since her wedding day was gone—the last material symbol linking her to the past.

But in its place a knowledgeable legacy far more important was reawakened as Allison, used to running Rose Mallow in its earlier days before the war eroded all of her resources, took full responsibility for the running of Bluegrass Meadors. She threw herself into all of the work, all of the chores, delegating to each woman her fair share of that work. But it was Allison who got up earlier and stayed up later, planning the day ahead. And when she needed advice, she went to Rad Meadors's journal, which soon became a guide for their daily lives.

Then the day finally came when Allison knew they could wait no longer. The weather was perfect and the tobacco fields were ripe.

That first morning of a new week, as the sun crept over the hills and began to light the meadows with its blinding rays, the four women left the cottage and followed the meandering path past the paddocks. At the edge of the field where the log curing barns were standing, Allison stopped.

Just as she had once carried Morrow in a basket to the woolen mill, so Allison brought her child to the fields in a basket. But this time the basket was much larger and deeper. And when she'd reached the poplar tree at the edge of the field, Allison took the rope, doubled it over, and anchored the basket to one of the limbs. She was careful to lift it only a few inches off the ground to allow for the circulation of air, yet it was close enough so that Morrow would not hurt herself if she happened to fall out.

Allison, Rebecca, Flood, and Madrigal were a strange-looking crew, dressed as they were in old workclothes found in the attic of the cottage. While the straw hats and veils provided little respite from the sun for their heads, so the gloves on their hands provided scant protection from the steady, unmerciful jolt of cutting the tobacco stalks.

After an hour, with little talk among them, Madrigal stood up and stretched her back. She gazed at the knife she held in her hands and then looked at the rows of tobacco waiting to be harvested. "I'd rather be back at the mill workin' ten hours a day," she complained.

"And I'd rather be havin' tea with the queen of England," Flood said, working beside her. "But since there's not much chance of either one, guess we'll have to keep on cuttin' the tobacco."

"And I could do with a cool drink of water about now," Rebecca said.

"What about it, Allison? You think we could take a break now?"

Allison looked at Madrigal and then back at the tobacco. "Let's finish this row first," she said.

The women went back to work, with the knives serving as machetes. Faster they cut, and when they reached the end of the row, Madrigal let out a whoop, threw down her knife, and walked toward the shade of the tree.

Rebecca came back with a cool bucket of water from the pump. And within minutes they'd all partaken of it, including Morrow, who had awakened from her nap.

Each day was the same, with the women getting farther from the cottage and the tobacco barns. An entire week went by, and all the while the grueling sun etched its mark on the women's faces despite their use of hats and veils. On wooden slab altars adjacent to the barns, they spread the ripe tobacco leaves to dry to a golden brown in the same uncompromising sun.

Several times, as the women worked in the field, Allison would glance up to see a man in the distance watching them. He never waved or spoke. He merely stood and watched. And then he would climb back into his buggy and disappear. Allison had no need to wonder who he was, for she recognized Royal Freemont, the neighbor down the road.

Once all the tobacco was dried, the four women hung the leaves in the well-ventilated barns for curing. And when that was done, they returned to the cottage, promptly fell into their beds, and slept around the clock.

In the cool of the evening, when the harvesting was over,

Flood sat on the porch with Allison and her baby. As Flood's attention turned to the barns at the edge of the razed fields, Allison said, "We'll have to see about the next tobacco auction, Flood."

The woman nodded. "I didn't think we could do it," she said. "Get it ready for market. But we did."

Allison noticed the sense of satisfaction on Flood's face. And she was hesitant about spoiling it. "I'll feel a lot better once the tobacco's out of the barns and in the warehouse."

"What are we goin' to do with the bare stalks, Allison?"

"First, we'll cut as much as we can for winter fodder. After that, we'll have to wait and see what the weather does. Rad—Major Meadors, that is—usually sets fire to the fields to get rid of the rest. But it's so dry around here that I'm afraid the fire might spread."

Flood nodded. "Whatever you think best, Allison, we'll follow up on it.

"Thank you, Flood." There was no need to say more. Once they'd left the prison, the two women had come to an understanding and appreciation of each other. For though Flood was supreme when it came to running a mill, she depended entirely on Allison in this alien environment of land, horses, and tobacco.

A few minutes later, Rebecca returned from milking the cow and Madrigal from the paddocks where she had been watching the foals. All four went into the cottage to eat their evening meal. When the dishes had been washed and put away in the cupboard, Flood, Rebecca, and Madrigal said good night. But, as usual, Allison lingered by the candlelight in the parlor and read from Rad Meador's journal.

For those weeks that swept August off the calendar and brought in a new month, the women were completely isolated, with no news of the war reaching them. Success now rode in almost every direction with the Union troops. In the Western campaign, Sherman took Atlanta and began his destructive march to the sea, burning plantations and fields, slaughtering animals, and leaving nothing behind to feed a hungry people. But the taking of that city had little effect on the Roswell women at Bluegrass Meadors. Another event was far more relevant. For about the same time, in a raid at Greeneville, Tennessee, John Hunt Morgan, the Kentuckian hero of the Confederacy, was finally caught and killed by Union cavalry. And in that group was one Major Rad Meadors.

As Allison lay sleeping, a group of ragtag men and boys, attaching themselves to the Paw-Paw Militia, was heading in the direction of Bluegrass Meadors to avenge Morgan's death. And in that group was a disillusioned Puckka Knox.

He had not gotten far from Louisville when his sister, Caddie, died. A week later, his mother, Rena, had followed. And with her death, the last restraints of civilization disappeared. Puckka was free to do what he pleased.

And it pleased him to join that group of deserters and bushwhackers that always follows in the wake of an invading army, culling the remains that a foraging army leaves behind. Those men, seemingly born to pillage and plunder if given the opportunity, were a source of embarrassment to both the Union and Confederate sides. But the South, so steeped in tradition and the gentlemen's code, was particularly aghast that any of her own could be capable of such behavior.

The men crept silently down the long, fenced lane of Bluegrass Meadors. In their hands they carried clubs wrapped in kerosene-soaked rags, ready to be ignited at a sign from their leader.

Puckka stood and looked at the brick mansion silhouetted in the moonlight. "I'll take the big house," Puccka said. "Anybody else want to come with me?"

But the leader held up his hand. "We're only goin' to burn the fields and the tobacco barns. That's all—a little calling card for the major."

"But what about the house?"

"That's not to be touched. Out of respect for the other brother, Captain Meadors, who's fighting on *our* side."

A few of the men grumbled, but in the end they obeyed their leader, igniting their torches and rushing through the fields, leaving a trail of fire that spread among the dry stalks. Quickly they struck and quickly they disappeared, while the aroma of burning tobacco rose on a golden cloud that spread over the land.

The skyline became an arc of flames, with a sudden breeze sweeping through the trees and carrying with it the sparks that threatened disaster to the entire plantation.

With the increasing glow upon the horizon giving a false dawn, Allison awoke. She rebelled at the idea of getting up, for she felt that she had only gone to bed a few minutes previously. But as she sat up in bed and rubbed her eyes, the odor of tobacco assailed her.

"Rebecca, Flood," she screamed. "Wake up! I think something's wrong."

She rushed to the window and looked out. The fear that had nagged at her during the entire harvesting of the tobacco became reality. The barns were afire and the wind, blowing from that direction, sent sparks, like a thousand tiny lights, toward the porch of the cottage itself.

"Madrigal, wake up! Flood, Rebecca, get the buckets. We've got to save the barns."

The nightmare began, with the women stumbling sleepily out of the cottage. Madrigal took up her position at the pump, filling the buckets with water, while the other three women ran back and forth in a vain effort to save the barns. But the water had little effect upon the fire. It continued to burn out of control, the log barns with their treasure and the stubble in the fields lighting up an area that could be seen for miles.

"Allison, you'd better get the baby out of the cottage. Looks like we might not be able to save it, either."

Allison, with her face blackened by the smoke, heeded Flood's warning. She left her place in line and rushed back inside the cottage just as the dry timbers supporting the porch began to smolder.

As Allison carried Morrow toward the redbrick mansion and placed the basket on the porch, Royal Freemont and his man, Big Caesar, raced down the drive in a carriage.

Without a word, they took their places with the women, pumping water and becoming part of the bucket brigade. But they, too, finally gave up on the barns, for the tobacco had been ruined. Instead, they turned their attention to the cottage, which was already on fire.

Three hours later, as the sun appeared on the horizon, all who'd fought the fire so valiantly were slumped on the porch of the mansion and looking at the ruins.

"It's all gone," Allison lamented. "Everything we worked so hard for."

"We don't even have a roof over our heads," Madrigal said.

Charred land in every direction greeted them. Only a piece of the tin roof and the stone chimney marked where the cottage had been. And the stubble in the fields was all that was left of the once flourishing tobacco crop. There was no trace, either, of the two tobacco-curing barns at the edge of the field.

"Looks like you'll have to move into the big house," Royal Freemont said matter-of-factly. He stood up and motioned to Big Caesar. "Got to go home now. Plenty of chores waiting for us there."

"Mr. Freemont—"

He waved his hand at Allison. "No need to say anything. Little enough we could do. Just wish we'd been here in time to help save the tobacco crop."

As the two men drove away, Flood said, "I feel exactly like I did that day when the soldiers burned the mill."

"But it wasn't Yankees this time," Madrigal said. "Big Caesar said it was retribution from some of the Paw-Paws wantin' to get revenge for Major Morgan's death. He heard it was Rad Meadors's bunch that cornered and killed him."

Flood looked up. "They could have burned Mr. Freemont's place, too."

"That's why they had to wait, to make sure they were gone, before they came to help us."

"Well, we've got the cow, Miss Allison. And the orchards," Rebecca said, trying to cheer her up.

"And we certainly won't go hungry this winter," Allison joined in, "with all the food we preserved. We're just lucky, I guess, that we stored the majority of it in the mansion's pantry."

"Well, are we goin' to do what Mr. Freemont said?" Madrigal asked. "Move into *this* house for the winter?"

"I suppose it's the only thing we can do," Allison replied.

Madrigal immediately stood up. "Then I know which room *I* want. It's the one at the head of the stairs, with the canopied bed and the sittin' room."

"No, Madrigal. That's the master bedroom. You can select one on the third level, as we all will."

"You sure are a spoilsport, Allison." Madrigal brushed

her blackened hands on her petticoat. And for the first time, she realized that even her dress had been lost in the fire. "What about our clothes? We don't even have a camisole left between us."

"Surely Major Meadors won't begrudge us the use of anything we might find," Allison said.

"I saw a trunk in the attic the other day," Madrigal confided, "when I was rummagin' around. There's the prettiest blue dress in it. Come on, Rebecca. Let's go up to the attic."

Rebecca looked at Madrigal. "We'd better wash ourselves off at the pump first. Otherwise, we'll leave a dirty trail all through the house."

"And we'd better do the same, Flood," Allison suggested. She winced as she pushed herself up from the chaise. Blisters lined both hands. The large bruise on her left leg caused her to limp awkwardly toward the pump where she and Flood joined Madrigal and Rebecca, already at work removing the soot and grime from their losing bout with the fire.

CHAPTER
27

The rains began in the night, falling upon the charred timbers of the cottage and spreading that peculiar acrid odor
through the air as the ashes and water combined.

Inside the redbrick mansion, Allison heard the steady
patter upon the roof, and she climbed out of bed to close
the window. For a moment she stood, looking out and
breathing the harsh-smelling air.

It was strange, Allison thought, that certain odors could
trigger memories long hidden away in the unconscious. She
remembered that day as a child when she'd watched the
servants making lye soap—with the steady dripping of
water over hickory ashes and then the boiling of the mixture
with tallow. She had wanted to help, but her mother had

sent her away to play under the magnolia tree, away from the cauldrons with their fires underneath.

But white-haired old Auntie Susie had allowed her to help, after all, sending her into the wooded area to gather sweet heart leaves to perfume the soap.

Allison smiled as she closed the window against the rain. With that childhood remembrance in mind, she began to plan yet another project even while she groped her way back to bed.

In the corner bedroom down the hall, only a few feet from the narrow stairs that connected the third level with the second, Madrigal O'Laney was still awake. All day, she'd kept her pains to herself. She hadn't thought much about it that previous night when she'd tripped over the water bucket. But by morning, she'd known that something wasn't exactly right. Her first thought when she woke up was that maybe she was going' to lose Caleb's brat. And she couldn't say that she was sorry.

The pains began to come closer and closer, causing her to grip the bedpost. And she clamped her teeth together to keep from making a sound, for she didn't want to wake up anybody if she could help it.

She had been careful not to confide in any of them about her condition. Not Flood, and especially not Allison. And if she could get through the night without any of them knowing, so much the better. Unless, of course, she began to bleed like Ellie.

For the next hour, Madrigal managed alone. Bands of escalating pain began to tighten around her stomach and spread to her back. Closer and closer they came together, until there was no respite, no separation of one pain from the other. It kept up with unrelenting insistence, causing Madrigal to regret her decision to manage alone.

Finally, in one long steady wrenching motion, Madrigal felt a part of her own body being torn asunder. Despite her vow, she cried out, but the sound behind the closed door was muffled by Flood's loud snoring reverberating down the entire hallway.

Gradually, the unbearable pain subsided. In relief, Madrigal lay upon the bed. She was weak—emotionally, physically—but the worst was over now. Yet there still remained a very necessary chore. Somehow, some way, before morning, she had to get up and dispose of the bloody sheets before the others found out. But the night was only half over. She still had plenty of time.

Madrigal slept off and on, with the steady downpour of rain hitting the dormer window and splashing onto the windowsill. She could feel the moisture upon her face, but she didn't have the strength to get up and close the window.

Shortly before dawn, Madrigal awoke. Lying in bed, she listened to the sounds around her. Outside, the crickets were chirping their nightly love song, and inside, Flood's snoring indicated that the household was still asleep.

Madrigal forced herself to crawl out of bed. She could wait no longer. Wrapping the quilt around her, she took the sheets that she'd bundled up earlier and started down the narrow backstairs. As one of the stairs creaked, she stopped. But no one challenged her.

A barefooted Madrigal trudged along the pathway that led to the charred cottage. And there, amid the ruins, she took a slab of wood, dug a hole in the soft, water-saturated soil, and buried the sheets.

When her chore was finished, she wrapped the now wet quilt around her and returned to the redbrick mansion.

That morning as the sun rose in the east and touched the tips of the trees shading the expansive lawn of Bluegrass

Meadors, Rebecca Smiley, on the opposite side of the hall from Madrigal, awoke. Quietly, she got up, dressed, and started downstairs to the kitchen to make a fire, as she was accustomed to doing. Halfway down the narrow stairway, she looked down and frowned. Dirty, wet footprints— small and dainty—marred the polished wood. Curiosity made her turn around and follow them back up the stairs. They stopped in front of Madrigal's door.

A puzzled Rebecca stood for a moment, and then, shrugging, she went back to her room and got a clean cloth to erase the marks along the hall and from each step. It wasn't any of her business if Madrigal decided to slip out at night, for whatever reason. But if she did it again, she would make sure that Madrigal was the one to clean up her own dirty footprints.

Rebecca had not been in the kitchen long when Allison brought Morrow downstairs. There was now no containing the child in a basket. She was far too active, crawling and climbing. Allison set her on a small pallet on the floor and gave her two wooden spoons to play with.

As Allison walked to the shelf to retrieve a bucket, she turned to the black woman. "Rebecca, will you please watch Morrow while I go to the barn and milk the cow?"

Rebecca nodded. But just before Allison reached the back door, she stopped her. "Miss Allison?"

"Yes?"

"I suppose I shouldn't say anything about it, but I cleaned up some dirty footprints on the backstairs this mornin'."

The alarm showed in Allison's face. "You think a bush-whacker came into the house while we were asleep?"

"No'm. It was Madrigal, goin' out sometime in the night. At least the footprints stopped at her door."

"But we made a pact that no one would leave the house

after we all went to bed unless it was absolutely necessary. And then we'd wake up someone. You think she spoke to Flood?"

"I don't know. Guess we can ask her later on when she comes downstairs."

"Ask her what?" A curious Flood, dressed in some old jodhpurs belonging to Rad Meadors, appeared in the doorway.

"Rebecca said that Madrigal went out during the night. Did she let you know, Flood?"

"No, she didn't."

"Well, that's strange. But surely she'll have an explanation when she comes downstairs for breakfast."

A worried Flood looked first at Rebecca and then at Allison. "I think I'll go back upstairs and check on her."

"Yes, that would be a good idea." Leaving the problem in Flood's hands, Allison swung the milk bucket over her arm and headed for the barn.

In the peacefulness of early morning, as she walked down the path, Allison observed the remnants of the fire—the empty fields and the charred timbers that served as blackened monuments to the tobacco barns and cottage. But the sense of devastation she'd felt the previous day had somehow vanished with the rain. They had lost the entire tobacco crop, but Allison had followed Rad Meadors's advice—to allow a few of the healthier plants to go to seed so that another generation of the burley tobacco could be planted in the spring. The seed was safe, and for that Allison was grateful.

The wind rose through the trees and swept over the fields. Allison shivered as four wild geese flew overhead. Summer had vanished overnight with the coming of the rain. And now a colder season was beginning, as evidenced by the premature activity of the animal world. Bushy-tailed squirrels with nuts in their mouths scurried in haste. And in the towering oak tree beyond the paddock, a large nest became visible on a lower limb, a sure sign that the winter would be a hard one.

In the barn, the cow was waiting to be milked, and Allison, after seating herself on the three-legged stool, filled the bucket with warm, fresh milk. She heard the horse neigh and the young foals kick in their stalls, but she paid no attention to them. It was Flood who was now responsible for feeding the animals and letting them out to pasture.

Twenty minutes later, the milk pitcher sat on the kitchen table and the three women began to eat their breakfast.

"Did you check on Madrigal?" Allison looked at Flood and waited for her reply.

"Yes. She won't be comin' down to breakfast," Flood announced. "She's feelin' rather poorly and says she wants to stay in bed this mornin'."

"I'm sorry. Is there anything we can do to make her feel better?"

Flood looked at Allison. "I think she just wants to be left alone, Allison. At least for now."

Rebecca looked at Allison and then back at Flood. No one needed to say a word. Somehow it was understood that something momentous had happened—something that Madrigal did not wish to share with the others. And so the three women around the table began to discuss the chores for the day, dividing them up among themselves. But as the day progressed, each woman, at some time, slipped upstairs, either to take Madrigal a little food or to check on her.

"Really, Allison, I'm all right," Madrigal insisted. "I'm just tired, that's all, from all the work these past two days."

Allison looked into Madrigal's pale, wan face—so like Ellie's during her worst time at the institute. "Of course, Madrigal. You just stay in bed today. It's not as if we have chores that can't wait. There'll be plenty of time for you to catch up later when you feel well again."

That evening, as the outside light grew too dim for Allison to continue working on the quilt she was making for winter, she rose from her position on the porch, folded the quilting frame, and started to take it inside.

"I think Madrigal's lost the baby," Flood anounced, not looking at Allison but rather gazing into the distance beyond the meadows.

"Rebecca thinks so, too, Flood. But she evidently doesn't want us to know. So, as far as I'm concerned, it's better if we don't ever mention it to her."

"I agree."

Flood left the porch and headed for the barn where she began to mix the sorghum and hay for the animals. She was still afraid of them and somehow they sensed her fear, for they became skittish every time she appeared.

But, like Madrigal, she kept her own secret to herself. There was no need to broadcast her fear of the animals to the others.

When Allison took Morrow downstairs to the kitchen to feed her, the hearth was cold, the candles unlit, and Rebecca was nowhere in sight. Allison had not seen the woman since early afternoon, and with the approach of night, she began to worry.

Along a stream a mile past the boundary of the meadow and apple orchard, Rebecca suddenly became aware of the dark, eerie shadows closing in along the bank where she sat. The weeping willows hanging over the water began to move with the wind, their pendants hanging like fingers rippling the murky waters where one large fish had teased her for the past hour with its constant jumping beyond the reach of her bamboo fishing pole.

To her left, she heard a twig break. She didn't look up for fear of what she might see. But the past two days had made her cautious. In haste, she pulled her string of bream out of the water, picked up her pole, and left the bank.

As she began to walk back toward the mansion, she realized the steps she heard were parallel to her own steps, with only a scant distance separating them.

She hated the stealthy manner in which she was being tracked. Finally, in a fit of exasperation, Rebecca stopped, picked up a large stick, and called out, "All right. Show yourself, if you're not too scared to."

She waited and then watched the limbs of a tree divide to reveal Big Caesar, Royal Freemont's man. Recognizing him from the night he'd come to help fight the fire, Rebecca was livid. "What do you mean, nigger, followin' me and scarin' me half to death? You coulda got your head knocked off just now."

"My, don't we sound sassy." He grinned at Rebecca, which made her even angrier.

"Don't you come a step closer," she warned.

He ignored her threat. "Looks like you been fishin', too."

For the first time she noticed the pole he carried, but her anger still controlled her. "And what if I have? The creek belong to you?"

"Not exactly. 'Cept you *did* take my fishin' hole from me. I been tryin' to catch that big one for the past two weeks, but I see you didn't have any luck, either."

"I caught me enough for our supper, anyway."

"What? Those skinny little things? They look like the ones I threw back in several days ago."

Suddenly, he held out the big string of fish he'd caught. "Here, why don't you take these with you? If I was you, I'd be too ashamed to go back home with that small mess of fish. Mr. Tompkins might laugh right in your face."

"Ha! You don't know what you're talkin' about, nigger."

Big Caesar winced. "I don't much like bein' called that, woman. I'd rather be called by my real name—Caesar."

"Doesn't matter. I won't be seein' you enough to call you *anything*."

"Then I can have my fishin' hole back?"

"I didn't see a sign with your name carved on it."

"Here, take the fish, like I told you, and stop your fussin'. Or else it'll be too late to cook 'em."

Big Caesar thrust his string of fish into her hand as Rebecca suddenly looked up at the sky. Big Caesar was right. It was late. Past time for her to get home.

He didn't wait for her to thank him. It was almost as if he knew the words would come out wrong no matter how she said them. Big Caesar disappeared. Rebecca stood still and listened to his footsteps until they were gone and the woods contained only the sounds of the katydids and the tree frogs tuning up for the night.

At the front window, Allison stood and watched a figure hurrying toward her. And when she recognized Rebecca, she felt a great relief.

CHAPTER 28

The war escalated, with hit-and-run tactics by small groups of Confederates diminishing the sheer power of cannons and artillery belonging to Grant and Sherman. Like will-o-the-wisps, the raiders appeared, did their damage, and then vanished before the men in blue could give chase.

At times, it appeared that the Confederates would be successful in winning back Missouri and regaining Nashville and Petersburg at Sherman's rear. Then, in the battle at Marais des Cygnes, in Kansas, the Federal cavalry caught up with Price's troops, and captured over a thousand men, including two generals and four colonels—officers the South could ill afford to lose.

While prosperity in the North flourished and fortunes

were made overnight, the South gradually grew weaker and hungrier, with a triumphant Sherman cutting a barren swath across the land to the sea. And in December of 1864, he presented an early Christmas present to Lincoln—the captured city of Savannah, childhood home of Allison Forsyth.

The rest of that hard, cold winter finally passed into the spring of 1865. And by April, when Allison and the others at Bluegrass Meadors were planting the tiny tobacco seeds into seed beds and protecting them from frost and damaging rain, a prison train filled with Union prisoners from Andersonville, Georgia, was being sent to Jacksonville by the Confederates, forcing the Federal army to take back their own since there was no food left to feed anyone, Northerners and Southerners alike.

All that remained was for the Confederate Army of Northern Virginia to surrender its arms and flag at Appomattox Courthouse. This was done on April 9. And with that action, the war was lost.

It was at the end of April that Royal Freemont brought the news to the women. And when he'd left, Allison and Flood sat down and cried, for they were the ones who'd lost the most in the war—husbands, home, and livelihood. But once they had mourned, they put their despair behind them, and for the first time since they had been loaded in wagons and taken to Marietta, they began to look to the future.

"Do you realize what this means?" Allison said. "We can all go home again. Just as soon as Major Meadors returns and pays us our wages."

"I hope he won't be too upset, seein' the barns and cottage gone," Flood said, gazing out over the fields, where the tender young plants were now six inches high.

Overhearing them, Madrigal said, "Well, it certainly wasn't our fault." She sat on the steps and lazily twirled a stick, making a design in the air.

"It would have been nice, though, if we'd been able to rebuild at least one of the barns."

"That's crazy," Madrigal said. "Nobody would expect a bunch of women to do that."

"But you forgot, Madrigal. Major Meadors thinks Flood is a man," Allison reminded her.

"Won't *he* be surprised when he gets home." Madrigal laughed and then stood up. "Come on, Flood, I'll help you get the foals in."

The two left the porch and began to walk toward the meadow, while Allison and a thoughtful, quiet Rebecca remained on the porch.

"Caesar said if the major doesn't get home by the time the tobacco is ready to be cured, he'll come over and help us put the barn up."

"Won't Mr. Freemont mind?"

"Not where you're concerned, Miss Allison."

"I should never have let it slip, Rebecca—my husband being dead. That was a tragic mistake."

"I don't know about that. We wouldn'a had the hog if you hadn't. And I sure did enjoy the winter sausage."

Allison laughed. "So did I. But I have an uneasy feeling. Royal Freemont doesn't give anything without exacting full value."

"Well, we'll worry about that after the major gets home."

"I wonder how long it will be."

"Probably in another month or so."

"Then we shouldn't be sitting here wasting time, Rebecca. There's so much to be done—the house, the books, the—"

Rebecca interrupted. "You act as if he's ridin' down the road this very minute. But he's not comin' yet, so you might as well relax. Why don't you go for a walk with Morrow while I step on into the kitchen and start our supper?"

"Go walk," Morrow parroted, getting up from the pallet where she had been playing and coming to tug at Allison's dress.

Allison smiled at the child, whose amethyst eyes were filled with excitement. "She's grown this past winter, hasn't she, Rebecca?"

The other woman nodded. "Like a weed. This Kentucky soil has really agreed with her."

"Well, she's brought enough of it onto the porch to plant an entire garden. That's certain."

Rebecca, already at the door, looked back. "A child's supposed to eat a peck of dirt before she's grown."

"Then Morrow is already ahead." Allison brushed the dirt from Morrow's hands, and then, holding on to her, she began to lead the child down the few steps to the ground.

In that quietness of the day when the sun makes several false starts before finally going down, Allison walked slowly along the tree-lined path leading to the long road. At intervals, Morrow stopped to pick a wildflower or to gaze at a glistening pebble at her feet. The child was precocious— a little over a year in age and already she was walking and talking, albeit not in complete sentences or so steady on her feet as one a little older.

During the walk, an unhurried Allison, allowing the curious Morrow to take her time, began to think of the other brother, Captain Glenn Meadors, who shared ownership in the plantation. She knew almost nothing about him except for the few entries in the major's journal. Yet, reading between the lines, Allison could understand why the two had fought on opposite sides in the war, for it seemed they agreed on little enough in life.

After the cottage burned and Allison and the others had taken shelter in the mansion, the redbrick house with its massive white columns seemed cold and impersonal. No family pictures gazed at them from the parlor mantelpiece; no recent evidence of women showed up except in an old hand-embroidered firescreen with the initials, SHM, to indicate the embroiderer, and the attic trunk full of old dresses and materials that a guilty Allison had used to clothe them all. Even Morrow was dressed in a blue calico print that she'd found in the trunk and used.

But she had bought the milk cow. And when Allison left Bluegrass Meadors, she would leave the animal there—surely a better-than-even exchange for the clothes.

She didn't know why she should think of Alma Brady at that moment. Perhaps it was the fine blue silk material—so similar to Alma's—in the bottom of the trunk that had reminded her. Allison hoped that Alma would eventually find her way back to Atlanta as she'd vowed.

Allison looked up to see Royal Freemont's carriage coming at a rapid pace down the road. She grabbed Morrow's hand and guided her to the grass growing by the side of the fence. Then she swung her onto the fence, and with her arms holding the child steady, Allison waited for the carriage to pass.

It was Big Caesar who was on the driver's perch. And he seemed in quite a hurry. He waved at Allison, but the carriage didn't slow down until it reached the back of the mansion close to the kitchen. An amused Allison looked at Morrow. "Well, Morrow, it looks as if Rebecca's beau has brought us something special."

Morrow's jabber made no sense to anyone but Morrow,

as Allison lifted her from the fence. The two continued their walk, turned around at the clump of trees, and began to head back toward the house. During that time, Allison continued her musings, turning over in her mind the relationship between her servant and Big Ceasar. Not that Rebecca's initial animosity for the man had subsided that much. But at least she was more civil toward him in her actions and her speech. And she did accept Big Caesar's gifts in a more magnanimous way than she had that first time with the string of fish.

Madrigal and Flood finished their chores in the barn and they, too, began to walk toward the house.

"What are you goin' to do, Flood, when you leave here? You think you can get your old job back at the mill?"

"I been thinkin' about that for a long time, Madrigal. There's no guarantee that the mill will ever be rebuilt. And if it is, they won't be hirin' women to run it. The men will be comin' back from the war. And that means there won't be any work for us. Either for you *or* for me."

"Then what's left?"

"You're still young and pretty. You'll find a man—maybe that nice Angus Smithwick if he's still alive. But me—I'm too old and ugly."

"You're not that *old*, Flood."

Madrigal's attempt to make Flood feel better brought a hardy laugh. "But I *am* ugly, and there's no denyin' that."

"It's a shame you're not a real man, Flood. Lots of men are ugly and they get by with it. They have more freedom, too. It just doesn't seem fair."

"I've thought about that, too, Madrigal. And I wondered what it would be like if I kept on pretendin' to be a man."

"What do you mean?"

"Well, we got out of that terrible prison by Major Mea-

262

dors's mistaken' me for one. And· nobody's found out any different since we've been here. I was thinkin' that if I didn't go back home but went to someplace where nobody knows me, I could get a piece of land to homestead or stake a claim at some gold mine out West."

"Can I go with you, Flood? To the gold mines?"

"No, Madrigal. You'd get into too much trouble. Better for you to go on back to Roswell. Besides, I'm not that sure that it's what I'm goin' to do. Depends on how much money we get for lookin' after this place."

The two joined Rebecca and Allison in the kitchen, where the bounty that Big Caesar had brought from Royal Freemont was being put away.

"What did Mr. Freemont send this time, Allison?" Madrigal asked.

Before she could reply, Madrigal had moved over to the box containing the yellow, newly hatched chicks. Quickly, she picked one up and held it to her breast.

Seeing it, Morrow squealed and headed toward Madrigal with her hands out.

"No, brat. You can't hold it. You'd squeeze it to death."

Morrow began to cry and went running back to Allison, who picked her up to comfort her. But Allison frowned at the red-haired girl who had spoken so harshly. "Madrigal, please. I'd rather you didn't call her that." Then Allison brought Morrow closer to the table so that she could look down at the noisy, fuzzy chicks in the box. The child stopped crying as Allison talked gently to her and allowed her to watch the chicks.

That night at dinner, Allison began to discuss their chores for the next day. Madrigal was assigned to help Rebecca set out the small tomato plants and potato slips that

Caesar had brought at the same time he'd brought the chickens.

"Why do *I* have to be the one to work in the garden?" Madrigal complained.

"Because you said you hated to cook or do housework," Flood answered.

"Well, isn't there something else that needs doin'?"

Someone would have to inspect the tender tobacco plants to make sure the hornworms or flea beetles had not attacked them. But Madrigal had done such a poor job of it the last time that Allison was hesitant.

"Would you like to cut out Flood's dress from the Indian muslin?"

"That would be a complete waste of time. She looks better in men's trousers."

"That might be true, Madrigal," Flood agreed, "but even so, I don't think I'd like to wear a dress that you cut out." She quickly looked at Allison. "If it's all the same to you, Allison, I'd rather you did it, if you're so determined I need one."

"Maybe Miss Madrigal would rather sit on a fine pillow all day even if she can't sew a fine seam." Rebecca sounded sarcastic.

"Yes, that would suit me just fine. I've done more than enough work around here to last me a lifetime."

"Then maybe you'd keep these eggs warm while you're doin' it. Even a settin' hen is accomplishin' *somethin'* while she's settin'."

Madrigal glared at Rebecca and then flounced from the table.

Seeing Allison so upset, Rebecca apologized. "I'm sorry, Miss Allison. I shouldn't have said that, I know. But it makes me boilin' mad to see how much work everybody else does around here compared to that girl."

"She hasn't been the same since that night she lost the baby," Allison said, attempting to excuse Madrigal's errant behavior, which had plagued them all.

"I like Madrigal. You all know that," Flood answered. "But she was like this lots of times when she was workin' at the mill. So don't try to find any excuses for her."

"We're all on edge," Allison said, "waiting for Major Meadors to return home."

Flood nodded and rose from the table while Rebecca began to clear away the dinnerware. Allison sat for a while longer and looked into the candlelight. In her hands she held the list of chores to be done the next day, but her mind was many miles away.

CHAPTER
29

Each afternoon, Allison looked down the long road for some sign of Major Meadors. And each morning, she arose with the determination to work a little harder. As if she were a child with a severe taskmaster threatening to look over her shoulder, she went over the ledger that contained the small transactions, the barterings that she'd done to keep the plantation in working order. But the burned cottage and tobacco barns continued to haunt her, and she worried that the man would blame them all for not saving the structures from the Paw-Paw Militia's arson.

Several weeks went by, with no one appearing except Big Caesar or Royal Freemont himself. Then, late one afternoon, Madrigal rushed into the parlor where Allison had just finished polishing the fine, old mahogany secretary.

"He's comin' down the road, Allison. The major's finally made it home."

"Quick, Madrigal, go into the kitchen and tell Rebecca to fix some refreshments. After such a long trip, I know the major will be hungry and thirsty."

This time Madrigal didn't balk at Allison's orders. She immediately raced into the kitchen, and Allison listened to the change in Madrigal's voice that was echoing through the house. She sounded like the old Madrigal from the days in the mill—sassy and bright, with a lilt to her voice—a far cry from the lethargic Madrigal of the previous months.

Allison rushed to the mirror and smoothed her hair. It was now long and pinned-up, rather than the riotous mass of curls that Royal Freemont had commented on that day she'd purchased the milk cow. She removed a pin and re-positioned it, and then taking a deep breath, she walked slowly to the front porch where she stood and waited, un-smiling, beside one of the Doric columns.

He rode down the long, fenced lane, his horse looking winded and spent from the long trip. The man was in uni-form—with the golden braid upon his coat sleeves tarnished by the wind and rain.

Allison frowned. The Roswell gray of the uniform could not be disguised despite the dust. She had seen it too many times—on her husband, Captain Coin Forsyth, and in the mill itself, where she had worked on the looms to weave the fine wool into cloth.

The man galloped to the porch, slid from the saddle and, seeing Allison standing by the column, swept his hat from his head. "Good afternoon, ma'am."

"Major Meadors?"

The man laughed as he tied his horse to the hitching post and then leaped onto the porch. "*Captain* Meadors, ma'am. Of the defeated Confederate Army of Tennessee. My compliments to you."

"You're not Major Rad Meadors?"

"No. I'm his brother, Glenn."

"But . . ."

Seeing the puzzled expression on her face, he said, "Oh, make no mistake. I was the one who got you out of the prison in Louisville." He laughed. "It was safer using my brother's name. Otherwise, *I* might have wound up in prison myself if they'd caught me in Union territory."

The full import of his words struck her hard. He was not the severe taskmaster of the journals, but one of their own, fighting for the same cause and rescuing them like a gentleman knight. With that revelation came a vast relief, yet it was tempered with the knowledge that his older brother would also be coming home any day. But if they were lucky, the captain would pay them their wages and they could all be on their way before he arrived.

Madrigal appeared at the door, and Glenn's attention was diverted. The red-haired girl smiled, looked straight at Glenn Meadors, and said, "I have some refreshments for you, Major—in the dinin' room."

He did not correct her as to his rank. Glenn used his hat to brush the dust from his uniform. Then he moved toward the heavy oak door that Madrigal held open for him.

Allison didn't follow the man inside. She remained on the porch, her mind reeling with the knowledge that the one who had written the journals, which she had studied so assiduously, was not the man she had pictured, but his older brother. No wonder she had been confused at first, trying to reconcile the charming officer who had brought them to Bluegrass Meadors with the no-nonsense, iron-hard words of the journals.

She looked out at the fields where the tender young tobacco plants were struggling toward the sun. Glenn Meadors had not noticed them. And he'd said nothing about the missing barns and the cottage ruins, still so visible despite the attempted cleanup.

But Major Rad Meadors would have noticed immediately. Allison knew that in her heart. Brushing her hand across her face as if to clear her mind from its jumbled thoughts, she began to walk inside the house. A shared laughter—Madrigal's lilting giggle and Captain Meadors's amused laugh—greeted her as she stepped inside the door.

She walked past the dining room where Glenn Meadors sat sprawled in a chair with Madrigal leaning over to pour him a stronger drink from the decanter. "Won't you join me, ma'am?" the captain called out to Allison.

"No, thank you, Captain. I must see to my chores."

Not stopping, she continued into the kitchen and sat down at the round oak table, rough-hewn by some local carpenter more than likely, with the backs of the oak chairs carved into stag horns—a masculine ambience at odds with the blue chintz curtains hanging over the windows.

Allison looked at the silently questioning woman standing beside the cupboard. "It's all a mixup, Rebecca. The man in the dining room is not Major Meadors at all, but his brother."

"I caught a glimpse of him, Miss Allison, past the kitchen door. He sure *looks* like the major."

"Of course he does, Rebecca. He's the same man who brought us here. But he's one of our own, a Rebel, who took a terrible chance to rescue us from that dreadful prison."

"Then why do you look so worried, Miss Allison? I'd think you would be happier to see the man who fought on our side."

"I *am* happy. But I'm worried, too, Rebecca, because I know the real Major Meadors is probably not far behind."

"It's the journals, isn't it?" Rebecca demanded. "You've been followin' that Yankee's advice all this time and wonderin' what he was goin' to say when he found out last year's tobacco crop was lost."

"That's part of it. But at least the spring tobacco is already planted and doing well. I'd feel a lot better, though, if the captain paid us for our hard work and we could leave before his brother gets here." She stood. "I'd better go to the barn and alert Flood. I'm sure he'll want to talk with her about these past months."

Allison left Rebecca sifting the ingredients for the night's bread. Instead of retracing her steps through the long hall of the house, Allison slipped out the back door.

As she walked along the graveled path that separated the brick-bordered beds of the herb garden, Allison noticed how quickly the plants had grown—shaped into a lover's knot design of gray-green interspersed with darker green. She made note of the thriving mint, thick of leaf and aromatic to the nose.

The pear tree at the edge of the walk was loaded down with white blossoms, a sure indication of a good crop ahead. And the grape arbor to the right held strong, sinuously twisted vines, with the new spring growth ending in spiraling tendrils that clung to the arbor and spilled over the sides.

The weathered wood of the arbor mirrored the weathered

Frances Patton Statham

siding of the barn, with its rusted tin roof a replica of the one that had covered the kitchen roof of the cottage.

Inside the barn, Flood, unaware of the homecoming, took a pitchfork full of hay and threw it into the wooden trough for the animals. She didn't mind the work when the animals weren't around. As hard as she'd tried, she hadn't made friends with any of them except for one of the foals. And that one—the colt with the star on his forehead—had no sense. Bigger than the others and more curious, too, he was always getting into trouble, jumping the fence and then standing back and waiting for Flood to come and lure him into the stall at night with a carrot from her pocket.

"Just look at him, standin' so tall," Flood had said to Allison one late afternoon several months previously. "Just like he's the king waitin' to be served."

"He's a beautiful animal, Flood," Allison had said. And from that day on they'd called him Standing Tall.

As Allison reached the barn, she noticed the animal had jumped the fence again. Inside, the smell of hay caused Allison to sneeze, the noise alerting Flood that someone had come into the darkened barn.

"Who's there?"

"It's me—Allison," she called out. "Standing Tall has just jumped the fence. You'd better get him into the stall, Flood, before he races down the drive."

Flood put down her pitchfork and walked over to the wooden bin where a bunch of dried winter carrots lay. She broke one off and headed out of the barn. Passing Allison, Flood said, "One of these days, Allison, that colt is goin' to sprout wings, he's so fast, and nobody will be able to catch up with him."

Ever since the colt had started jumping the fence, Allison had lived with that nightmare. She knew the colt was valuable—it didn't take much of an eye for horseflesh to know it—but he was wayward, too. And sometimes as she watched him prance and caper in the meadow, she felt sorry that her brother Jonathan wasn't there to begin training him.

Looking at Flood, dressed in the old jodhpurs and shirt, Allison realized that she even walked like a man. But now, perhaps it wasn't necessary for Flood to maintain the deception. Yet, if Captain Glenn Meadors wasn't any more observant than the day he had hired her, it probably would be just as well not to call his attention to that fact.

Flood lured the colt toward the barn, and at last, when the door to the stall was closed and Standing Tall was nibbling on the carrot, Allison said, "We have a visitor, Flood. Well, not really a *visitor*. One of the owners of Bluegrass Meadors has just ridden in—Captain Glenn Meadors."

The alarm on Flood's face spread over her broad cheekbones and turned her brown face a slight ashen color. "Oh, Lord, I was hopin' it would be the other one—the major. What did he say when he saw the barns and cottage gone?"

"He acted as if he didn't even notice."

"I can't see him, Allison—until we go over exactly what I'm to say."

"But we've gone over it numbers of times, Flood."

"That was between *us*. I'll forget everything once I'm in front of a total stranger."

Allison smiled, then she explained the mixup again, this time for Flood's benefit. "So you see, Captain Meadors isn't a total stranger after all."

Flood refused to be comforted. She was still subject to being questioned, regardless of which brother had come home first.

Nevertheless, Flood began to calm down by the time she

and Allison reached the path that ended in the herb garden behind the kitchen.

Once Flood had washed her hands, the two sat down at the old oak table to go over the carefully kept figures Allison had written down. She went over each entry with the large, heavyset woman, pointing out all of the negotiations—the money they'd made selling butter and extra milk from the cow; the bartering for seeds to plant in the vegetable garden; the debit of cloth used to make their clothes.

And when she felt that Flood was well acquainted with the transactions, she closed the book and said, "The captain will more than likely ask to see you after supper."

Again Flood showed her trepidation. "Then I won't be able to eat a bite, I'm so nervous."

"You'll do fine, Flood. But you must remember to ask for our wages so that we can make plans to go home as quickly as possible."

That evening, as the sun was setting, Allison put the finishing touches to the dining room table, placing the fine old silverware at one end. She lit the homemade tallow candles in the candelabra, patinaed by age, and watched the flames flicker over the linen cloth, touching the small basket of flowers in the center with their pale glow and then colliding with the dark shadows at the other end of the long table.

When the dinner was ready, a slightly drunk Glenn Meadors sat down alone in the dining room while the others took their places at the oak table in the kitchen. But before they began to eat, the man called out.

"You'd better hurry and see what he wants," Flood said to Madrigal while putting down her fork.

Madrigal was soon back in the kitchen. "He said it's lonesome in the dinin' room by himself. So he wants us to join him at the table."

Everyone looked at Allison. "What should we do?" Flood asked.

Allison glanced at Rebecca, who was busy feeding some broth to Morrow. For the first time since the four had begun sharing a table, there was an awkwardness, and Allison hesitated. The old lines had been drawn again, separating black from white.

Rebecca sensed her mistress's hesitation and she quickly spoke up because of it. "I'll stay here in the kitchen with the baby. Go ahead, Miss Allison."

Madrigal did not wait for the others. She immediately grabbed her plate, walked into the dining room, and took the chair nearest to the captain.

Allison and Flood both hesitated at the door. Glenn waved them inside the dining room, too. "Come and sit down," he urged. "And I hope you know a few rounds of 'Bonnie Blue Flag.' Tonight might be the last night I can mourn the death of the Confederacy before my brother walks in and spoils it all."

There was a spirit of conviviality at the table that night. And once the meal was over, the singing began. Tears came to Allison's eyes while they sang the forbidden words, with Glenn's slightly inebriated voice leading them. Then, in chameleon fashion, Glenn's mood changed and the tears were replaced with laughter.

For Allison, sitting in the fine old Hepplewhite chair with its needlepoint cushion, it was a pilgrimage into the past with the charm of Rose Mallow and the comfort of her childhood home in Savannah. That night, in the glow of the candles, she remembered her soldier husband, Coin Forsyth. Her compassion caused her to overlook the condition of the man at the far end of the table. And she accepted the fact that by the end of the meal, Glenn Meadors was much too drunk to discuss business.

The entire evening had gone by without a word said about their hard work on the farm or the compensation due them. But perhaps his homecoming was not the appropriate time, after all.

As Allison took a candle and made her way up the stairs to the attic bedroom, she vowed she would get Flood to speak with the man first thing in the morning.

But by morning Captain Glenn Meadors was gone. And so was Madrigal O'Laney.

CHAPTER
30

Glenn Meadors had noticed more than Allison gave him
credit for. And if he chose not to mention the absence of
the tobacco barns and the cottage, it was his own decision,
made as he first galloped down the drive, for he had more
important things on his mind.

Bluegrass Meadors had never meant as much to him as
it did to his brother Rad. It held no special magic for him.
It was merely a place to live until he was grown and could
get away, to see the real world—of cities, of boomtowns
made from gold, of men living on the exciting edge, gam-
bling with life the same way they gambled with cards.

The war had caused him to leave a little earlier than he'd
planned, but his days with the army had magnified his

earlier yearnings. Glenn had no desire to spend the rest of his life on an isolated plantation in Kentucky when an exciting world was out there waiting for him.

In fact, he would not have returned to the house at all if he hadn't wanted something—the strongbox and its contents buried in the herb garden. Even retrieving it before Rad returned had been a gamble.

But he didn't feel guilty taking his mother's jewels and the family money from that box. After all, he was leaving the whole plantation to Rad—a decent-enough exchange. The only thing he *hadn't* planned on taking with him was the redhead, but she had been quite persuasive.

Madrigal clung to Glenn as the two galloped through the dark, past Royal Freemont's place. She, too, was searching for something different. And if her journey into the future began with a handsome Confederate officer, so much the better. Of course, she knew that the liaison made in the herb garden, as she helped him dig up the strongbox, wouldn't last forever. But, like Tom Traymore, the man was the means to an end.

Madrigal, seated behind Glenn Meadors, giggled and tightened her arms around the man's waist as the horse flew down the road. "Do you remember when we first passed by Mr. Freemont's house and you wouldn't let us stop to get water?"

Glenn kept his eyes on the road. "Yes. And I remember your sassy comment about a galvanized Yankee. I think you were trying to get back at me, too, and I had a hard time maintaining the charade."

"Mr. Freemont's been nice to us since then—because of Allison. I wonder if he'll marry her."

A startled Glenn turned his head and almost bumped into

Madrigal's face. "How can he do that with her husband still living?"

"Oh, Captain Forsyth is dead. She's a widow."

"But what about Mr. Tompkins?"

"Flood? Oh, Glenn, you never even noticed, did you?" Madrigal giggled again. "I guess now that we're gone, I can tell you the truth. Flood is a *woman*, though she doesn't much look like one. When you first hired her, she was dressed in her dead husband's clothes."

Glenn Meadors's laugh matched Madrigal's. "Well, she certainly hoodwinked me." He was silent for a moment and then he said, "So all of Flood's talk about her family was just a ploy. Aren't any of you related?"

"No. We just banded together on the prison train."

"Then it's just as well I *did* leave home before Rad gets back. I can see him now, when he finds out I hired a bunch of women. And Confederates, too. For him, that's almost worse than having the tobacco crop burned."

A tinge of loyalty prompted Madrigal's next words. "Well, it wasn't our fault—about the barns. I told you what happened."

"You're right. The blame should be laid where it belongs—square at Rad's feet. I heard he was in the cavalry that captured Morgan. That was enough to have the whole place burned down."

The sound of a wagon coming down the road caused Glenn to grow cautious. "Hush now, Madrigal. No more conversation. We've got a long way to ride to get to the train station."

"What are we goin' to do with the horse?" she whispered.

"Leave him in the stables with Rad's name on him. Let *him* pay the livery fee."

An hour later, the sun was up. As Allison walked into

the kitchen to feed Morrow, she was unaware of the captain's disappearance with Madrigal or of Major Rad Meadors's approach to St. Louis, a three days' distance from Bluegrass Meadors.

But by ten o'clock that morning, Allison, Rebecca, and Flood had learned of Madrigal's defection. They stood on the porch and gazed down the drive as if somehow she might reappear.

"I can't believe she'd do such a thing," Rebecca said. "Goin' off with that Captain Meadors. Mark my words, she'll be awful sorry one of these days."

"Well, I'm awful sorry *now*," Flood said. "But not about Madrigal. You realize the captain left without payin' us? What are we goin' to do, Allison?"

"We'll wait for his brother to come home. And in the meantime, we'll continue working."

Rebecca and Flood went to the tobacco fields, while a sober Allison walked inside the house to work on the quilt that Royal Freemont had paid in advance for her to make. With Morrow playing beside her, Allison began to sew. But an uneasiness caused her to become clumsy with the needle. She pricked her finger, and as blood appeared, she quickly dropped the material and put her finger to her mouth.

Morrow looked up from her play. "Hurt," she said, and walked over to her mother to pat her on the arm.

"It's all right," she assured Morrow, drawing her close and hugging her. But it was not all right, for the pain had found a place to lodge beyond the small wound in her finger. With the captain's disappearance, Allison had begun to worry anew, to wonder what would happen to them all and especially to the sweet baby standing at her knee. Allison's situation was no better than it had been at Rose Mallow, when all her money was gone and she'd felt so alone. But now because of the child, she bit her lip and forced a smile. "Go back to your dolly," she said, "and let Mommy work on the quilt."

Out in the field, as Flood and Rebecca inspected the tender young tobacco for the insects that could cut down a plant overnight, the black woman was worried, too.

Rebecca knew that if it had not been for Miss Allison planning and scrimping and thinking up ways to get a little extra money, they would not have survived the winter. And it had made her mad, seeing the drawn, desperate look on the beautiful, kind face of her mistress when she realized that they were in peril again, just like those awful days at Rose Mallow. Allison Forsyth deserved better than that.

Making up her mind, Rebecca walked to the part of the field where Flood was working. "I've got a plan, Flood," she said. "And I hope you'll go along with it."

Flood took her stick, knocked off an insect from a tobacco leaf, and stamped it into the ground. "What is it, Rebecca?"

"Major Meadors will be comin' home soon, more than likely. And when he gets here, he's got to be set right about you. Can't have him thinkin' you're a man or that Miss Allison is your wife."

The conspiracy between the two began that night. Rebecca set two places at the kitchen table and one in the dining room with the good silverware. A fire burned in the marble fireplace, its glow matching the candles blazing in the silver candelabra.

"What's this, Rebecca?" Allison asked as she came downstairs after putting Morrow to bed.

Rebecca gazed out the window as she spoke. "I set your place here in the dinin' room like I used to at Rose Mallow."

"That's ridiculous. I'll eat in the kitchen as usual."

Allison leaned over to blow out the candles, but Rebecca stopped her. "Miss Allison, wait a minute. I wasn't goin' to tell you, but Flood and I had a conversation when we were out in the field today."

"Well, I suppose you're going to tell me what it was about?"

"Flood doesn't want to hurt your feelin's any more than I do, Miss Allison, but the truth of the matter is that she just isn't comfortable eatin' with you."

"But we've eaten every meal together since we got here. What has happened so suddenly to make her change her mind? I think I'll just go and find out."

"No, Miss Allison. I wouldn't do that if I was you. It would only embarrass her, havin' to talk about it. You just sit down where you belong and I'll bring your plate in a minute."

Rebecca took over as she had that day so long ago, when they had returned from the memorial service at the church. And Allison, feeling hurt and ostracized, sat down at the table in the dining room.

"Well, Rebecca, how did she take it?" Flood asked when the other woman appeared in the kitchen.

"She's powerful hurt, Flood. But it's for her own good. We can't have her eatin' in the kitchen like a hired hand when the major walks in."

"I wish we could tell her . . . "

"No. That'd spoil everything, if she knew what we were doin'."

"I reckon you're right. But I sure don't want her to think hard of me after all she's done these past months."

The pattern was set. From that evening on, Allison took her place in the dining room apart from the other two. And as Flood and Rebecca took care of the outdoor chores, so

Allison took care of the ones inside, except for the milking of the cow, which she refused to give up. But in the separation, an almost imperceptible change came over Allison. She was again the mistress of a fine plantation, with demeanor and manners to prove it. And Rebecca was glad to see the return of that slight aloofness, that regal setting of the head that indicated her aristocratic background.

For a week, the weather was unusually nice, with the sun shining down on the healthy green tobacco plants and highlighting the freshly whitewashed fence that Flood and Rebecca labored to finish in record time.

"It's always important to make a good impression," Rebecca said as she and Flood began painting the final stretch of fence closest to the house.

"But I've got a feelin' the major won't think much of the pretty fence once he sees what's happened beyond it."

"I'm countin' on the tobacco plants to soften him up a bit. The field sure does look pretty right now."

In less than twenty-four hours, the warm spring weather had changed into blackberry winter, with a sudden chilling rain coming down in torrents, sending rivulets through the fields and threatening to wash away the young vegetable garden.

Late on the second afternoon of the rainstorm, a worried Allison stood at the dining room window and peered out. A strong wind bent the tree branches and dark clouds swirled low over the meadows. A sudden flash of lightning, answered by an immediate roll of thunder, caused her to back away from the window and seek comfort before the hearth.

As the darkness crept into the room, Allison removed the firescreen and held a candle to the flame so that she might light the candelabra on the table. As if the light were a signal, Rebecca brought Allison's dinner to the dining room.

"Doesn't look like the storm's gonna let up any time soon," Rebecca said.

"But I don't think the fields can take much more water," Allison replied.

"Big Caesar said the creek's overdue to flood its banks. When it happened four years ago, it ruined all the crops around here. That, and the hail."

"Then we'll just pray this isn't the year for it to happen again."

"I hung up a rabbit foot on the back door, too. Just in case we need a little extra luck."

While Allison began to eat her soup and bread, a mud-spattered Rad Meadors urged his horse past Royal Free-mont's place. A flash of lightning caused Bourbon Red to shy. Seeing the limb split from the tree directly in front of him, Rad was tempted to turn around and seek shelter at Royal's. But he had come too far to stop now. He wouldn't be satisfied until he reached the house he hadn't seen in over two years.

Yet the house and meadows had always been with him— an image in his mind—even in the darkest moments of the war. And each time he passed by a house that had been put to the torch, he became angry at the senseless loss and tragedy that caused men to destroy what they loved.

Even now he wasn't certain what he would find once he reached the long drive. Perhaps Bluegrass Meadors had been destroyed, too, despite Glenn's brief letter assuring him that it was still standing and being looked after.

He continued down the road that began to look like one of the small streams that he had splashed across often enough traveling from one line of battle to another. But this night there were no scouts lurking behind trees to watch his progress or to take aim at the enemy uniform.

By the time he finally left the road and approached the drive, Rad's horse snorted in anticipation. Reaching down and patting him on his flank, Rad said, "So you remember the meadows, too, old boy."

Overhead, the heavy limbs of the trees dripped with rain and the mist diminished visibility as Rad strained to see some sign of life beyond the drive. Then a tiny light flickered in the distance and the tired horse, without further urging, broke into a trot.

Despite the poncho, Rad Meadors was soaked through and through. And his bones ached with the cold. But he kept going toward the light—and home.

CHAPTER

31

As a gust of wind blew down the chimney and threatened the fire in the fireplace, Allison, still seated at the dining table, wrapped the soft lavendar shawl around her. She was dressed in gray and lavender, suitable colors for a widow. But the effect, with her amethyst eyes even more startling by candlelight, was one of delicate, haunting beauty, a chiaroscuro of light and darkness touching only part of the face and begging for further revelation.

Rad Meadors stood in the hallway and quietly observed the woman. Because of the storm, she evidently had not heard him enter through the front door. At first, he felt like an interloper spying on the woman. But that was ridiculous. This was *his* house and the woman was the one who didn't belong. Yet there she was, quietly sitting at his table and acting as if it were her rightful place.

He moved forward into the doorway and cleared his throat. "Good evening."

Like a startled deer, Allison looked up and saw the tall, dark man, dripping wet, with a dark poncho covering his body and his dark hair plastered to his head. He was the Dark One, with blackness surrounding him, his massive frame and his haunting dark eyes bringing a dim remembrance to her out of another time and place. She felt his strength emanate and spread into the room like some visible entity, filling the corners and empty spaces and calling upon the room to be a witness to his presence.

"Major Meadors?"

He nodded and stepped inside the threshold. "At your service, ma'am."

She was visibly relieved at his identity, for she was alone in the house. Immediately, she rose from the table. "My name is Allison—a member of the family your brother hired to look after Bluegrass Meadors. Welcome home, Major."

He gave a curt nod to acknowledge her welcome. "Has my brother arrived yet?"

Allison hesitated. There was no need to keep it from him. "He was here a week ago, and then he left again."

"And your husband? Where is he?"

Again Allison hesitated. "One of the colts jumped the fence. Flood has gone out to find him and bring him back."

She watched the major walk to the sideboard, where he poured a glass of golden liquid from the decanter and downed it in one large draught. Then he poured another and carried it toward the hearth. He took one sip, but, instead of finishing it, he placed it on the mantelpiece.

"Have you had anything to eat?" Allison asked.

"No."

"Then I'll go to the kitchen and prepare a plate for you."

"Thank you."

He was tired, as evidenced by the monosyllables of his speech and the stiff movements of his muscles as he knelt by the hearth and deliberately rubbed his hands. With piercing eyes, he stared into the fire as if to conjure up a burning mirage hidden within the flames.

As she reached the door, Rad Meadors's voice stopped her. "Take your time. I'll change into dry clothes before I eat."

"Of course."

Allison left the room and sped toward the kitchen. The kettle hung over the dying embers, keeping the soup warm; and the freshly baked bread, its odor still permeating the air, was wrapped in a linen napkin, the same as it had been each night that week—an extra portion reserved for the owner of the house in case he came home without warning.

Outside, the wind rose, whistling and flapping against the back door like some uncouth clod at a country barn dance. The rope and pulley of the well in the middle of the herb garden creaked and moved back and forth in a squeaking rhythm. And down by the creek the rising water already covered the trunk of the old, low-lying willow tree where Rebecca had first met Big Caesar.

Allison looked out the kitchen window and strained to catch some sight of Flood and Rebecca returning from the creek. When she didn't see them, she said another prayer for their safety amid the terrible storm outside.

Waiting for Rad Meadors to reappear, Allison began to worry about Morrow. So she took the candle from the kitchen table and tiptoed up the backstairs to the attic to check on the child, who was afraid of storms.

Morrow slept peacefully in the small bed. With her thumb in her mouth and the rag doll Allison had made for her lying on the pillow, she looked the picture of serenity, without a worldly care.

Touching the angelic face, Allison bit back the tears. It wasn't fair. Coin, her baby's father, should have been the one returning home from war that night. They would have given him such a joyous welcome—all the love they had stored up for father and husband. Instead, the child was fatherless and the man downstairs was a total stranger to Allison.

Tenderly, she removed the thumb from Morrow's mouth, tucked the quilt around her, and then walked downstairs again. Once Allison had reached the kitchen, she heard Rad Meadors's step in the other direction—coming down the elegant winding stairs that still showed the signs of an indented hoofprint on one of the risers. When Allison had first seen it, she wondered which of the brothers had once ridden his horse into the house and up the stairs.

And she still wondered as she walked into the dining room with the bread tray. When she returned with the tureen of soup, she saw that the man was already seated in the chair at the head of the table, the place where Coin should be sitting.

Allison knew it was wrong to resent this powerfully built stranger. The war was over, but there was a part of her that could never forgive and forget. She had lost too much to be magnanimous in defeat. But she disguised her feelings as she served him, for it would not do for him to realize how she felt about him.

After serving him, Allison replenished her own bowl, which had grown cold, but instead of sitting down at her original place, she began to walk out of the room.

"Where are you going?"

"Back to the kitchen."

"But you haven't finished your own meal. Sit down."

Allison glared at him. He had given her an order as if she were one of his lackeys. But in the end she did as she was told.

He paid no attention to her but took the fresh, sweet butter she had churned and slathered it on large chunks of bread. He finished his bowl of soup in record time and Allison, without asking if he wished another serving, laid down her napkin, got up, and took his bowl to the sideboard where she ladled a second helping, equally as large as the first.

Halfway through the second bowl of soup, Rad Meadors spoke again. "The barns are gone."

Allison refused to be intimidated by the accusation. "The cottage, too," she said without apology.

"And last season's tobacco crop—what happened to it?"

"It was lost also."

The major's face became a thunderous image, a twin to the one raging outside. "My Lord, I didn't get much protection for my money, did I? Is there some other disaster waiting for me to uncover?"

Less than two years before, the man's tone of voice would have devastated Allison and brought tears to her eyes. But too much had happened. She was a totally different woman, tempered by the events that had taken nearly everything away from her. But she still had her pride, if nothing else. And if the man seated opposite her were not able to treat her as a gentleman should, then she had no recourse but to set him straight.

In the candlelight, her eyes took on a fierce glow. Her head lifted and she stared directly at the man. "There are certain things that you will find out soon enough, Major. I had hoped that as a gentleman, you would wait and discuss it with my . . . with Flood Tompkins. But since you chose to accuse me to my face, then I think there are several facts that you should know."

Surprised by her attack, he laid down his soup spoon and stared at her.

"I understand that you were in the regiment of cavalry that killed Major John Hunt Morgan. In direct retaliation for that crime, the Paw-Paw militia came in the night and burned the barns and the tobacco crop that had been harvested. The wind swept the sparks toward the cottage, so we were unable to save it, either. And the only reason you're sitting in your house tonight, Major, is because the militia didn't choose to destroy it, too, out of respect for your brother, Captain Meadors."

"Well, perhaps I was hasty—"

"Just a moment, Major. I haven't finished."

Once Allison had started, there was no stopping her. She rose from her chair and continued. "As to your paying us, we have not received a single picayune from either you or your brother. When he hired us, he left without giving us anything. And when he returned last week, we expected to be paid for our hard labor—for the harvesting of the tobacco last August and for the planting of the new crop in April. Instead, he left again in the dead of night.

"But tomorrow I'm sure you'll be able to settle with Flood so that we can be on our way south. I don't use the word *home* because we don't know whether our homes are still standing.

"Oh, and by the way. Since the cottage was burned with our few possessions in it, we have been staying in the attic rooms and wearing the old clothes found in a trunk. But

Flood will discuss anything we might owe *you* when you settle with her . . . *him* tomorrow."

Throughout the entire barrage against him, Rad Meadors sat dumbfounded. Then the cry of a baby changed the heated atmosphere. Allison's attention was diverted.

"Please excuse me, Major. I must see to my child."

He stood up. "One answer, please, before you go."

"Yes?"

"Just where did my brother find you?"

"In the military prison in Louisville."

Rad Meadors groaned as Allison left the room. He might have known. His brother had done it again—put him into an extremely unpleasant situation and left it up to him to set things right again.

Rad walked over to the mantelpiece and took the unfinished glass of whiskey and downed it. But he felt no better. His homecoming was spoiled.

Now his tiredness overwhelmed him. He left the dining room with the candelabra and walked slowly up the stairs to the master bedroom. Overhead, in the attic, he could hear the baby still crying, while outside the thunder and lightning continued.

A lantern flickered in the meadow as Flood and Rebecca returned with Standing Tall, the unrepentant colt. Seeing the two, with the colt, pass under his window, Rad was thankful, at least, that the colt had not been lost, too.

He closed the window, locked his door, and went to bed. At his side, he laid his loaded revolver. If he had to sleep in his own house with a bunch of criminals, then he would be prepared in case they came to murder him in the night.

While Allison waited for Flood and Rebecca to return, she cleaned up the dining room and the kitchen, but somehow she couldn't bring herself to go to bed until she knew the other two were inside the house.

Finally, the back door opened, and Allison was immensely relieved to see the two women. "Did you find the colt?"

"Yes," Flood said, shaking the rain from her cap before stepping inside. "He was down at the creek."

Rebecca came into the kitchen directly behind Flood. She removed the wet shawl and hung it on the peg beside the door. Looking at Allison, she announced, "There's another horse in the barn. Has the major come home?"

"Unfortunately, yes."

Flood frowned. "Why do you say that, Allison? Isn't that what we've been hopin' for ever since the captain and Madrigal left?"

"He's a hard man, Flood. Tomorrow, you'll have to be extra careful when you talk with him. And don't let him intimidate you. Just get our money so we can leave right away."

"You didn't like him, Miss Allison?"

"I hated him on sight, Rebecca."

"Seems to me you didn't much care for Captain Forsyth, either, the first time you met him."

"That was entirely different, Rebecca. At least *he* was a gentleman. More than I can say for Major Meadors."

At Rebecca's questioning look, Allison added, "There's a world of difference in a Yankee."

"But they still *bleed* the same as a Rebel, don't they, Miss Allison?"

Allison turned on her servant. "I don't know what's gotten into you, Rebecca. It sounds as if you're trying to take up for the man when you haven't even laid eyes on him."

"I guess that will be remedied tomorrow," Flood said. "Unless he wants to see me tonight."

"No. He's already gone to bed. And if you'll both excuse me, I think I'll do the same."

"Guess we'd better go, too, Rebecca. Tomorrow will be comin' much too soon to suit me."

"Well, not for me. The sooner the better. And I think I'll pack my few things tonight."

With Allison holding the candle, Flood and Rebecca followed her up the backstairs to the attic. And once in the attic, Allison walked along the hall, lighting each one to her door.

"Good night, Flood. Good night, Rebecca."

"Good night, Allison."

She went inside her room, checked on the sleeping baby, and then climbed into bed. During the night, the storm gradually subsided, but the hours until dawn were filled with unpleasant dreams. When a tired Allison finally awoke, she blamed the major for her restless night.

CHAPTER 32

Rad Meadors awoke with a start. He grabbed for his revolver and then, realizing where he was, relaxed. He was not hiding in some bivouac with the enemy surrounding him. He was at home, in his own bed.

Slowly, he arose and looked out the window. The sun was shining again, but the debris and tree limbs scattered on the ground served as a reminder of the previous night's storm.

The words spoken by the woman at the dining table had haunted his dreams. All during the night, they had laced in and out of his consciousness—the indictment for his part in the capture of his friend, Morgan, who had chosen to fight on the losing side.

In earlier days, Morgan had been like a brother to him, with none of the rivalry that marked Rad's relationship with his younger brother Glenn. He hadn't been surprised when Glenn had gone over to the Confederates. But with Morgan, it was different.

Somehow, as the two had left home to go in opposite directions, Rad had felt a foreboding that the next time they met it would be a battle to the death. Thank God he hadn't been faced with fighting his own brother. The trauma of the battle with Morgan would forever be a scar in his mind and side. That was enough. He didn't need Glenn's blood on his hands, too.

Rad walked to the ewer basin and poured some fresh water into it to splash onto his face. The war was finally behind him. The only thing that mattered now was Bluegrass Meadors. And the sooner he started to bring it back to its former glory, the better. His first priority was to settle up and get rid of the family whom Glenn had hired.

With that in mind, Rad shaved and dressed for the day.

In the early light before the sun had time to drink up the moisture from the plants, Rad, dressed in jodhpurs and shirt, with his comfortable old black riding boots, walked to the stable, saddled his horse, and took a tour of the land. He carefully noted the condition of the young tobacco, the whitewashed fence, the paddocks and meadows, and the sites where the cottage and tobacco barns had once stood. Despite their loss, the situation could have been much worse, as the woman had pointed out the previous night. He would concede that at least. But there was so much to be done—things that only an owner would see to after the three years of neglect.

The smell of the meadow, the shape of soft morning clouds just beyond the rim of the horizon brought an excitement to Rad. It was always this way, after he'd been gone—as if he were seeing the place for the first time. How he loved the land and the horses that had once grazed in the pastures and raced in the derbies—fast as the wind, bringing honor to Bluegrass Meadors. If he were lucky, it would be that way again.

Once the tour was completed, Rad galloped back down the lane to the barn, and a few minutes later, he returned to the house.

The odor of bacon frying wafted through the house and drew Rad toward the dining room. Once he'd eaten, he would go over the books with the Tompkins man, dig up the strongbox from the herb garden, and then take the family to the train station in Louisville. While he was in town, he would hire some good help to bring back with him. And it certainly wouldn't be a bunch of convicts.

"Good mornin', Major."

Rebecca was in the process of setting the dining room table when the man walked in. "Your breakfast will be ready in a few minutes, sir."

He noticed there was only one table setting as opposed to two the previous night. His curiosity caused him to ask, "Where is Mrs. Tompkins this morning?"

"If you're talkin' about Miss Allison, she's in the kitchen with the baby."

"And Mr. Tompkins?"

"He just left to go to the tobacco field to inspect the damage from last night's storm."

"After you bring my breakfast, I'd like for you to go and get Mr. Tompkins. I won't be needing him after today. You can tell him to be in my office in half an hour, with the books."

"Yes, Major."

A worried Rebecca walked into the kitchen where Allison still sat at the table, holding a glass of fresh milk for Morrow. "Well, Rebecca, what did you think of him?"

"It's not so easy to tell, Miss Allison. He appears hard, but somehow I believe there's a softer side to him, too."

"Well, we certainly won't be here long enough to discover it. Has he asked to see Flood?"

"Yes'm. Right after breakfast."

"Good. Then I suppose after their conference, we'll be on our way."

"I reckon so."

As soon as Morrow finished breakfast, Allison took her upstairs. The quilt for Royal Freemont and his new suit of clothes were ready. Now all she needed to do was to get them to him before they left. Perhaps, if the major sent the three women to Louisville in the carriage, they could stop off at Mr. Freemont's house.

While Allison began to pack her few items of clothing and the little rag toys she'd made for Morrow, Flood Tompkins, with the ledger in her hand, walked into Rad Meadors's office.

She removed her cap and stood before his desk. "You sent for me, Major?"

"Mr. Tompkins?"

"Just call me Flood. Everybody does."

"Have a seat. We need to come to an understanding as to money owed. I presume you kept good records?"

"All transactions are listed in the ledger, Major." Flood proceeded to hand over the book to Rad.

She remained silent while he scanned one page and then another. Puzzled, he looked up at intervals, turned to another page, and then looked back at the previous page. "I find this highly irregular."

"In what way, sir?"

"It seems you've been mainly on a barter system ever since you got here. Tell me what this entry means: 'Money advanced from Royal Freemont.' Am I to understand that you borrowed money from my neighbor?"

"You'll have to take that up with Allison, Major. She's the one who dealt with him. She purchased the cow, too, with her own money."

"Damn! If you expect to charge me for some poor cow Royal unloaded on you, I won't pay. What's the cow's name? Daisy Belle?"

"I don't know, sir. You'll have to ask Allison."

Rad Meadors's temper got the better of him. "What are you, man? A henpecked husband? Don't you even know what went on these past eight months? Will I have to take it up with your wife to get to the bottom of all this?"

Flood looked extremely uncomfortable. "I think you should know some things, Major. And the first one is that Allison Forsyth is not my wife."

With Flood's confession, Rad closed the ledger and, for the first time, took a long, close look at the person sitting before him. He narrowed his eyes and then commanded, "Stand up and turn around, Flood. Slowly."

She did as she was told.

"My God! You're not even a man. You're a *woman*."

"Yes, sir."

Rad sat down again as if the realization were too much for him. "My brother hired *women* to run this place. I can't believe even *he* would be so stupid."

"Be that as it may, we did the best we could."

"Tell this Allison—whatever her name is—to step into my office. The sooner we finish with this mess, the sooner I can have you off the premises."

A few minutes later, Allison stood at the open door. "You sent for me, Major?"

He said nothing at first. Instead he stared, long and hard. "You're wearing my mother's dress."

It was the same gray that she had worn the previous evening. Allison wondered why he hadn't recognized it then. "I have subtracted its value from the money you owe us." And then her manner became just as accusing as his. "If you remember, I told you last night that all our possessions went up in flames when the cottage did."

"Yes. Well, come in and sit down. As soon as we make some sense out of these jumbled figures, you can all be on your way."

"The records are kept in the same manner as *your* ledgers, Major."

"How do you know? Did you feel called upon to snoop in my office while you had the run of the house?"

"Your brother, Captain Meadors, gave them to us, when Flood—when I requested information on the harvesting and planting of tobacco. So now that that's cleared up, what else puzzles you?"

"If you bought a milk cow from Royal Freemont, I can only say you paid far too much for her. No one gets the best of Royal."

"You're speaking of Daisy Belle, of course?"

Rad's worst fears were corroborated. "So that's the one he unloaded on you."

"Not at all. But in case you wish to see the cow, she's now in the grazing pasture."

One by one, Allison went over the items. And when Rad could find no significant fault with her accounting, he dismissed her and closed the book.

He walked to the toolshed adjacent to the corncrib, retrieved a shovel, and then began to dig in the soft earth in the herb garden a few feet to the left of the well. The ground was still soggy from the rain, and the great clumps of earth were heavy as he hoisted them carefully to the side.

Then the shovel struck metal. Working quickly, Rad removed all dirt from around the box, drew a bucket of water from the well, splashed it onto the box to get rid of the mud, and then carried the strongbox into the house.

He set it on his desk and opened the lid. The box, containing the family jewels and all the gold, was empty except for one thin slip of paper.

An incredulous Rad reached inside to recover the paper. And he recognized his brother's handwriting.

Brother Rad,
As you can see, I have taken my share of the family fortune. Call me the Prodigal, if you like, but I have gone to see the world and I won't be back. Bluegrass Meadors is all yours—a fair exchange, don't you think?
Glenn.

Rad jammed his fist against the strongbox, and his face showed his anger. He stifled an oath and began to pace up and down. Glenn had not only done something with the money he'd sent to hire decent help, but now he'd left him almost penniless. Paying taxes on the property would take almost his last cent. So how was he going to pay what he owed to the women? There wouldn't be any ready cash for four more months—until the tobacco crop was harvested and sold.

Allison brought down her bundle from the attic room. And then she went into the kitchen where Rebecca had been watching Morrow. As mother and daughter walked again into the long hallway, Rad Meadors stood at his door and watched them. It was his first sight of the child—small, angelic-looking, a replica of her mother, with the same blond coloring.

Allison looked down the hall and saw him. "We're almost ready, Major. Flood is bringing her things down right now."

Rad nodded. "As soon as he . . . she comes downstairs, I want to see you both in my office."

Allison did not think his request was out of the ordinary. In fact, she expected it—for he had not yet paid them. "Of course." Allison picked up her bundle from beside the stairs to carry it toward the front door.

"Go walk," Morrow said, breaking loose from Allison and running ahead toward the open front door.

Hampered by the bundle, Allison called out, "No, Morrow. Stay here, darling."

But the child was headstrong, recklessly running toward the porch and the high brick steps. In a lightning-quick movement, Rad was down the hall and onto the porch. He overtook the child moments before she reached the first step. He swooped her up into his arms. "You'd better obey your mother next time," he admonished.

In his arms, the child stared at Rad with wide amethyst eyes. Puzzled, she reached out and touched his face. "Dada?"

There was something about the trusting child that caused his heart to lurch. And for the first time, he looked toward the woman and felt a deep sympathy for her and her child.

Then Allison stepped forward. "I'll take her now, Major. Thank you for reaching her in time."

But he held the baby a moment longer. "Just who *is* her father, Allison?"

"Captain Coin Forsyth, of the Confederate army."

"Where is he now?"

"He was killed in the Wilderness campaign in Virginia."

Rad returned the child to Allison. Somehow, it just didn't make sense, this woman with her obvious breeding winding up in prison. But he had no time to mull this over. More immediate matters were pressing upon him.

"Did you want to see me, Major?"

Flood Tompkins stood in the doorway.

"Yes. You two come into my office, please."

They followed him back down the hall and into his office. Flood and Allison, with Morrow in her arms, stood and looked at each other while Rad turned his back to them and stared out the window at the tobacco field. In silence, they waited. When he finally turned around, his face had lost its former softness. And in its place was the thunderous, black visage of the previous night.

"You might as well unpack your things. You'll have to stay until the tobacco crop is in."

"I don't understand, Major. I thought you were just rarin' to get us off your property quick as you could."

He looked from Flood to the silent Allison. "It seems my brother has done us all a disservice. I have no money to pay you until August. You have a choice of either leaving today, without remuneration, or staying until the tobacco is sold."

"That isn't much of a choice, is it, Major?" Allison's voice was low and accusing.

"No, it isn't." He didn't apologize. He merely stared from one to the other. "Well?"

"We'll talk it over with Rebecca," Allison said. "She's in this, too."

Allison and Flood left Rad Meadors's office. There was little need, beyond mere formality, to talk it over with Rebecca. Allison knew that, in the end, the three would stay on.

CHAPTER 33

Bluegrass Meadors became a busy place, with Rad anxious to alleviate all signs of neglect in the least possible time. He worked from morning to night and showed no mercy to the women, driving them with the same impatience that he showed for himself.

"Flood, I want you to start removing the lower leaves from the plants. Be in the field at sunup."

"Rebecca, the garden needs weeding. As soon as you finish that chore, you can join Flood in the field."

"Allison, take the carriage and go to Royal Freemont's house. Tell him I need to borrow Big Caesar for the day if he can spare him."

On and on the orders came, with the three women so

exhausted at night that they went to bed almost as early as Morrow did.

A week after the strict regimen had begun, a tired Allison, sitting in the kitchen with the other two, yawned. "We might have been better off if we'd taken our chances and left when we could."

Rebecca smiled. "That man's always in a whirlwind, impatient to be gettin' things done. He and Big Caesar sure did put that barn up in record time."

"Now I'm beginnin' to understand why Captain Meadors didn't stay around," Flood added.

The three were silent again until Allison spoke up. "I was wondering about Madrigal today. You think she's all right?"

"She's a survivor. Always has been."

"But I still worry about her."

"You'd be better to worry over yourself, Allison. I got a feelin' this is goin' to be a long, hot summer for all of us."

The days passed; the tobacco grew. And the second barn was raised. One morning, just before breakfast, Rad Meadors stood near the fence and watched Standing Tall kicking up his heels and then galloping up and down the length of the white fence in record time. He had broken him of jumping the fence, but Rad knew he needed to begin more serious training with the animal, for there was racing blood in his veins.

Smiling to himself, Rad pulled up a blade of grass and began to chew on it. He catapulted over the fence and walked through the meadow to the tobacco field. Everything had been going so smoothly lately. He had to hand it to the women. He had driven them hard—as hard as he had his men in battle. Each day, he'd added a little more to their workload and then stood back, waiting for them to complain. So far, they had refused to do so. But it was just a matter of time. They couldn't keep up the pace he'd set for them. But they were a stubborn bunch.

Rad reached the tobacco field. From a distance, the plants looked healthy and green, their sturdy, strong leaves branching out to drink up the sun. Then he saw a wilted plant amid one of the rows.

Frowning, he walked over to the plant and knelt to examine it. His breathing became irregular as he tried to refute what he saw. But there was no denying it. Like locusts that arrive on the wind and strip entire fields of wheat in a matter of hours, the flea beetles, tobacco's worst enemy, had invaded the field overnight. And Rad, kneeling in the dirt, realized that his entire tobacco crop was in peril.

Swiftly, he rose and headed purposefully back to the house. He took little time to wipe his boots on the boot bar. He pushed open the door and yelled, "Flood, Allison, Rebecca. Leave what you're doing and get to the tobacco field immediately."

And then he was gone.

"Oh, Lordy, did you hear that?" Rebecca said, turning from the oven. "And just when breakfast is about ready."

"Something's happened to the tobacco. I feel it," Allison said.

"Then we'd better get out there," Flood said, "since we've got a stake in this crop, too."

Breakfast was forgotten as the women went to the field. Like an invasion, the beetles came, while Rad and the three women tried to beat them off the tender, succulent plants. At times, it seemed as if the battle would be a losing one, for when one beetle had been killed, two more appeared on the same plant.

"I can almost hear them chompin' away," Rebecca said, taking a particularly vicious swipe at one of the insects.

All day the women stayed in the field, leaving it only long enough to get water or, in Rebecca's case, to bring the bread she had baked that morning. Allison was faced with an added chore—that of watching Morrow, who was playing under one of the trees. Bringing a glass of milk and a piece of bread, Allison sat on a quilt underneath the tree and fed Morrow. And when she returned to work, she saw, with a sense of relief, that the baby had gone to sleep again.

It was sundown by the time they reached the last row. Despite the bonnet shielding her face, the harshness of the sun had done damage to Allison's delicate, fragile skin. But Rad Meadors had eyes only for the tobacco. As the sun finally disappeared behind the grove of trees to the west, he stood, leaning on his stick, and surveyed the field, now covered in the white phosphate dust. "Well, we did it. We saved the crop. We can all go in now."

"I'll take the baby, Miss Allison."

"Thank you, Rebecca. I'm not sure I'd even have the strength to carry her."

That night, after a cold supper, they all went to bed and slept for twelve hours—all except Morrow, who awoke at her usual hour. Seeing Allison still asleep, she climbed from her own small cot and got into the larger bed with her mother. And there she waited and watched for Allison's eyes to open.

Finally, she grew impatient. Hearing a noise downstairs, she scooted down from the bed, pushed the latch of the door, and, with a sense of freedom, began the dangerous descent from the attic stairs to the kitchen.

Rad heard a noise above his bedroom, followed by a child's cry. He rushed out into the hall and hurried in the direction of the attic stairs. And there he found Morrow sprawled at the bottom and crying as she attempted to get up.

"Morrow!" Allison awoke with the noise, saw the empty cot, and then the open door. Frantically, she ran into the hallway, and with her bare feet making no noise, she flew toward the steep steps. "Morrow!"

The man holding the child in his arms looked up at Allison. She stood at the head of the stairs—a slender figure in a white lawn gown, with her long blond hair hanging over her shoulders. She had not taken the time to put a shawl around her. But she seemed unaware of her own appearance as she traversed the distance separating her from her small child.

"Is she hurt?"

"A slight cut on her chin," Rad said, wiping the blood with the hem of the child's gown. "But I believe she's all right otherwise."

"I was still asleep. I didn't know she could open the door by herself . . . "

All at once, Allison became self-conscious. She was standing in front of the major, with her nightclothes on. He, too, was in a state of undress, with only his jodhpurs on. His chest was bare, proclaiming a masculine virility with his large, muscled arms. Allison avoided his searching dark eyes as she said, "I'll take her now. Thank you for rescuing her."

Rad frowned as he remained at the bottom of the stairs and watched the woman disappear toward the attic. The stairs were steep—too steep for an exploring child. He hadn't given it any thought before. But with the accident, Rad realized that something needed to be done. Either the woman would have to maintain a closer watch on the child or else he would be forced to find a safer place for them both.

Rad went back to his room, finished dressing, and then walked down the wide winding staircase to the main floor.

Rebecca was already in the dining room, setting his regular place with the china that he remembered from his own childhood. The china had gathered dust in the beveled glass cabinet once their mother had died and there was no woman in the house to see to the formality of living. But now, with the three in residence, things had begun to change—not only on the plantation itself, but in the house, too.

Rad was aware of the scent of fragrant blossoms wafting from the front parlor, where the fine furniture, covered for so long with white sheeting to protect it from dust and sun, now stood, polished and waiting to be enjoyed again.

Suddenly feeling a need to learn something more about these women occupying his house, Rad looked at the woman who had come into the dining room and was now pouring his coffee.

"Rebecca, something puzzles me."

"What's that, Major?"

"I've been watching all three of you women and you don't seem to be the criminal type. Tell me what you did—what crimes you're guilty of. Not that it will make any difference to me now," he quickly assured her. "You're all good workers, regardless of the past."

"We were arrested for treason, Major. By your own General Sherman's orders."

"You mean you were all spies?"

"No. There was a textile mill in the little town of Roswell where we lived. And once the men who worked there left for the army, the women took their places at the spindles and looms. When General Garrard took the town, he burned the mill and arrested the workers for making cloth for the Confederate army."

Rebecca was careful to watch the reaction on the man's face before she continued. The frown encouraged her to wait for the question that she sensed was the real reason why he had inquired.

"And Allison Forsyth. She was a mill worker, too?"

Rebecca smiled. "For just two days, Major Meadors. Captain Forsyth was dead; we had no money left—just the baby and that large old mansion about to fall down over our ears. The only way Miss Allison knew to raise enough money to leave Rose Mallow and take us back home to Cypress Manor in Savannah was to swallow her pride and ask Mr. Roche, the manager, for a job. But she hadn't counted on the mill being burned so soon."

She waited for any other questions, but for the moment the man seemed to have lost interest. A disappointed Rebecca, wondering if she had done more damage than good on behalf of her mistress, set down the silver coffeepot and brought in the platter holding the eggs and bacon.

As soon as Rad had filled his plate, he said, "That will be all, Rebecca."

"Yes, sir."

The woman began to leave the dining room, but then the major's voice stopped her. "Rebecca, I'm going into Louisville after breakfast. I'm not sure when I'll be back. If the three of you want to do as little work as possible today, I won't complain. Yesterday was an extremely hard day for all of us."

"It sure was, Major Meadors."

Rebecca saw the carriage leave. And two days later, she saw it return. During the time between, the three women rested, with Allison, helped by Rebecca, attempting to eradicate the effects of the sun from her tender complexion.

"If you don't take better care of yourself, Miss Allison, you're goin' to be black as me," Rebecca admonished, slathering milk clabber over Allison's face.

Allison laughed. "You used that same argument, Rebecca, over ten years ago."

"Well, looks like you haven't learned any sense in the past ten years—at least when it comes to your skin."

"Ten years ago, I was a young girl. Now I'm a widow. Beautiful skin just doesn't seem to matter to me anymore."

"You act like your life is over. Well, that ain't true. And I'll tell you another thing, too. The way Mr. Freemont looks at you, I think it won't be long before he comes over and asks you to live in *his* house. That is, if the major will allow it."

"Stop talking such nonsense, Rebecca. Hurry and get this terrible-smelling clabber off my face. I have more important things to do than sit here wasting time."

"Such as?"

"Well, taking Morrow for a walk, for one thing."

Less than a half hour later, Allison and Morrow were winding their way across the meadow to the shade tree when Rad came down the drive. Seated in the carriage with him was Big Caesar. Allison waved as the carriage passed by.

"Da-da," Morrow said.

"No, darling. That's the major. Can you say 'major'?"

"Da-da," Morrow repeated, oblivious to the exasperation she caused her mother.

To take Morrow's mind off the man, she said, "Let's go to see the chickens. I need to gather the eggs before we go back inside."

Later, with the eggs safely tied up in her apron, Allison began the walk back to the house. She was careful to hold on to Morrow with her other hand to make sure the child did not stumble again. Her little face was still bruised from her fall down the stairs, but the cut looked much better. And Allison was relieved that no scar would remain as a permanent reminder of the accident.

"Miss Allison?"

She heard Rebecca's voice calling from the kitchen steps near the herb garden. "I'm coming, Rebecca."

The black woman rushed down the path to meet Allison. "Here, let me take Morrow. The major wants to see you in the parlor immediately."

"The parlor? You're sure he isn't in his study?"

"He's in the *parlor*, Miss Allison. And I think you'd better not keep him waitin'."

"Be careful with the eggs," she said, also handing over the apron to the woman.

"Smooth your hair," Rebecca admonished. "You look a shambles."

Allison glared at the woman. "You certainly are bossy today."

"It's my right to be. Remember, I've looked after you almost from the time you were born."

"When you were all of eight years old."

"Stop sparrin' with me and go on into the parlor."

A reluctant Allison went inside the house. The past two days with the major away had been blissful. Now she wondered what new work he had dreamed up to keep them all busier than ever.

CHAPTER 34

"You wished to see me, Major?"

She stood in the open doorway of the front parlor and waited to be acknowledged. Despite her outward, self-assured demeanor, there was a certain vulnerability about her that could not be disguised. It showed in her eyes—those incredible amethyst eyes the color of fine Venetian glass—and in the small flutter of her hand that reminded Rad of the graceful movement of a willow branch bending to the wind.

Abruptly, he stood up and walked to the window to give himself time to regain his composure and the formal manner of the previous weeks. And when he turned around again, he indicated the slipper chair beside the settee where he had been sitting. "Sit down, Allison."

She was not prepared for his voice, so harsh and so distant. "If it's all right with you, I prefer to stand."

"It is *not* all right, so please take a seat."

Allison slowly moved to the chair, but her eyes challenged him in an accusing manner. As he gazed back at her, she didn't waver. Suddenly, there was something else beyond the challenge that bound the two together in the uncomfortable silence that filled the room. But Allison waited, watching him, determined not to give in as some are prone to do, to say something inane because of another person's refusal to speak.

He moved from the window and took his place again on the settee opposite her. "Your face is burned."

It was not what she expected to hear from him. "Yes, but it's not surprising after our day in the tobacco field."

He nodded as if agreeing with her. "I've gotten Royal Freemont to let me hire Caesar for the rest of the season. That should ease matters with the tobacco crop. From now on, you will not be required to work outside in the sun. Instead, you will be responsible for the smooth running of the house."

"What about Rebecca and Flood?"

"They are to continue as they are."

"I'm sorry, Major, but the three of us are in this together. In the past, we've shared the chores equally, and I fully expect to continue doing so until we leave here."

As a passage of cloud obscures the waning moon and then moves on, a sudden darkness appeared in Rad's eyes. "You don't have a choice, Allison. You're not three women trying to hold things together until the owner comes home. I *am* home and in full charge, make no mistake. There's no need to tell me what you will do and will not do. *I* give the orders around here now."

Allison's face showed her anger. She stood. "Well, I think you've made yourself perfectly clear, Major. So if that's all, then I'd like to finish my chores for today."

"No, that isn't all. I've decided that you and your child are to move from the attic into one of the larger bedrooms on the second floor. Even if you have no regard for your baby's safety, *I* do. And I don't wish a repetition of several mornings ago. The next time she might not be so lucky."

A chagrined Allison gripped the back of the chair with her hands. What could she say? He was right, of course. It was another indictment against her—this time, as a mother. She finally looked up, swallowed, and said, "Which one?"

"The large corner room at the end of the hall. The baby should rest better in the summer heat because of the cross ventilation of the windows."

Allison did not give up without a fight. "Morrow is still a baby—with fretful times of crying. Won't she disturb your sleep by being on the same floor?"

"After trying to sleep through the hellish noise of war, a baby's cry isn't going to disturb me, I assure you."

"Then I'll move our things down this afternoon. Are there any further orders?"

"Yes. The dining room table is to be set for two. Beginning tonight, you will have your meals in the dining room with me."

She opened her mouth to protest, but Rad dismissed her. "That will be all, Allison. Until tonight."

She whirled around, her petticoats rustling as she swept from the room. Rad watched her go and then sat down again.

He should have known about the woman, been more observant of her—especially her soft, cultured speech. But he'd had to be hit over the head first by her servant, Rebecca Smiley, before he noticed.

His two days in Louisville had been eye-opening—both at the military prison and then at army headquarters, waiting for the reports to come through.

Yet Rad knew he shouldn't have been surprised at what he discovered, for innocent civilians in the corridors of war had always suffered as much as those fighting in the battlefields. In one way, though, it was worse. For civilians were the defenseless ones, without guns, without redress from a military tribunal.

He knew, too, that the atrocities were not completely one-sided. Although it was easier for Allison to believe the worst of the Yankees because of her own experience, she had not seen the devastation done by Morgan and some of the others to their own people. Perhaps one day she could gain a true perspective, but not now. She was too tied up in her own hurt. And he couldn't blame her.

Rad Meadors left the parlor and went outside to find Big Caesar. For the next week, they would both be busy cutting down the timber to cure, for the eventual replacement of the cottage.

In the attic, Allison began to pack her few dresses and Morrow's things. A few minutes later, she was on the second floor in the bedroom Rad Meadors had designated for her.

As she began placing her belongings in the beautiful old clothespress opposite the burled walnut bed with its high curved pediment reaching almost to the ceiling, she realized the room was much more suitable for Morrow. Hidden by the lace ruffle that fell gracefully from the bed to the floor was a small trundle bed, where Morrow could sleep.

There was something feminine about this room that reminded Allison of her own at Cypress Manor, with the little extra room adjacent to it, where the marble stand holding pitcher and basin stood near the dressing table. Even the old china chamberpot, decorated with pink roses, was vaguely familiar.

Looking at the room and its annex, Allison was glad that there was nothing in it to remind her of Rose Mallow. It was better that way—better not to recall a reality that had vanished as suddenly as the seeds of a dandelion scattered by the wind. Better to remember the girlish dreams half-born in the mind. They were much easier to live with.

Allison looked out the window as Rad Meadors disappeared beyond the orchard. Despite her bravado, she was afraid of him. For she knew in her heart that one day he would force her to deal with that reality—all the things she had buried in some deep, dark cavern never to be explored again. And at that moment she hated him for it. It was almost as if he had willingly gone out of his way to evoke some response, some feeling from her, to bring her out of the numbness that had enveloped her ever since that day of the memorial service when Captain Coin Forsyth's soul had been offered up to God for safekeeping.

The slight breeze through the open window grazed Allison's face. She felt its cooling touch upon her flushed cheeks. But then the soft sweet music of a bird began, bringing back memories. "Hush, little baby . . . "

Quickly, Allison pulled down the window, shutting out the sound and the grief from her heart.

That evening, when the shadows had spread over the meadows and invaded the house, Allison lit the candles on the dining room table. She had seen to it that the silver candelabra, ornate with the trappings of some English silversmith, was squarely in the middle of the table. She had done as Rad Meadors had ordered and now the two places were set, far apart, one at each end of the long, polished table.

She stood in front of the fireplace, which was filled with the scent of fresh green leaves. Even Rebecca seemed to be in league with the man, for when Allison had walked into the kitchen, she had been shooed out with a sharp scolding.

"*I'll* serve the dinner tonight, Miss Allison. Just like I used to at Rose Mallow. And I don't need your help. You go on into the dining room. I'll be there in a minute."

Now, she stood, waiting for the major to appear and feeling sorry for herself. She had been banished from the kitchen, from the cameraderie between Flood and Rebecca. But she certainly didn't feel at ease at the same table with Major Rad Meadors.

"Good evening, Allison."

"Good evening, Major."

He started to correct her and then thought better of it. "Are you ready to be seated?"

"Yes."

He walked to the end of the table and held the chair for her as if she were some honored guest. "Thank you."

Rebecca chose that moment to come in with the large tray of food. Allison noticed that the woman had raided the pantry of some of the delicacies they had put up in Mason jars the previous summer, when the threat of winter was uppermost in their minds. Once Rad had been served, Allison took little. Frugality had become a way of life to her.

Rebecca said nothing about the small helping. She was too busy examining Allison's appearance. She was gratified that her hair was in place and her dull gray dress with white collar flattering to her trim figure. Even her burned complexion, framed in the soft glow of light, was barely noticeable. There were only two things wrong. One, Rebecca knew she could fix. The other would have to be left up to the major.

Before Rebecca departed to the kitchen, she pushed the candelabra aside so that the view from one place to the other at the end of the table was unobstructed.

Allison glared at Rebecca, but it did no good. Only Rad seemed to notice her silent protest.

"There's no need for you to be aggravated with Rebecca, Allison. If she hadn't seen fit to move the candles, I would have done so myself."

Allison made no comment. Keeping her silence, she picked up her fork and began to eat slowly.

"This won't work, you know."

She gazed up in surprise.

"You think you're going to freeze me out by your silence so that I'll banish you back to the kitchen."

Allison smiled in spite of herself. "Is it that obvious?"

"Yes. Something I might expect of Morrow, but certainly not her mother."

His comment made her ashamed. "I'm sorry. But somehow I can't . . . I just can't . . . "

"I understand, Allison, how difficult it is for you to sit at the same table with a Yankee, especially after what has happened in your life. But if two intelligent adults cannot sort things out and make some effort toward reconciliation and understanding, then there's no hope for the nation. We will always be divided."

"We were divided long before the war began, Major. And

it will take more than a few platitudes for the breach to be healed. If it ever is . . . "

Rad smiled. "I have no wish to solve the nation's ills tonight, Allison. I'm only asking for a truce for the next several months."

"Yes, of course. Once the tobacco is harvested . . . "

"What are your plans when you leave here?"

"I'll take Morrow and go back to Savannah, to Cypress Manor. That is, if it's still standing."

"You have no desire to return to Roswell?"

"No. I have no relatives there. Only sad memories."

Rad nodded. "Tell me about your childhood in Savannah."

Allison hesitated. She knew that he was just making conversation to pass the time at the table. She put her animosity behind her and responded as she would have if she had been dining with a friend instead of an enemy.

"It was quite ordinary. We were a small family—just my brother, Jonathan, my parents, and me. My mother died when I was ten years old, and once my brother had left to study under the Reverend Pratt, my father began to tutor me himself. We spent many long hours together discussing philosophy and reading the classics. . . . " A faraway look enveloped her as the candles flickered and burned. She was traveling where Rad could not follow—deep into the past. Suddenly, the hiss of tallow melting brought her back with a start.

"And you? What about your childhood?"

"Quite ordinary, also. My own mother died in childbirth with another son. Glenn was eight and I was twelve. My father never got over the loss." His eyes narrowed. "There's something about you that reminds me of her."

"It's the dress, if you remember."

"I must confess that I was quite irate when I first recognized it. But no. There's something else about you—your blond hair, perhaps . . ."

"You don't look at all like your brother."

"No. Nor my father, either. I used to wonder if he hadn't found me somewhere and brought me home—a waif by the side of the road. And then I found a picture of an uncle who went out to California. And I stared at my own image. It was quite a relief, I assure you, to one small boy to find someone in the family he resembled."

Rebecca stood in the shadows and listened unashamedly to the conversation. She counted on her fingers the number of weeks before the tobacco crop would be harvested. And she prayed that it would be long enough.

CHAPTER
35

September's fire spread over the land, with the leaves of trees bleeding red. The golden tobacco leaves hanging in the log barns were seared by the same heat that fanned through the apple orchards, changing colors from green to gold and then to scarlet. And on the distant horizon, the sun, like a burning-red ember, scorched the earth with its heat.

In the corner bedroom of the redbrick Kentucky plantation house, no breeze stirred as Allison sewed the dress that she had cut out long ago for Flood.

Their work on the land was finally finished. At that moment, Rad and Big Caesar were loading the cured tobacco onto the wagon to take to the auction barn. In another day or so, the women would be paid from the proceeds and then they could be on their way.

While Allison sewed, Morrow played in the annex, content to use the remnants of material that Allison had given her to dress her rag doll. And while she played, she jabbered and sang, causing Allison to smile as she listened.

At the knock on the open door, Allison looked up. "Come in, Flood. I'm almost finished."

The large, heavy-set woman, still dressed in trousers and shirt, walked inside. She looked at the table where a shabby valise from the attic sat open, waiting for Allison to finish packing her own clothes.

"Well, it won't be long now," the woman commented.

"No, it won't. In another day or so. But I never thought the time would ever come. I suppose the children of Israel felt this way, too, leaving Egypt."

"Let's just hope we won't have to wander around in the wilderness for forty years like *they* did, before gettin' home," Flood said.

"It shouldn't take us more than a week to ten days," Allison said. Then she laughed. "I never thought I'd ever look forward to riding on a train again."

"But it will be different this time. We can get off and break the trip whenever we want."

"And order hot food at the railroad hotels, too. No more foraging in the woods for berries or nuts."

Allison snipped the last thread from the hem and turned the dress right-side out. "Well, now, this is the moment of truth. Let's see if it fits you, Flood."

The woman took the dress into the annex. "Run along to your mother, Morrow. Flood has to change clothes."

The child picked up the scraps from the floor, packed them in a small case, and, with the doll in her arms, walked into the bedroom. A child's wicker rocking chair sat under one of the windows. Morrow dropped the case, climbed into the chair, and began to rock her doll to sleep.

Before Flood had time to put on the dress for Allison's inspection, Rebecca walked up the stairs and called out, "Mr. Freemont's in the parlor, Miss Allison. Said he needs to see you right away."

"Serve him something cool to drink, Rebecca. And tell him I'll be downstairs in a few minutes."

Royal Freemont felt awkward. He was dressed in his Sunday summer suit, even though it was the middle of the week. He laid his straw hat on the settee beside him.

He would just as soon be having a tooth yanked out by the local barber than to be where he was at that moment. But he had made up his mind. And there was nothing to do but speak his piece.

He was sorry now that he hadn't taken the mint julep Rebecca had offered him, since he was thirsty. But he didn't want to run the risk of spoiling things with Allison—in case she disapproved of drinking spirits while the sun was still high in the sky.

Royal's fresh paper collar was already sticking to his neck in the heat. But he didn't dare touch it, for fear that it might fall apart with the least bit of tugging.

He never thought he would ever want a woman again. His wife, Lily Mae, had been a nagger, and frankly, rest her soul, he'd had more peace with her gone than at any time when they were married.

He guessed it was the cow that did it—the Forsyth woman calling his bluff about Daisy Belle. And when Big Caesar gave her one of his prize cows, that sort of clinched it. Whether it was an animal or a human being, Big Caesar could always tell good bloodlines.

"Good afternoon, Mr. Freemont."

The man jumped up from the settee with such force that his hat fell to the floor. "Miss Allison," he said, trying to ignore the hat sprawled at his feet.

She didn't seem to notice as he bent to pick it up. She sat down in the blue slipper chair. With those wide, serious eyes that resembled the purple haze on a soft spring morning, she looked at him and said, "The suit fits you well, Mr. Freemont. I hope you're pleased with it."

"That I am, Miss Allison. And with the quilt, too. You're a fine seamstress."

He cleared his throat as he took his place again on the settee. "You may wonder why I'm here today, Miss Allison. Well, I tell you, I like what you do so much that I've come with another request."

Before he could continue, Allison said, "That's very kind of you, Mr. Freemont. But if it's something that will take awhile, I won't be able to help. You see, I'll be leaving here within the next day or so."

The sound of a wagon coming down the long drive forced Royal to forget his carefully rehearsed speech. Instead he blurted out, "That's exactly why I'm here, Miss Allison. Seeings you're a widow woman with a small child, your future don't look too bright. So I'm offering to marry you— to give you and Morrow a home. My house needs a woman's touch, too," he added.

Royal looked at the carefully arranged bouquet on the tea table in front of the fireplace. "My house ain't had fresh flowers in it since Lily Mae died."

Allison attempted to disguise her surprise, but she was not successful. "I'm sorry, Mr. Freemont. I had no idea . . ."

When he saw Rad Meadors coming up the steps, he

stood. "No need to say anything now, Miss Allison. Think it over. And I'll come back tomorrow for your answer." He grabbed his hat. "I'll see my own way out," he said, and disappeared into the hallway.

A bemused Allison was still seated in the slipper chair as the doors opened and closed. A brief conversation between the two men was soon replaced by the sound of Royal Freemont's carriage headed back down the drive.

"What was that all about?" a curious Rad inquired, standing in the doorway of the parlor. "Royal acted as if he couldn't get away fast enough. Did I interrupt anything?"

Allison had a difficult time trying to remain serious. Rad was Royal Freemont's friend, and she was determined not to say anything to cause embarrassment, especially after Royal had been so kind to them through the winter and spring.

"As a matter of fact, you did—Mr. Freemont's marriage proposal."

Allison sailed past Rad and out of the room, then walked up the winding stairs to her room, where Flood was keeping watch over Morrow.

"Well, did the dress fit all right, Flood?"

"Oh, yes. It's a fine dress, too. Only I'm so used to wearin' trousers . . . "

"But those days are over now. You'll get used to being in dresses again.

"Maybe."

That evening at dinner, Rad was unusually quiet.

"Did you get a good price for the tobacco?" Allison finally inquired, to break the silence.

"The auction isn't until tomorrow." He frowned, and

Allison made no further attempt to make conversation since he seemed to prefer the silence.

There had been no need to light the candles, for the sun was late in setting. But now the shadows invaded the room. And although Rad didn't seem to want to talk, he appeared to be in no hurry to leave the table. Allison tried not to show her impatience, even though the meal was over.

Finally, Rad stood. "That was an excellent meal, Allison."

"I'm sure Rebecca will be delighted to hear that you enjoyed it."

He left the dining room, and a few minutes later, as Allison took the dishes to the kitchen, she heard a horse gallop down the drive.

In the kitchen, while Allison and Rebecca put up the clean dishes, Rebecca said, "So what are you goin' to do, Miss Allison? You goin' to marry that Mr. Freemont?"

"No, Rebecca. You know I'm not. I don't love him. But I wish I did. It would make things so much easier for Morrow and me."

"And when did *you* ever take the easy way out?"

Allison laughed. "I presume, then, that you think I should tell him no when he comes back for his answer tomorrow?"

"Not any of my business. It's up to you."

Again Allison laughed. She could read Rebecca so well. There was no need to ask her what she thought. Her mouth, the way she held her head and stood with her arms crossed, gave her away every time. "Still, I hate to hurt his feelings."

At her words, a satisfied Rebecca turned her back to put up the kneading board. She gave a sigh of relief at Allison's intentions. But she was uneasy, too. She would have thought the major would have said something to Allison before now. Especially with just two days left. But Rebecca had done all she could. It was now up to the major.

The two left the kitchen and made their way up the stairs. "Did the major say where he was goin' tonight?" Rebecca asked, pausing at the landing where the two usually parted company.

"No, he didn't. But then I'm not surprised. And it really isn't any of our business, Rebecca."

"Good night, Miss Allison."

"Good night, Rebecca. I'll see you early in the morning."

Allison went to bed, but she was restless. Morrow was restless, too, waking off and on and finally asking for a drink of water. As Allison climbed out of bed and walked into the annex to pour water from the pitcher, she saw Rad's horse from the window. A few minutes later, the sound of the man's footsteps up the winding staircase indicated that Rad had already put the horse in the barn and come inside the house. Not really realizing that she had been staying awake and listening for his return, Allison relaxed and went to sleep.

The next day passed slowly, with the major away at the auction. All afternoon, Allison kept busy, dreading her encounter with Royal Freemont. But it was Rad who finally returned, while there had been no sign of his neighbor.

When the two sat down to dinner that evening, Royal still had not appeared. To Allison, that was a puzzling thing. Just as Rad's behavior for the past two days had been puzzling. During the meal, Rad took no interest in casual conversation. In silence, he stared at Allison as if she were a total stranger and not the woman who had sat at his table these past few months and seen to the running of his house.

Finally, he got up. "Twenty minutes from now, I'd like

to see you with Flood and Rebecca in my office." He didn't wait for a response from Allison, and she offered none.

"Look's like the time has come," Flood said. "And I can't say I'm sorry."

"I'll be happy to leave here, too," Allison agreed. With Morrow beside her, she allowed Flood and Rebecca to go ahead of her. By the time she appeared in the doorway, Rad Meadors had already begun to talk.

"I want to thank you for all the work you did here on Bluegrass Meadors. Without you, I doubt that it would still be standing or that we would even have a crop of tobacco to sell this year. Here are the envelopes with your pay. I hope the money will see you through the next few months until you can get home and find other work."

Rad gave the first envelope to Flood. "Thank you, Flood," he said. "You did more than your share of the work load." Then he turned to Rebecca. "The same goes for you, Rebecca. I'll miss your cooking."

"Thank you, Major."

Now it was Allison's turn. With the last envelope in his hand, he walked toward her. She also waited for a thank-you. But it seemed to get caught in his throat as he suddenly thrust the envelope into her hand. "This is your share, Allison."

He looked at her as if he were about to say something else. But then he abruptly turned his back and returned to his desk. "Caesar will take the three of you into Louisville first thing tomorrow morning."

The abrupt dismissal, after all her work, her constant care of the house and the herb garden, canning and preserving—and not even a thank you for all of it—made Allison furious. She picked up Morrow, to leave the room as

quickly as possible, to follow Flood and Rebecca out of the
man's presence.

His voice called her back.

"Yes?"

"Oh, there's one more thing, Allison.

"If you're still looking for Royal Freemont to pay you a
visit, you can forget it. He's not coming."

CHAPTER
36

Once again in the early morning light, the soft haze swept over the meadow, giving an impressionistic view to the distant background of grass and trees and orchards. But in the foreground the features of the landscape were etched in strong, focused lines and curves—the white-graveled drive, the brown and yellow leather carriage, the impatient horse attended to by Big Caesar.

Allison stood on the steps for a moment, drinking in the view like a spectator who knew she would never pass this way again. She was also a part of the picture, dressed as she was in the familiar soft gray calico with the lavender shawl over her arm. Beside her sat the shabby valise that Royal Freemont had given her as a bonus when she'd made the quilt to his liking. And at her side stood an excited Morrow, a small replica of her mother, with identical features and hair and dressed in an identical dress made from an extra panel of material that Allison had removed when she was remaking the dress.

"Go bye-bye," Morrow said, seeing the waiting carriage.

"Yes. Soon," Allison agreed.

Coming down the backstairs, through the kitchen, and into the front hall, Flood walked slowly, carrying a bundle hoisted over her shoulder. For a moment, she stopped. Then she shored up her courage and went out to face Allison. She was wearing the same working trousers and shirt that she'd worn the day before.

When Allison saw her, she said, "Flood, I thought you were going to wear the dress I made you."

Flood had an apologetic look on her face. "It's not that I don't appreciate what you did, Allison. It's a beautiful dress. And it fits me fine. But the truth of the matter is, I just don't feel comfortable in a dress. Guess I got so used to pretendin' to be a man that I hardly want to go back to bein' a woman.

"In fact, I stayed up most of the night thinkin' about what I was goin' to do." Her face grew a little redder, as if she were dreading what was coming next. "Would you be *too* upset, Allison, if I didn't go back south with you and Rebecca?"

"What would you do, Flood? Stay here in Kentucky?"

"No. I think I'd like to go west and stake a claim in the gold-minin' area. I could do that, you know, if I kept on bein' a man. Of if that didn't work out, I could get me a little piece of land and homestead, now that I've got the hang of farmin'."

"You don't want to go back to Roswell?"

"Well, it was like I was tellin' Madrigal one day. I couldn't get my old job back even if they were to rebuild the mill. All the jobs would more'n likely go to the men comin' home from the war. So there's nothin' left for me there."

She looked at Allison as if waiting for approval.

"You have to follow your heart, Flood. And if your heart tells you to head west, then you don't need anybody else to tell you what to do, do you?"

"But I sure would like to go knowin' I had your blessin'."

"You have it, Flood. I assure you." Allison reached over and gave Flood a hug. "Thank you for everything you did. And may the Lord bless you wherever you go."

"Thank you, Allison."

Allison brushed a tear from her eye. Trying to disguise her emotions, she said, "I wonder what's keeping Rebecca?"

"I think she went down to the orchard to pick a few apples for the journey."

"Pony. Want to see pony," Morrow begged.

Flood looked at the impatient child. "If you want to take Morrow for a walk, I'll stay here and wait for Rebecca. We'll put the things in the carriage for you and then call when Caesar is ready to leave."

"I suppose that might be best. Morrow will certainly be penned up for a long time once we start traveling."

Allison left the house and began to walk past the white fence toward the meadow where the colts were romping. The mare that Glenn had left in the livery stable in Louisville was also in the meadow, but Rad's horse was nowhere to be seen. In fact, Rad himself was nowhere in sight. Allison decided she should have been prepared for that. But somehow she wasn't.

It seemed only good manners for the man to wait and see them off. But, of course, they had been no more than hired help to him. It was only friends who saw each other off, bidding each other good-bye and godspeed. Perhaps she should be grateful that he had even thought to arrange transportation to the railway station for them.

Rad stood by the weeping willow that jutted from the creekbank into the water and allowed his horse to drink. He couldn't understand his feelings. Particularly his anger with his friend, Royal. He had no right to be angry with him, just as he'd had no right two nights before to act like a jealous husband and tell Royal to stay away from Allison Forsyth.

Now he had only a few minutes to decide what to do. Big Caesar was waiting for him to return from his ride before leaving for Louisville. He gazed back toward the house. Only a few minutes more and Allison would be out of his life forever—unless he acted fast.

Suddenly, Rad made up his mind. He threw his leg over the saddle and urged Bourbon Red into a gallop. As he rode across the fields, he saw the woman strolling hand in hand with the child. And in a burst of speed he headed straight toward her just as Allison turned around to walk back to the house.

"Allison, wait!" he shouted.

At first, she didn't see him because the sun was in her eyes. "Wait," he shouted again when she continued walking.

This time she saw him, coming toward her with incredible speed. Quickly, she bent down and picked up Morrow to protect her from danger at the rapid approach of the rider.

She looked up at the large, powerful man in the saddle. His magnificent horse snorted, as if breathing fire through his nostrils, while a trail of dust obliterated the landscape. The two stood—a man and a woman, challenging each other, with their destinies suspended like the silken threads of the spider's web in the ancient oak tree, subject to the whim of the wind.

"You can't go, Allison. You know that."

His voice held a quiet strength at odds with the pawing animal digging clumps of earth with his hoofs, while the colt Standing Tall, as if sensing some momentous happening, took off, running parallel to the fence in a burst of energy, his speed proclaiming kinship with his sire, Bourbon Red.

"Stay here with me, Allison," Rad slid from his horse and stood before Allison, towering over her still.

She was silent, forcing him to say the things he had vowed never to say to a woman. "I want you to marry me. I need you, Allison."

"To need someone is not enough."

Allison's voice was sad as she began to walk away.

"No, it isn't," Rad agreed. "But what about love? Would you stay if I told you that I love you?"

Morrow struggled to get down from her mother's arms. Allison hardly noticed as the child wandered toward Rad, pulled up a dandelion, and brought it to him. "Da-da," she said, holding up the flower to him.

He stooped down, took the flower, and picked up the child. "You see, Morrow wants to stay. What do you say, Allison?"

She looked in the direction of the carriage where Rebecca was loading her valise. And she looked again at Morrow, content in the man's arms.

"I'm not sure I'll ever be able to love again—the way a woman should love her husband . . ."

"Nothing will ever be the way it should be, Allison. Ever again. The war has taken care of that. And I suppose I'll always be jealous of your captain and your love for him. But if you decide to stay, I promise to care for you and the child with as much love as he would have shown you if he had returned home from the war."

Flood and Rebecca were already seated in the carriage. Big Caesar, trying not to notice what was going on between Rad and Allison a short distance away, adjusted the reins, got down from the carriage, kicked one of the wheels, then climbed aboard again.

"Well, Allison, which is it to be?"

Her voice was so low that Rad had trouble hearing it. "If you want me to, I'll stay."

Rad, holding his breath until she gave her answer, breathed again. And there was something unfathomable in his serious eyes as he said, "Thank you, Allison. You won't ever regret it, I promise."

"Is it all right if Rebecca stays, too?"

"Of course. We'll need her more than ever now. And Caesar will be particularly glad of that."

With Morrow still in his arms, he took Allison by the hand, and they walked together from the meadow to the waiting carriage in the driveway.

"Rebecca, may I see you for a moment?" Allison asked.

The black woman wasted no time in getting down from the carriage. "What is it, Miss Allison?"

They walked beyond the terrace on the other side of the porch. And when they were nearly out of sight, Allison said, "Major Meadors has asked me to marry him."

Rebecca's white teeth were evident in the broad, satisfied smile. "It was high time. And what did you tell him?"

"I said yes, Rebecca. But that presents another problem."

"Such as?"

"If I don't go to Savannah, then you'll be traveling by

yourself. That is, if you still want to go. But I'd rather have you here with Morrow and me. You have a choice, Rebecca. What do you want to do? Stay here with me or go back to Cypress Manor?"

It took a split second for the woman to decide. "If it's all the same to you, I'll stay and continue workin' for you. I sure don't want to be in Miss Araminta's employ, I can tell you that."

"Then it's settled. We'll need to get our things out of the carriage."

"I'll see to that, Miss Allison."

They left the terrace, and Allison watched as Rebecca approached the carriage. A short distance away, she heard the woman's lilting voice. "Caesar, take the valise and that bundle down from the carriage. Miss Allison and I have decided to stay here at Bluegrass Meadors for good."

"I hear you, Rebecca!" the man said, swinging down from the carriage to do as he was asked.

Still feeling surprised at the turn of events, Allison walked to the carriage where Flood waited. But before she could say anything, Flood beat her to it. "I guess he's finally asked you to marry him. Well, that's exactly what Rebecca and I prayed for all along."

Allison laughed. "I wish you'd told me. Then perhaps I wouldn't have been so surprised."

Allison reached out and took Flood's rough hand. "Be careful, Flood. And if things don't work out, you can always come back to Bluegrass Meadors."

"That's awful kind of you, Allison. But my second sight is workin' hard today. And it tells me we won't ever see each other again. But you'll be happy. I see that much. And I'll find my gold. So don't worry about me."

Allison watched the carriage moving down the long drive-way. She stood with Rad Meadors by her side.

"My mother's wedding dress is in the locked chest in the attic. You'll find the key hanging on the white silk loop behind the door."

"How soon? I mean, when do you wish the ceremony to take place?"

He hesitated. "I don't want to rush you, Allison. But if it isn't quite soon, the neighbors will begin to gossip. I have no wish for them to talk about us."

"Does that mean—"

"Tomorrow, Allison. Or day after tomorrow. But no later."

He wasn't even giving her time to get used to the idea. He walked away, retracing his steps to the meadow where his horse was still saddled. She watched him stride toward the fence, leap over the top rail, and call to Bourbon Red with a whistle.

Allison left the steps and walked inside to find Rebecca. She was in the kitchen, and with Morrow content to remain with her, Allison walked back to the bedroom down the hall from the one occupied by Rad Meadors.

She put off going to the attic as long as she dared. But if she was going to wear the wedding dress, then she would have to see to it right away. With each step up to the attic, she thought of Coin and their wedding day.

She remembered Royal's words from two nights before. A future none too bright. A widow woman with a small child. "Coin, forgive me," she whispered. "I don't know what else to do. I'll always love you, but there's Morrow to think of—and he loves her."

Allison found the key on the silken loop as Rad had said she would. With trembling hands, she walked to the large old trunk under the attic window and unlocked it. "Please, don't let it be lace," she prayed as the trunk lid swung open with a grating creak. "Anything but lace."

Her prayer was unanswered. The ecru lace dress and headpiece rested in layers of rice paper, waiting over the years for some other bride to lay claim to the family heirloom. With tears falling down her cheeks, Allison unwrapped the exquisite dress and held it up to the light, while her mind remembered another wedding day and another groom who had sworn his eternal love.

CHAPTER
37

Coin Forsyth rode into Roswell in the middle of the night. His horse had grown lame, and when he reached the long driveway below Vickery Creek, he got down and led the horse the rest of the way.

He had dreamed of this for months—his reunion with Allison and the baby after such a long, dismal separation. There was so much he wanted to do to make up for being away. He knew Allison must have had a hard time of it, as they all had—the women and children, forced to be self-sufficient while all the men were fighting.

But it was over now—the lost cause, with the specter of slavery somehow overlaying the real reasons behind the conflict—the right to govern oneself, the right to trade without suffering the enormously high tariffs the sectionalists in Washington had imposed upon the South. The war had settled nothing. Now, with Lincoln dead and the radicals in power, there would be even more inequities, more hardships. But whatever befell them, he and Allison would brave it together.

The moon shone down on the few creek pebbles remaining to line the drive. Bits of mica gleamed at intervals to point the way toward the house through the deep woods.

On each side of the road, the trees and shrubs loomed in rampant growth, spilling over onto the driveway and broadcasting a dark, eerie gloom despite the moonlit night.

Soon now, Coin would have his first glimpse of Rose Mallow, and his anticipation caused him to hurry, impatiently tugging at the reins to draw the winded horse along with him.

The September air carried a slight chill as the mist from the river floated and curled in varied patterns, obscuring and then framing his journey homeward. Reaching the small copse of trees, Coin watched for the mist to part enough for him to catch his first glimpse of the house.

He smiled and waited. In great swirls of gray, the fog rolled out, rising higher and higher, sweeping clean the view down the distant stretch of road to the steps of the wisteria-vined porch.

Coin drew in his breath. Nothing was as he remembered it—the boxwoods, the circled drive. Even the shutters hung on their hinges, with the slight breeze causing one of them to knock against a broken windowpane. In the deadly drench of moonbeams, Rose Mallow appeared a ghostly shell of its former beauty. One column lay propped against the porch. He could see that a step was missing, and the magnificent old oak door, once a bastion against intruders, was warped and partially open.

"Allison," he called out, forgetting his intention to knock first so as not to alarm her. "Where are you?"

An owl hooted in the distance at the night's disturbance. "Allison," Coin shouted again, but in his heart he knew that it was useless to call her name. The house was deserted. Allison, his wife, was gone.

"Allison, you're beautiful."

She heard the deep, masculine voice from the hall as she descended the winding stairway. For a moment, she hesitated, for Rad Meadors, dressed in the full military uniform of the enemy, was looking up at her and following her progress. She swallowed, then quickly moved down the last three steps and finally took the arm offered to her.

Allison's lips moved, but no sound came. She wore the ethereal lace gown, with her face half covered by the small veil—with tiny forget-me-nots woven by hand into the pattern—that teased the viewer with only a partial glimpse of the woman's beauty. And in her hands she held the pink roses and white baby's breath that Rad had sent up to her room by Rebecca earlier.

The reality of this day—her wedding day—was shadowed with dreams. She held on to the remembrance of another time, another plantation house, and a sandy-haired boy also waiting for her to appear. But her heart told her that she was marrying a man this time. Not an innocent boy. And perhaps that was what disturbed her most.

There would be no wedding trip immediately, for all money had to be put back into the land and the horses. Rad's only concession to the special day was the wedding cake and punch prepared by Rebecca and waiting to be shared with their two guests, Mr. Falcon, the minister, and his neighbor, Royal Freemont.

By evening, they would be alone. It seemed so callous to eat dinner together the same way they had done for the past several months and then to move immediately into the master bedroom. But Allison had little choice. Rad would never understand that, even though she'd been married before, a woman was shy on her wedding night.

Rebecca sat in the small room off the parlor and held Morrow. She was pleased at the way the parlor looked, with the greenery arranged around the mantelpiece and on the hearth. Big Caesar had outdone himself, combing the woods for the waxleaf magnolias and bringing back enough branches to fill half the room. The candles were lit, too, giving the parlor a festive air.

While the minister stood calmly by the hearth, Royal Freemont sat on the settee and fidgeted, crossing first one leg and then the other. But when Allison appeared in the doorway, Rebecca saw the man become still, with a wistful look on his face.

The minister smiled and motioned for the bridal couple to step forward in front of him. Then the ceremony began.

With the familiar words, Rebecca, too, was caught up in the past, for she had been with Allison on the day she had married the young Coin Forsyth. Six bridesmaids in rustling pink dresses; Miss Araminta, dressed in blue, as the matron of honor; Mr. Jonathan giving her away, since old Mr. Biggs was already bedridden by a stroke. What a full, lively house that had been. Nothing had been able to spoil that beautiful day, despite Miss Araminta.

And Miss Allison had looked so lovely in her traveling costume, leaving with Mr. Coin late that afternoon to board the ship in the harbor for Newport. Rebecca shook her head to clear it and to regain the present. It wouldn't do to let the past come between Miss Allison and her marriage to the major.

" . . . And do you, Rad Meadors, take this woman . . . "

"I do."

" . . . for richer, for poorer, till death do you part?"

The minister stared at Allison and waited for her answer.

As if her mind were a thousand miles away, a startled Allison looked up. The minister nodded in encouragement.

"I do."

The ring was a small gold one, removed from Rad's little finger and placed on Allison's left hand. There was no other to use, for the family heirlooms had been taken by Glenn. And once he had placed his own small ring on her finger, he continued to hold her hand in his.

" . . . I now pronounce you man and wife. Whom God hath joined together, let no mortal put asunder. . . . "

Rad stood and looked down into Allison's eyes, which were veiled by the lace. With a suddenly impatient movement, he drew back the veil to see her face in all its beauty. Again he was the dark one, a stranger standing in the house, magnificent in his strength, with his presence overpowering the room.

He bent down and touched her lips with his own for the first time. It was a dangerously restrained kiss that promised a much fuller exploration later when they were alone. Allison felt the shock like a bolt of lightning splitting a tree and shattering its heart.

Then the minister's voice broke the spell. "Congratulations, Rad. You have a fine bride."

Then it was Royal's turn. He cleared his throat and averted his eyes from Allison. "Be good to this woman, Rad. Or you'll answer to me."

Rad laughed and gripped Royal's hand in friendship. "You mustn't let Allison hear that, Royal. The first argument, and she might flounce out of my house—to yours."

"I think the refreshments are ready," Allison said, overlooking Rad's remark. "Would you care to come into the dining room, Mr. Falcoln? Mr. Freemont?"

Rebecca left Morrow in the kitchen with Big Caesar while she saw to the wedding cake and punch. Allison stood at Rad's side, but the conversation of the three men suddenly switched to horses and tobacco, and the bride was momentarily forgotten.

"You've got a fine-looking colt in the pasture, Rad," Mr. Falcon commented. "Will you be grooming him for the races?"

"Yes. In fact, Caesar and I plan to start training him some time next week."

"I've got a better colt than Rad," Royal bragged. "He's going to give Standing Tall a run for his money a little later on."

Rad laughed. "I always did enjoy a little healthy competition, Royal. It makes winning all the sweeter."

"Yeah. I noticed that, my friend," Royal replied.

"May I propose a toast to the bride and groom," the minister said, holding his punch cup high. "As these two have put away sectional differences and become united in wedlock, may these divided states be reunited into one country."

For Allison, it was a bitter cup, a bitter toast. A frowning Rad, noticing that Allison did not drink, said, "You didn't drink to the reverend's toast. Is there something wrong?"

Allison forced herself to smile. "I don't believe it's protocol for a bride to drink to her own health."

Quickly, she held up her full cup. "But I *will* drink to

all brave men everywhere—including the three in this room."

"Hear! Hear!" The men had no such hesitation as Allison. They drained their refilled punch cups, all the time wishing for something a little stronger.

The two men were not encouraged to stay, once the brief celebration in the dining room was over. As they said their good-byes, Rad turned to Allison. "I'll see both of them down the drive. It won't take long." But Rad walked toward the kitchen, and Allison, the silver tray in her hands, heard him call to Big Caesar, "Get my horse for me, Caesar. I've decided to escort the reverend to Royal's house."

Soon the house held only Allison, Rebecca, and Morrow. "It was a beautiful ceremony, Miss Allison. You and Mr. Rad sure do make a handsome couple."

Allison looked down at the lace wedding dress. "Somehow I don't feel married to him, Rebecca."

Rebecca grinned. "You will, Miss Allison. By tomorrow mornin', you'll feel like a wife again, that's for sure."

"But I'm afraid, Rebecca. I think I've made a dreadful mistake."

"Well, what do you want to do about it? Pack your bag and have Caesar take us to the station?"

"You know I can't do that. I made a promise—a vow."

"Then, if you won't leave, I guess you'll just have to keep that vow."

The two looked at each other, and Allison knew that Rebecca was right. She couldn't run away from Rad Meadors. He would find her and bring her back.

"I think I'll go upstairs and change clothes."

"Then I'll help you." With Morrow between the two women, they walked slowly up the wide stairway.

An hour later, with the wedding dinner waiting on the

dining room table, Rad had still not come home. A furious Allison, looking at Rebecca, said, "I'm not waiting any longer." She got up from the table. "I'm going for a walk. Will you please put Morrow to bed for me?"

"Of course. The major asked me to, anyway."

"I don't even believe the major is planning to come home tonight," Allison complained. "So I might as well sleep in the same room with Morrow."

Allison left the house by the front door. A few raindrops fell onto the leaves of the surrounding trees. At the sound, Allison looked up, but she saw only a small cluster of clouds to the east. Nothing to get excited about or to cause her to turn around and go back inside the house. She had braved a few raindrops before. And it was not as if she were wearing the lace dress that had once belonged to Rad's mother.

Allison crossed the meadow and began the trek along the creekbank. In front of her, the sky was relatively clear. But behind her, clouds began to gather in dark, swirling funnels. She continued walking until she reached the creek, where she sat down on the grass and peered into the green water.

For some time, Allison was content to sit, feeling nothing but the wind on her face. Then it changed from a gentle zephyr to a more insistent breeze, slapping against the hem of her gray dress and lifting the old willow tree's branches like a broom to sweep back and forth across the rippling water. Suddenly, it was dark.

With her mind on other things besides the weather, Allison finally became aware of the change when the first crack of thunder sounded, bringing with it a jagged streak of lightning on the other side of the creek.

Startled, she stood and turned in the direction of the house. She saw the dark clouds swirling, the solid sheet of rain in the distance bearing down upon her, threatening to catch her in its fierce lashing. And behind her, the sound of thunder grew increasingly louder.

She was caught with no shelter from the storm. She had not meant to walk all the way to the creek, had not meant to stay out this long. What if Rad returned and she wasn't in the house? Would he think she'd run away from him? Perhaps she had, in her own way.

Allison gathered up her skirts and began to run just as Rad urged his horse over the fence and headed toward the creek. "Allison, where are you?"

All around her, the telltale smell of sulphur permeated the air, the bolts bursting upward through the sky and down to the meadow at the same time like a sleight-of-hand trick, with the human eye unable to tell where the flame started and where it stopped.

In one great burst of light, the horse and rider appeared directly in her path. Unable to get out of the way, she stopped, helpless, as the horse, equally startled at her appearance, suddenly reared.

Allison closed her eyes and waited for the hooves to hit her. But instead, strong arms gathered her up and she was in the saddle with Rad. Behind her, a tree split, the noise of a great limb hitting the ground. But she didn't look back.

The great horse seemed to have no difficulty, even with a double load. He jumped the fence and continued going, straight to the steps of the plantation house.

The front door was wide open, revealing the candlelight that flickered and threatened to be snuffed out with each sweep of the wind through the front hall.

"Rad?"

The man was like a demon possessed. He rode the horse inside the house, through the hall and up the wide stairway toward the second floor. With the ring of a horseshoe against one of the treads, Allison remembered the earlier indentation. Now it was no secret how it had gotten there. Rad Meadors, in a dark temper, must have done it.

Like one looking on and not believing what was actually happening, Allison felt herself slide from the saddle. But a split second after Rad slapped the horse on the flank to get rid of him, he returned his attention to Allison.

He lifted her in his arms and said, "So you were running away from me, were you?"

She didn't deny it. Instead, she said, "Rad, put me down."

He ignored her demand. "No wife of mine runs away on our wedding night."

He leaned over and kissed her wet, parted lips—not in the same gentle manner of the afternoon wedding ceremony, but with all the force of a man who had waited much too long to claim what was rightfully his.

As Rad slammed the door to the master bedroom, a grinning Caesar stopped the horse as the animal bolted onto the porch. Then he led him to the stables.

The white gown draped over the master bed was brushed to the floor by impatient hands. And the wet gray dress clinging to Allison found the same fate.

Outside, the storm continued, with bursts of lightning outlining the man and the woman in each other's arms.

That night, anger was replaced by tenderness, lust with love, as Rad Meadors taught Allison the pleasures of the body, bringing her to ecstasy and beyond.

CHAPTER
38

Pheenie Peters sat in a rocking chair on the porch of the Roswell commissary store and slowly chewed his tobacco. He nodded as he listened to Coin Forsyth. At one point, he got up, walked to the edge of the porch, and spat. Then he took his place again with the other three men.

"Bedford's sister, Ellie, was in the group shipped north," he said, pointing to the man in the farthest chair. "He tried to find out what happened to her, but never did."

Coin looked in Bedford's direction. "Did you contact the war department?"

"I went as far as Marietta, where she was put on a train, but a man there said it wasn't no use tryin' to find her. They took her across the Ohio River. I thought once of goin' along the train tracks up Nashville way and askin', but then Martha, my wife, said it would be a waste of time. If Ellie wants to come home, she will."

"If she has enough money for the fare," Coin added.

"You plannin' to go after Miss Allison and the baby, Captain?"

Coin looked again at Pheenie. "Yes. There's a carpet-bagger who wants to restore Rose Mallow, so I'm selling it to him. I don't want to do it, but there's no other way I can raise enough money for the trip."

"When do you leave, Captain?"

"Next week, after the sale of the house."

One of the other men said, "Well, if you ever find out what happened to Alma Brady, let me know. Me and Henry, her husband, were good friends, and when he was killed at Snake Creek Gap, I sorta made a promise to 'im to look after her."

Coin Forsyth left the porch of the commissary and began to walk home. It was a foolhardy trip, he knew, starting out when he had no idea where he was going. But he could follow the tracks; talk with people in Nashville and Louisville; go to the newspapers, and consult the official war records. Even then, Allison could have left the train at any point, and he would have no way of knowing. But he had to go. He knew he would never rest until he discovered what had happened to his wife.

In one week's time, Coin Forsyth boarded the train in Marietta to begin the long search for Allison, Morrow, and Rebecca.

At Bluegrass Meadors, Allison settled down to being the mistress of the large plantation house. The families who had worked for Rad in the past returned, one by one. Soon, the small houses were filled and the crops were growing—cotton, tobacco, corn, and other vegetables. Rad threw himself into the work as if by laboring harder than his own help, he could erase the ravages of war and bring prosperity to the area that was still divided by old animosities.

Once his uniform had been relegated to the trunk in the attic along with the family wedding dress that Allison had worn, Rad never spoke of the war to her.

And when he hired an overseer to live in the new cottage built closer to the creek, he and Big Caesar were able to spend more time with the horses, racing them along the sandy track behind the paddocks and clocking Standing Tall, faster than any of the others.

Winter passed, with layers of snow covering the meadows. Then spring came. The apple trees bloomed, the burley tobacco seed was sown in cold frames for the new season, and Allison waited for June and the birth of her child.

One evening, during the last part of June, Rad and Allison sat at the dinner table and listened to the storm outside. With rumblings of thunder in the distance answering the sudden flashes of lightning, Rad smiled and looked at his wife.

"Do you remember our wedding night, Allison? It was the same sort of storm as tonight."

Allison laughed. "How can I ever forget? Probably no civilized bride in history was ever taken up to her wedding chamber on horseback."

"My mother was," Rad answered.

"Do you mean your father . . . "

"How else do you think that first hoofprint was embedded in the wooden staircase?"

"I didn't know. I thought perhaps *you* were the one who

made a habit of riding your horse down the hall and up the steps."

With the glow of candles lighting Rad's face and softening the sharp angles, the man lowered his voice so that Rebecca, going back and forth to the kitchen, would not hear. "One day, our own son will look at the second hoofprint and realize the passion of that night when *he* was conceived."

"Were you . . . I mean, did your father . . . "

"I was born nine months later, so I must have been conceived on my parents' wedding night, too." Rad smiled again. "If you were hoping for another blond-haired child like Morrow, I'm afraid you're going to be disappointed. I have a feeling that this child will be his father's son."

Seeing the briefest frown flicker on Allison's face, Rad said, "What's the matter? Is it not to your liking that a son might resemble his father?"

For a moment, Allison didn't answer. She set her fork down and gripped the table. Then, breathing easier, she said, "Have you thought that the baby might be a girl?"

"The next one, perhaps. This one will be a boy."

Allison did not reply. She watched Rad as he finished his meal. When he had drained his glass and placed his napkin on the table, he looked up again. "Is anything wrong, Allison? You've hardly eaten anything at all tonight."

"I'd like to go to our room now, Rad."

"Allison." Rad immediately stood up and came to her. "Have the pains started?"

"Yes, Rad."

"For how long?"

"For the past several hours."

"Rebecca," Rad shouted. "Leave what you're doing. Your mistress needs you right away."

Allison was gathered up into Rad's arms, but she protested, "I can still walk, Rad."

"No. I'll carry you up the stairs. Rebecca," he shouted again, and hurried from the dining room.

Not far from Louisville, at the Asylum for the Insane, Coin Forsyth waited impatiently in the anteroom of the director. His heart was heavy with grief. He had traveled for nine months, checking every lead, every trail that might take him to Allison.

On the day he'd found Marcus Stagg, he had almost challenged him to a duel. But it wouldn't do to kill a man who was already under a death sentence.

Realizing that he was going to meet his maker sooner than he wished, a poor Marcus, wrapped in blankets to ward off the trembling chill, seemed intent on confessing to anyone who would listen every sin he'd ever committed or thought about.

"Yes, I remember the woman well, Captain Forsyth. She was beautiful, with those large lavender eyes, that beautiful moonbeam hair. I was going to take her, too, that day. Not for the mill, but for my personal use. But then I saw she was sick—and had a sick baby. So she stayed on the train."

The man, sitting propped up in the chair of the seedy rooming-house room, developed a fit of coughing. A scarlet stain seeped onto his handkerchief, and he was unaware when Coin quietly closed the door.

Coin's conversation with Stagg outside of Nashville had been over three months ago. Now, as he waited for Dr. Woodwoth, he was desolate. What heartbreak to find Allison at last in a place where the people were chained like animals, with no hope of ever seeing the outside world again.

Coin looked up as the door opened, revealing a stout, gray-bearded man in a white coat.

"Mr. Forsyth?"

"Yes?"

"My assistant told me you were waiting to see me about one of the patients here, Allison Forsyth."

"My wife."

The man's rheumy voice sounded sad. "I'm not sure if you should see her in her present state. She's a pitiful sight, but I guess in the circumstances she has a right to be."

"I'd like to see her, Doctor."

"Well, if you insist. But only from a distance. You realize, of course, that you will not be allowed to take her out of the asylum."

"Not even if I vow to care for her myself?"

"Not even then."

Coin followed the man, walking along the cloistered outside porch to a dingy stone building where the door was locked and chained. The director took a key, opened it, allowed Coin to follow him inside, and then relocked it.

A babble of voices rose in the air, with a wail resembling an animal. Then a man's voice cried out, "Repent! Repent! Armageddon is at hand!"

They went through another door, with a burly attendant unlocking it and keeping guard. "She's in the small room before you, Mr. Forsyth. You may look inside for a moment, but I won't open the door. She tried to kill one of the guards just last week, so we're keeping her in isolation for the moment."

The woman sat in the corner of the padded room. Her body rocked back and forth, with her long, dull hair hanging over her face and obscuring her features. In her arms

355

she held two rag dolls. "Hush, little baby, don't you cry. Mama's gonna sing you a lullaby."

"She lost both her children," Dr. Woodwoth whispered. "But she's content with the dolls now."

"No, Morrow! You mustn't eat Lovey Lou's porridge. Mama will give you some, too, when your turn comes."

At the name Morrow, Coin turned from the small window, his grief welling up in his throat. It was too unbearable to see her like this. His beautiful Allison was gone—replaced by a hag crooning to her rag children.

"Where did you find her?"

"Wandering by the train tracks."

Coin nodded. "I think I've seen enough. I'm ready to go."

But there was something that worried Coin. The mention of two children. At the last moment, Coin turned around and walked back to the window. The woman's hair was now pushed away from her face, and her eyes met his as he gazed into the opening.

"Henry? Is that you, Henry?"

Her eyes were not the color of amethysts; her hair, streaked with gray, still had dark patches. "Doctor, that's not my wife," Coin said. "It's someone else."

"It's been a long time, Mr. Forsyth, since you've seen her. People change, especially in a place like this."

"But the color of eyes remains the same. That's not my wife," he reiterated.

The doctor peered through the small opening. "Woman, what's your name?" he called out.

The woman looked at the two faces staring at her. "Allison Forsyth," she said, and burst into hysterical laughter. Then her face became sad. She went back to the corner, sat down, and began rocking back and forth. "Hush, little baby, don't you cry. Mama's gonna sing you a lullaby."

The faces at the window were forgotten as Alma Brady returned to her world of fantasy, which she inhabited with her two rag children.

At Bluegrass Meadors, Rad paced up and down in the hallway. He had been up the entire night and now the dawn was beginning to edge its way over the hills. The rain had stopped some time during the night, but Rad was hardly aware of it, for he had been listening for another sound— a baby's cry.

When it came, Rad gripped the arms of the straight chair and tears came to his eyes. He wanted to rush into the room, to tell Allison how much he loved her—that he really didn't care whether the child was a boy or a girl. *She* was the one who mattered to him.

He stood outside the closed door and waited for what seemed an eternity. But it was a mere twenty minutes later when Rebecca finally opened the door. She smiled and said, "You can come in now, Mr. Rad."

He walked slowly, carefully toward the bed where his wife lay. "Allison?"

Her large amethyst eyes held joy mixed with pain as she looked up at him. "You were right, Rad. We have a son. Would you like to see him?"

"In a moment. I just want to be with you for a while, darling. I didn't think I could stand it, being separated from you for so long . . . not knowing . . . "

He stood by the bed, his hand reaching out to touch her. And Allison, seeing him like this, wondered why she had ever been afraid of him. How could she ever have thought of him as some dark, sinister stranger? He was her dear husband and a kind father to Morrow. For the past nine months, he'd treated the child as if she were his own. But Allison was glad that she had been able to give him flesh of his own flesh and blood of his own blood.

"Rebecca, will you please bring the baby to me? It's time his father saw him."

The black woman rose from the chair beside the cradle and brought the tiny bundle to the canopied bed. Allison smiled up at Rad and pushed back the blanket to reveal the face of the baby.

"He's your son, Rad, as you can see. You were even right about his coloring, too."

Rad looked from the fair-haired woman to the dark-haired baby. Tenderly, he took the child in his arms, but his eyes soon returned to Allison. "Darling, thank you," he whispered. And his entire being proclaimed his vast love for his wife.

That same evening, Coin Forsyth arrived in the town of Louisville, which was less than twenty miles from Bluegrass Meadors.

CHAPTER
39

In the small mining town of Nugget Canyon, Madrigal O'-Laney awoke with a frown. It was already dark and from the clatter coming from the saloon downstairs, she knew the miners were getting impatient for her to make an appearance.

"You better get your backside out of that bed, Madrigal. Mr. Sudderth said he wasn't payin' for you to sleep all afternoon—alone, that is."

"But I'm not feelin' well, Sally Jean. How am I gonna sing and dance when my head's 'bout to split?"

"Drink this cuppa coffee. Sadie put a little rum in it for you. Says there's nothin' to perk you up any more'n a little hot drink."

"Then *you* drink it, Sally Jean. I don't want to be perked up."

Sally Jean sat down on the bed. "What's the *real* reason you don't want to go downstairs tonight, Madrigal? Is it that Wolf Perkin again?"

Madrigal's eyes blazed with anger. "He nearly ruined my life two years ago. And I'm sure not givin' him the time of day. I don't care how much he spends in the saloon. I'm not sittin' with him, and I'm not bringin' him upstairs. Ever."

Sally Jean was sympathetic. Now old and plump, with faded red hair, she watched over Mr. Sudderth's girls like a mother hen. Madrigal was her favorite, though. Maybe it was because the girl reminded her of herself years before, when her hair was still burnished copper and her skin was smooth and white.

"Here, baby. Drink your coffee and then I'll lace up your corset for you."

Soon there was a knock on the door. "Madrigal," a voice called out. "Mr. Sudderth says he ain't waitin' any longer. The piano player's playin' his last tune before you come onstage."

"Tell him to hold his horses," Sally Jean yelled. "She'll be down soon as I get her ready."

The plump woman turned to Madrigal and, in a much softer voice, said, "Now don't sashay your bustle too much. Else you'll have all those miners up onstage with you."

"I'll remember."

Downstairs, the saloon was filled with cigar smoke that swirled upward toward the gaslights, barely reflected in the large glass mirror hanging over the bar. The rowdy miners were already getting drunk, for it was Saturday—the one day out of the week that they put up their shovels and mining pans and came into town with their gold dust for the assayer's office. The rich veins along the canyon had almost run out. Soon they would all have to go farther west, and then Nugget Canyon, like so many others, would become just another ghost town.

But tonight all cares were forgotten. The men crowded into the saloon, taking up the places at the bar and the gaming tables, to await the entertainment and to get drunker.

Seated at one of the tables at the back was Coin Forsyth, who had arrived in town only an hour and a half earlier on one of the mule-drawn mail-carrying stages called "the jackass mail."

His search for Allison had reached a stalemate in Louisville. The prison where the Roswell women had been kept had burned to the ground and all records of the women had been lost in the fire, too. If it had not been for a chance conversation with a former guard at the prison, Coin might have given up. But the guard had provided him with a new lead, bringing him west to look for the man who might have taken Allison out of the prison.

"Glenn Meadors pretended to be someone else, but I knew better," the former guard had confided to Coin. "He was a Confederate captain, not a good thing to be in Louisville at that time. Coulda been hanged if he'd been caught. But I remember the four women he signed out of the prison and one fit the description of your wife, if I recollect rightly."

"Where can I find this Glenn Meadors? Does he live near here?"

"Used to. But he pulled up stakes and went west. Said he wasn't ever comin' back."

Now, Glenn Meadors's trail had grown cold, but Coin

had finally located one of the four women, Madrigal O'-Laney. He was impatient to talk with her, but the owner of the Gold Nugget Saloon told him he'd have to pay his money and wait until after the evening show. Without blinking, he had pulled out his last roll of bills, which assured him of being alone with the woman.

After waiting all these months for some news of Allison and the baby, Coin was able to disguise his impatience for a short time longer. But the other men in the saloon were not so prone. They began to slap their hands against the tables and to call Madrigal's name. "We want Madrigal," they shouted, and nothing would appease them but for her to appear.

Jebadiah Calcott, the old-timer seated beside Coin at the far table, laughed and leaned toward the newcomer. "She'll be onstage soon—a right cute little gal, singin' and dancin'. Old Sally Jean taught her all of her songs. Good thing, too. Sally Jean's got so fat, you'd have to hoist her with a pulley to get her up those steps."

The music began; the green-tasseled draperies opened, and Coin saw a saucy, young redheaded woman prance onto the rustic stage. Draped over the bar, Wolf Perkin also watched Madrigal. He was determined to have her that night. She'd been avoiding him, but she wouldn't be able to anymore.

Onstage, Madrigal smiled, blew a kiss to the audience, and, with a swish of her green boa dyed to match the fancy green dress, began to belt out the lyrics of her opening song. "Mable loves sable; Erma loves ermine; Goldie loves golden charms. But all I ever wanted to be wrapped in, was my man's arms . . . "

It was not so much the lyrics but the motions she went

through that brought down the house and caused the men to dream of being that man.

The show went on, with the men getting rowdier and drunker and the songs becoming more risqué. Yet Madrigal, outwardly gay and calm, glanced uneasily toward the bar where Wolf Perkin leered at her.

Then the curtain finally came down and she rushed behind the stage.

"Hold on, Madrigal. Where do you think you're goin'?"

"I got a terrible headache, Mr. Sudderth. I'm goin' back to bed."

"Not yet, you don't, girl. I hired you to mingle with the customers. So get on out to the front. There's a man that's paid a lotta money for you to sit at the table with him. . . . "

"If it's somebody named Wolf Perkin, I quit. Here and now. You can have your old costume back . . . "

"It ain't Wolf," he assured her. "So don't get so het-up."

Warily, she glared at him. "Who is it?"

"Some new fella by the name of Forsyth. Now be a good girl and go on out, Madrigal."

"If I was goin' to be a *good* girl, Mr. Sudderth, I wouldn't be workin' for *you*."

She looked up and saw Wolf walking toward her. Quickly, she said, "Where did you say the man is?"

"I'll take you to him."

Madrigal followed the owner, but Wolf stopped them. "Madrigal, you're to spend the rest of the evening with me."

She looked from Sudderth to the intimidating man towering over her. Her voice was smooth and sugary. "I'm so sorry, Wolf. But Mr. Sudderth here tells me I have a better client. Maybe I'll be free another night."

Wolf pulled out a bag of gold dust. "Here, Sudderth. I'm

buying Madrigal for tonight. Let the other man have someone else."

"Can't do that, Perkin. I've already taken the man's
money."

"Well, give it back to him."

"That's not the way I do business, Perkin. Just hold on
to your money and come back another night."

Sudderth shoved Madrigal past the angry man, and as
she appeared on the main floor of the saloon, the men began
to whistle.

"Which one is he?" Madrigal asked, scanning the room
through the dense smoke.

"The sandy-haired man standing up at the far table."

She stared at him for a moment as the smoke cleared
enough for her to get a better view. "Why, he looks exactly
like Allison's husband, Captain Forsyth, from Roswell,
Georgia. But he's supposed to be dead."

"A lot of dead men come west," Sudderth said in a dry
tone. "Easier that way."

"No, you don't understand—"

"Hey, Sudderth, who's the high bidder tonight?" a voice
called out.

"I am," Wolf Perkin said, directly behind them. He
threw his bag of gold at Sudderth's feet.

The owner ignored Wolf and nodded toward one of his
bouncers. He wanted no brawls tonight, especially with
Wolf Perkin involved. The man was in an ugly enough
mood to ruin his entire Saturday night take.

Sudderth walked to the table where Coin was waiting.
"Mr. Forsyth, this is Madrigal, the girl you asked for. She's
yours for the rest of the evening."

"Won't you sit down, Madrigal?"

But Madrigal still stood, gazing into the man's face, as

Sudderth left. He was older, but the features were the same. She had stared at him long enough in church every Sunday when she was little to recognize him anywhere. "Do you have a wife named Allison?" she blurted out.

Coin's eyes lit up, and his voice was eager. "Why, yes, I do. I've been searching for her for the past two years. Do you know her?"

"Yes. And Morrow, too. Flood Tompkins and me were on the same—"

Suddenly, a shot rang out. The clink of glasses at the bar ceased. At the gaming tables, men looked up from their cards, then they relaxed and continued as if nothing had happened.

"You were saying . . . " Coin prompted the young woman before him.

Madrigal's mouth hung open for a moment, but no more words came. The red-haired girl in the fancy green silk dress reached out for the table. But it eluded her as she slumped to the floor.

"Madrigal!"

"Somebody's shot Madrigal!" another voice cried out.

Sudderth, looking about the room, saw Wolf Perkin lurking in the shadows. And he held a gun in his hand. "Get that man," he shouted, pointing to Wolf.

Wolf backed away toward the door. "Stay where you are," he warned. And looking at Sudderth, he added, "I told you no one else was gonna have her tonight. You shoulda listened to me." Wolf lifted his pistol again, but this time a shot rang out from another source and blasted the man who had shot Madrigal in the back.

As some of the men rushed to Wolf, a frantic Coin knelt beside Madrigal. His one chance to find Allison was now ebbing away with Madrigal's lifeblood. "Where is she?" he begged. "Tell me where I can find my wife."

"Flood," she whispered. "Shirt-tail Canyon . . . "

"Move aside, mister," a gruff voice said. He looked up to see a large, fat woman hovering over him. She nodded to one of the men beside her. "Pick her up and bring her upstairs. And call Dr. Masoni."

"I don't think it's any use to call the doctor, Sally Jean. She looks done for, if you ask me."

"I didn't ask you, Marvin. Go find the doctor while we get her upstairs."

Sudderth, seeing the pall settle over his customers, called out, "The next round of drinks is on the house. Everybody, belly up to the bar. Horace, play something on the piano while Hercules drags Perkin's carcass on over to the sheriff's office."

In the space of a few minutes, the Gold Nugget Saloon was cleared of all signs of the brawl with the exception of a little blood seeping through the sawdust on the floor.

"Sorry about that, stranger," the old-timer said to Coin. "But it's just another Saturday night as far as we're concerned. Can I interest you in a game of poker?"

"I don't think I have the stomach for it," Coin replied, leaving the table and finding the stairs.

While Horace, the piano player, played especially loud, Coin sat on the landing above and silently watched the comings and goings. The doctor appeared but didn't stay long. Finally, a wet-eyed Sally Jean came out of the room and closed the door behind her.

"Excuse me," Coin said, following her down the hall. "Is she dead?"

The woman nodded.

"Did she say anything . . . at the end?"

"No."

His disappointment welled up in his throat, threatening to choke him. He'd come so close. "She tried to tell me something. Please. Did she say anything at all? Even one word . . . "

"I don't know who you are, mister," Sally Jean said, "or what you wanted from Madrigal. But whatever it was, she can't help you now."

"Wait," he begged, reaching out to touch her plump arm. "Madrigal mentioned a flood. Do you know what she was talking about?"

Seeing the look of desperation in Coin's eyes, Sally Jean softened. "She had a friend she talked about sometimes. Name of Flood Tompkins. Made it big in the goldfields, I understand. Does that help?"

Flood. So that was a person's name, not a disaster they'd been through. Coin suddenly smiled. "Yes, it does. Thank you, ma'am." He looked at the woman's face, puffy and red with tears. "I'm sorry. About the girl . . . "

Sally Jean's voice cracked as her memories took over. "You'd never know it, but I looked like that once. . . . " She turned her back to Coin and waddled slowly down the hallway to her own room.

There was nothing left to do but to return downstairs. Coin had only one more piece of money in his pocket. With a purposeful stride, he went back to the table where the old-timer was still sitting. "If you don't mind, Calcott, I'll take you up on that game of poker."

CHAPTER
40

Along a canyon ridge encircled with the gold of the sun, soft, white cumulus clouds began to gather in intensity as if to prompt a memory of rain in the dry red earth.

In the valley below, a quiet, meager stream glinted with the golden particles that had escaped from the hills. For Flood Tompkins, sitting on the porch of her house and viewing her domain, there was nothing in the bare landscape to remind her of the lush greenery of the Georgia hills.

She had been lucky, finding the special vein of gold that had been overlooked time and again by other miners. But her sixth sense had told her where to look, even as her sixth sense now told her that a stranger was heading her way up the canyon.

The big brown mansion was almost finished. And she didn't care that some people had watched its progress and pronounced it a monstrosity. She was rich enough to have anything she ever wanted. The house now had real windowpanes, brought by ship to California and hauled overland to Shirt-tail Canyon. The stained glass decorating the heavy oak front door had come the same way, as well as the cupola and gingerbread trim of the porch.

But Flood was proudest of all of the statuary in the garden—the cast-lead deer and bears—the evening shadows giving them a real-life look. She liked to sit on the porch at twilight and imagine some grizzly coming down from the hills or some wild fawn coming into the garden to nibble at the leaves of the tender plants.

Now she sat and watched. The lone rider on his mule finally came into sight. But Flood wasn't afraid. Her loaded pistol was in the holster that she'd worn from the first day onward in the mining camp.

Down below, Coin Forsyth stopped to rest his mule. He looked upward at the sprawling brown house that sat like a giant squat toad on the land. The glint of gold decorating the dome of the cupola caught the last vestige of the sun and caused his eyes to water. Quickly, he looked away.

"Yes, old man Tompkins was awful lucky, I can tell you that, finding that lode. He don't come down to the mine much anymore. Just sits on his porch and watches—and waits for the wagons hauling all his geegaws from California."

Coin smiled as he remembered his conversation three

days ago with one of the workers at the Tompkins' Mining Company.

"You think he'd mind if I go up to see him?"

The man grinned. "He'll let you know whether he wants to see you or not. If he doesn't shoot by the time you get to that big break in the trail where that lead panther stands guard, then you'll probably be all right. Otherwise, you'll have to leave a message in the panther's mouth for his housekeeper to come and get. That's what we do if we need to send a message to him."

Coin got back on his mule and continued his journey up the ridge. And just as the worker had said, he approached the bend in the trail where the six-foot-high mountain panther jutted out.

He stopped. Looking from the cast-lead animal to the ridge above, Coin had the feeling that he was being watched. It was not so much that he saw anyone. But it was the same feeling he had in battle—some instinctive, primitive response that caused the hairs on the nape of his neck to stand on end.

Feeling foolish, he waved his hand toward some unknown being and slowly edged his mule past the statue. No shot rang out as warning, so he continued along the rocky trail that eventually widened into a passable road.

"Hallo!" Coin shouted. His cry was taken up by the mountain and echoed along the canyon. "May I come up . . . up . . . up . . . up?"

His voice was repeated in triplicate, spreading over the vast wilderness.

"Yes . . . yes . . . yes . . . yes," the echo responded. And Coin, receiving the go-ahead, kicked the mule to urge him up the incline.

Like Madrigal, Flood recognized the older Coin Forsyth.

For a moment, as he climbed down from the mule, she began to wonder if she hadn't made a mistake in allowing him to come up the trail. But then he had never known her in Roswell. But even if he had, she looked vastly different now.

"What can I do for you, stranger? You lookin' for a job? If you are, then you've made a wrong turn. My foreman, McKenzie, does all the hirin'.'"

"No, Mr. Tompkins, I'm not looking for a job. I'm looking for something much more important to me—my wife, Allison Forsyth. I'm Captain Coin Forsyth."

"And you think she's here, Cap'n?" Flood hedged.

"No. But Madrigal O'Laney said you might know where she is."

At Madrigal's name, Flood took her hand from her pistol. "Come onto the porch and have a seat, Cap'n."

Coin tied his mule to the hitching post and walked up the steps.

"You must be plumb frazzled if you came all the way from Nugget Canyon. Would you care for somethin' to drink?"

"Thank you."

"Tillie," she called out. "Bring our guest a glass of cold buttermilk."

While Flood waited for Tillie, she said, "How's Madrigal?"

Coin hesitated. "She's dead. She was killed a month ago by a man named Wolf Perkin." He saw the hurt come into Flood's eyes. "I'm sorry."

Flood quickly masked her sorrow. "But you didn't come here to tell me about Madrigal."

"No. I'm trying to find my wife. She was in that group of women arrested by Sherman at Roswell, Georgia, and sent north. Madrigal was evidently with her, but she died before she could tell me what happened to Allison. You're my last resort, Mr. Tompkins. Please, if you know anything at all about those women, I'd appreciate any bit of information, no matter how small."

Tillie came with the buttermilk, and while Flood watched the man gulp it down, she wrestled with her conscience. How much should she tell this man? Should she say that his wife had married another man and that it was best for him to forget about her? But what of Allison herself? Perhaps she hadn't married Major Rad Meadors after all.

Coin took his handkerchief and wiped his mouth as he set down the empty glass. "You know something, don't you?"

"She's probably still in Kentucky. Between Louisville and Lexington, at a plantation called Bluegrass Meadors."

"Owned by Captain Glenn Meadors? But I was told he pulled up stakes and came out west."

"He did—before his brother came home from the war. But we all worked for the major. I stayed until the tobacco crop was harvested, then I left. That's all I can tell you, Cap'n."

Flood was suddenly impatient. She didn't want to answer any more questions. And she certainly didn't plan to volunteer any more information. "If you'll excuse me, that's all the time I can give you. And you shouldn't wait any longer if you plan to get off this ridge before nightfall."

He had traveled so far, wasted so much time coming west, when less than six months ago he had been less than twenty-five miles from her. He looked at his mule, at the round pan and pick tied to the side. He had no money left.

"You wouldn't mind, would you, if I saw your foreman about a job for a while?"

"It's all right with me, Cap'n. Tell McKenzie that Flood sent you." She watched him walk down the steps. "Good luck, Cap'n," she called after him. She lingered for a few minutes longer on the porch and then watched him disappear down the trail.

With a heavy heart, Flood opened the door with the stained-glass oval and called out, "Tillie, I'm ready for my supper. And I have a hankerin' to eat on the green-and-gold royal china from that English porcelain factory."

Months later, at Bluegrass Meadors, Allison sat opposite Rad at dinner. They, too, dined on old porcelain, but theirs was a family heirloom that had been shipped downriver on one of the early riverboats that had brought Rad's mother as a prospective bride to the redbrick mansion.

It was springtime again and the tobacco had been planted in the fields. But Rad's mind was on the horses and the upcoming race at Saratoga Springs.

"You have your trunk packed, Allison?" Rad inquired.

Allison smiled. "Yes. Rebecca still has the children's things to pack. Then we'll all be ready."

Rad's dark eyes softened. "You'll be the most beautiful woman at Saratoga this season."

She laughed in a teasing manner. "Thank you for the compliment. But I daresay all the stylish clothes you bought for me will go to waste. You'll only have eyes for your horse, Standing Tall."

"For only three minutes, darling. But once he wins the race, you'll be the love of my life again."

"You could still go without us, you know. I wouldn't mind staying here with Rebecca and the children."

"No. My family goes where *I* go. I would never think of

leaving you here alone." He smiled again. "Besides, this is the honeymoon we never took."

"It's a rather large entourage, don't you think, for a honeymoon?" Allison teased. "A maid, two children, two horses, and a trainer."

"But we have a separate suite on the riverboat just for us. And Rebecca will be well paid to see that the children don't disturb us during the night. I don't mind sharing you in the daytime, but by sunset you're mine—all mine."

"But—"

"The discussion is closed, my darling. So finish your soup."

Allison picked up her spoon, but she was too excited to eat. Rad had worked so hard during these past months and now he had a chance to win the big race at Saratoga. Big Caesar had already gone ahead with the two horses, Standing Tall and Liberty's Son. Both had proven to be excellent thoroughbreds, but it was on Standing Tall that Rad's hopes rested.

"Isn't Royal coming over tonight?" Allison inquired.

"Yes. Such a shame he's not going to Saratoga, too. But that's luck for you—having your best horse suddenly strain a tendon. Anyway, he's promised to look after things here for me while we're gone."

"That's generous of him."

The conversation after that was light and casual. And once the dessert had been served, Allison left the table to go upstairs and check on the two children, Morrow and Jonathan, who had been named for her brother at Rad's insistence.

That night, as Allison slept beside Rad in the canopied bed, she dreamed of Coin. It was strange that, without her bidding, he had begun to occupy her dreams lately. But that night he was especially real, and by morning, as the first shreds of light came through the lace curtains at the window, Allison had a sudden need to lean over and look at the man beside her.

"Have I suddenly grown horns, my love?"

Rad's deep, sleepy voice gave her a start. Quickly, Allison replied, "No, Rad—only a dark, stubbled beard."

She reached out and touched his face. Suddenly, she was in his arms. "Rad," she protested. "It's time to get up."

"So it is," he admitted, loosening his hold on her. "But let me remind you, the trip this morning is the only thing that has saved you."

An hour later, Allison stood on the porch and waited for the carriage to pull up. The purple haze in the meadow and the tiny, tender plants of burley tobacco spread before her called up memories of earlier, harder times. She looked at Morrow standing so sweetly beside Rebecca. And her eyes sought out her dark-haired son, Jonathan, squirming in Rebecca's arms.

Perhaps her dream of Coin the previous evening had been an omen, showing her that the past was gone and she could face her future without fear. Gazing about the familiar landscape, Allison realized that she was happy again. Kentucky was her home now. She had roots here—a husband who loved her and a son to inherit the land after him.

The happiness showed in her face as Rad came into sight with the carriage. But as the carriage containing Allison and her husband and children began its trek down the long, fenced drive to the road leading to the river landing, Coin Forsyth arrived by train in Louisville. Soon after Allison had looked back to catch one last glimpse of the house, Coin began to walk toward the livery stable to hire a carriage and to inquire the way to Bluegrass Meadors.

CHAPTER 41

The large riverboat paddles groaned and turned, digging into the water like the giant waterwheel bringing power for the looms and spindles of the woolen mill along Vickery Creek.

It was already dark. The children were in bed, and Allison, taking a turn on deck with Rad, stopped to watch the faint fairy lights sparkling along the banks of the river as the boat passed by.

"You're a thousand miles away, Allison."

Rad's chiding voice in her ear brought her back to him. She smiled and reached out to tuck her hand in his. "I'm putting the last ghosts to rest, Rad."

"Good."

He stood patiently beside her. He made no attempt at conversation, for somehow he realized that the beautiful woman beside him was struggling with the last vestige of the past. He had watched her progress these past months, refusing to say anything even though his jealousy urged him to have it out with her once and for all. But his cautious side—the one that had kept him alive during the war—told him that he would lose more than he gained if he did so.

"I was remembering," she confessed, "the waterwheel—and wondering whatever happened to Théophile Roche, the mill manager."

"He's filed a war reparations suit against the government for seventy-five thousand dollars."

A surprised Allison looked at her husband. "Then they didn't hang him, after all."

"Evidently not. But that's probably his only consolation. He won't get any money for the burned mill."

"But how do you know this, Rad?"

"I have my sources in Washington," he answered, and then changed the subject. "Are you ready to go inside?"

"Yes. It's getting a little chilly on deck, isn't it?"

She had stayed out far longer than she'd planned. But Rad had not seemed to be in any hurry. It was almost as if by knowing what was ahead, it would be all the sweeter by delaying their night together as long as possible.

Inside the large, elegant stateroom, the gaslights gave a soft glow to the opulent furnishings. The large bed, draped in blue damask and ecru lace, had a soft blue painting of clouds and sky overhead. Seeing it, Allison couldn't decide whether it might have come from some Italian palazzo or a New Orleans bordello.

Once the lights were out and the small porthole opened to catch the sounds of the river at night, the origin of the furniture didn't seem to matter. What mattered to Allison was the man lying beside her.

She felt his hands drawing her close to him, and with the touch of his lips, she remembered her wedding day and the sudden shock that first time he had kissed her.

But she remembered their lovemaking, too—more passionate than anything she'd ever dreamed of—on that night when she had first become his wife.

Now, as he began his lovemaking all over again, each sensation was new, yet a bond of pleasure united her to that one night.

"Allison, I love you more than life itself," he whispered. "Don't ever leave me."

There was something vulnerable about Rad tonight. She had seen it in his eyes at dinner. Had felt it on their walk on deck. And now, as his body trembled with anticipated ecstasy, she finally understood what she meant to him. And understanding it, she wanted to give him more of herself than she had ever done before.

"I love you, Rad," she whispered.

But the old jealousy haunted him and forced him to cry out, "More than you loved Coin Forsyth?"

Allison hesitated. But then her voice was strong and sure. "Yes. More than I've ever loved anyone."

"Show me," he whispered.

From the passive one she had been, allowing Rad to make love to her, she became the active one—changing places with him and making love to him, arousing a new passion in both of them that seemed perfectly natural, that begged and ached for fulfillment, that teased and brought partial relief, only to hold back and then begin all over again—once, twice, while the lights along the riverbank appeared briefly through the porthole—with two souls brought to the precipice by the alien sounds around them.

And when Rad could stand it no longer, he changed places with Allison, who finally cried out from the sheer ecstasy of it. This was what Rad had sought from that first night, a visible sign that his lovemaking was not for his pleasure alone.

And when they were both spent, they lay in each other's arms and slept.

The paddlewheels quieted, the riverboat drifted toward the dock along the levee, and the river current received its cue to rest.

In the morning, as Allison opened her eyes, she saw Rad's face staring down at her. "Good morning, my love."

"Good morning, Rad." Suddenly embarrassed as she remembered the night, she stared up at the ceiling bordered in garlands and cherubs.

Rad laughed and turned her face toward him. "It's too late for modesty. Last night, I discovered your true nature."

His teasing caused her to smile. "And I've discovered something about this bed."

"What's that?"

"I think it must have come from a New Orleans bordello. Else I would never have behaved the way I did."

He laughed again. "Yes. We'll blame it all on the bed." He gave her a playful smack. "Get up, wife. Your husband is hungry."

By late afternoon of the next day, Rad's family was safely ensconced in the elegant resort hotel while he made his way out to the racetrack paddocks to check on Big Caesar and his two horses.

Allison did not expect to see Rad again, except for brief

periods until it was time for the race. So she contented herself with her children. In the meantime, she was oblivious to the heads turning as she walked past. But Rebecca, seeing the murmurings of small groups here and there on the grounds, swelled with pride and stood a little taller.

On the second afternoon, Allison, realizing the children were restless, took a stroll through the gardens with Morrow, Jonathan, and Rebecca, dressed in her stylish black and white uniform.

"Who *is* she?" a voice inquired.

"We made inquiries of the concierge," another voice answered. "He pretended not to know until my husband put a rather large bill under his plate."

"Well, tell us. Who is she?"

"Major Rad Meadors's wife, from Bluegrass Meadors in Kentucky. I'm told she was some Southern belle from Savannah, a widow he met during the war."

"That wasn't very loyal of him, was it?"

"His family has always had a bit of renegade in it. You probably remember his father from past seasons. And they say the two brothers fought on opposite sides."

And so the voices and the gossip went, while Allison briefly nodded, her parasol shading her delicate complexion and her silk skirts making a ladylike, swishing sound as she passed by.

Then the day of the races dawned and an excited Allison dressed carefully for the event. She lifted her hat from its box and coaxed the drooping feathers into their former position.

In her mirror, she saw Morrow dressed in her blue silk dress embroidered with lace, the same lace decorating the long pantaloons that stopped just short of her shiny black slippers.

Her hair hung in long blond curls, with a blue silk hat covering her head. And as she sat and waited, Morrow looked from the parasol that she casually spun back and forth on the floor to the mirror and her mother's image.

"Mommy has a hat just like mine," she said to Rebecca. "See?"

As soon as Rebecca's attention was diverted, Jonathan toddled over to Morrow and grabbed at her parasol.

"No, Jonathan," the child scolded. "Boys don't carry parasols. Only girls do."

A loud protest came from Jonathan, bringing Rebecca's attention back to the baby. "Come here, Jonathan," she coaxed. "Time to go for a ride."

They left the hotel in style, with a small blackamoor in attendance and a footman in red livery carefully winding the carriage toward the racetrack. In the back of the carriage was a large basket, holding delicacies from the hotel kitchen and cool water from the springs.

"Oh, Rebecca, I'm so nervous," Allison admitted.

"No need to be. You're the prettiest woman here in Saratoga, just like the major said."

Allison laughed. "I was thinking of Standing Tall. If he loses the race, it will be such a blow to Rad after all his work."

Unknown to either Rebecca and Allison, Rad was holding a serious discussion with Big Caesar at the paddock. Standing Tall was entered in the fourth race, but now there was a possibility that he would have to be pulled from the running altogether.

Rad knelt down and ran his hand along Standing Tall's fetlock. "When did you first notice it, Caesar?"

"About an hour ago, Major. I put a poultice on it right away, but the swelling hasn't had time to go down."

"You think Liberty's Son kicked him?"

"Never has before. But then there's a filly in the next stall."

Rad swore. "Just our luck." He stood up. "It seems such a shame to have come all this way for nothing."

"He can still run, Major."

"But can he win with this handicap? That's the question."

"We won't know till he's tried."

Rad knew that Allison would be arriving soon and he wanted to be in their box to greet her. "Caesar, we've worked together for this entire year. You know just as much about Standing Tall as I do. So I'll leave it up to you to watch him for the next hour. If he's no worse, then let him run. Otherwise, I'll listen for the announcement dropping his name from the race."

"Yes, Major."

Rad walked rapidly down the dust-covered trail and passed other horses, their owners, and their trainers.

"I hear you got a great horse, Meadors. You plan on winning today?"

Rad forced a smile. "If your own horse, Brown Beauty, stumbles out of the starting gate, I might have a chance."

The man roared with laughter, adjusted his cap, and stuck his large cigar back into his mouth.

The carriage holding Allison and the children arrived a few minutes before the opening ceremonies. And once again, with the little blackamoor leading the procession and carrying a small footstool, heads turned as Allison made her way toward the box where Rad was waiting.

Coin Forsyth stood at the edge of the crowd and looked at the lineup. His finger ran down the list until his eyes lit on the line: Standing Tall, out of Bluegrass Meadors. Owner: Rad Meadors, Kentucky. Trainer: Caesar.

With the roar of the crowd, the first race began. But Coin

wasn't interested in the horses, only in the man whose two-year-old was running in the fourth race.

By the time the second race began, Jonathan was already crying and Morrow was thirsty. Seeing Rad's frown, Allison said, "Rebecca, you might as well take the children out on the green. Maybe they'll be more comfortable in the shade."

Rebecca was glad to leave the confining box. She was nervous, but it was because of Big Caesar. He was younger than she was, yet it didn't seem to matter to him. Just as it hadn't seemed to matter when she'd been less than civil and called him those names down by the creek. Now he wanted her to be his woman, and she had halfway promised. "If you win at Saratoga, I'll be your woman, Caesar."

That had been six months ago. Now she was sorry she'd said that because she didn't know whether she wanted Standing Tall to win or not. And that was a terrible thing to say, after all the major's work.

"Come on, Morrow. Let's go and get something to drink from the carriage."

"Then can I play with my hoop on the green?"

"If you promise not to get your pretty dress dirty."

Once their thirst had been satisfied and Morrow's hoop retrieved from the carriage, Rebecca found a bench under one of the tall trees. While Jonathan tore the flower from Rebecca's dress into shreds, Morrow was busy rolling her hoop up and down on the green. Other nursemaids and children peopled the landscape, claiming their own spots from usurpation while the roar of the crowd in the background went unheeded.

A sandy-haired man strode purposefully across the green, and as Rebecca watched his progress, she felt a sudden chill, like a ghost stepping across her grave. And as he came closer, her heartbeat increased. "Oh, Lordy, it can't be," she said, but her eyes told her what her heart denied.

The man stopped and stared at the black woman. "Rebecca! Rebecca Smiley. Is that you?"

"Mr. Coin?"

"Yes." He rushed to her, and his face held all the anguish that had been stored up for the past three years. "Where is she, Rebecca? Where is Allison, my wife?"

"She thought you were dead, Mr. Coin. She—"

The blond-haired child, unheeding of the man, dashed up to Rebecca. "I fell on the grass, Rebecca. Do you think Mommy will be angry that I got my pretty dress dirty?"

"No, child. It'll be all right. Now run on back and play with your hoop."

Coin's eyes followed the child. There was no need to tell him who she was, for she was the image of Allison. "Morrow?"

"Yes, Mr. Coin."

CHAPTER
42

The fourth race began, and Rad breathed a sigh of relief as Standing Tall rushed from the starting gate. He had not told Allison of the horse's injury, for he didn't want to worry her. But now that the race started, he wondered if he hadn't made a mistake. He should have prepared her since there was little possibility that the horse might win.

"Rad, there's something wrong with Standing Tall, isn't there?"

Her voice, as well as her observation so early in the race, startled him. "Yes. But I didn't want to worry you."

She reached over and took his hand. But her eyes stayed on the horse that faltered and then fell behind. "Is it anything serious?"

"A swollen fetlock. But it will heal eventually."

"Good. Then it doesn't matter if he loses this race, does it?"

His eyes left the horse briefly as Rad gazed at Allison's profile. He tightened his grip on her hand. "I suppose not."

After that, he felt better.

Rad was hardly aware of the horse's name until the announcer repeated it. Falling so far behind, Standing Tall now seemed determined to gain ground. Rad picked up his binoculars and began to watch as the horses bunched together on the far side of the track. And then Standing Tall came from nowhere, edging past one horse and then the other, until he was running neck and neck with the two front contenders.

By now, Rad was standing, straining to catch a glimpse of the horse. Everything was forgotten but the horse and the race. And Allison smiled as she remembered Rad's words: "For only three minutes, darling. But once he wins the race, you'll be the love of my life again."

As in all of life's important moments, the dimension of time became suspended as Rad and Allison watched the race. The minutes were an eternity in the mind, while on the track Standing Tall, in the colors of blue and gold, rode to victory.

"Ladies and gentlemen, Standing Tall, out of Bluegrass Meadors, is the winner by a nose."

Allison was swept into Rad's arms and kissed soundly in front of some of the more sedate viewers. "Come on, darling. Let's get down to the winner's circle."

But Allison hung back. "No, Rad. You go on. Let me watch from here."

But Rad insisted. "I want you, darling, beside me."

Coin Forsyth was swallowed up by the surging crowd.

He managed to fight his way to the railing as the jockey rode Standing Tall into the winner's circle. And Coin waited to catch sight of the owner, the man who had stolen his wife.

While Coin watched, a tall, self-assured man with hair the color of soot appeared. And by his side stood Allison. Coin drew in his breath. She was more beautiful than ever and a radiance shone in her face. Suddenly, all anger vanished from Coin's heart, to be replaced by an inordinate sadness.

He had seen enough. He turned from the railing and retraced his steps past the crowd and toward the bench where he'd left Rebecca. She was still sitting there, hugging the crying little boy in her arms.

"Did you find her, Mr. Coin?"

He hesitated. "I saw her. From a distance." He suddenly cried out, "I can't ruin her life again, Rebecca. For Allison, and Morrow, too, Coin Forsyth is dead. Do you understand?"

Rebecca didn't speak. She merely looked toward the child on the green.

But Coin's voice was insistent. "You never saw me, Rebecca. Promise me you'll never let Allison know I'm still alive."

"I promise, Mr. Coin." Rebecca's voice broke. And just as she shouldered her burden, Rebecca understood the great sacrifice that Coin Forsyth had just made for Allison in the name of love.

"But where will you go?" she asked. "Back to Roswell?"

"No. There's nothing for me there. I think I'll go to Canada instead."

She watched Coin Forsyth linger for a moment to drink in a final view of the beautiful little girl whom he had never seen before. Then he disappeared beyond the acres of carriages, with their drivers waiting for the owners to return.

A few minutes later, with a lovely flush giving color to her delicate, porcelain face, Allison walked onto the green.

"What's the matter, Rebecca? You look so glum. Didn't you hear? Standing Tall *won*."

"Did he, Miss Allison?" Rebecca attempted a smile. "That's sure good news."

Rad laughed at the puzzled look on Allison's face. "It's a mixed blessing for Rebecca, Allison. You see, Caesar told me Rebecca promised to be his wife if Standing Tall won the race today."

Rebecca got up, the sleeping Jonathan in her arms. "I'm takin' on a heavy burden, that's for sure."

"Oh, Rebecca, I'm so happy for you," Allison said. Her amethyst eyes were bright. "There's this little piece of land Rad gave me. It would be perfect for a wedding present . . ."

Rad laughed. "Let's go on to the carriage, Allison. Sounds as if you're just as anxious to get back to the Meadors as I am."

He reached out to take his sleeping son from Rebecca as Allison called to Morrow, "Come along, darling. Your father says it's time to go home."

Allison returned to Bluegrass Meadors where she had found a second love. But each July, as the heat bleached the earth and the breezes stopped singing through the apple trees, Allison left the redbrick mansion with its white Doric columns and went down to the creek to be alone by the old willow tree.

And on that same day, in other small towns and villages along the rail lines from Nashville to the gates west, the survivors of the train called "Sorrow" remembered July 5, 1864, and dreamed of going home.

In Roswell, the mills were rebuilt and the town bound up its grievous wounds. Rose Mallow became a showplace, while the old shack where Madrigal O'Laney was born finally fell down of its own accord.

Today, historians continue to search for some trace of the four hundred and fifty Roswell women who were uprooted by that long-ago war.

Their memory still haunts the land.

AUTHOR'S NOTE

The small town of Roswell, situated on the banks of the Chattahoochee River twenty miles north of Atlanta, contains some of the most beautiful antebellum homes in Georgia. Founded by Roswell King, a wealthy businessman from Darien and Savannah, it was originally a summer colony, an escape from the malarial fever of the great coastal plantations. The town archives contain the history of many families who settled there, including the James Bullochs, whose daughter, Mittie, married Theodore Roosevelt, Sr., and became the mother of a U.S. president. Her wedding at Bulloch Hall was the social event of the 1853 season.

But *The Roswell Women* is not based upon this wealthy upper class. Rather, it is based on the mystery of what happened to four hundred and fifty women and children—workers in the King textile mills—at the time of the Civil War.

When General Kenner Garrard, who served under General William Sherman, arrived in Roswell in July 1864, prior to the siege of Atlanta, he found three Confederate mills in operation—one, a woolen mill with a French flag flying overhead, and two cotton mills—in full production. He was ordered by Sherman to burn the mills, arrest the workers for treason, give them nine days' food rations, and ship them north across the Ohio River.

The Roswell Women is a fictionalized version of what might have happened. It traces this actual trail of tears from Marietta to Nashville, Tennessee, to Louisville, Kentucky, and into Indiana.

The disappearance of the Roswell women is cloaked in mystery. Old military diaries with conflicting stories, orders written by General Sherman in the field, newspaper reports filed by Northern war correspondents, an accounting discrepancy in the number of women arriving in Nashville from Marietta, and advertisements sanctioned by a provost marshal, offering them as bond servants, are only bits of a puzzle waiting for completion. The women's voices are still silent, for history has turned up no personal accounts written by the women themselves.

It is my hope that by telling this fictionalized story of one little-known event of 1864, I have made readers aware of a continuing tragedy throughout history—of countless numbers of women and children caught in the corridors of war.

FRANCES PATTON STATHAM
Atlanta, Georgia
October 1986